Acclaim for
HIDDEN CURRENT

"Sharon Hinck has outdone herself with this tale of reclaimed mystery and redemption. As a dancer myself, I loved the rhythm and lyricism of Hinck's masterful prose and the perilous quest of her protagonist to learn Truth. *Hidden Current* dances on the page."
  —TOSCA LEE, *New York Times* bestselling author

"Rhythm and dance can move a world, and *Hidden Current* shows how it might be done. A lovely story, told through the eyes of a character who must find her true strength in faithful, trusting service. *Hidden Current* combines a creative, sympathetic interweaving of the dancer's art with intriguing worldbuilding and a strong faith element. Well done, Sharon Hinck."
  —KATHY TYERS, author of the Firebird series

"*Hidden Current* made me want to leap up and dance with joy. The characters, setting, and creatures were exquisite, and the Maker touched my heart. One of the most beautiful stories I've ever read."
  —MORGAN BUSSE, award-winning author of The Ravenwood Saga

"Sharon Hinck's *Hidden Current* is absolutely beautiful! I was instantly drawn in by her intriguing island world held in place by dancers. This story is one of discovery, truth, and a lovely, fresh allegory that will touch readers' hearts. If you enjoy Christian young adult fantasy novels with danger, adventure, and a hint of romance, you're going to love it!"
  —JILL WILLIAMSON, Christy Award-winning author of Blood of Kings

"*Hidden Current* enthralled me! Sharon Hinck brings characters to life like no one else! The characters' paths collide and propel them on an adventurous, imaginative quest. *Hidden Current* is bursting with intrigue, danger, betrayal, redemption and hope—everything readers want in an epic tale! *Hidden Current* is unputdownable!"

—ELIZABETH GODDARD, bestselling author of the Uncommon Justice series

"Sharon Hinck's writing has a way of transporting readers to spectacular new worlds while, at the same time, connecting to the heart of reality. Her books deliver escape and relevance, adventure and compassion, questions and answers—all in the midst of clever, character-driven storytelling. I wholeheartedly recommend *The Dancing Realms* series."

—WAYNE THOMAS BATSON, author of The Door Within trilogy and The Myridian Constellation

"Mystery. Danger. An intriguing world unlike any you've been to before. What's not to love about a story like that? In *Hidden Current* you'll find all that and so much more! These characters are some of author Sharon Hinck's best ever in a story that will live in your heart long after you've read the last page."

—MICHELLE GRIEP, Christy Award-winning author of the Once Upon a Dickens Christmas series

"A fanciful world, endearing characters, insidious evil... *Hidden Current* swirls together high adventure with spiritual truth in an elegant dance set to the heartbeat of the Maker's love for every creature under His care. Truly a beautiful story worth savoring over and over again."

—CHAWNA SCHROEDER, author of *Beast*

HIDDEN
CURRENT

Books by Sharon Hinck

The Secret Life of Becky Miller
Renovating Becky Miller

Symphony of Secrets

Stepping Into Sunlight

The Sword of Lyric Series
The Restorer
The Restorer's Son
The Restorer's Journey
The Deliverer

The Dancing Realms Series
Hidden Current

HIDDEN
CURRENT

THE DANCING REALMS
BOOK 1

SHARON HINCK

to Kyrie, Soren, and Alethea

"And Hilkiah the high priest said to Shaphan the secretary, 'I have found the Book of the Law in the house of the LORD.' And Hilkiah gave the book to Shaphan, and he read it."

—2 Kings 22:8 (ESV)

1

DESTINY IS MEASURED IN INCHES. ONE MOVE IN THE WRONG direction or one faulty gesture can erase a lifetime of preparation. The weight of that truth tightened my muscles as I lined up for class with the other novitiates. Beneath the taut, hooded scarves covering our hair, we looked alike: wide eyes anxious and alert, cheeks hollow from years of relentless training, identical blue tunics and leggings. We were the remnant, the few dozen women who had endured each level.

I raised my chest against the gravity of my fear. One week stood between me and the pure-white fabric of final acceptance into the Order. This was a time for determination, not doubt. A slight breeze through an arched window cooled my cheeks. Outside, the primary sun lit the tiled courtyard, while the subsun hugged the horizon, painting the stone with pinks and reds.

An attendant opened the studio door. Time for class and another chance to prove myself. I pressed into the floor with my toes, rolling through the tendons of my bare feet, careful to maintain even spacing as I took my place in the vaulted room. Cold marble threatened to cramp my feet, but soon I would be worthy to dance on the warm bare earth of Meriel.

If I passed the pattern test.

If the saltars approved me.

If I made no mistake during the next week.

Saltar Kemp limped to the front of the class, rhythm sticks clenched between arthritic fingers. She studied our silent ranks, eyes narrowing as she sought out flaws. Was I the exact number of inches from the women to either side of me? Did my leggings settle just above my anklebone? Was my spine perfectly aligned?

I held my breath.

Her eventual smile encompassed the room, fine lines bunching on her wizened features. "You must remember to breathe. Such concentration is good, but too much tension is as bad as none." She tapped a slow beat with her sticks. "Four counts to breathe in. Four counts out. That's better. Now begin nolana pattern three."

My heart rose. I loved that pattern. I loved all the patterns. I thrived on the challenge of memorizing them, reversing them, repeating them in endless variations.

We began to move to our saltar's counts. I slid one leg to the side, foot caressing the floor, then lifted the leg, balancing, rotating, careful to match my movements to the other dancers.

"Remember." Saltar Kemp's hoarse voice melded into the steady clacking. "Your feet will push the earth to turn our world. It is a holy calling. You do well to tremble within, but keep your faces calm."

We lunged and poured our bodies forward. We moved like channels of water, divided as if by an unseen boulder into two streams that circled the room, arching, flowing, reaching.

A ripple disturbed the flow. The novitiate in front of me opened her left arm instead of her right. The saltar's sticks clattered to the floor.

We all froze.

"Novitiate Alcea Blue, step forward." The saltar who was usually our most gentle now gave no quarter. No hint of frailty colored her voice. Alcea walked forward, the bend of her shoulders pleading for forgiveness.

"You may leave. Your designation is removed. Your time in the Order is over."

None of us dared gasp, and I bit my cheek to keep my mouth shut. We'd witnessed dismissals dozens of times over the years, but this was only one week from our final test. And—my heart clenched as Saltar Kemp's words sank in—this was more than a demotion to servant. Alcea was being completely cast out.

"Please." Her voice quavered. "May I at least stay on as an attendant?"

Remorse flickered in Saltar Kemp's eyes, but she hardened her jaw. "Did you think your constant questioning of authority would go unnoticed? The flaws in your dance are not your only failing."

Breaking all protocol, Alcea ran from the room, her sob ringing against the cold walls. Pity swelled behind my ribs. Each of us grew up without a parent's love. We forfeited hope of husbands, children, or any community but the Order. To sacrifice so much and lose it now. . .

I closed my eyes, listening for the four counts that would signal our return to the pattern. When fear or doubt arose, there was always the pattern. The pattern comforted. The pattern never changed.

Hours later, my skin wore the sheen of sweat and triumph. I'd survived another class. So close to admittance to the Order, the chance for failure only grew. If an experienced dancer could be cast out because she had a reputation for raising questions and she made a small error, I needed to guard myself each second of the days that remained.

As we left the practice hall, we filed past the former novitiate huddled on the floor. Tears stained her cheeks. Dismissed from the Order, even her name was stricken. We couldn't speak to her or offer the silent comfort of a touch. Still, my hand reached out, and I hoped the small gesture conveyed sympathy.

"Calara Blue, a word please." Saltar Kemp's call snapped me back to reality.

Head down, I hurried to the doorway where she waited. Had she noticed my wavering? I peeked at the saltar's expression.

She cast a grim glance down the hall, but then dusted off her hands and relaxed her frown as she addressed me. "We have an absence in faculty for next hour's first form. Please regarb and teach them. I'll inform you of other schedule changes tomorrow."

"Of course." I turned toward the stairs leading up to the dormitories. Saltar Kemp touched my arm. "And not a word about this to the students. Explain only that you're substituting."

"I understand."

"Please." A desperate whisper came from the former novitiate. She unfolded from the floor and approached the saltar. "I can teach the last class before I leave. Let me say goodbye to the children."

Saltar Kemp stared past her, stepped back into the studio, and closed the door.

THROUGHOUT MY RUSH TO PREPARE AND THEN TEACH THE first-form girls, an unsettled confusion twisted in my stomach. I hurt for the rejected woman, feared for my own place, and then felt ashamed of my selfish fear.

At suppertime I had no appetite, so I bypassed the communal hall and slipped outside to find solace in the Order's gardens. Stone troughs held cultivated flowers, grasses, and vines. Whenever I walked among them, they offered me a rare and treasured moment of peace. Reeds and ferns and berries and flowers, even the stinging leaves of the lanthrus—each held its own beauty. Cobblestone surfaced all the ground, muting the slight ripples that rolled through the earth. I paused before my friend's namesake, the alcea flower. As I leaned forward to smell the delicate blossoms, my eyes pooled with tears I dared not cry. I was no longer allowed even to think her name. Was it possible that a woman I ate and slept and danced with for so long could be erased so completely? Would I become nothing to those I left behind if I failed my test?

I plucked a flower and let my lips brush its soft petals. I couldn't use her name, but I would honor her in memory each time I saw her namesake.

A gust of wind sent cold fingers across the back of my neck. I pulled my linen cloak closer, following the stone path under a trellis archway. Outside the Order's wall, a full view of the sunset stretched out in a panorama. Violet streaks warned of a coming storm, and dark clouds approached.

Past the wide ring of fields that separated the Order from Middlemost, the nearby town spread around it like flower petals. Garrisons, meeting halls, kitchens, and storage buildings came first, with layers of homes and small shops forming a larger circle. The town basked in the blessing of the Order rising at its core, as did our entire island.

Beyond Middlemost stretched forests and plains, farms and grazing land, with vast distances separating the many villages we served. Even farther—a journey of weeks or months, depending on who spoke of it—the rim villages stubbornly scrabbled a life from the undulating lands near the sea.

How had I been so lucky? If not for the Order's rescuing me, I could be suffering in the poverty and chaos of a rim village today. Although we didn't speak of the outside world, everyone knew life beyond the Order was governed by strife and uncertainty.

I followed the path around a bend of the courtyard's outer walls and heard the murmur of voices ahead of me. When I rounded the curve, a laborer in coarse trousers and a stained leather vest blocked my view of a woman standing beyond him. He crouched to pick up a sack, allowing me to glimpse her.

I gasped.

Alcea's blue eyes stared into mine. Terror lit her face as she pulled the hood of her cloak forward. The man spun, his hand moving to a longknife in his belt. His fair hair was playful and windswept, but his eyes glinted steel. If this man thought to prey on a castoff, he would rue the day. I hurried toward them. "What are you doing here?"

His dismissive gaze swept me before he handed Alcea—no, I must only think of her as the castoff—a bundle. "Thank you," she whispered.

He spared a terse nod and pointed to a mark on a parchment map. "It's only three days' journey to Salis. You'll find help there."

She leaned heavily on a walking stick. A bandage wrapped her right ankle and foot. Tossing aside all the rules, I touched her shoulder. "What happened to you?"

The man turned his dirt-streaked face in my direction. Anger pulsed along his unshaven jawline and he sneered. "As if you don't know."

My foot felt for the path behind me, and I edged back a step. Had he caused her injury? Violence seemed like a familiar acquaintance to him.

"She doesn't know," the former novitiate said to him. "None of us did." Her quiet voice betrayed a brokenness far worse than the slump of her once-proud back, or the way she favored her right leg. She raised her palm to me in farewell. "You've been a good friend. Be careful."

I nervously scanned for any sign of a prefect or saltar. "And you." I mouthed the words, throat constricted.

She limped away, and I directed my frustration at the man. "Who are you? Why is she hurt?"

"Brantley of Windswell. Who are you?"

I raised my chin. "Calara Blue."

"Not your designation. Your true name. Before you were sold to the Order."

A memory tugged, a whisper, a word, but I tamped it down. "We have no life before the Order. We speak of nothing outside." My designation was a point of pride. The calara reed reflected so much of what a dancer must be—well rooted, yet supple. The calara patterns were some of the most complicated.

He snorted. "A shadow of a shadow. Named for a pattern that's named for a plant."

How dare he scorn me? He was a rough man from some midrange village, or even the rim. He hadn't the least understanding of our work. "You haven't answered my question. What did you do to her?" My gaze followed the path across the field that my former classmate had taken away from the Order.

He crossed his arms and leaned back against the wall. "The saltars hobbled her. Sliced the tendon. They do it to all the castoffs. Can't have novitiates dancing anywhere besides the Order after they leave."

The turmoil that had churned in my stomach all afternoon pressed up into my throat. "No. Never! How dare you?" She must have injured herself while preparing to leave. But why invent such a ridiculous story?

He condemned the whole Order with his answering glare. Condemned me. "Why should I expect you to see facts in front of your nose? They don't even allow you to think for yourself."

An ugly lie. "The Order preserves our entire world. If they—"

"Ah, the benevolent Order."

My core muscles tightened, holding back nausea. I clung to anger for strength. "You mock our calling. What essential vocation do you claim?"

"One of the landkeepers is ill. I'm filling in for a few weeks." He shifted his weight, a subtle change, but obvious to my dancer-trained eyes. He was lying.

I stepped closer. "I should report you to the saltars."

He tossed back his head and laughed. "And confess that you spoke with a castoff?" With the speed of a harrier prey bird, he pushed away from the wall and grabbed my arm. He tugged me close. He smelled of the sweet ocean . . . an aroma I hadn't known in years.

My heart pounded an unsteady rhythm.

His voice was a low growl. "You may think you could expose me, but you'd do well to remember I'm an equal danger to you. You forgot to treat Alcea as invisible. One word about this, and you'll be the next hobbled castoff." He shoved me aside and strode away from the Order toward the uneven buildings of Middlemost, careless of where he placed his feet.

I rested a hand against the cool stone of the outer courtyard wall, shaking. He was right. I'd breached a primary rule. I didn't dare speak of any of this. But what if he was a danger to the Order? There were rumors of enemies from the rim seeking to disrupt our work.

Drawing on my discipline, I uncurled my spine, lifted from the center of my head, and found my alignment. My lips would remain sealed for the time being, but I would stay alert and watch for any sign of Brantley lurking nearby. Meanwhile I needed to remain focused to prepare for my test.

Hurried footsteps approached from the courtyard. An irritated prefect appeared, his hair damp with sweat. "Saltar Kemp is calling for you. Her office."

I gave a submissive nod, hoping to hide my fear.

He didn't wait for a response, but walked away, expecting instant obedience.

Before following the prefect inside, I let my gaze travel up to the building encircling our world's center. Dozens of windows on the outer ring overlooked the courtyards and the tangle of Middlemost below. A huge brass telescope perched on the rooftop parapets. It was as though I was on stage, every misstep on display. Someone could have seen me talking to the dismissed novitiate. Was the destiny to which I'd given my life about to crumble?

WE ALL DREADED A SUMMONS HERE. AS I STOOD ON THE threshold of the saltar offices, an attendant pushed past me and deposited a heavy bound book of parchments onto the table in front of Saltar Kemp. The saltar sighed and rubbed the back of her neck, but didn't see me. I hugged the doorway while cobbling together a defense in case anyone had reported seeing me speak to the castoff novitiate.

Attendants hurried from table to table. To the left, High Saltar Tiarel's private office door stood open. Her large desk was covered with books, papers, and brass tools for measuring stars, winds, and waves, shining symbols of her power. Ignoring the activity in the large outer office, she stood by her picture window looking out at the dancers in the center ground. Balconies allowed other people glimpses of their work from above, but only the High Saltar enjoyed a direct view from her office. From the stiff set of her shoulder blades, whatever she saw didn't please her.

"A pattern should never be disrupted once it begins," Saltar River shouted at Saltar Tangleroot, drawing my attention to the opposite side of the room. A young, sharp-edged teacher, Saltar River bore no resemblance to the flowing pattern for which she was named. She terrorized the students in form five, and I still cringed when I remembered her classes. She was the tallest saltar, a detriment for a dancer when uniformity was prized. Yet somehow she'd risen swiftly through the ranks of dancers. Now she towered over Tangleroot, peering down her hooked nose.

Saltar Tangleroot shrunk into herself but stood her ground. "The High Saltar is never wrong. This storm will be too severe if we don't contain it. We can't wait." She paced to the window facing the courtyard and studied the sky. Their arguing created a harsh contrast to the peaceful tapestries adorning the walls.

"Calara Blue, where have you been?" Saltar Kemp's gruff voice made me flinch. My reckoning was at hand.

She beckoned me toward her table.

I tiptoed forward. How could I convince her to let me stay?

When she registered my worried expression, she gestured toward the window. "Don't let this ruckus concern you. The High Saltar will make a wise choice. She always does. Although I question this directive." She picked up a massive book and opened it with a thump.

An attendant brought Saltar Kemp a mug of water and retreated. She sipped it and winced, the tiny wrinkles around her mouth bunching. "Needs more filtering." She offered it to me. "Here. Taste this."

I obediently took the mug and sipped. A hint of sweetness and citrus lingered in the water.

"I'm correct, am I not?" she asked.

"You are." She wouldn't ask my opinion if she were about to cast me out, would she?

A beleaguered attendant passed behind her chair, and Saltar Kemp grabbed his arm with her arthritic fingers. "Return this to the kitchen and get me some drinkable water." She leaned back. "The first-form prefect reported that you did an excellent job teaching this afternoon. The saltars have recommended that you continue to work with the first form, taking over their final class of the day."

The commendation startled me so much, I swayed back on my heels. "I'm . . . I'm honored."

Saltar Kemp rubbed the bridge of her nose. "I objected of course."

Disappointment squeezed my ribs. She'd been my greatest advocate in my progression through the ranks and my favorite teacher, yet she didn't trust I could teach the first-form girls?

"I'm sorry I haven't earned your faith," I said quietly.

She drew her chin back and frowned. "Don't be ridiculous. I'm sure you'll do fine. However, it's unfair to add duties the week before your final test. You need to rest and review the patterns."

Her fingers traced illustrations on the open pages before her. "You can refer to these lesson plans. Tomorrow the class is scheduled to study the history of the Order."

Relief poured over my muscles like warm liquid. She still believed in me. Yes, the task would add to the mounting pressure, but I could handle it. I smiled. "I'm happy to help."

She handed me the book and studied my posture. It must have held too much confidence because she leaned forward, planting both hands on her desk. "I suspect there may be some on the panel who hope you fail your test. I won't be able to protect you. You'll have to be flawless."

I knew that already. The problem with perfection is that it wasn't a fixed point. Each time I neared it, it danced away, tantalizing and mocking.

The book weighed heavy in my arms as I plodded up one flight to my dormitory. Recruits too young to begin training were housed on the upper floor with their keepers. At the age of seven, they entered the first form and moved down to the fourth floor beside the second and third forms. Every few years, I had celebrated the move to the next level down— nearer to the ground and nearer to my destiny.

Flickering torches lit the hall with yellow light. My feet glided over stone floors polished smooth by generations of novitiates. Everything about the Order spoke of perfection. I followed the curved hall, bypassing several balconies that overlooked the center ground. The steady beat of drums guided the dancers below through perpetual patterns. They'd work faithfully through the night, holding storms at bay and keeping our world turning.

I hugged the book to my chest, visualizing my deepest hope. In one week, if I proved worthy, I would join them.

Farther down the hall, I opened the door to the sleeping quarters for the fifteenth form, women of about one and twenty. Our beds were made of shredded cattail plants stuffed inside lumpy ticking. Dozens of these mats covered the floor around the edge of the room, leaving the center area open. Damp leggings hung from rope strung across the rafters. Dancers sprawled throughout the room, stretching their splits, bandaging blisters, and massaging aching knots in neck or calf. Windows supplied the natural light of dusk, and a few torches gave extra illumination in preparation for the night. Their smoke combined with wet wool and the perfume of flowering branches someone had set on the windowsills.

Conversations rose and fell, more subdued than usual. Today's dismissal had frightened us all, which was probably Saltar Kemp's intent. Did she really feel a need to remind us of the seriousness of the upcoming test?

Several women saw me enter and called out.

"Calara, you weren't at supper. I was worried."

"One of the prefects was looking for you. Did he find you?"

"Where were you?"

I offered vague answers. The women of our form became sisters as we lived, worked, studied, and danced together. But in class we competed against each other, determined to prove our worth. We'd also been trained to report any infractions. When any careless word could be recounted to a prefect or saltar, our trust for each other remained tenuous.

I eased to the floor beside my friend, Starfire Blue. Free of her hood and the tight regulation braid, her auburn hair swirled around her face like torch flames. I marveled—and rejoiced—that she'd risen through the forms in spite of her irrepressible and sometimes irreverent view of life. She sat in a straddle stretch, resting forward on her elbows, but she popped up to tap the book in my lap. "Were you assigned extra study? You didn't make any mistakes in class, did you?"

"Saltar Kemp asked me to teach the first forms this week."

Her eyebrows drew together. "Has the saltar been soaking her head in sweet water? How will you manage?"

I rolled my shoulders. "I'll be fine. If I don't know the patterns by now, no review session will fix that."

A break in the rhythm rising from the center ground caused all of us to turn our heads toward the door. High Saltar Tiarel must have made the radical decision to interrupt a pattern before it was complete.

"The storm must be worse than it looked," Starfire said. Two women raced to close shutters, deepening the darkness in the room. A new drumbeat began, full of nervous triplets.

I didn't have time to indulge my worry about the coming storm. Instead, I took up a spot on the floor near one of the torches, struggling to read the history lesson notes in the weak light of the flame.

Much later, when my sister novitiates had retired to their mats, I rubbed my burning eyes and put aside the heavy book. I slipped out to the nearest balcony. Overhead, angry clouds blocked the stars, releasing bursts of rain. Uneasy groans rose from the lowest level of the stone tower as the wind stirred deep waves far beneath us. We'd always endured occasional storms, but harsh weather had become more frequent and severe in recent months.

In the center ground, rows of white-clad dancers sculpted precise lines and angles. Their arms urged the storm past, while their feet trampled the earth that turned muddy beneath them. Their movements were powerful, beautiful. I usually drew comfort from watching them, but not tonight. Was Alcea out in this storm, or had she found shelter somewhere in Middlemost? Was Saltar Kemp feeling even a flicker of guilt for sending her out? And Brantley's outrageous accusation . . . Had someone really wounded her? Or had he?

"I thought you'd be here." Starfire slipped up beside me and held a hand out to catch the rain. "Hard to believe we'll be dancing out there in a week."

The thought once thrilled me, but now turmoil whirled through my mind, as if borne by the harsh wind. "Star, have you ever heard rumors about what happens to the castoffs?"

She shivered and backed into the alcove where the rain couldn't reach her. "It was sad today, yes?" She tugged me away from the edge. "You're getting soaked."

"I know we're supposed to erase them from our thoughts, but . . ."

Starfire gave me a quick embrace. "You're too tenderhearted. Remember Saltar River's favorite proverb. 'Distraction will approach like carrion birds at the worst times . . .'"

"'. . . Wave it off and keep your focus true,'" I finished. "Thanks. You're right. I have too much on my mind already." I took a calming breath of the chill wet air and followed Starfire back inside. While the drums progressed through the storm pattern, I pictured each step and imagined myself on the field with the other dancers, pouring myself out on the center ground to keep the world turning.

LATE-AFTERNOON SUNS HEATED THE UPPER-FLOOR HALL. After a full day of training, it took all my effort to gather energy to teach. A prefect I didn't recognize stood by the doorway, his brutish forehead emphasizing a perpetual glower. Sweat prickled along my scalp as I fought off my worry about what he might report to the saltars.

I managed a welcoming smile to the seven-year-olds sitting on the floor around me. Their scarlet tunics were a bit rumpled, and halos of fine hair escaped from their braids. Yet their backs were tall as they sat, feet drawn up, soles together, and knees pressing to the floor as if their legs were little wings.

"Our world, Meriel, appeared one day on a vast ocean with no boundaries. For generations this island world rode the currents, unstable and ever-moving underfoot."

The girls stared with mouths gaping like fountain fish. Were they excited and eager to learn, or weary from their long day of chores and instructions?

I opened the book Saltar Kemp had lent me and showed them a drawing penned by a saltar from generations past. "Then the Order learned the secret to keep our world in place, rotating around itself. They created the center ground where the ripples are the most subdued, and built this wondrous edifice as a huge ring of protection. They coated the surrounding land with brick and stone to steady it."

I turned a page and held up the next illustration for the girls to see.

"Every day the dancers' feet touch the land, teaching it what to do. Each pattern was inspired by a crucial element of our world and can be used to nourish those very things. A flower, a vine, a star, a river. When you came to the Order, you were given your new name. Each year you succeed, you earn a new designation color that becomes your second name. You've been chosen among all others to study the patterns. One day, if you work very hard, you'll join the dance."

"Have you danced in the center?" one of the little girls piped up, scooting a few inches forward.

I stood and gently slid her back into place, keeping the curved rows of students concentric and even. "Not yet, but that is my deepest hope. I take my test in six days."

The girls' intakes of breath reminded me of the wind gusts yesterday afternoon.

"Are you scared?" one of the girls asked. A smattering of freckles adorned her cheeks, and her fiery hair reminded me of Starfire.

I weaved around the semicircles of students, touching a slumping shoulder here, coaxing a chin up there. "I can trust my training. As can each of you. Each year you will have a saltar to teach you. They are the most experienced and wisest of the dancers. If you listen to them carefully, you'll learn all the beautiful patterns that govern our world."

I returned to my place at the front of the class and lowered to my knees, turning another page of the book. "Here you can see the oceans that surround our world. Nothing but dangerous sweet water stretching into infinity."

"I like the sweet water. I liked to swim in it." A girl with golden hair and a particularly messy braid spoke wistfully, directing her gaze out a window.

Her mention of swimming made it clear she came from a rim village, and she was one of the youngest of the group.

I shot a nervous glance at the prefect in his blood-red tunic. His glower darkened as he listened for my response. "But now you know the truth," I said firmly. "The sweet water is harmful. We capture clean rain or purify what we gather from the ocean wells."

She looked ready to argue so I kept talking. "As I was saying, after our world appeared—"

"It didn't just appear. Meriel was made." The same girl leaned forward slightly.

"No, it simply appeared."

Her mouth pursed, and she shook her head. "My grandmother told me there are old stories about a Maker. She told me—"

I interrupted before she could make more injudicious statements. "What's your name?"

"Nolana Scarlet."

"Well, Nolana, the Order is a special place. When we come here, we put aside our past. We don't speak of our families, our villages, or any part of those old lives."

I continued with the history lesson, rushing through pages of the book to give no more opportunity for questions. We covered all the material but still had time left before the end of class.

"You've all done a wonderful job listening today. As a reward, I think we could use the remaining time to learn part of a pattern. What do you think?"

Around me, the girls scrambled to their feet, fidgeting and scuffing small bare toes against the floor. Getting them into position was like catching needles as they shook loose from trees and spun to the ground. Was this why my first-form teacher was always so grumpy?

Once I had them positioned correctly, I picked up a hand drum from the side of the room and beat the fern rhythm. "First, close your eyes and listen. Hear how the drum speaks to your feet. In the same way, your feet will one day speak to the earth. Today we'll only learn the first eight counts, because they need to be perfect."

I scurried around, coaching, correcting, demonstrating the proper shape of the foot, the stretched line of the leg, the generous arc of the arms. With careful repetition, the girls established the curling frond shape, and practiced the traveling turns moving out from the center line until one girl lost her balance and bumped against another.

The girls giggled, and I laughed with them.

From the doorway, the prefect cleared his throat and crossed his arms. I hurried the students back into position, resenting his reminder of the strict standards of the Order. The sense of fun fled from the girls' eyes. After scurrying into place, their once-limber muscles now tightened with anxiety.

At last, a bell from the dining hall rang three times from the first floor. The girls lined up by the door. I was tempted to collapse in an exhausted heap, but instead I picked up the history book. As the girls filed out, the prefect grabbed Nolana's arm. Her scarlet tunic disappeared against the bulk of his crimson garb. "You're not going to supper. You've already been warned about heresy."

I crouched beside her and wrapped a protective arm around her. "She wasn't speaking heresy. She was only asking questions."

"She's been warned. Time in the storeroom will help her remember."

A tremor moved through her tiny frame, and a tear dripped from Nolana's downturned face.

I had hated that dark storeroom with its musty air and uncertain passage of time, and most of all the horrible solitude. I'd learned to do nothing to draw attention to myself—an important skill.

I gave her a squeeze meant to comfort while pulling her out of the prefect's grip. Her tunic fell off one shoulder, revealing a mottled bruise.

I shot up and squared off with the prefect. "Has someone beaten her?"

The lout shrugged. "Only when she deserves it."

Fury burned like the second sun, heat traveling up my neck to warm my cheeks. "She's only in the first form." I squared my jaw. "Besides, she danced beautifully today, and that's the most important measure of class ranking. And look at her. She can't miss a meal. She's new here and far too thin. Perhaps you are inexperienced in the work of prefect and didn't realize that."

His fat lips bent into a sneer. He didn't bother to answer, but simply shoved me aside, grabbed Nolana's arm again, and dragged her into the hall.

If I protested any more, he'd only take out his anger on Nolana. I had no power to stop him, and he knew it. Helpless, I trudged down the stairs.

Entering the long dining hall, I moved slowly to my place. Saltar Kemp nodded to me from her seat at the high table. What would she do when she received the prefect's report? My small burst of anger and courage melted out of my bones, and my hand shook as I picked up a mug of water. I'd flourished through years of study at the Order, dedicated to its noble work. Why, with only six days left until my test, had everything begun to change? Starfire Blue passed me a basket of saltcakes. I placed one on my plate, then took an extra and hid it in the pocket of my tunic. Perhaps later I would be able to bring it to Nolana.

Or perhaps after the saltars heard about my class, I would be locked in a storeroom somewhere too.

SALTAR RIVER SURPRISED US WITH AN EXTRA EVENING class, claiming it was her benevolent gift to help us prepare for our upcoming test. I was convinced, however, that she longed for one last chance to torture us. We held extensions as she counted out the beats until our muscles shook. Then we took turns crossing the room with running leaps. Saltar River stared down her beak-like nose, eyes narrowed to catch any error. I propelled my weary body into the air, cursing the gravity that made me plummet back to the floor.

Dawn Blue, whose jumps evoked envy, leapt higher than ever with her focus upward. A moment of inattentiveness cost her. The floor shifted a hair's breadth, and she landed wrong. Her knee torqued. The sickening snap echoed through the room—the sound of another dream lost forever. My heart contracted like her crumbled body on the floor. Two dancers ran forward, risking River's wrath to help Dawn Blue from the room. I stared after them, faint from shock and legs barely able to support me—until River ordered us to finish the sequence. Without a glimmer of remorse on her angular features, Saltar River finally dismissed us.

Too exhausted and demoralized for conversation, all the novitiates staggered to bed. In the darkness, I felt for the saltcake I'd saved for Nolana. Only smashed crumbs remained in my tunic pocket.

Even though my body screamed for rest, I couldn't sleep until I brought her some food and comfort. The sideboard in the kitchen always held leftovers from a meal. No one would miss a few bits of food.

Hands in front of me, I felt my way to the door, tiptoed into the hall, and made my way downstairs by the last flickers of dying torches. After navigating the empty dining hall, I reached the kitchen. A few embers still glowed in the massive hearth, giving me enough light to find a bowl of persea fruit. Their knobby skin was easy to peel without a knife, and the meaty flesh would fill Nolana's stomach.

I grabbed two perseas and padded back toward the dining hall. A whisper of sound made me freeze. A shadow moved behind the partially open kitchen door. I wasn't alone.

A saltar or prefect? But why would they hide behind a door?

I turned and ran toward the back door. Heavy feet pounded after me. Arms surrounded me, and a rough hand covered my mouth.

"Not a sound. Understand?" A shake punctuated the harsh words.

Terror paralyzed me, but I managed a tiny nod. The grip loosened, and I spun to face my attacker.

"You!" I gasped.

Brantley of Windswell glowered. "Quiet. Do you want to bring down the wrath of the Order?"

"What are you doing here? Stealing food? Don't they feed the landkeepers down in the village?"

In the orange glow of embers, his pointed gaze fell to the fruit in my hand. "I haven't taken anything. You on the other hand . . ." His words trailed off in a veiled threat. We were a danger to each other. Again.

He must have reached the same conclusion. A wry smile pulled at the corner of his lips. "You're quite the little rule breaker, aren't you?"

"These aren't for me." Why was I explaining myself to a landkeeper? "What are you doing in the Order? It's not allowed."

His teeth flashed a predatory grin. "Call a prefect."

My fingers tightened around the fruit. How could I explain my nighttime roaming to a prefect? Besides, this renegade would probably invent a tale implicating me in something worse than an after-hours snack. The saltars would banish me from the Order. A tremor rattled through my frame.

Under the shadows cast by his unruly blond hair, his grin faded and his eyes held something that might have been regret. He sighed. "Get out of here. And don't tell a soul you saw me. Agreed?"

What option did I have? Every part of my body and mind were depleted, and I wanted to get away from him and continue my errand. My only hope of doing so was a truce. "Promise me you aren't going to cause trouble for the Order."

He tugged my arm and hustled me ahead of him toward the dining hall. "It's clear. Go now."

I hesitated at the threshold, peering out into the dark dining hall. "I'm serious. I want your promise that you aren't an enemy of the Order." I glanced over my shoulder. He had disappeared back into the shadows.

I couldn't take the time to worry about his lurking. Instead, I wove past tables until I bashed my shin on a bench. I sucked in a breath, then hurried on. I hugged the wall of the broad stairs, winding past my floor and upward to the fourth floor. Muffled coughs and sniffles punctuated the silence from behind the closed doors of sleeping quarters. Feeble torches were spread farther apart, so I felt my way along the wall.

I'd lived on this level for several years, but with my heart pounding in my ears I struggled to remember which door indicated the right storeroom. The one used to punish young novitiates was small, musty, and bug-ridden, with shelves containing nothing soft to cushion the imprisonment.

I found a wooden door sealed with an iron bar. I pressed my ear to the surface, listening for tearful whimpers. What I heard was worse. A tiny voice hummed a forlorn melody with scattered notes like a morning bird song. I shifted the bar and opened the door.

"Shhh. Nolana, someone might hear." My pulse sped faster. "Singing isn't allowed."

From the corner of the closet, Nolana hugged her knees, studying me with hopeful eyes. "Can I come out now?"

I chided myself for offering the girl false hopes. I did a quick scan of the halls in each direction and handed her the fruit. "No, I'm sorry. You'd only get in more trouble. But I thought a full tummy might help you get through the night."

She tilted her head. "Why can't I sing?"

"When did you come to the Order?"

She shrugged. "Feels like forever. But I think it was last week."

Poor thing. She was completely new. No wonder she didn't understand all the rules yet.

"Singing is not allowed because melodies tempt dancers to move beyond the pattern. The drums are all we need. They keep us precise."

A door or shutter creaked in the distance. I didn't dare linger. "Try to sleep, and stay quiet. When the prefect lets you out, don't raise your eyes to his face, and don't argue. I'll see you in class tomorrow."

Such a feeble comfort to offer. In my earliest weeks here, even though I was thrilled to be accepted as a novitiate, I had been battered by homesickness, endless rules, and strangers who seemed harsh and cruel.

I knelt in front of her, whispering. "You must trust the Order. Put away all thoughts of your old family and village. It makes life easier."

She blinked. "I think I'll talk to the Maker."

I shook my head. She had to be taught to set aside those harmful myths so she could fully embrace the Order.

At my frown, she dipped her chin. "Don't worry. I'll be tiny quiet."

THE NEXT MORNING, I PREPARED MYSELF FOR TROUBLE. MY evening wanderings had been a foolish indulgence. Patrolling soldiers may have captured the trespassing landkeeper. Had he talked, looking to make me the scapegoat for his law breaking? I slid into my spot beside Starfire in the dining hall and joined the others passing bowls of porridge. From the center of the Order edifice, the reassuring drums beat the daily turning pattern that began each new day and ensured our world remained locked in place, spinning around the axis of the Order. But even the familiar rhythms couldn't calm me today. At a table farthest from the kitchen, the little girls of the first form gathered. Nolana wasn't among them.

"Have you learned all their names yet?" Starfire dipped her saltcake into the porridge.

"What?" My stomach cramped, and I couldn't coax it to welcome any food.

She tilted her head toward the scarlet novitiates. "The little girls you're teaching. There are so many of them."

By contrast, our table held yet another empty space after last night's injury. "And each year their number will shrink." I didn't bother to hide the melancholy in my voice.

High Saltar Tiarel tapped the head table with a rhythm stick, and I flinched.

Starfire shot me a curious glance as the soft murmurs of conversation stilled.

"Saltars, dancers, prefects, novitiates, and attendants." The High Saltar's chest puffed out and she lifted thin eyebrows at the room. Each syllable proclaimed that her words carried a vital portent.

My muscles tensed, and I stared at a knot in the wood of the table, trying to grow smaller. Tiny quiet, as Nolana would say. Would I be shamed before the entire Order?

"We've had news of an uprising from a rim village. Some of their men may be heading this way to disrupt our work." She sniffed, her pale brows drawing together. "For those who are new here, rest assured that we've faced these ragtag rebellions in the past without any interruption in our rhythms. The soldiers of Middlemost will keep us safe. However, until further notice, please remain within the Order edifice." Her stone-gray eyes flared, revealing a brief glimpse of buried rage.

I still braced myself, so tense that blood couldn't reach my limbs. Had my choice brought danger on the Order? I knew I should have reported my encounter with Brantley. Her next words might yet condemn me.

"Now as you finish your meal, Saltar Kemp will play a rhythm and challenge you to state the pattern's name as fast as possible." Tiarel's eyes turned flat and cool again, the gray of shadow instead of the glint of steel. She took her seat and passed her sticks to Saltar Kemp.

My breath released in a rush, and blood tingled back into my arms and legs. Bright spots like star rain cascaded across my vision, and I swayed.

Starfire elbowed me. "What's wrong with you today? You should have listened to me. Taking on a teaching task is too much for you. Just look at yourself."

I bit my lip and nodded.

"Well, you best gather your bearings before morning stretch. The saltars are watching everything."

I studied the faces of the saltars at the head table. None looked my direction. Perhaps I was safe for the moment. Except that I still had to prepare for my test, avoid the mishaps that had cast off two of our form in two days, face the prefect I'd dared to challenge yesterday, ascertain Nolana's welfare, and decide if I should report Brantley's presence—even if that would mean my dismissal.

In the practice hall, I approached Saltar Kemp. "Do you know which rim village is rebelling?" Brantley had told me he was from Windswell. If Windswell renegades were moving to attack Middlemost, I would tell Saltar Kemp about Brantley, no matter the cost to my standing.

She stroked her thinning hairline, just visible along the edge of her hood. "Undertow. But don't spare it another thought. Remember, your priority is the test."

Relief fueled my smile. Whatever Brantley's reasons for lurking around the Order, they had nothing to do with a rebellion or with me. "Of course. Thank you."

"Stop by my office before you teach this afternoon. I have some parchment you can use for keeping track of the novitiates' progress."

I took my place on the floor and began stretching. Undertow. Why did that name feel familiar? It wasn't Brantley's village, and that had been my only worry. Yet a tug of memory nagged at me.

LATE IN THE DAY, I CHANGED OUT OF MY SWEAT-DRENCHED leggings, tunic, and hood, and into my teaching garb. Arms laden with the history book, spare parchments from Saltar Kemp, and a willow pen, I hurried upstairs toward the first form's practice hall.

In the stairwell, dozens of girls from the sixth form held buckets of mortar and worked it carefully into the fine cracks that spidered across the walls. Because of the subtle motion of our world, repairing the stone was a constant chore, especially after storms. How did people manage closer to the rim, where the ground rolled so unpredictably?

I wound past the girls, chiding myself for the question. Novitiates weren't allowed to think about the world outside the Order.

A different prefect stood by the door today, an older man I'd seen occasionally. Novitiates rarely interacted with the prefects, so I didn't know his name, but I was grateful the rotating schedule had brought someone other than the brute who had observed yesterday. Nolana had returned to her class, her gaze downcast, her spirit subdued.

The Order required exacting standards. I'd always understood that. Yet the last few days I'd seen the power of the Order crush those with the slightest flaws or mistakes. Had the rules become harsher, or was I noticing it more? Perhaps it was normal to have doubts before the test. I wished there was someone I could ask.

Using advice and supplies from Saltar Kemp, I asked each girl her name and created a chart. A few misspoke—so new they blurted out their old names. A small frown from me was enough to correct them. The willow pen was supple in my hand, and when I pressed carefully, it wrote fine green characters on the page. They deepened to a chocolate brown as they dried.

I quizzed the girls on the previous day's history lesson and drew small marks by the names of those who needed extra help. Nolana answered each question posed to her without a hint of argument, although she still stared out the window far too often.

After reading another chapter on the triumphant establishment of the Order and the original High Saltar of generations past, I allowed for a few minutes of discussion.

"This morning Saltar Tangleroot began to teach us the fern pattern. The one you taught us yesterday." Reseda Scarlet bounced in place, her braid flicking forward over her chest.

Filipena Scarlet giggled. "We surprised her."

"She didn't know how we could learn so fast," Nolana said, a faint smile briefly erasing the shadows under her eyes.

I grinned. "Well, if you work hard at your history each day, perhaps I'll give you a head start on some more patterns. It's always good to impress your saltar."

In the distance, the muffled drums from the center ground finished their pattern. We all waited, and soon a new rhythm began. Gale pattern. Of course. The High Saltar wanted to stir up fierce wind to prevent rebels from traveling toward Middlemost. Within a few hours, the weather would turn.

The supper bell rang, and the girls filed out. I lingered in the empty room, strolling to the window ledge. Smoke rose from the smithy's fire down in Middlemost, but there was no sign of approaching invaders. Carts rolled on narrow streets, some pulled by farmers returning home after a day of selling produce, others harnessed to sturdy ponies with short legs who could navigate the shifts of earth underfoot. Beyond the Order's wall, an entire world went about its business. What were their lives like?

Frightened at where my thoughts were running, I checked the door, reassuring myself I was still alone. Then I looked outside again, letting my gaze follow a road that wound toward vast forests. Where did it go? Who lived along its path? Were they happy?

If I were a harrier bird, could I see all the way to the rim from here? Or perhaps if I had one of the High Saltar's viewing tools? If I looked through the rooftop telescope, would I glimpse the wild and untamed ocean that always threatened us?

My hand caressed the leather cover of the history book. I pulled out the chart tucked into the front. Each of the girls came from villages and families whose names they could no longer speak. Did they understand the sacrifice they'd made by pledging to the Order?

I tore off a small corner of the parchment. With tiny letters, I wrote "Undertow?" and stared at the name. Then beneath it I wrote one more word: Carya.

I folded the fragment several times and hid it in my pocket.

THE MORNING OF OUR FINAL TEST, TENSION HUNG OVER our sleeping quarters like the jaws of a forest hound about to snap down on our necks. I rolled my shoulders against the taut fear. Around me, the other women managed their nerves in varying ways. Some fell quiet, others chattered. A few reviewed patterns, using their fingers to walk through movements on their palms. Others coaxed an inch more flexibility from their spine or legs.

For me, the past few days had been a blur of training, teaching, and burying my questions and doubts. I was exhausted, but today I needed to grasp determination with both hands.

Starfire tucked and tied her hood scarf three times before being satisfied. "Have you ever thought about being an attendant instead of a dancer?" she asked. "I would be great helping in the laundry."

I laughed. "You don't get to choose your assignment. Remember how much you loathed kitchen duty when we were in our form nine year?"

"Scrubbing pots is better than this pressure." She grabbed my arms, panic widening her eyes. "What if I do so badly that I'm cast out?"

I hugged her. "You won't. Trust your training." I hoped the words reassured her more than they did me. Each breath I took fluttered in my chest, leaving me shakier than the last.

A prefect tapped at our open door. "It's time."

A bubble of panic caught in my throat. My stomach twisted into a hard knot. I shook out my arms and legs and rolled my head side to side. Nothing could shake loose the foreboding that gripped me.

We filed downstairs and entered the practice hall. Ranks of novitiates sat along one side of the room, creating a rainbow of tunics. They would watch with a sharpened intensity all day, dreaming of their turn before the Order, when their destiny would be fulfilled or crushed.

The saltars sat on benches at the front in their most formal robes, wide cuffs with intricate embroidery hiding their hands, tiny silver stitches adorning their hems and collars. Although they held their expressions still and severe as befitted their role as our judges, their postures held none of the tension of the students. They almost looked smug and eager to destroy our dreams. I quickly banished that disrespectful thought.

Saltar River stood, displaying her impressive height. "A momentous day. You have all prepared diligently. If you fail, the saltars will determine your future fate. Some may be allowed to remain as attendants or work in Middlemost to support the Order. Those deemed the most flawed will be cast out." She allowed a gleam to light her eyes. "The novitiates who pass their final test will be invited into the Order. But only on a trial basis. No dancer can truly be judged until she dances in the center ground. I hope this news will only fuel your desire for excellence."

I stared straight ahead, jaw tight. So even if I was accepted, I couldn't be secure in my place as a dancer? I'd heard that after her injury, Dawn Blue had been sent to work for a tanner down in Middlemost—a loathsome job. Would that be my fate as well?

Keep breathing. No distractions.

"Let us begin with star rain pattern." The saltar nodded to the drummer in the corner. The deep, throbbing beats were so much stronger than the clacking sticks used in practice. I embraced the sound, summoning courage.

As a group, we performed each pattern requested, striving to dance with more power and skill than ever before. The first hour steadied me. Familiar work and physical exertion quieted some of my nervous energy. My joints softened and my muscles grew more supple.

But as time passed, the patterns became more challenging. The gale pattern had never been a favorite of mine. The dance included a series of jumps in place, landing with our feet tight together, then adding a spin in the air with the fourth jump. By the time we finished all the repetitions, we were panting. That made the delicate alcea movements that followed even more difficult. I fought to glide smoothly into a sustained pose, leg extended behind me, without letting my chest heave for breath.

During the next two hours, my body tired, but the greater challenge was to keep my mind alert. A slip in concentration could cause a disastrous mistake. Under the gimlet eyes of the saltars, there was no place to hide. The saltars took turns walking among us as we danced. During the summer cloud pattern, I noticed Saltar Kemp touch Tangleroot Blue's arm and whisper in her ear. The novitiate silently left the room, spine curved in defeat.

Don't lose focus.

If I worried about the fate of others, I'd be throwing away my own destiny. I completed my turn and knelt, holding the final pose, arching back, heart lifted toward the ceiling. My muscles burned and my heart pounded. I had invested every ounce of strength. Whether I had succeeded was now the saltars' decision.

When the group portion of the test finished, the High Saltar ordered us to wait in the hall. I immediately claimed a spot on the floor, lying on my back and letting my spine lengthen as my muscles released their tension. Then I hugged my knees to my chest, feeling the sweet ache as I stretched more deeply. One by one, novitiates were called in for individual testing.

When Starfire Blue was called, I watched the door until she returned. She came and settled beside me, pale and shaken.

"Well?" I whispered.

She wiped moisture from her forehead. "Calara, do you think anyone at this point has said, 'No, thank you,' and walked away?"

I forced a small chuckle. "Those are your nerves talking. Think of all the women who would love to be in your place." Still, the image took root. Would a woman ever be offered a place in the Order and turn it down? Where could she go?

"Calara Blue." The prefect's voice snapped me to my feet, and I smoothed my tunic. As I walked to the door, one of the other women stretching on the floor thrust her leg in front of me.

I stumbled over her, my ankle twisting as my weight came down hard. Pain speared me. I whirled to see who had tripped me.

"Sorry." Furrow Blue shrugged. "Didn't see you."

Furrow had never been a close friend, but I hadn't expected deliberate sabotage. "You—"

"Calara Blue." The prefect gave his final call.

There was no time to confront Furrow. I rolled my foot a few times, then put a little weight on it. Only a sprain. I limped to the door, then forced myself not to favor the leg as I entered.

Novitiates learned the patterns in ranks of dozens, carefully matched for size. Now I stood alone in the large hall, exposed and vulnerable.

High Saltar Tiarel nodded to the drummer, who began a pattern. For a few counts I couldn't identify it. Panic flared upward from my throbbing ankle. Four more counts and I was supposed to move, but in which direction?

The rhythm grew clearer. I hid a smile. Calara pattern. Of course. The strong and supple reed that was my namesake.

I threw myself into the movements, gliding forward and back, sweeping my arms overhead. Each step jarred my ankle, but I ignored everything except the perfection of the dance. Still, I was relieved no jumps were included in this pattern. If they had been, my ankle would have collapsed. As it was, the last section of spins that circled the room jammed sharp knives into my foot each time I pushed into another turn. Sweat mingled with a few escaping tears and rolled down my face, but somehow I completed the steps.

Yearning surged through my muscles as I held the final pose, stretching at an angle toward the vaulted ceiling. Would I be found worthy?

Inches from my calling, a strange impulse intruded.

Run!

Memories flickered across my vision. Alcea limping away, Nolana huddled in the dark storeroom, Brantley's accusations, Saltar River's cruelty. Then I saw a woven hut built on undulating land, a woman's face, careworn and tear-streaked—hands reaching toward me.

My heart cried a desperate plea. *You don't belong here.*

I forced every thought into stillness. These doubts were another test, and I hadn't worked so hard only to fail now. I leaned a bit more weight on my sore ankle and let the pain distract and steady me.

Still, I worried that my thoughts had broadcast my doubts. Had my eyes flickered with those memories? Had the frowning panel members noticed? I commanded my face to mask every thought, every fear.

With the last beat resonating off the walls, I bowed my head, completing the pattern. Then I walked to the center of the room and faced the panel of saltars.

They fired questions at me, designed to test my knowledge but also to assure my loyalty and dedication. History came easily, since teaching the first form all week provided a review. Botany had always been a favorite, so I had no problem naming various plants and explaining the design of the patterns that carried their names. Constellations weren't difficult since Starfire and I often slipped out to the courtyard after the subsun disappeared and watched the sparkling patterns emerge overhead. I answered each question with swift confidence.

High Saltar Tiarel leaned forward, her lips a tight line and her thin eyebrows arching. "Why are the dancers the most important people on our world?"

"Without their work, our world would float aimlessly. The dancers are vital to the survival of everyone." And oh, how I longed to join their work . . . to be important.

The High Saltar met my wide-eyed earnestness by raising her pointed chin another inch. "Why have you endured fifteen years of training?"

"Because there is no room for flaws in the work of the Order."

The High Saltar pursed her lips. "Which novitiate would you name as unworthy to be invited into the Order?"

"Furrow Blue," I blurted without thinking. Then I despised myself for my petty vengeance, no matter how justified. Had a life dedicated to nothing but the patterns made me as heartless as the saltars? A few younger girls in the watching rows giggled. I cleared my throat. "I mean . . . Everyone in our form has worked very hard, and I wouldn't—"

"That is all." The High Saltar crossed her arms.

My test was over. But how had I done? I could read nothing on the severe faces before me.

I walked to the door, wincing inwardly with each step. As soon as I was outside the door, I sank to the floor, rubbing my ankle and finally allowing myself a small moan. Starfire came and sat beside me, putting an arm around my shoulders. "See, working in the kitchen doesn't sound so bad now, does it?"

I gave a broken laugh. "Did they all look grim when you finished?"

She nodded. "They always look that way. I'm sure you did great. Do you want me to find an extra scarf so you can bind up your sprain?"

I shook my head. "We aren't done yet, and I don't want to draw any attention to myself. Not that way."

We both stared at the mottled purple colors rising on the swollen skin of my ankle. The injury would be impossible to hide.

I found a place near the stairs and rested with my leg braced up against the wall. As blood stopped pooling around the sprain, the ache eased. I should be able to survive the day, as long as we didn't have any more dance tests.

After what seemed like weeks, a prefect summoned us all. Starfire let me lean on her until we reached the threshold. Then I walked as steadily as I could manage and took my place. A few more women had been dismissed at some point during the afternoon, but our rows still held many hoping to be chosen.

I lifted my chest. I'd given all I had. If I wasn't found worthy, that was my fate.

High Saltar Tiarel rose, hands tucked into the wide sleeves of her robe. "Novitiates, I want to thank the saltars who have trained you throughout all fifteen forms. The quality of your work today is a testament to their dedication."

The rows of students to the side tapped their fingertips against the floor in a sparkling rhythm of acknowledgement, raising a sound like a soft rainfall.

"I also commend each of you who passed your test." She opened a roll of parchment. "The novitiates who will be invited to move to the dancers' arc of our building and take their place in the grand patterns of the central ground are—"

A commotion rose from the outer courtyard. Angry voices advanced. Metal jangled beyond the windows. Heavy boots stomped into the inner courtyard. A soldier burst into the rehearsal hall, shoving aside the prefect who was trying to hold him back.

"High Saltar, I must speak with you. Now." His tunic was torn, his breastplate streaked with blood.

Her eyes flashed with the white heat of a smithy's flame. I expected her to sear him with a rebuke. Instead, she gave a terse nod. "In my office."

She strode toward the door. In spite of the surprising sight of an armed soldier within the Order, my focus fixed upon the parchment that held my future. The High Saltar carried it crushed in her fist as she left.

THE SALTARS ALL TALKED AT ONCE, AND FROM THE SNIPPETS
I overheard, it was clear no one knew how to proceed. Some of the
bolder students ran to the doorway. From my position, I could see the
High Saltar and the soldier disappearing around the curve of the hall.

Commotion continued from the courtyard. While the other teachers
argued, Saltar River strode straight across the room to the ground-floor
windows. The blue novitiates parted for her like windblown grasses, and
we followed in her wake, pulled forward by curiosity and dread.

Burly men roamed the courtyard, bristling with swords and knives and
dented shields. On a rare outing into Middlemost, I'd glimpsed soldiers
patrolling the streets, but we'd never seen any on the Order grounds.
A bearded soldier with a blood-soaked bandage tied around his thigh
shouted at a thinner man with a polished helmet, perhaps someone of
higher rank? I couldn't distinguish his words over the noise. Arguments
rolled among the men like tumbling rocks.

The men near the courtyard wall took up positions by each entry and
window. Their movements held more than agitation and anger. These
soldiers had the stiff joints and jerky motions of fear.

The bearded man shook his head, abandoning his argument, then
noticed us through the windows. A leering grin spread across his hairy
face. He elbowed another soldier and pointed.

Saltar River whirled toward us. "Novitiates! Withdraw to your sleeping
quarters until further notice."

What about the test results? I longed to ask, but didn't dare.

As students lined up to leave, I noticed Nolana's troubled face. I approached her and knelt down. "You don't need to worry. The soldiers protect our Order. You'll be all right."

Her lashes swept her cheeks, and when she looked up at me, her eyes held depths beyond her years. "No." Her words came out breathy and edged with sorrow. "They took me from my village."

"You mean soldiers escorted you when you journeyed here?"

Her feathery brows drew together, as if puzzled by my ignorance. "They took me. They killed my papa and took me."

I drew back. "That's impossible. The Order would never—"

"Scarlet novitiates, proceed." Saltar Tangleroot hustled her charges out, leaving me staring after them.

The poor girl was so confused. Why would she create an evil tale like that? We all knew that the soldiers served the Order, and the Order served our world. Perhaps in her homesickness she'd had nightmares. I'd experienced many my first year here. I needed to warn her not to talk about her bad dreams. She couldn't afford to get into more trouble.

The other forms filed out in neat rows, and we followed them upstairs. I leaned heavily on the railing, each step pain upon pain. When we reached our room I collapsed on my mat in relief. Using the fabric from a spare hood scarf, I tightly wrapped my ankle. I wasn't the only one suppressing moans and rubbing sore muscles and joints. The adrenaline of performance bled away, and the disappointment of not knowing the results grated like grit against blisters.

Starfire Blue mustered enough energy to roll onto her stomach and prop on her elbows. "Do you think they added this disruption as a new part of the test?"

The thought had crossed my mind, but I shook my head. "This couldn't have been planned. Those soldiers are angry and afraid. And bleeding."

"Will they tell us what's happened?"

"They'll say we aren't to think about anything beyond the walls of the Order."

Starfire huffed. "Then this doesn't count. They are *inside* the walls, and they ruined our test day. And what about supper? I'm starving."

My stomach grumbled at her words. We hadn't eaten all day. Were we supposed to ignore our hunger and prepare for bed? Or would the official results be announced soon?

While we waited, we took turns using the washrooms down the hall. The water buckets on the counter were low. Apparently the attendants had been diverted from their schedule too. I used a sparing amount of water to splash my face, then used a clean linen cloth to rub my skin as well as I could. If I knew we were done for the day, I'd gladly peel off my sweat-drenched hood scarf, tunic, and leggings and change into comfortable nightwear, but I thought it best to stay prepared for a summons. After years of consistent schedules, none of us were equipped to deal with the unpredictable, so after washing up, we stayed dressed and ready, resting on our mats, too dejected for conversation.

Fatigue overcame my anxious speculation, and I dozed until Saltar Kemp appeared in our doorway. "Blue novitiates, I'm very sorry that we'll be unable to complete the proclamations or gather for a meal this evening. You may prepare for bed." Her wrinkles seemed deeper, her skin tinted gray.

Furrow Blue sat on her mat near the door and turned to the saltar. "What happened? Why are soldiers here?"

I was grateful for her boldness—so much that I almost forgave her for my injury.

Saltar Kemp's mouth drew down and she sighed. "Since this was such an important day for you, perhaps you deserve to know. The soldiers were visiting midrange villages to collect the Order taxes. Foleshill refused to supply the produce required, and after some . . . opposition . . . the soldiers retreated here to consult with the High Saltar."

Unthinkable. Perhaps the backward rim villages might be reluctant to offer their due to the Order, but the midrange towns knew it was an honor to share in our work by donating provisions. Families there were honored to send their finest girls to train.

Saltar Kemp met the gaze of girls around the room, taking in our varied expressions of confusion, disbelief, and concern. The grooves around her mouth deepened. "I know. A tragic and inexplicable event. It will be dealt with, I assure you. Get some sleep. The soldiers will be gone on the morrow." She withdrew before we could ask more questions.

No wonder we were taught not to think of the world beyond our walls. Clearly, even with the sacrificial efforts of the Order, chaos threatened to infect some villages. Yet another reason I needed to be chosen. I ripped the hood scarf from my head, unbound my braid, and raked fingers through my hair. Bone-weary, I didn't bother changing. I curled up on my mat and surrendered to sleep, a sleep disturbed by cramping muscles, the throbbing of my ankle, and tormenting dreams.

THE NEXT DAY AT BREAKFAST I SHOULD HAVE BEEN RAVENOUS but struggled to force down a few bites of porridge. Even Starfire picked at her food, shredding bits of persea into her bowl.

"Calara, I don't think I want to be a dancer. What do you think they'd do if I respectfully declined?"

"When they call your name, your doubts will flee," I said softly.

"And what if only one of us is picked? We'll never see each other."

Seeing the mess she'd made of her persea, I handed her my fruit. "Don't exaggerate. The dancers aren't in complete seclusion." Although with their separate wing, private dining hall, and regimented schedule, the dancers rarely interacted with the rest of the Order.

Starfire's chin tucked down. "You are my best friend. I want you to know that. If we . . . if I don't . . . if only one of us is accepted and we can't speak again . . ."

"We would find a way. But we won't need to. We'll both be accepted. So eat something. You'll need your energy."

Starfire crinkled her nose. "Or we could both decline and go off to discover the world."

Suddenly the thought held appeal. Those winding paths glimpsed from the upper window, the haunting questions about my birth village, the teasing thoughts that had invaded even my final test. Were the answers out there somewhere? But after all these years of hard work and the uprisings in the tumultuous outer world, how could I abandon the Order? Everyone knew the world beyond our walls held danger and chaos. I would scrub floors or mortar the walls. Anything to stay.

The High Saltar left her place at the head table and came to stand before the room, regal, confident. Dozens of spoons lowered, hands stilled, and muted conversations died.

Tension built in my jaw, chest, and stomach. When I noticed the tightness, I used my training to release the muscles. Even with my best efforts, I barely coaxed my ribs to expand and draw in air.

"Traditionally, testing day is also a time to announce promotions and other changes. I'm pleased to share a few new positions with you now."

She rattled off assignments without one mention of yesterday's disturbance. I supposed that made sense. We'd been taught since the first form: by willing it to be so, we erase the problem from our minds. Bad things simply didn't happen in the Order. My admiration for her swelled. She embodied the ability to create her own truth.

She continued. "Finally, Saltar River has been named as my new Sub-High Saltar, and Saltar Fern will take her place teaching the fifth form."

I groaned. The High Saltar and her assistant were the ones who interacted directly with the dancers. I'd hoped to be done with Saltar River.

"Now I'll call the names of the dancers joining the Order. When your name is called, please come forward. Pine Blue, you are now Dancer Pine. Welcome to the Order."

Across the table, Dancer Pine's face lit with joy. She scrambled off the bench and hurried to stand before the High Saltar. An attendant gave a stack of neatly folded items to High Saltar Tiarel, who handed them to the new dancer. White leggings, white hood scarf, white tunic, and a white robe—the clothing that would mark her as a dancer of the Order.

"Do you pledge your service to the Order, in obedience to our vital work?"

"I do." Her voice squeaked, and then was drowned out by our fingers tapping the table like a downpour of congratulations.

As she was led away by the attendant, I leaned forward, pulse quickening. I could see myself stepping to the front, tipping my head in deference to the saltars, boldly making my pledge, receiving my new name, my new identity.

"Gale Blue, you are now Dancer Gale . . ." Calmly, the High Saltar called each successful candidate forward.

One by one, our table emptied, and as each new dancer stepped forward, my breaths became tighter.

Tiarel's chin lifted. "We have one more dancer to announce. The rest will be given their new assignments later." At our table, Furrow, Starfire, and I were among those still not named.

Starfire's panicked gaze met mine. "I hope it's you," she said softly.

Whatever the outcome, everything in our lives was about to change.

"Calara Blue, you are now Dancer Calara." The words rang in my ears, and, for a second, I forgot how to move.

Starfire stood with me and gave me a quick hug. "Don't worry," she said. "We can still meet in the courtyard to watch the stars. I'll look for you."

I nodded and walked to the front, so dazed that I didn't feel my ankle . . . or any other part of my body.

Someone's voice came from my throat, pledging to serve the Order. When the new clothes were placed in my arms, the soft fabric drew me back to a semblance of reality. I hugged the folded items to my chest, bowed to the saltars, and followed the attendant for a few steps.

I paused to look back. Furrow stared at the table, her face shadowed with despair. I ached for her and was glad to know I could sorrow for her even though she'd hurt me. Of course it was easy to feel compassion for another's suffering when all my dreams had come true.

Starfire gave a small wave, genuine happiness for me shining on her face. She was a true friend, able to share my joy. My heart caught on a thought. Would I have been able to celebrate with her, if she had been chosen and I wasn't? I didn't know.

I followed the attendant through a side door into a hallway I'd never entered before. Light filtered in from generous windows set high above.

As my feet trod the cold marble, the sense of fulfillment swelled in my heart until I thought I'd burst. Delicate banners hung along the wall, beginning with scarlet and passing through all the colors of my past fifteen years. Shyly, I touched the final blue banner, saying goodbye to my life as a novitiate. As the hall curved, rows of doors on both sides came into view, each with small symbols etched into the wood.

The attendant led me to one adorned with the carving of a series of calara reeds. She opened the door. "Regarb and wait here until you're summoned. This will be your sleep quarters now."

I entered, expecting to find the other new dancers, but the tiny room was empty of other people. A plump ticking rested on a platform. A row of pegs provided storage. A box with a wooden comb, leather hair ties, and a stack of linen cloths hugged one side of a long shelf set into the wall.

It had never occurred to me that dancers had their own rooms. The air felt empty and cold. How would I sleep without the comfort of others nearby? The isolation would be unbearable. Perhaps the dancers who worked in the central ground at night needed quiet and seclusion to sleep during the day. Or perhaps this was one more deprivation to help us focus solely on our work.

More questions flooded me. When was the schedule announced? When would I get my first chance to dance barefoot on the earth of our world? Did the assignments vary? If I were assigned to dance each night, how would I slip away to meet with Starfire?

No time to dwell on inquiries. I'd been given an order. I tugged off my clothes and changed into the new white fabric, finer and softer than anything I'd worn before. After hanging my old things on the pegs, I studied the long robe. Was it only worn on formal occasions? Who could I ask?

A tap at the door interrupted my fretting.

"Are you ready?" an older woman called out while already pushing her way into the small room. Her plump frame seemed massive after my years with reed-thin novitiates. White curls bounced around her head like my childhood memories of sea froth.

She sized me up while brushing a bit of nonexistent lint from my tunic.

"Am I ready?" I repeated, unsure.

The elder attendant smiled. "All the new dancers wear the same dazed expression. Don't fear. You'll feel at home in no time. I'm Ginerva, your assigned attendant."

"Ginerva?" There was no pattern by that name, no flower or constellation. And she gave no designation. "Just Ginerva?"

"Well now, they won't be allowing me to include my village name, will they?"

I blinked a few times. "Do I wear the robe?"

She grabbed it from my hands and hung it on a peg. "Not today, child. It's time to gather in the common hall." While she spoke, she grabbed my blue clothes and bundled them together, taking them with her. "Follow me."

I padded after her farther along the hallway. She stopped to push her bundle into a basket set in an alcove. "Laundry there," she said crisply. "Blankets once a week. I'll bring fresh clothes each morning, never you fear. But I won't be picking up after you, you hear?"

By now we'd reached arched windows that gave a view into a huge open room. She waved me to the door, also arched and propped open. "Away with you." She stopped herself, squeezed the bridge of her nose, and gave a funny cross-eyed squint. "You can find your way back to your room, yes?"

"Look for the reed carvings on the door?"

She beamed. "You'll do." Then she waddled down the hall, leaving me to step across the threshold into my new life.

A RANK OF WINDOWS IN THE REHEARSAL HALL OF THE
dancers' wing framed a wondrous view of the movement in the central
ground. Drawn to the magical sight, I wove my way across the room past
a few other dancers who were warming up. I stopped inches from the
panes. For the first time, I witnessed a pattern unfolding, so close that if
I could reach through the glass, I might feel a billow of fabric as women
spun past. Soon I would be among them.

Enthralled, I paid no mind to the other white-garbed women chatting
quietly in the room, until the sharp clack of rhythm sticks and scurrying
motions pulled me back to reality. I smoothed my new tunic and exchanged
a nervous smile with Dancer Pine, and offered respectful nods to a few
other experienced members of the Order.

High Saltar Tiarel entered, and the dancers slid into neat lines. I found
a place in the back row with the other new dancers from my form. How I
wished Starfire could be here to share this moment, as we'd always hoped.

Saltar River positioned herself behind one of the High Saltar's
shoulders like a severe shadow. "New dancers, step forward."

For a dancer, there was never room for error. But now, more than ever,
the demand for perfection set all my nerves on fire. Whatever awaited, I
hoped I would be worthy of my calling.

As pale as our new tunics, we filed to the front.

"Face the Order and state your name."

One by one we introduced ourselves to the rest of the dancers, speaking
our new designations for the first time.

High Saltar Tiarel addressed the room. Her cold gray eyes warmed from slate to the shade of a forest hound's fur. "These new dancers have passed their test and pledged their loyalty. They are your sisters. Dancer Pine, you may remain here to practice with the next shift. You'll be the first to join in the dance. The rest of the newcomers, follow Saltar River."

Disappointed to be torn away from the central ground, I obediently followed the others to yet another common room, this one full of long tables and benches.

"Line up," Saltar River ordered.

We glided swiftly to our places, spines tall, chins level, shoulders back. Surely the standards would only be more stringent now. None of us wanted River's disapproval on our first day. When we were novitiates and revealed any weakness, she designed brutal dance combinations in punishing repetitions to strengthen us. Only for our good, I reminded myself, hoping the resentful thought hadn't registered on my face.

The saltar crossed her arms. "We introduce new dancers into the shifts gradually. Never more than one new person at a time. We can't risk inexperienced dancers making an error and harming our world." She paced along the row, stopping in front of me, her attention snapping to my swollen ankle.

I wanted to hide my foot behind the other, but I didn't move.

She shook her head and made a tsking sound. "Dancer Calara, you'll be the last to join a shift, since you need time to heal."

Despair clawed at me. I'd waited so long. I was so close. Yet perhaps her decision was a mercy. How horrible to enter the grounds and falter or fall my first time.

I dipped my head in acknowledgement. "Thank you, Saltar."

She sniffed and stepped back.

After pulling a parchment from her tunic pocket and unrolling it, she read a seemingly endless list of rules, procedures and schedules. I tried to memorize the important facts, but my thoughts kept straying to the central ground so tantalizingly close.

That night Ginerva fussed over my ankle, smothering it with a sweet-scented poultice. She massaged the bruised joint, wiggled it every which way, and finally wrapped it tightly. Her concern and attention, so foreign to me, loosened my tongue and I found myself confessing my impatience to join the dance.

She laughed. "Hush, girl. Believe it or don't, you'll soon be hoping for fewer shifts instead of more. Hard work, it is. Sure, you all look pretty as white songbirds flitting about, but it's no playtime. Some even say . . . well, you'll see."

I tried to coax more nuggets of information, perhaps to delay being left alone, but she briskly tidied the bedding, lit a candle on the shelf, closed the shutters, and left like a cloud skittering before a wind gust.

Curled on the too-soft mattress, I stared at the flame, trying to convince myself this was a lovely room. Even though I was separated from my friends. Even when I missed the scents of drying wool and the murmurs of conversation. Even when the stark emptiness offered no encouragement to bear up under the weight of my calling. I should be grateful. This small cell wasn't at all like the storeroom of the first form where my seven-year-old self was once tortured by solitude and shadows. No, not similar at all.

AS THE DAYS PASSED, I KEPT UP IN REHEARSALS, GOT reacquainted with older dancers I'd known slightly from novitiate days, and settled into the new schedule. Abundant meals and an endless supply of candles, unheard of in the school, were only part of the benefits of our elite status. Attendants carried buckets of hot water from the kitchen to the washroom, allowing us to indulge in warm baths in several large tubs. Instead of tedious chores, all our time was dedicated to dance or rest.

Under Ginerva's care, my ankle grew stronger, and I expected to be assigned to a shift soon. Every spare moment was spent near the windows at the back of the rehearsal hall staring out at the ground as I mentally performed each step with the dancers.

Not everything in my new setting was paradise, though. Our rigid schedule and solitary rooms allowed little opportunity for interaction. Complaints or curiosity about the outer world were never encouraged in our training, but here the restrictions on our conversation, our expressions, our very thoughts were even more enforced. Meals could have provided a bit of chatter, but after we ate, Saltar River led us in reciting proverbs of the Order.

"The power of the Order is sufficient to shape the world."

"As the true wind guides the currents, only the worthy may direct our course."

"In the same way the dance bends to the drums, bend your will to obey the saltars."

"All that is of importance rests within the walls of the Order."

"Imagine perfect patterns, and you will perform perfect patterns."

I dutifully spoke the words, waiting for the proverbs to chase away the last fragments of my doubt. Instead, the words tasted empty, and I found myself longing to exchange a surreptitious eye roll with Starfire. I reassured myself that I would find the fulfillment I longed for once I danced in the central ground.

That evening, Ginerva rubbed salve into my ankle, rotated it gently, and congratulated me on the improvement. Then she poked my ribs. "Still too thin. Now I'm knowing you do nothing but practice dancing, watch dancing, and think about dancing. Didn't anyone tell you they keep baskets of fruit and bresh for you all?"

I reassured her I planned to retrieve a snack and keep my strength up.

After she bustled around the room and left, I opened the shutters. The stars throbbed in tones of blue and green, the signal that we were due for star rain.

Starfire was sure to slip out to the courtyard on a night of star rain. I was longing to learn where she'd been assigned and to tell her all my new experiences.

I picked up my candle and wound my way toward the dining hall where an unobtrusive door led outside. If anyone questioned me, Ginerva's reminder of food would be a fine excuse.

One of the shadowed tables did indeed hold a variety of fruit and the crusty, buttery bresh—so much more delicious than the saltcakes served in the school. I nibbled one and carried a spare for Starfire. After a quick glance around, I eased through the door and into a private courtyard.

I wasn't alone. Dancer Iris, a gentle woman several years my senior, sat on the edge of a planter watching the sky. At the soft snick of the door closing, she startled. Her posture relaxed when she saw me.

"Come to watch the star rain?"

I hovered by the door. "Is it allowed?"

She beckoned me closer. "Of course. Few of the dancers can be bothered, but I try to enjoy an occasional light show."

When she shifted to make room for me, the sound of metal against stone drew my attention to her feet. She tried to hide the shackles under her long nightwear gown, but my gasp stopped her. "What . . . ?"

She avoided my gaze, leaning back to study the sky again. "They don't tell you everything when you graduate into the Order, do they?"

Clasping my hands in my lap, I pressed back my dismay. "What happened? Why?"

She sighed. "At rehearsal, I asked a question that Saltar River believed was impertinent. A week of leg bands has reminded me of the importance of perfection and respect."

The resignation in her voice chilled me. Even in the mottled starlight, raw sores were evident on the skin where the heavy iron rubbed.

"It's nothing," she said. "They'll be removed tomorrow."

"My attendant gave me a salve for my ankle. It might help," I offered. "I'll bring it to your room later."

"Thank you." She stood and walked awkwardly to the door. "I'll leave you to enjoy the star rain."

Any other time, I would have loved for her to linger and tell me her experiences as a dancer, to warn me of errors to avoid. But not tonight. I longed to see Starfire. After witnessing Iris's suffering, I needed the reassurance of a friendly face even more. As soon as the door closed, I hurried to the low wall separating the secluded courtyard from the larger garden of the school. The stone was uneven enough to provide footholds for my bare toes, and I scaled the wall and landed on the other side without crushing the bresh in my pocket.

A small animal stirred in the dried leaves behind one of the planters, and I darted deeper into the shadows of the building. Leaving the dancers' courtyard was probably frowned upon, but the risk was worth a moment with my friend.

I wrapped my arms around myself in the chill evening air, scanning the area for any sign of Starfire. While I waited, I leaned against the wall and gazed at the dancing tapestry overhead. The pulsing lights grew, then exploded and shook off their colors in a sparkling cascade. Their beauty coaxed me away from my questions and fears. Green swirled and transformed into blue, which contracted and then leapt outward and showered golden dust toward the earth. I reached out my hand to catch the tiny particles. They tickled my palm before their vibrancy faded and left only sand. As a child, the star rain had always comforted me. Tonight it raised my spirits again. I laughed and tossed the star rain back into the air. Awe and wonder stirred my heart, and overwhelming gratitude swelled under my ribs. The beauty made me want to thank someone, as if the stars had been given as a gift. But where was a giver to thank?

More and more pinpoints swelled and burst, spiraling with magic fragments of color. Over the entire garden, over all of Meriel, light painted the air in designs more lovely than any of the Order's patterns.

No, I must not allow such thoughts. The patterns of the Order were perfect.

A door creaked.

I pressed my spine against the stone and held my breath.

A woman in a long brown attendant's gown stepped lightly into the garden. She moved like a dancer.

"Starfire?" I whispered.

She whirled, her wide grin greeting me.

"I hoped you'd come," we both said at once, then laughed and hugged. I clutched her a second longer, drawing a deeper sigh than I had in days.

"Tell me everything." I dragged her to a bench, jabbering breathlessly. "Where are you working? And everyone else? And do you happen to know how Nolana is?"

"Wait. I want to know how you are. Is your ankle better? Have you danced in the central ground yet?"

I shook my head. "You first."

Her mop of auburn hair picked up glints from the sky's performance. She shoved a few locks back with one hand, revealing a bruise on her cheekbone.

"Starfire, what happened?"

"Nothing." She looked away. "We best talk fast in case we're interrupted. I was assigned to serve a tender in Middlemost. But I still get lodging here."

"A tender? Do you even like ponies?"

She laughed, although for the first time since knowing her, a bitter thread tinged the sound. "They aren't so bad. The tender isn't very kind. But then, there are a lot of angry people in town."

She would loathe pity from me, so instead I nudged her. "You'll put him in line fast enough."

Now her laughter was genuine. "I will, at that. Let's see, Furrow was allowed to join the new class of Blues. She might make it yet in another year. But can you imagine repeating last year?" She shuddered, then launched into a quick report of the other news I'd missed while sequestered with the dancers.

I soaked up the gossip like a reed does water. Some from our class were working as attendants in the school, a few had reentered the Blue class, others had simply disappeared. She knew nothing about Nolana, having little interaction with the novitiates since she spent her day in Middlemost and attendants ate in the kitchen.

"Speaking of kitchens . . ." I unearthed the bresh and handed it to her. She tore off a bite and offered me some.

I shook my head. "I've eaten my fill. Enjoy." While she ate I told her all I dared about my new life. Boasting about luxuries would be unkind. Sharing my uncertainties would betray the Order. I was left with little to say, but she seemed to enjoy hearing about my motherly attendant and tidbits about my rehearsals. "And I'm expecting to be scheduled for my first real shift soon."

"Morning, late day, or night?" she asked. "If it's late day, I could watch for you from a balcony after supper."

"I haven't been told yet." I walked to the arched trellis that framed a view of Middlemost. The waning star rain cascaded over the town. "Seems like a long walk each day."

She pulled up the hem of her dress. "I wear shoes now."

My heart contracted like a bruised muscle. She was even further from the exhilarating dream of dancing barefoot on open earth. Again, I hoped she wouldn't notice my pity.

She shrugged. "At first, young men harassed me as I was leaving the tender's stables at the end of the day. But there's this kind landkeeper who offered to walk me back to the Order. Said some of the plants do better if they're pruned at night, so he was coming this way."

A tingle stronger than a shower of star rain prickled my skin. "What's his name?"

"Brantley of Windswell. Oh, and I heard—"

A shutter slammed open, and a prefect poked his head out of a ground-floor window. "Cook is looking for an extra attendant to help with some baking for tomorrow."

Starfire sprang to her feet, blocking me from the prefect's view. "Coming."

I realized my white clothes stood out—shouting my presence to any casual glance.

"Good to see you," she whispered. "Best run."

When the man's head disappeared, I raced to the wall, climbed, and landed safely in the dancers' private courtyard. A particularly brilliant burst of color slowed my steps. The star rain was dissipating, but another swirl of light overhead coaxed me to enjoy the last of the show. Once more, I felt a sensation behind my heart that was half appreciation for the beauty and half an unfamiliar yearning—but I had no idea what I yearned for. Probably to dance. Certainly that would ease this beautiful ache.

Green and blue lights braided around each other, coiled, and unfurled. I laughed and ran to the center of the courtyard, letting the sparkling fragments fall over me. I swirled with them, spinning low with bent knees, then lengthening and stretching upward as I continued to turn. I leapt upward, as if I could join the stars in their dance, then arched back, arms open and welcoming to the light.

A gust of wind tossed the last of the star rain upward and over the roof of the building. I drew a slow breath of appreciation. Time to get to bed.

I turned toward the door as a form in the shadows shifted behind a potted tree.

"Iris?" Had she been watching my carefree dance? Had I broken a rule? Would she report me?

A masculine throat cleared, and Brantley stepped forward. "Sorry. Didn't want to interrupt you."

His grin was far from apologetic, and an appreciative spark lit his eyes. He looked as rough-hewn as I remembered, and he carried a coil of rope over his shoulder.

I frowned. "What are you doing here? And don't tell me you like pruning at night. That lie might fool Starfire, but I know you're here to cause trouble."

"So is that how you dancers talk to the earth and sky?" His arms sketched a mockery of my movements.

My face heated. Had he watched me the whole time I'd played in the star rain? "No. We use precise patterns. Not that it's any of your business. The work of the Order stays within the Order."

He stepped nearer, glaring down at me. "I know far too much about the 'work' of the Order. But you insist on being blind to it all."

I stretched to my full height. Even so, I still needed to tilt my chin upward to confront him. "I don't want to hear more of your lies. Are you even a landkeeper?"

His eyes narrowed. His muscles tensed, and I braced myself for a blow.

Instead, he seemed to make a decision. He sighed, gentling his expression. "You're right that I have a reason for being here. Besides work."

I didn't want to hear a confession from him. If he revealed a plan against the Order, I would have to tell someone, and then I would have to explain what I was doing talking to a stranger in the dancers' courtyard. He was putting me in an impossible situation, and I didn't appreciate it.

He sank onto a bench. "My niece is in the school. My family asked me to check on her wellbeing."

I knew very little of men. Truth be told, I knew very little of anything or anyone, except dance. But his concern seemed genuine. I shifted my weight from foot to foot. "Which form?"

He stared at me blankly.

"Which color?" I asked.

He shook his head.

I let my breath out in huff. "How long has she been here?"

Creases puckered along his forehead. "She'd be new. Only a few weeks."

I offered a reassuring smile. "I taught the first form briefly before I left the school. All the girls are fine. Happy, fulfilled, and learning their calling."

His scowl deepened, or perhaps it was only the darkening night sky. He surged to his feet. "Good to know. Good night, and sorry again for interrupting you." Hitching the coil of rope higher on his shoulder, he strode out of the courtyard.

Long after he disappeared, I continued to stare after him, bemused. There was a sweetness to his quest. How much comfort would I have felt, those early days at school, if someone had checked on my welfare?

A stray breeze swooped down and tossed fallen star particles, reigniting their light in a last flicker of colors, reminding me of my spontaneous dance. Odd. I'd danced under the steely, critical gaze of the saltars for years, and never felt as self-conscious as when I thought of Brantley watching my private celebration.

7

THE HEM OF HIGH SALTAR TIAREL'S FORMAL ROBE POOLED on the floor as she sat on a low bench. Tiny perfect stitches. I had ample time to study them as I knelt at her feet in a private alcove near the entry to the central ground. Traditionally, she met with each new dancer before and after their first shift, and my turn had finally arrived. I should have appreciated the honor of time with her, but instead my muscles quivered with impatience.

"Throughout your training you've been kept from touching the earth with your bare feet. It takes great effort to keep our world turning and to keep it from flying loose into chaos. We didn't want you to interact with our world until you learned the controlled and careful way to speak with your movements."

I'd heard all this many times, but I nodded, keeping my gaze respectfully low.

Just tell me which patterns we'll be performing and let me go warm up.

Her gray stare assessed me and her thin eyebrows angled down. "We have applied only the best practices to your training. You, in turn, have proven yourself both capable and loyal. Now, Dancer Calara, there are secrets we can only reveal to you at this important moment."

My chin shot up. "Secrets?"

She rested her hand on the side of my face, then brushed her fingers down the white sleeves of my tunic, like sharp bare twigs scraping against a wall.

"Some dancers—not all, of course—have strange experiences as they encounter the earth. They hear from the ground beneath them."

"Hear the ground?" No saltar had ever taught us about that.

"If it happens to you, don't be startled. Continue your pattern. Continue to coax the earth to the bidding of the Order. Some of our most effective dancers have this sort of connection with our world, but it is an added challenge to overcome. After your first shift, you will meet with me and tell me what you experienced. You will speak to no one else about anything you hear or feel. Understand?"

No. I bit my tongue, trapping the word behind my teeth, then breathed out, "Of course."

She let go of my arm and pressed the heel of her hand against my forehead. "Go and move our world."

I rose to my feet in one smooth motion, grateful my ankle felt strong and whole. After a bow, I joined the other dancers lining up in the rehearsal hall. Iris was loosening her joints with large leg swings. She smiled as I took up a position beside her. Her ankles were free of the shackles, but even with the salve I'd shared, red sores testified to the toll they'd taken. "You'll be fine," she whispered.

I clung to her reassurance as I reached down to press my hands into the floor, deepening the stretch through my legs.

As the doors to the central ground opened, weary dancers and drummers exited and brushed past us into the tower. I shook out my limbs to loosen my muscles, but they fought me with their tension. After all my impatience, I was suddenly terrified and wished that time would slow down. I needed one more rehearsal. One more class. One more of Saltar Kemp's pattern drills.

Too late now. The more experienced dancers for this shift headed out into the fresh air, and I followed them.

The primary sun was setting, and we would spend our first hours in the soft glow of the subsun, and then the sparkling stars of twilight and early evening. I glanced toward the balconies. Since this was the late-day shift, perhaps Starfire would get a chance to watch.

As I found my place in the formation among all the other hooded women, I realized Starfire might not be able to pick me out in the group even if she did watch. We were uniform in physique and identical in garb, as was needed to create perfect patterns.

Then my scattered thoughts were swept away by the warmth of Meriel's dirt beneath my feet. After years of marble and cobblestone, the softness welcomed me. I curled my toes, enjoying the sensation of the soft earth shifting. I spared a moment to absorb the vast ring of the Order building looming above us and the open sky far overhead.

In the stillness before the first beats of the drums, the earth trembled slightly under my feet. Or perhaps it was only my eager nerves. I unlocked my stiff knees and found my balance.

A soft rolling sensation moved beneath me, as if the earth chuckled. A place in my soul responded, the same place that played in the star rain and kissed the new blossoms in the courtyard gardens. Warmth coursed through my chest.

Thank you for letting me touch you, strong earth. I'm here to speak to you.

The rhythm began, many quick counts followed by a pause, and then repeating. The sound evoked water sloshing back and forth in a bucket. Current pattern! This was the moment for which I'd prepared my entire life, and the first pattern was the powerful central theme that turned our world. Although the rules required I keep my face expressionless, inside my smile beamed. Destiny, indeed.

We began to move with small running steps to one side of the field, gave a wide sweep of our arms, then ran back across. Although it had been a lifetime since I'd seen ocean waves, or been rocked in a mother's arms, the dance stirred those memories and more.

My body exulted as we moved on to the first variation of the pattern, adding a leap at the end of the rapid steps, landing like a soft exhale at the end of the phrase. The earth coaxed me higher with each jump.

The rhythm progressed to a driving, rolling pace, and our group loped in a wide circle bordering the entire area. I felt it. I felt the earth give way as my feet pressed back against it. Around me, the blur of white dancers swirled me along. In my mind's eye I saw images of our world, alone amid an endless sea. Our island turned around its axis, refusing the tug of deep ocean waves. Beyond the walls, miles and miles of field and forests, rivers and villages joined the dance, oblivious to the imperceptible movement that we experienced with such amazing power.

Yes! The world was ours, we set the direction, we charted the course, we—

Shackled! A deep voice rang through my mind, with a groan that shuddered through my bones.

I stumbled. My feet automatically recovered and kept moving, but I lost my place in the pattern. What came next? Ahead of me, Iris continued the steps confidently, and I followed her. We leapt lightly past the window of the High Saltar's office. The bright white of her formal robe stood unmoving near the glass.

Had she seen me stumble? And that voice. Was this what the High Saltar had warned me about? A sound older, stranger, more powerful than any human speech. One simple word had left me shaken. I kept dancing, watching the others, searching them for a reaction. Their faces remained stoic.

We spiraled into a tight group in the center, and I drew comfort from being surrounded by others, breathing together, muscles reaching and straining together. Kneeling, we continued our swaying movements.

Release My world!

The voice was deep and heavy, as if projecting from the heart of a boulder, or sung from the ocean depths. I shuddered as the words rocked through me.

Tiarel's warning played through my memory over the rumbling. "Coax the earth to the bidding of the Order." But the strength of the voice made folly of her command. I could as easily tell one of the suns to stop traveling across the sky.

The other dancers rose, and Iris nudged me. A few of the women sent me worried glances.

"I'm sorry," I whispered . . . to Iris, to the Order I was failing, to my dreams that were spiraling out of reach.

Somehow I stumbled to my feet. Years of repetition served me as I moved into the next variation, yet my movements lost their smooth texture. My feet feared each new step, worried I'd stir another proclamation from the voice. For several minutes I danced as though the ground were coated with embers.

The voice gentled, a mere echo of what I'd first heard. *My people have forgotten Me.*

The sorrow in the voice pierced my heart and made me want to weep and tear my tunic. Rocking side to side, rolling through my heels, I projected my thoughts toward the earth, but found little to say.

"I'm sorry, sorry, sorry," I said silently. "Don't speak again, please, please, please."

Perhaps the earth had mercy. Perhaps I'd been overwrought and only thought I'd heard words in the thrumming of the drums. At any rate, no more voices interrupted the pattern.

We completed current and grabbed a few breaths before the drums began the next rhythm. We paced through the slower furrow pattern to urge crops to grow, followed by pine and willow to nourish the trees. Even though I imagined the forests throughout our world strengthened and heartened by our dance, I couldn't return to my original feelings of joy and satisfaction. I couldn't be sure when the voice would speak again, and how I could cope if it did.

Much later, when we finished yet another series, I was surprised to see the torches alight. I stood poised, alert, ready for the next cue, but the drummers stood, stretched, and left the ground.

"We're done." Iris touched my shoulder.

I blinked a few times, struggling to return to reality. We lined up and filed inside. In the jostling of dancers exiting and entering, Iris was able to grab my elbow and pull me aside. "Whatever you do, don't tell the High Saltar what happened to you out there."

"But she said . . ."

"Calara, I've seen what happens." Her warning tone was almost as adamant as the words I'd heard in the dance. "If she saw your mistakes, blame it on nerves."

A cold breeze crept through the doorway from the center ground, and I shivered. Iris hurried away before I could ask her to explain. The experience had already terrified me. Why did Iris have to stir even more fear in me? If I couldn't trust the High Saltar, then I couldn't trust the very ground I walked on.

My lips coaxed into a wry smile. And apparently the ground I walked on *was* unpredictable.

As the energy of exertion and surprise wore off, my whole body slumped with fatigue. I longed to steal away to my room. I trudged across the large rehearsal room.

When I reached the door, High Saltar Tiarel waited, posture more rigid than usual, face implacable.

How much had she noticed? What should I tell her?

I kept my gaze down, finding the reliable stitches on her hem once again.

For years I'd depended on the instructions of others. Routines, schedules, precise orders. I had little practice relying on my own instinct. Yet in that moment, the very fiber of my being sensed danger.

She grasped my chin in a painful grip and tilted my face to meet her gaze. Deep eyes probed my soul and stripped me bare. "Well?"

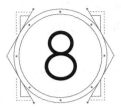

8

THE WALLS OF THE REHEARSAL HALL GLARED DOWN AS I struggled to think of an answer for High Saltar Tiarel. "It was an honor to dance in the center ground," I said in a carefully neutral tone.

The High Saltar's impatient hiss reverberated in the room that had rapidly emptied of the other dancers. She tightened her bruising grip on my lower jaw. "What did you hear?"

A tremor ran up my spine at the memory of the deep voice, but I met her gaze with all the childlike naivety I could muster. "I heard the drums. I heard our feet against the ground. And once I thought I heard the howl of a forest hound in the distance."

Her eyebrows lowered, suspicion and threat sliding across her brow. She pushed my chin aside and allowed me to step back. "Report to my office in the morning."

After an obedient bow, I slipped away and ran all the way to my room. How had my lifelong dream become such a nightmare? A part of me wanted to keep running—into the outer gardens, down to Middlemost. Perhaps Starfire could find me work tending the ponies.

How could I fulfill my purpose when I didn't know whom to trust?

My door stood open, and I rushed in and tumbled onto my bed, gasping for breath and fighting back tears. The scent of clean, pressed linen reminded me that there had to be a way to put things right, to regain the smooth order of my life. But how?

Ginerva was lighting candles on the shelf. "So dearie, how was your first . . ." When she saw how distraught I was, her lips formed a worried circle. She sat beside me, opening her arms. I let her enfold me while a few frightened sobs quivered from my lungs.

"There, there." She patted my back. "You'll be fine. Mayhap a bit overwhelming, but you'll get used to it. Of course it's a huge adjustment. You've worked your whole life for the experience. Trust me. I've seen many women serve here, and I knew right away you had the strength for the work. You'll be fine."

I pulled back. Tender hazel eyes welcomed my confidences. She'd cared for dancers for years. She would know what I should do.

"I heard something. A voice. I—"

Alarm squeezed Ginerva's features and she placed a finger over my lips. "Hush. Don't ever speak of it."

"That's what Iri—what another dancer told me. But why? The High Saltar wants me to tell her—"

"No!" She pulled a handkerchief from her sleeve and mopped my tears.

I stilled her hands. "Please, tell me why."

She rose and peered out into the hall before closing the door and returning. Even though we were alone, she whispered, heightening my sense of danger. "Tiarel has been trying for years to find women who can hear the voice—and more importantly can help her command it with more power. She sends them out again and again. Some go mad. Some disappear. There are rumors of a well in a room beyond her office, cut down to the ocean, and it's not used for drawing water."

Horror tightened the muscles of my face.

She sank beside me again. "There, there child. I've gone and upset you more. I'm sorry. Don't be worrying about those tales. Only you must understand why you can't tell her."

"But how can I hide it? I'll have to tell her. She's the High Saltar. Besides, I'll be on another shift soon. What if the world talks to me again? I can't . . ."

"That's just it, dear one. You didn't hear the voice of the earth or the sea."

She wasn't listening, or perhaps she couldn't believe me. I eased away and confronted her. "I'm telling you, I heard it. So strong that I nearly fell.

So compelling I almost couldn't finish the pattern."

She patted my hand and pressed her lips together, seeming to struggle with a decision. "If you heard Someone speak to you, it wasn't our natural world. You heard the Maker."

Poor dear woman, still steeped in the myths of the rim villages. Now I was the one to pat her hand. "Ginerva, I won't tell anyone what you said. But you know that to speak of these lies is heresy."

She cupped my face in her palms, her touch so gentle and different from Tiarel's. "Little one, I've trod this earth for three of your lifetimes. I've served here for decades, and have tried to help the dancers when I can. I've seen the world beyond the Order, and more importantly, I've had glimpses into the true nature of the Order. Tiarel is growing desperate. That's why she's been sending out regiments to wrest girls from their homes."

My hands clenched. Nolana had claimed she was stolen away. But that couldn't be true. "Families vie to have their girls accepted—"

"She's always searching for the ones who might grant her more control over the world." With a flutter of fingers she waved away my interruption and spoke rapidly. "And it's why more villages are rebelling. They've been bled dry by her taxes and now have lost lives trying to protect their families."

"Then why would she send any dancers away? If she needs more, why wasn't Starfire accepted? Or Alcea, Furrow, and Dawn?"

Ginerva shook her head. "She thinks only the most perfect and skilled dancers can master the voice. She culls those who she believes to be weak of spirit, but allows most into the Order—at least until she can test them in the center ground. And many girls don't come willingly. Think back. Think about the days before you were brought here."

I stepped back. "We aren't allowed. There is no life before the Order."

Through tiny cracks around the door of memory, a sensation emerged, one revived by the current pattern I'd just performed. The sheltered warmth of being rocked in loving arms. The faint melody of a lullaby. Then a later moment, the image of my mother's arms reaching for me, horrified tears streaming down as I was wrested away, the copper taste as a soldier struck me, silencing my desperate scream.

I gasped. How had I forgotten? "Th-th-they took me?"

Tears watered Ginerva's eyes. "It takes years of control to plant the lie so deep."

She waited quietly while everything I knew and believed crumbled like sunbaked clay, leaving me grappling in the dust for something to grasp.

"But our work here? Maintaining the world."

She shrugged plump shoulders. "Perhaps a part of what the saltars believe is true. And part is a lie."

"A lie," I whispered. All the years of reverence to the very people who had torn me from my family. All the longing to earn approval. Something inside me shriveled and died, even as I tried to hold on. "Maybe they had to. Maybe the suffering is worth it for the greater good." But the words were dry grit on my tongue.

"All I know is that if Tiarel learns the voice spoke to you, you'll suffer a terrible fate. Can you hide it from her?"

"I don't know."

"You must. Or you must flee."

MY EXPERIENCE IN THE CENTER GROUND AND THE ONSLAUGHT of new memories kept me awake all night. I had been taught to despise the peasants of the rim, but as memories unfurled, I remembered the sensation of diving into sweet water and riding the waves as they carried me back to the tangled fringes of vegetation that lined the shore. I remembered riding the shoulders of my father, laughing and grasping for persea from a branch overhead.

As I tossed in my bed, I stopped resisting all the doubts about the Order that had gathered recently like lead weights on a scale. Brantley's accusations about how castoffs were treated no longer seemed so farfetched, nor Nolana's plaintive testimony of being stolen from her family. I couldn't countenance Ginerva's belief in a Maker, but I did trust that she'd seen more of the inner workings of the Order than I had, and her fear for me was palpable. Perhaps there was truth to even the dark rumors of a hole into the ocean where unworthy dancers were cast. I couldn't deny I'd witnessed harshness and cruelty, all in the name of the Order.

None of this helped me make a plan, however. When the first sun sent the faint glow of predawn light through my shutters, I still didn't know what to say when I met with Tiarel. Even if I hid my experiences, I'd soon face another assignment out on the central ground. I couldn't endure another encounter with that powerful voice. Couldn't hide its impact on me forever.

I grabbed a cloak and tiptoed down the empty hall and out to the dancers' courtyard. Not even the servants were awake yet. The night dancers would be finishing their lonely shift soon, but for now, the Order seemed almost deserted. Overhead, stars faded as deep violet softened the dark sky. I wished I could fade from sight as easily or find my old village and make a new life. But how? I didn't know how to navigate Meriel. I wouldn't even be able to find Salis, the town where Alcea sought refuge. Should I just run until my legs gave out?

A thump interrupted my thoughts. It came from beyond the wall of the school's gardens. I tiptoed to the wall and climbed enough to peer over. A rope dangled from the first-form sleeping quarters several stories above, and beneath, a man untangled a bundle from his back. My eyes adjusted to the dim light and I squinted.

Brantley was holding Nolana.

He wasn't checking on her welfare. He was stealing her back.

I gasped.

At the sound, he pushed Nolana behind him, facing the threat with his knife at the ready. He clearly wasn't expecting the danger to be my disheveled head peeping over the wall. His alert defensiveness shifted to an expression of exasperation. "You again? Whatever you do, don't raise an alarm. Please."

A kernel of hope flared in my heart. He'd helped Alcea when she was cast out. He'd known the nearest villages. I climbed the wall and jumped lightly to the cobblestones before him. "I won't. On one condition. Take me with you."

BRANTLEY HEFTED A PACK OVER ONE SHOULDER AND tucked his knife back into his belt. "Don't be ridiculous. Go back to your precious Order. Just give us time to get away." He grabbed Nolana's hand and strode toward the arched trellis where wisps of morning fog hovered over the grass beyond.

The little girl tugged him to a halt. "Uncle Brant, she was my nice teacher. We have to help her."

He swept Nolana into his arms and jogged out of the gardens, ducking sideways into the relative shelter of the outer wall.

I followed, running lightly. "I can't stay here."

He scanned the windows of the Order, then measured the distance to Middlemost. "Got yourself into some trouble, did you? All the more reason we don't want you along. Besides, once I deliver the girl to her mother, I'll be traveling fast."

"I can keep up. I'm stronger than I look."

He sized me up. White tunic and leggings, pristine cloak, light leather slippers, no supplies. The planes of his face were as hard-edged as the stone that formed the Order's walls. "No."

Nolana whispered something in his ear.

He rolled his eyes. "Where are you heading?" he asked me.

I swallowed. Good question. Where could I go? "I . . . I'm not sure."

"Glad you have a plan." His sarcasm burned through me, but the longer I kept him arguing, the more chance I had to convince him.

"Just bring me along until I'm safely away from the Order. I don't care where you're going."

Nolana leaned her face against his bristly cheek. "Please, Uncle Brant?"

His steely gaze met mine in an angry challenge. "If we're caught, it will be on your head."

"Understood." Brave words, but if Nolana was captured because of me, the guilt would be unbearable. "Don't worry. I won't slow you down."

His only response was a snort. Then he adjusted his hold on Nolana, scanned the surroundings once more, and ran toward town.

My cloak fluttered behind me as I tore after him, determined to stick like a pale shadow. We reached the first row of houses and shops, and he wove past a bakery where puffs of smoke from the chimney indicated early-morning work. We passed an empty fruit stand and the smelly barrels of tallow behind the chandler. He continued rapidly down a narrow street of taverns and into the alley behind a row of stone cottages with thatched roofs.

The uneven cobblestones bruised my feet, but I stayed close. He was breathing hard from the run, and I took a bit of smug satisfaction that I wasn't winded at all. Of course I wasn't carrying a little girl and a pack, either.

He glanced back once to be sure I still followed, but whether he was relieved or disappointed to see me was hard to say.

Finally, he opened the side door of an inn and slipped inside. I was close enough to sidle in behind him.

A heavyset cook stood before a massive hearth, stirring a pot that exuded a burnt and sour odor. She raised her eyebrows at our hasty entrance into her kitchen, but merely held out her hand. Brantley gave her a few tokens from his pocket, and she nodded and turned back to her cooking. Kettles caked with residue stacked along the side of the room, and a rodent scurried from the corner and glared at our intrusion. I bit my lip, hoping we wouldn't be staying long enough to eat anything here.

Brantley lowered Nolana and led us from the kitchen into a dining hall. Rows of empty tables canted at awkward angles with rough benches and chairs shoved underneath.

A woman in a coarse brown dress stood staring into the dead ashes of a cold fireplace.

"Brianna, I was able to get her out this time," Brantley said.

The woman turned, a joyous sob wrenching from her when she saw Nolana. She fell to her knees, opening her arms as Nolana ran to her, their movements a beautiful dance of reunion and love. Brianna stroked her daughter's hair, kissed every inch of her face, and they murmured reassurances to each other. An empty place in my heart throbbed with longing. Would I ever belong to someone with that sort of love? My only place of belonging had been the Order, and now I was adrift even from them.

Brantley cleared his throat and stepped closer to Brianna. "We have to get both of you on your way."

Brianna lifted teary eyes, her blonde hair a tangled frame around her face. "Of course." Her gaze shifted to me and my dancer garb. Her jaw hardened. I wore the uniform of the Order who had stolen her child, no wonder she instantly despised me. "Who is this?" she asked.

Not an easy question to answer, as even offering a name was a quandary. In fleeing the Order, I could no longer call myself Dancer Calara.

"Call me Calara." The name felt odd on my tongue without the designated color or rank, but at least it held some familiarity. "I've left the Order," I added to reassure her.

Brianna's expression didn't soften. She rose and hefted her daughter to her hip, ready to fend me off as if I were a ravening forest hound.

Brantley pulled out a chair and waved me toward it. "You stay here. You'll draw too much attention. I need to get them out of Middlemost."

Panic made my eyes flare. "You said you'd bring me with you."

His ocean-blue eyes met mine, but I couldn't read what I saw in their depths. Betrayal or honesty? "Trust me," he said. "I'll come back for you once they're on their way."

The cook poked her head in from the kitchen. "Just heard some soldiers pounding on a door up the street. Get hid or get out. Can't have them finding you here. Didn't pay me enough for that."

Brantley ran to the front door of the inn and peered into the street. "Too late." He scanned the room. "Upstairs?"

The cook waddled to the stairway and crossed her arms. "Oh, no you don't. Worse for me if they find you in one of my rented rooms."

Heavy thumps sounded on the door across the alley, and deep voices demanded entry. Metal scraped, and in the distance a baby wailed and was quickly hushed.

Brantley ran to the dining hall's cold fireplace and stepped into the wide hearth, staring upward. "Here. Climb."

Brianna didn't hesitate. She lifted Nolana, and the girl somehow disappeared upward. With a boost from Brantley, Brianna followed. How had they done that?

He beckoned to me. The splintering of wood and a woman's startled cry from next door propelled me to Brantley's waiting arms. Above me, uneven stone climbed to the chimney's crown. The silhouettes of Nolana and her mother stood out against the early dawn light. Nolana had found enough footholds to scramble up, while Brianna moved more slowly, bracing her back against one side and her feet against the other.

Brantley linked his hands. I placed my foot in the makeshift stirrup and let him hoist me high enough to grip an outcropping stone inside the chimney. Greasy soot coated every surface and years of acrid ash choked my nostrils. My feet grappled for purchase on the slick stone.

I made my way up until I was even with Brianna. Our backs pressed against opposite sides of the chimney, and I was grateful for the strength of my legs that wedged me securely in place. But were we high enough to give Brantley room to hide, and who would boost him?

Beneath us a chair scraped. He stepped up from its seat and grunted as he hefted himself high enough to be out of sight of the approaching soldiers. The chair scraped again, disappearing as the cook shoved it back to a table.

Fists pounded the front door, and the cook grumbled. "Hey, what's all this noise? My guests pay for a good night's rest."

"We have orders to search every building," one of the men said. "Stand aside."

The cook's voice faded as she moved toward the kitchen. "Well, be quick about it. My porridge is burning."

I scarcely dared to breathe as booted feet tromped throughout the inn and then mounted the stairs. Doors crashed open, voices rose and fell with questions and demands. Their heavy-footed search made the whole inn shake.

One of Brianna's feet skidded, and a bit of ash loosened and fell to the hearth below. I wrapped an arm under her leg to give her more support. The edge of a brick dug into my back, and my thighs cramped with the effort of holding my position. Nolana had climbed enough to poke her head out the top of the chimney. The modest inn suddenly seemed as dizzyingly tall as the Order tower. I was grateful our bodies created a net that could catch Nolana if she fell. Unless her weight pushed us all down to the ground.

"Are you done yet?" the cook called as footfalls stomped down the steps. "What's all this about?"

"A dancer went missing. Have you seen one?"

I drew in a silent gasp, and my legs quivered. They weren't after Nolana. They were looking for me.

"Ha! What would one of them be doing, flitting around in town? They keep to themselves, they do," the cook answered.

I wanted to kiss her flour-smudged face. I also silently thanked the darkness of the chimney that kept me from seeing Brianna's expression. As Brantley had feared, I'd complicated the rescue. I pressed my head back against the grimy stone, guilt squeezing my throat.

The soldiers moved on, and still we held our cramped positions. Finally the cook called from below. "They've gone."

Brantley sprang to the ground.

"Nolana," I called softly. "You can come down now."

A hiss sounded from Brianna. "That's not her name."

"I'm sorry. What's her true name?"

"None of your business, dancer." The sneering word held weeks of pent-up resentment.

We inched our way down the chimney, where Brantley assisted us to the hearth.

Blinking in the light of the dining hall, I brushed soot from my hands. My cloak and leggings were coated with the stuff, too. As streaked and filthy as my soul felt. I'd been an eager and faithful part of the Order that was harming our world, and now even my effort to leave had further endangered the others.

The cook stood near the foot of the stairs, waving a few sleepy customers back up to their rooms. "I'll ring when breakfast is ready. Go away with you. Excitement's over."

Again, I wanted to thank her for protecting us, until she turned her angry visage toward us. "You four. Get out now."

Brantley fumbled in a pocket for more tokens, but the cook pinched her face into a threatening stare. "You don't have coin enough for me to risk everything. Get out or I'll call the soldiers back myself."

Brianna held her daughter to her chest. Dark rivulets lined the path of tears down her face as she turned to Brantley. "What now?"

He pulled fingers through his hair, the blond curls darkened by layers of soot. "We have to hide somewhere. We'll go back the direction they've already searched." Even though Brianna waited hopefully for his next idea, he looked confounded, weary, even fearful.

I had to find a way to help. This was all my fault. "I have an idea."

Frowns turned my way, except from Nolana, who offered an encouraging smile of trust. "My friend works for the tender. She could hide us."

As a testament to how desperate he felt, Brantley didn't argue. "I know the place."

He cajoled a few saltcakes from the cook, then led us out into the streets. The first sun was fully risen now, and its brightness felt like a threat. Running, ducking, hiding breathless in dark alcoves, we listened for the sounds of soldiers or even alert shopkeepers or tradesmen who might give us away. Eventually we made our way to the stables. The tender hadn't risen yet, and the ponies seemed unimpressed with our presence as we crept inside. A few blew breathy greetings or shook their heads making manes fly. We made for the far end of the stable, climbed a pile of hay and burrowed in at the back, hoping no pitchfork would find us when the tender fed his steeds.

"So where is your friend?" Brantley's breath tickled against my ear.

"She'll be here." I hoped. My suggestion led them here, and now Starfire wasn't at work. Would my effort to help be a complete failure?

Brantley put a protective arm around Brianna, shooting an accusing glare at me. "Are you sure she won't betray us?"

"I'm not sure of anything anymore," I said quietly. I sagged, hugging my knees. As my breathing slowed back to normal, energy bled from my muscles like blood from a wound. This idea was all I had to offer. My own safety was no longer important. I had to help the others escape Middlemost. The aggressive search through town was my fault. "Maybe I should turn myself in. Perhaps they'll stop the search."

"What would they do to you?" Brantley asked, a little too eager to consider the suggestion.

Hobble me? Send me out to the center ground over and over until I went mad? Throw me down a hidden well to disappear in the deep ocean?

"They kill the bad ones," Nolana said, her wispy, innocent voice so wrong for the dark words she shared. "The prefect told me."

I bit my lip. "He was trying to scare you. I'm sure they don't . . ." No, I wasn't sure of anything. Only that we were in danger, that my entire world had turned upside down, that everything I'd taken pride in was now a source of shame. "Let's focus on getting you and your mother away from here."

Brantley plucked a piece of straw from my hair, his teeth flashing in the dimness of our stable hiding place. He seemed to find me a source of humor, an object of mockery. I couldn't blame him. Surely, I looked ridiculous.

When he focused on his sister and niece, his expression turned serious. "I've enough tokens to rent a pony. Bri, you'll be able to reach Windswell well ahead of any searchers."

"What about you?" Brianna asked him.

"I'll head a different direction and lead them away from you."

Which left me on my own. How long could Starfire hide me in the stables—if she ever showed up, and if she was even willing? And once I found a way out of Middlemost, where would I go?

The clang of a bucket outside hushed us into tense silence. Light flickered over us as the stable door creaked open. I wished I dared stand and peek over the haystack to see who had entered, but I couldn't risk it.

Grain whispered into troughs. Ponies snorted. "You're hungry this morning, Ablehoof." Starfire laughed.

Relief washed over me, and I eased to my feet. Starfire was making her way toward us, and there was no sign of the tender.

"Star," I hissed.

She startled and dropped her bucket, then squinted into the shadows where I stood. "Who are you? What are you doing here?"

I clambered over the hay and slid to the floor in front of Starfire. "It's me. Calara. I need your help."

She grasped her chest and gave a relieved laugh. "You scared me worse than a saltar on test day. What are you doing here? And why"—her gaze coasted over me head to toe—"do you look like that?"

I brushed stable grime from my tunic, only spreading the smudges. "It's a long story. I have friends who need help."

Brantley emerged, and Star's eyes grew rounder.

"I need to rent a pony," he said. "I have the coin."

Star backed away a few steps, shaking her head. "The tender handles those transactions. You'll have to wait until he wakes."

I reached out to Starfire. "Remember the girl in first form I was worried about? She was stolen from her family to be brought to the Order. He's trying to help her and her mother get away."

Starfire rubbed her forehead. "A few weeks ago I wouldn't have believed the Order would take a child against her will. Was anything we were told the truth?"

Tears caught in my throat. "I haven't figured that out yet."

Starfire closed the distance between us and hugged me. "Maybe I can help. The tender is probably sleeping off another night of drinking. If your friend pays enough, he may not care that I helped a customer on my own." She tossed back her auburn mop of hair and grinned at Brantley. "You protected me on my walks back to the Order in the evenings. I owe you. Ablehoof is the fastest we have."

"Thank you." Brantley dipped his chin.

"Are you sure you won't get in trouble?" I asked Starfire. She'd been a true friend throughout the years. Could I bear even more guilt if she suffered because of helping us? Why did all my choices seem to bring others pain?

Lines around her eyes tightened, accentuating the dark circles, but she hid it with a short laugh. "I studied at the Order. Think I can't manage a drunken old tender?"

Brantley didn't allow time for me to wrestle with misgivings. He paid her a generous amount, got Brianna and her daughter settled, stocked a saddlebag with supplies, and led them out of the stable. While he was giving them directions for the best route out of Middlemost, I huddled with Starfire in the stable, absently stroking the warm muzzle of a dappled pony.

"When I left for work this morning, there were soldiers at the Order. Big ruckus." Star frowned and nudged me. "It's you they're looking for, isn't it?"

"Perhaps." The enormity of my choice to flee rolled through me, leaving hopelessness in its wake. The soft jangle of tack and muted clopping of hooves faded into the distance, and my heart sent a wish for Nolana's safety.

Brantley strode back into the stable. He shook his head, sending up a cloud of straw dust. "With the pony they'll reach help sooner. You may have actually had a good idea this time, dancer."

"Don't call me that." My voice broke. I wasn't a dancer. I wasn't a novitiate. I wasn't even a worker like Starfire. I'd run from my role, the role I'd prepared for all my life. Now I was nothing.

Brantley leaned against the stable doorframe and crossed his arms. The streaks of soot and dirt didn't look as harsh against his coarse, travel-worn clothes as they did on mine. His sturdy boots, longknife in his belt, sack of supplies, and strong jaw all spoke of confidence and strength. Unlike me, he knew who he was and where he belonged.

He sighed, gaze raking over me. "Now, what are we going to do about you?"

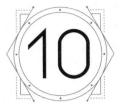

10

TWO DAYS LATER, PUNISHING RAIN BEAT DOWN ON Brantley and me, soaking through my cloak. Although it was midday, clouds blocked both suns and created a gloom like a shuttered chamber. The ground roiled unpredictably under my feet, nothing like the subtle shifts of the Order's grounds. I struggled to avoid falling.

Ahead of me, Brantley sprang over a large fallen tree and tromped forward at a relentless pace. I struggled over the trunk, tangling in the long, narrow skirt of my peasant garb.

"I can't move in this," I muttered, missing the freedom of the tunic and leggings I'd worn most of my life. The wind cast my words forward for Brantley to hear.

"You should be grateful Starfire found you a disguise," he tossed over his shoulder without slowing.

I *was* grateful. Grateful for her help and his. Even though I'd complicated his rescue of Nolana, ultimately he was too kindhearted to leave me behind. After he sent his sister and niece safely on their way, he let me accompany him as he fled the town a different direction. We crisscrossed pastures and forests, stopping only for quick drinks or a bite of saltcake. His plan was working. The soldiers struggled to follow our trail.

The hard pace hadn't bothered me, but the raw earth and open spaces made my stomach churn. Trees and underbrush grew in haphazard clusters so different from the tidy arrangement of the cultivated stone beds in the Order's gardens. Everything was foreign. Nature was wild and fierce and uncontrolled.

Today's thunder reinforced that impression as it grumbled downward.

Pine trees shook like wet hounds, flinging more water into our faces. In the past two days, the weather seemed to attack us at every turn. Was the High Saltar ordering the dancers to produce storm patterns to punish me for leaving? Or was the Order's ability to shape the weather another lie and this was simply a normal hardship of traveling in the wild? If only I knew what to believe.

"Stay here," Brantley said.

I dragged my gaze upward, dashing raindrops from my face and tucking wet strands of hair under the equally wet hood of my cloak. Brantley waited beside a low outcropping of jagged stone. I hurried under the small shelter, crouching to escape the downpour. "I need to check how close the patrol is," he said, then disappeared before I could protest.

Why risk stumbling into the middle of armed soldiers? Brantley was far too reckless. Surely we'd kept our pursuers busy long enough with our circuitous route. Wasn't a steady pace rimward the best plan now?

Even if Brantley had waited for my response, I wouldn't have raised those queries. Years as a novitiate had taught me unquestioning obedience. The attitude served me well traveling with the landkeeper. Brantley's earlier exasperation and reluctance toward me had mellowed into grudging tolerance because I refused to slow his pace or complain.

Except about this wretched dress. I hiked up the hem to wring water from it, a futile effort when everything I wore was soaked.

Footsteps sounded nearby. That was fast. Perhaps Brantley had decided not to venture too far back in this miserable weather.

I was about to call out to him, but men's voices and heavy footsteps stopped me. Cold dread clenched all my muscles, and I crouched even lower in the rocky alcove, trembling in the effort to hold still.

"I'm telling you, we've lost her trail," one man said, so near I could hear him brushing rain off his leather-clad arms.

"I'm not telling the High Saltar that," said another.

"But she could be anywhere in the wide world. For all we know the dancer could still be hiding in Middlemost." The man's voice took on a whine like an untrained first-form child. "What's so special about this one, anyway? We bring the Order new girls all the time. So what if a few run off?"

"Dunno, but Saltar High and Mighty sure has a nettle in her backside about this one."

Leather creaked and their steps moved back the way they'd come. Their retreat could be a ruse to draw me out, so I pulled farther back under the stone, trying to shape my body into the rock, to dissolve into it like salt into dough. I would never leave this haven. I'd hide here until I grew old and gray.

They won't take me back. They won't take me.

I squeezed my eyes shut, only to confront images of the outcomes I feared most: soldiers dragging me back through the doors of the Order, a sharp knife cutting my tendon as Tiarel smiled, being forced out onto the central ground while the voice of the world thundered and condemned me.

I shrank into a tighter ball. Why was I even running? I had nowhere to go. Nowhere to belong. I was only delaying the inevitable. The cold stone offered no comfort, and my body trembled.

Minutes or hours later, Brantley found me shaking uncontrollably in the crevice. He peered into the darkness. "You all right? Dancer?"

He'd never bothered to call me Calara. The rare times he spoke to me, he called me 'dancer,' in a tone that made the title sound like a curse. This time, though, his voice held only concern. My throat clogged and my eyes burned. I couldn't speak.

His hand thrust toward me, and I recoiled.

He eased as far under the outcropping as he could. The warmth of his body reached out to me like a comforting fireplace.

Still, I couldn't stop shivering.

"They've gone," he crooned. "Let's move. Now's our chance to lose them for good."

I nodded, but my limbs wouldn't unlock.

He placed a cautious hand on my shoulder. When I didn't flinch away, he rubbed small circles and made tsking sounds that reminded me of Ginerva comforting me after an exhausting rehearsal.

"I'm sorry," he said. "I wouldn't have left you if I'd known they were so close. Gave you a start, did they?"

I blew out a breath, my muscles beginning to soften into usefulness again. Somehow I found words. "Did you hear them? They're going back to the Order."

He gathered my hands in his, rubbing warmth and life into them. "Great news. So let's cover some ground. We're not far from Foleshill. We could stay there tonight."

I frowned. He wanted to reach a village so he could leave me behind. "No, not Foleshill. They weren't paying their Order tax, so it's likely Tiarel has sent more soldiers there."

His hands stilled. "And how would you know that?" Even in the shadow of the overhang, I could see his speculative gaze, hardened with renewed suspicions.

My ribs sagged. Was there anywhere in this world I could go where I wouldn't be thought of as an enemy? "I was a novitiate. I heard about rebellions sometimes."

Brantley edged back. "So where do you suggest we head, dancer?" The sneer had returned.

I convinced my legs to move and followed him out of the shelter. Rubbing my finger and thumb together, I remembered the smooth texture of a small corner of parchment, long since lost, and the tantalizing words I'd once penned. "Undertow."

His eyebrows disappeared under the tangle of hair that dripped over his forehead. "A rim village? Why?"

I hated to share my fragile and uncertain hope, but if I didn't give him a reason, he'd abandon me in Foleshill. "I'm not sure, but I think it may be where they took me from." One tear escaped, blending with the rain covering my face. I scuffed a few of the moldy leaves underfoot. "I may even have family."

A heavy silence followed my admission. Then Brantley sighed. "You couldn't have mentioned that before? Do you understand it will take us weeks to reach the rim? And now we're on the wrong side of the island."

"Did you have another place in mind?" I asked.

"My plan was to lead any searchers away from the road to Windswell until it would be safe for me to return."

"So in the meantime, we could journey to Undertow?"

He gave me a long look, but didn't answer. Instead, he hefted his pack and trudged forward, muttering and complaining to himself and occasionally kicking a stick out of his way.

I followed behind, a sudden gladness casting off the gloom of the day. In the wake of his irritation, his flare of suspicion had washed away, and we now had a destination.

OVER THE NEXT FEW DAYS, HE CONTINUED TO MUMBLE about all the trouble I'd caused and never missed an opportunity to cast aspersions on the Order and all dancers, yet we settled into a grudging partnership. I tended the fire and foraged for cattail roots and edible greens, grateful for the botanical lessons I'd had as a student in form seven. Brantley rustled through bushes trying to flush out small game. One evening a bog rat peered from the underbrush on the edge of our camp. Brantley flung his knife with impressive accuracy, and we had spit-roasted meat for our supper. As we sat in the glow of the small fire, licking our lips and savoring a warm meal, the world seemed to shrink into the small circle of flame, safety, and companionship.

"So tell me about your family." Brantley's tone held none of his usual contempt, only curiosity.

I swallowed my last bite and hugged my knees. "I can't remember much. We weren't allowed to think about anything that came before the Order."

He made a scoffing sound, but without his customary fury, so I dared to continue.

"I have glimmers of riding my father's shoulders. Of my mother. I remember her reaching, crying." I shivered. "I hadn't thought about my home village in years."

Brantley unrolled a blanket from his pack and draped it around my shoulders. "So you were my niece's age when you were taken?"

Was that a hint of compassion?

"Younger. They told me my family sold me, didn't want me, and that the Order was now my family. And they gave me a purpose."

And what of that purpose now? A skewer twisted inside my ribs. Would I ever find a place to belong again? Eager to change the subject, I poked a stick at our fire, drawing pops and sizzles. "Your turn. Tell me about your family."

I didn't look at him, but his voice held a smile. "My mother is a force of the sea, steering the waves and constant as the horizon. She raised us to defend the weak."

"Us?"

"My brother Cole and me." As if a hand tightened around his throat, his words choked off.

"Brianna's husband?"

"Mm-hm." The companionable mood had splintered and the silence hung heavy now, broken only by crackles from the dying fire.

The stretching time threatened to snap, so I braved another question. "What happened to him?"

"The Order happened to him." He surged to his feet, snatching up his pack, and moved to the far side of the fire. He curled up with his back to me.

I huddled under the blanket while the cold of the ground seeped into my soul. I shouldn't fool myself. His resentment may have faded a little, but I was still the enemy in his eyes. How would I endure the coming days? I still needed his help to find Undertow. And what then? Would anyone there remember me?

I turned my face to the stars, feeling lost among their multitudes.

AFTER WE WERE FAR FROM ANY MIDRANGE VILLAGES AND curious eyes, I changed back into my dancer garb. The fabric was hopelessly stained, and Brantley insisted I rub dirt on the parts still white so I wouldn't attract attention. Ginerva would be horrified at the state of my clothes, but at least I was able to climb trees and gather fruit with more ease.

I'd never gone so many days without taking class, and my body began to protest. One morning I left Brantley dozing by our fire and slipped away to stretch. I didn't dare perform full patterns, but I at least regained some suppleness in my muscles. I settled into a daily routine of early waking, washing beside whatever river or pond we'd camped near, limbering my body, then returning to help Brantley strike camp.

I lost track of the days. Sometimes I believed I'd always slept under the stars and spent every waking hour of my life hiking through forests and across prairies. Ages ago when I'd stared out of the upper window of the Order, I'd wondered where the roads led. Now I'd traveled those paths and far beyond.

One evening, dusty clouds gathered overhead like an angry mob, hiding the sinking suns. Gusts of wind harassed our small fire. Brantley added a few dry twigs to the blaze and settled with a sigh. I pulled my rough cloak around my body and huddled closer to the flame.

"You're very quiet." Brantley poked at the fire and sparks flew up.

"I'm sorry."

"Wasn't a complaint. Just an observation."

I shrugged, not sure how to respond. Our fire needed more sticks, so I opened my cloak along the ground, protecting my hands from the earth as I pushed myself up.

Brantley chuckled.

"What?" I asked.

"You always do that. You're coated with grime, but you don't let your prim little hands touch the ground."

I sniffed and headed off to gather more wood. He didn't need to know the truth. I wore my light slippers constantly and avoided touching the bare earth with my hands so that I wouldn't be assaulted again by the voice of our world. Perhaps out here, far from the central ground, the connection with our island wouldn't be as strong, but I couldn't risk it. Madness lay that way.

I wound deeper into the woods, collecting any dry limbs the trees had cast off. Many were too damp to burn, but I was determined to find a good supply. It was one way to earn my keep. Besides, I was tired of Brantley's frequent mocking and teasing. What would it take for him to respect me?

The trees parted and I entered a small clearing, then pulled up short. The sticks fell from my hands.

Across the clearing, a huge forest hound bristled, clearly as startled as I. His eyes gleamed gold and alert in the twilight. He was the size of a pony, his haunches almost at eye level. His muzzle wrinkled as he bared his teeth.

I held my breath, fear snarling around my limbs. I'd never seen one of these creatures, although their mournful calls rose in the distance on nights when I'd prowled the Order's gardens. As young novitiates, we were told stories about the many people slain by these furious beasts.

Never taking his gaze from me, he moved silently to the right, then rolled his shoulder and paced to the left. Back and forth, each zigzag brought him nearer. He was hunting me. His hypnotic, silent advance was meant to paralyze his victim, and it was working.

I couldn't outrun him, and I held no weapon.

You are a dancer.

The thought brushed through my mind, bringing with it the memory of patterns I'd learned to affect every aspect of our world. Could it work with this creature? No one had ever taught me a forest hound pattern.

Softly, I began to mirror his walk, stalking first to one side and then the other, always meeting his stare, always drawing slightly closer. His crinkled muzzle relaxed and his ears pricked forward. As his hostility lessened, my own fear also fled.

"That's right. There's no need to be angry," I breathed. "This is your land. I'm only passing through."

Soon I was within a handbreadth of him, close enough to smell the musky odor of his coat. His thick fur was multi-colored and would surely gleam in the glories of sunlight. Even in the dimness I caught hints of bronze and copper mingled among the grays and browns.

Nose to nose, his hot breath poured over me like a blessing. I opened my arms. "You are a beauty, aren't you?"

He dipped his head and nuzzled against my chest. I giggled, welcoming his affection and echoing his actions. I hugged him, rubbing my face against the soft underfur of his neck.

A twig cracked somewhere behind me, and the forest hound pulled back, every hair standing up. In two mighty bounds he disappeared into the trees.

I stared after him, awestruck and grateful for the encounter. Then the enormity of the experience snipped the invisible string holding me upright and I sank, boneless, to the ground.

"What . . . ?" Brantley sounded as if someone were strangling him.

I turned to look at him. One hand pressed against a sturdy tree trunk, his other held his knife. His skin shone pale and bloodless. "What were you doing?" he choked out.

I understood his shock, but his horrified expression made me want to laugh. I eased to my feet and walked back to where my pile of kindling waited. "I startled him, but I explained I didn't mean him any harm."

"You *explained*?" A vein throbbed on his temple.

I picked up the branches and padded back to our fire.

Brantley followed, every stomp punctuating a firm rebuke. "Don't wander off like that. You could have been eaten. Or you could have run into a patrol. You wouldn't manage to tame a bunch of soldiers with your strange . . . whatever it is you do."

He kept talking, and I hid a smile. I poked new branches into the flames and let warmth swell inside my chest.

He'd been worried for me.

Not only that, I'd discovered that even though I had no place to belong, perhaps my dancing still had a purpose. I kindled that precious ember of hope.

"WE'RE LOST." I BALANCED ON ONE FOOT WHILE DISLODGING pine needles from my shoe, my mood as prickly as my toes.

Brantley brushed tousled bangs out of his eyes. All the scuffs on his leather vest and smudges on his tunic and trousers blended into a dappled camouflage that matched our surroundings. In every direction, mottled green underbrush battled for space with spicy pines and tangled willow. "We're not lost." He set his jaw to emphasize his declaration. With food scarce, a new leanness enhanced the strong lines of his face. He looked trail worn, but it suited him.

He bounded over a fallen tree and reached back to help me. I scrambled up and he grabbed my waist to lower me to the ground. Inches away from him, my skin warmed with awareness.

I pulled away and dusted off my hands. "Do you know where we are?" I squinted into the distance through the crowded branches.

"No."

"Then we're lost."

He growled. "Not knowing where you are is not the same thing as being lost, if you know how to get to where you're going. And I know how to get to the rim from anywhere."

I arched a skeptical brow his direction. "We've been wandering in circles."

"I'm looking for a stream. Once we find one, we follow it seaward. Everything eventually flows to the rim."

The opposite of all I'd been taught. Everything flowed toward the Order. Not rivers, but everything important, all the hopes and highest aspirations of our world. Everyone desired to move inland, to serve the

Order. And here I was heading as far from the center ground as possible.

I sank onto a rock, stretching my legs. "How can I help?"

At my weary question, he turned a frown my direction. "That depends. Are you able to keep walking? You're looking even scrawnier than you used to."

"Thanks," I said dryly. "And yes, I can keep walking, but we'll need food soon."

Brantley rummaged in his pack and pulled out some rope. He eyed a promising tree and, after a few tosses, was able to secure the rope and use it to climb. His boot skidded on one branch, and I held my breath as bits of bark rained down. After a short scramble, he found his footing, and with a few grunts propelled himself higher. Was he hoping to find fruit in the high branches? If so, he was looking in the wrong tree.

"Do you see anything?" I called.

He leaned out, grinning. "Yes!"

The triumph in his voice made me smile in spite of my hunger and exhaustion. He seemed so at home out here where things were wild and uncertain. He climbed down and sprang to the ground from the lowest branch. A few needles and a pinecone had caught in his hair.

I reached out and picked off the pinecone, then brushed away some of the needles. My fingers caught in a snarl of his curls.

"Ow!" He grabbed my hand and untangled me. When he stepped back, he kept his grip on my fingers. I studied the familiar ridges of his knuckles, the broken nails, the scraped skin of his hands. Hands that had comforted me, provided for me, supported me. Warmth seeped through his skin into mine. He smiled crookedly, and a bemused expression followed across his brow.

He dropped my hand and stepped back, clearing his throat. "We'll have a chance to clean up soon. I spotted a home not far from here. And we're not near any villages, so it should be safe to meet someone and trade for supplies."

I blinked a few times, shaking off the awkwardness. "We've avoided anyone since the soldiers by the outcropping. I don't like the idea of talking to strangers now."

Brantley coiled his rope and stuffed it into his pack. "This far out, no one will know about the soldiers' search."

I nodded slowly, though I was not reassured. "Which way?"

"Follow me. And let me talk first. You're out of your element."

A flare of resentment added energy to my steps as I followed him. I could have reminded him that I'd kept up with him just fine, and that I was now as accustomed to living in the wilds as he was. So much for that strange connection I'd felt a moment earlier. He still dismissed me as weak and useless. I'd begun to think of him as a friend. That almost proved his belief in my foolishness.

The scent of wood smoke gave the first hint that we neared a habitation. We slowed our steps, and Brantley crouched behind a bush, beckoning me to join him.

Nearby, buried in overgrown vines, a small home hid under the trees. More shack than cottage, it was made of supple willow branches woven together. Here in the midrim, the movement of the ground was more evident than in Middlemost, and buildings clearly needed to be flexible. As if in affirmation, a wave rolled under us, and the cottage rippled with only a slight moan of protest. The surrounding garden was even more chaotic than untamed nature—if that were possible. Bits of herbs and vegetables struggled against weeds and nettles. Uneven paths wound drunkenly through the plots. If not for the smoke rising from a crumbling chimney, I wouldn't believe anyone had lived here in ages.

"As a landkeeper," I whispered, "it must break your heart to see a garden so untended."

Brantley rubbed his jaw, drawing a rasping sound. "I'm not actually a landkeeper."

I rolled my eyes. "You lied? There's a surprise."

He grinned. "Hey, I managed not to kill any plants while I worked at the Order garden."

I sized him up. Soldier? Builder? Smith? I knew nothing about him. He could even have a wife and children. A tiny pang pierced my chest. "So what do you do when you aren't sneaking and skulking?"

He chuckled. "I don't skulk."

I crossed my arms, waiting.

"I'm a herder."

I wrinkled my brow. "Who's caring for your flock while you're sneaking and . . . sneaking."

His eyes twinkled. "Oh, they're fine. Perhaps I'll introduce you when we reach the rim."

A glimmer of warmth tickled behind my ribs. Maybe he wouldn't drop me at the first rim village we encountered. I wanted to ask him more about himself, tried to find words to inquire about a wife or children, but he focused on the hut again, and the moment was lost.

Brantley began to rise, but the door of the shack swung open, and he ducked. At least he had the sense to observe before entrusting our lives to a stranger.

And the woman who emerged was stranger than strange.

Matted hair stormed away from her face in all directions. Wrinkles ravaged her skin. Her clothes were a parody of dancer garb—a tattered tunic and leggings that ended in torn strips. Around her neck, a green scarf stood out among the muddy colors of her garments. She muttered to herself, then stomped a bare foot on a patch of dirt. "Why don't you listen?" she shouted.

She waved her arms, then limped in a lopsided circle. I stared at her bizarre behavior, transfixed. She moved forward and back, then hopped sideways several times. An ugly scar marred the skin of one leg.

"What's she doing?" Brantley whispered.

Her arms painted a circle as she turned.

"It's a pattern . . . of sorts." Horrible, broken bits of patterns. Nausea rose in my throat. The poor creature had once trained as a dancer.

She stopped her rotation facing away from us, grabbed her head, and shook it side to side. An unearthly shriek rose from her throat, full of confusion, longing, and despair.

Beside me, Brantley sank lower. "I don't like this."

"I agree. Let's keep moving."

The woman sank to her knees, placing her palms against the dirt. "I tried to tell them, but they wouldn't hear." She pulled her hands away as if the ground burned her, and gripped her head again. "No, no, no, no, no. Don't say anymore."

I pressed a hand to my throat. She'd heard the voice, just as I had. Was she hearing it now? Perhaps she was one of the dancers that the High Saltar sent into the center ground again and again, only to have her senses overwhelmed. If not for Brantley helping me, this could have been my fate. The poor woman.

I rose to my feet. Brantley glided into the cover of the trees, but I couldn't follow. Instead I took a step toward the woman.

Brantley returned, grabbed my arm, and hissed. "Where are you going?"

"She's wearing a scarf of truce. She won't hurt me."

The woman was moving again, a few steps of lenka pattern, and then awkward jumps as she attempted star rain. Without pause she shifted to other steps that made no sense together. Bits of subsun rise with night breeze. She made clicking sounds against her teeth, keeping a semblance of rhythm.

I wrenched away from Brantley and entered the clearing. Now I recognized the middle of furrow pattern. When her steps turned in my direction, the woman's jaw sagged open. She blinked several times, as if assuming I was an apparition.

I eased into the movements from where she'd left off, blessing her ramshackle garden with steps that beckoned rain and growth. She resumed her clicking sounds and joined me. As we finished the pattern, she gave a deep, happy sigh.

Then she glanced at my feet. "No!" she shouted. "You dance with your feet covered? How dare you?"

As if she were my saltar, I stood before her with my gaze lowered. "I heard the voice of the earth in the center ground and was overcome. I dare not touch the bare earth again."

She giggled. "The voice. The voice. Oh, yes. Ginerva tried to warn me."

"You knew Ginerva?"

"We all knew her. She wasn't my attendant, but when she saw what was happening she tried to help. Too late. Too late." She chortled.

Her laughter seemed to teeter on a thin edge of rationality, and I feared if I said the wrong things, she would spin into incoherence again. "My companion and I have traveled a long way, and we wondered if we could trade for some food."

She tilted her head and stared at me for a long moment. Then she took a step closer and touched my face, my tunic, the hair that had pulled free of my braid, as if assuring herself I was real.

"From the Order? You came to bring me back?" Her voice turned childlike and wheedling.

"No. I'm sorry. I'm only passing through. Can you help us?"

She squinted, then poked me. "Us? How many are you?"

I signaled Brantley to advance, and he walked slowly toward us, arms outstretched as if seeking to calm an untamed pony.

She lurched backward. "Invasion!"

"No," I soothed. "A friend. See?" I took Brantley's hand, wishing I could make him look less alarming.

The woman limped at a run to her shack and emerged with a shovel, which she waved wildly from side to side. "Send him away."

"I'm not leaving you with her," Brantley told me in an undertone. "She's dangerous."

I squeezed his hand and released it. "I need to speak with her. Please. Go to the edge of the woods. I'll call if I need help."

"Are you mad?" His brow lowered, and his expression promised a lecture from him later about taking unnecessary risks.

"Please. You're upsetting her."

He rubbed the nape of his neck, then shook his head and strode back to the woods, muttering. A small smile tugged my lips. He truly had become protective, and if I were honest, I might admit his concern felt . . . reassuring.

The woman poked her shovel toward Brantley's retreating figure a few times, then lowered it.

"What's your name?" I asked her.

"Dancer Subsun." Her chest straightened and spine lengthened in spite of her injured leg.

"It's an honor to meet you. I'm . . . I was . . . call me Calara."

She sniffed and tossed aside her shovel, leaning her weight on her good leg. "A castoff?"

Close enough. I nodded. "It's hard to make a new life after the Order."

She jabbed my chest with a gnarled finger. "The voice, the voice. It's too big to fit inside us, isn't it?"

My eyes widened. "Like the whole world is speaking."

She rubbed her temples. "Not the world. The Maker. You heard Him."

Even after so much effort by the Order, it seemed the myth wouldn't fade. Nolana, Ginerva, and now Dancer Subsun, all spoke of a Maker as if his existence were a forgone conclusion.

"I heard *something*," I said cautiously.

"It's Him! And oh, how I long to hear again. Please can't you take me back to the center ground? He told me something . . ." One finger twirled a gray strand of hair, and she looked upward as if trying to draw a memory from the sky. Then she gasped and grabbed my upper arms. "The letter! That's what He said."

Her sudden change of subject lost me. "A letter?"

"*Find the letter.* He told me that once." Her face lit with eagerness. "My legs can't take me far, but you can still walk. You have to find the Maker's letter . . . or was it a book?"

The only books I knew were stored in the saltars' offices, and they certainly didn't speak of a Maker. "I wouldn't know where to look."

"No, no, no! You have to try." Urgency burned in her eyes, then her spine hunched and she winced as if in pain. "Why won't you understand?"

"I'm only trying to reach a place where I'll be safe." A difficult enough task.

She cackled. "Too late. You heard the voice. Nowhere is safe. Now you must seek the Maker." For a fleeting moment, sanity cleared her troubled eyes. Her grip on me gentled. "Find the truth. He told me it's there. Someone has to find it."

Her plea held echoes of the sorrow I'd felt in the center ground. A world lost, a Maker forgotten, and a deep longing for restoration. I couldn't make sense of it.

"I can ask about a letter as we travel, but what do I do if I find it?"

"You'll know." Madness blew across her eyes as quickly as it had left. "Promise me. Promise you'll find the letter. Seek the Maker." She shook me, words clawing over each other.

Brantley was right. She was deranged and dangerous. I couldn't help her, and we certainly couldn't get aid from her either.

"Of course. I'll look." I pried her fingers from my arms and patted her hands. "I'll go now. If any soldiers come through here searching, please don't tell them about us."

I eased back a few steps.

A canny gleam lit her crooked smile. "Too late, too late. Soldiers have already been this way. Someone is angry." Her laughter rose to a hysterical pitch, then broke off into a moan as she grabbed her head. Limping, she headed into her shack.

I slipped away while I had the chance, shaken more than I wanted to admit by her confusing warnings and the news that soldiers could be near.

After joining Brantley at the edge of the clearing, I told him about the conversation.

"Seek the Maker?" he scoffed. "That's helpful advice."

"Your niece told me she talks to the Maker."

"Younglings talk to imaginary friends. Doesn't make them real."

"I wonder. The voice I heard . . . could it be . . . Someone instead of something? The Order taught the Maker is a lie and myth, but I can't trust the Order."

"I agree you can't trust the Order, but that doesn't mean you should start chasing myths."

"But what if—"

"We need to keep moving." He hitched up his pack, ducked under a branch, and set a new course straight into the thickest underbrush.

Just as well. I didn't want to argue with him, especially since I didn't know what to believe anymore.

"I'm hoping," he tossed over his shoulder, "what she told you about soldiers was a delusion. But we still better avoid any more settlements until we reach the rim."

I followed, my stomach knotted with hunger and my legs weary from our relentless pace. At least those were experiences that my time in the Order had taught me to endure. However, there were new problems I had no training to address: my questions about the voice, the Maker, and the letter that Dancer Subsun seemed to think would give me answers. Brantley might dismiss it all as nonsense, but I resolved that if we found people we could trust, I would ask my questions with or without his help. *Release my world!* the voice had told me in the center ground. A deep yearning built in me. I had to understand what I'd heard and find a way to dance on bare earth again without fear.

COLD RIVER WATER RUSHED OVER MY SHOES, LAPPED AT MY ankles, and splashed my shins. Every muscle, bone, and joint clamored a complaint, and I let the water soothe away the leading edge of pain. I scooped up a handful for a drink. The river held rainwater, but I tasted a hint of sweetness, probably from seawater seeping up from below.

"You'll ruin those ridiculous shoes." Brantley kicked off his boots and settled on a boulder, dangling his bare feet in the creek. "The water's not going to hurt you."

"My choice." I turned away, not wanting to explain that even a creek bed could be hazardous for me to touch. We'd both grown more irritable as days had passed with little food, and I pressed my lips together to keep from lashing out at him.

A splash sounded as he came up behind me. "Traveling will be that much harder if your shoes are wrecked and you have to go barefoot." Brantley's breath brushed hot against my ear.

He had no idea. Traveling would not be harder; it would be impossible. My very sanity would be threatened if my bare skin was forced to touch our world.

My shoulders sagged. I couldn't afford to let these thin slippers fall apart. I tromped to the bank and wiped my shoes on a wide burdock leaf.

Brantley watched me with a puzzled frown. "I didn't mean to chase you out of the water."

Should I explain? Could I? Or would he assume I was as mad as Dancer Subsun?

"Dancers only touch the raw earth after a lifetime of preparation, and only in the central ground. I can't risk . . . communicating . . . with the earth out here."

He barked a laugh. "And here I was about to ask you to do some of that dancer stuff"—he wiggled his fingers—"and drum us up some berries or something."

I sighed. "It doesn't work like that."

"I thought the Order controlled everything."

"I'm not in the Order anymore, in case you hadn't noticed." I loathed the bitter edge to my voice. He'd sacrificed a great deal to escort me to safety and didn't deserve my irritation. I drew a steadying breath. "I'm sorry."

"No, I'm sorry." He rubbed the back of his neck. "Don't mean to take it out on you."

I managed a small smile. "We've found a river, so there's reason to hope."

He sloshed over to me and stepped up onto the bank. "That there is. As soon as we reach the rim, we'll have full bellies. Roasted copper fish, smoked sea trout." He licked his lips and grinned.

I didn't share his confidence. Who would help a runaway dancer and a herder wanted by the Order's soldiers?

Brantley flung droplets at my face, jarring me from my pessimism. "Cheer up. We're not lost anymore."

I scooped both my hands in the water and threw it his direction, dousing the front of his shirt. "So now you admit we were lost?"

His laugh was rich and deep. "Let's go, dancer. The ocean is calling."

I shivered. The Order taught us the sea was vast, dangerous, and so honeyed that its water led to illness. I couldn't match Brantley's eagerness to reach the shore, but it could lead us to Undertow and maybe even my family. A mother's gentle encouragement, an uncle's laughing eyes, a sister's hug. Who knew what I might find? The hope stabbed me with a pang as sweet as ocean water.

"Lead on, herder," I answered.

His enthusiasm fueled my steps with new lightness as we traced the riverbank. Overhead, a harrier bird glided, banked, and dove beyond the trees. The pines and willows swayed to the subtle motion of the ground, changing heights as deep waves rolled beneath us. Songbirds caroled delicate melodies. Even the whir of insects sounded happier. I was able to ignore my gnawing hunger and the pervasive fear of pursuit. A tiny kernel of anticipation sprouted in my soul.

Late in the day, the trees parted, the river widened, and we came to a sight that stole my breath.

The primary sun rested low over an unending expanse of ocean, sparkling with shades of amber and peach. Gentle turquoise currents played tag with the shore, where tangled plant roots disappeared into the water.

Brantley noticed my awe and clapped an arm around my shoulders, drawing a deep, satisfied breath. "Always pains me to be away from the sea too long. She's beautiful, isn't she?"

I tore my eyes from the sea for a moment to look at him. His smile was broad and relaxed, and a contented sigh lifted his chest. He was the happiest I'd ever seen him.

I followed his gaze back out over the vastness. A thrill of amazement whispered over my skin. "The water really does go on forever."

No wonder the Order fought so hard to keep our world secure. What would it be like if our island pulled loose to spin aimlessly through the limitless waves? A shiver of dread rippled up my spine, yet I also felt a tug to embrace the dance of ever-shifting froth, playful wind gusts, and soaring seabirds.

Brantley moved closer to the edge and rubbed his hands together. "Now we can get some food."

I turned in a slow circle on the short band of earth where we'd emerged from the forest. I surveyed the matted woven weeds where water lapped along the rim, the river we'd followed, and the emptiness before us. No sign of habitation, no fruit trees, no berry bushes. Where did he plan to find food?

I perched on a fallen tree, a safe distance back from the edge, my gaze drawn again to the shifting colors of the setting sun reflected on the water.

Brantley rummaged through his pack and pulled out a thin wooden whistle. He blew a few notes, a repeating pattern. Then he kicked off his boots, tossed aside his cloak, and pulled off his vest. Had he gone mad?

When he took off his shirt and flung it to the ground, I looked away.

Could proximity to sweet water drive a person to madness even if he didn't drink it? I was too tired to run back upriver, and too tantalized by the ocean to want to leave, but I was worried about my companion's erratic behavior.

He sat at the edge and dangled his feet in the water, scanning the horizon.

"What are you doing?" I finally called from my safe spot near the woods.

"Patience," he said.

I waited, watching the shifting colors of the subsun reflecting on the waves. After several minutes, my stomach grumbled a reminder that Brantley had promised he'd find food. I stood, determined to broach the topic, but a ripple moved off to the side and drew my attention. I blinked a few times. One low wave moved against the rest of the lapping current and headed our direction.

Had Brantley's tune called forth new waves in a similar way that dancers spoke to the earth?

A shape rose from the surface. I wanted to dash to Brantley and pull him back from the edge, but I was paralyzed and only managed to squeak.

He didn't hear me over his joyous laughter.

A creature lifted a head and chest from the water. It moved toward the shore with the agility of a river fish, but its long neck supported a head with floppy ears, a tapered muzzle like a forest hound, huge violet eyes, and a mouth shaped into a perpetual smile. Instead of fur, its blue-gray skin was so smooth that water beaded and rolled away from the portion of its body that broke the surface.

He should have retreated to safe ground, but Brantley yelled, "Navar!" and dove into the water. Or had he fallen? The strange fish dipped its snout down and up several times, then stretched out, submerging most of its shape.

I clutched my throat and tiptoed a few feet closer to the edge, riding the rocking movement underfoot caused by the creature's wake. I expected to see Brantley devoured. Instead he appeared on the far side of the creature and propelled himself up on its back in one smooth movement.

Arms outspread for balance, Brantley stood—stood!—on the slick body and shook wet hair from his eyes. "Meet my friend Navar," he called. Knees slightly bent, he maintained a balance that any dancer would envy. "Isn't she a beauty?"

Navar raised her head again, turned her long neck to peer at Brantley, and bobbed her muzzle up and down. After Brantley twirled a fist in the air a few times, his mount faced forward and propelled the two of them in a wide circle. The sun silhouetted Brantley's muscled form, his chest full of sea air, profile rising to meet any challenge. Together, he and Navar looked like a mythic being born of water and sky.

"We'll be back soon with supper," Brantley shouted.

Then with dizzying speed, they shot across the water and faded from sight toward the horizon.

Sinking to the rolling ground, I dredged my memory for any childhood knowledge of huge aquatic beasts. The sweet scent of ocean waves tasted familiar in the back of my throat, but I couldn't conjure any recollections similar to the scene I'd just witnessed. Brantley treated Navar in the way a tender would treat a favorite pony. I shook my head, half in awe, yet still half afraid.

How could Brantley plunge into the wide ocean, leaving the safety of our world? How could I trust the beast would bring him back? As shadows stretched longer, I shivered. Sudden solitude lowered over me like the dusk. The expanse of water made me feel very small and alone. Not knowing when—or if—Brantley would return hollowed my chest. I hugged my shins, resting my chin on my knees.

I thought I'd begun to know Brantley. Determined, reckless, teasing, strong. I'd learned many sides to him as we'd traveled and grown to appreciate most of them. Yet I had no idea of the level of his courage. My blossoming affection for him now seemed like a silly girl's fantasy. I was far from worthy of a man like him. I was a castoff. Worse than a castoff. I'd fled my calling. Abandoned my vow. Besides, I couldn't daydream about joining my life with any man. I was, after all, a dancer—of a sort. Odd how that pledge to forsake family, future husband, or children made less sense to me with each day away from the Order.

The subsun angled until the glare hurt my eyes. Shaking my head with a heavy sigh, I rose and proceeded to set up a camp in the hopes that Brantley would return. I gathered wood and lit a small fire to help him find his way back. For hours I stoked the flames alone, watching the subsun sink toward the horizon. Then a sharp whistle pulled my head up.

Out across the water, Navar darted side to side while approaching. Brantley adjusted his stance to her movements and called out occasional instructions. I couldn't fathom what he was doing.

Then Navar dipped her head deep under the water and tossed it upward. Water rained down on the shore, along with the slippery splashing sound of fish slapping the ground. Three more times, the creature angled, dipped, and butted small copper-colored fish into the air. Supper fell at my feet, and I raced to gather up the fish and deposit them by our fire. I laughed as my tunic was soon wet from the wriggling catch.

Meanwhile, Navar floated right up to the edge of the island. Brantley stroked the beast's neck and murmured praise, then leapt lightly to the tangled mat of vegetation and strode toward me.

The creature vanished like a dream, and if not for the fish scattered nearby, I would have believed I'd imagined it.

Brantley stretched. "Told you I'd get us some dinner. Took longer than I thought. Used to be we'd find schools near the coast, but . . ." He trailed off as he noticed my baffled expression. "What's wrong?"

I shook my head. "I've never seen . . . I didn't know . . ."

"I told you I was a herder."

Which had conjured images of him tending land animals in a midrange pasture. "What is that . . . creature?"

"Navar? She's a stenella. Don't tell me you haven't seen one before." He grabbed his knife and efficiently gutted one of the fish. "How did you imagine a herder from a rim village provided for his family?"

I felt more ignorant than a first-form novitiate, so I ducked my head and peeled bark from a stick to skewer the fish. Why couldn't I remember more from the handful of early years before I was brought to the Order? Had people of Undertow herded fish toward shore this way? Perhaps even my father? What else had I forgotten?

I set aside my worries as the scent of crisping fillets rose from the fire. After days of hunger, the tremendous gift of food pushed everything else from my mind. We ate in companionable silence. The meat was flakey and tender, with only a hint of sweetness. Somehow the citrus-honey flavor of the sea didn't bother me as much as I had expected. I smiled to myself. Saltar Kemp would be horrified if I became accustomed to unfiltered sweet water.

After we'd eaten our fill and stoked the fire, Brantley leaned back on his elbows with a sigh. "You can't tell me you'd rather live inside the cold walls of the Order or the stiff cobblestones of Middlemost."

The mat of tangleroot that formed the ground this close to the edge rolled unevenly. I wanted to grab the surface to steady myself, but kept my hands folded in my lap. "I'm not sure I could get used to how much everything moves out here."

"This is nothing. Try riding the rim when a storm blows through."

I didn't want to imagine that and shook my head.

He leaned back and studied the sky. "Seems the weather hasn't been as bad the past few days. Think the High Saltar has given up on harassing you?"

"I hope so. I'm not important enough for her to bother with." The memory of her eyes burning into mine, demanding descriptions of my experience, argued against my optimism.

"Well, get some sleep. Tomorrow we'll follow the rim toward a village. I think we may be close to Whitecap."

Dense undergrowth stretched into the distance along the shore as the ground bobbed unpredictably. Walking the edge would be even more daunting than our hike from the center. "Is Whitecap near Undertow?"

He must have noticed the weary edge to my voice. He sat up and unfurled his cloak, draping it around me. "No, but traveling will be easier now."

I squinted again at the shore. "It will?"

"Sure, now that we can travel by water."

"By water?" I tossed away his cloak and stood to confront him. He didn't think I would leave the safety of land, did he? Ridiculous!

Ignoring my alarm, he chuckled and surged to his feet. He threw an arm around me and planted a brotherly kiss on the top of my head. The warmth of his body so close to mine stirred an errant wish for something more than a casual touch. Something I'd never known to miss until now.

Before I could examine those thoughts, he flopped beside the fire again. "Stop worrying. Tomorrow you'll learn how to ride."

My throat tensed in a choking grip as my pulse pounded so hard my breath came in rapid sips.

Ride? I couldn't even swim.

13

"YOU DON'T HAVE TO SWIM, ONLY RIDE." BRANTLEY'S CURLS
were more unruly than usual in the morning light, probably because
he'd spent the last hour raking his hands through them in frustration as
we argued. He'd coaxed, badgered, and offered reassurances as if I were
a nervous child.

I refused to budge.

Navar had answered Brantley's whistle and hovered near the shore for
the first half hour, then lost interest and drifted away in languid circles.

"At least come closer to the water." Brantley held out his hand. With
his feet planted wide on the matted tangleroot, he rode the ripples that
undulated beneath the edge. "Are you sure no one ever taught you to swim?"

I shook my head. I'd had flickers of memory from my early childhood
at the rim, even of playing in the sea, but my time in the Order had erased
that knowledge fully, and planted only fear and disdain for the ocean.

Brantley's eyebrows cocked upward. "My niece could swim like a
stenella when she was four years old."

His efforts to shame me didn't work. I could admit Navar was beautiful
and intriguing, but that didn't mean I would trust my life to her. Terror
still gripped me in a relentless fist.

With a low growl, Brantley strode toward me.

I skittered back a few steps. Had he grown so frustrated that he would
simply throw me into the waves?

He stopped, a flicker of hurt skimming over his features before it
disappeared beneath the surface. He offered his hand again. "Come sit
near the edge. Get to know Navar. Can you do that much?"

He was relentless. Maybe if I made a small concession, he'd stop pressuring me. I ignored his hand, but tiptoed to the rim. After spreading my cloak over the tangleroot, I sat, carefully removing my shoes before easing my feet into the ocean.

The water was warmer and thicker than river water, almost like cream. It lapped my shins like a puppy's tongue. It didn't seem so dangerous. Yet still, my fingers clutched the tangleroot through the fabric of my cloak until my knuckles turned white.

Brantley settled beside me. I scarcely noticed, so intent on preventing an errant wave from knocking me loose. He gave a low whistle, and Navar extended her head and sailed toward us.

I sucked in a sharp breath and leaned back.

"There you go. You're all right," Brantley murmured. I wasn't sure if he was speaking to Navar or me. The stenella turned her bright gaze my direction and nodded her head.

Brantley stroked her long muzzle. "You can touch her."

That would mean letting go. I couldn't do that with an abyss stretched before me.

Brantley glanced down at my clenched hands and sighed. He edged behind me and wrapped his arms around my waist. Warm, strong muscles embraced me. "I've got you."

As his chest rose and fell calmly into my back, my fluttering breaths slowed to match his. I convinced one of my hands to reach forward.

Navar's skin was soft as the finest leather. She emitted a low chortle, then wove her sinewy neck side to side in a subtle dance. I released tension from my shoulders, and gradually my neck relaxed enough to swing my head side to side in fluid oval shapes that mirrored her movements.

Her eyes brightened, and she bobbed her head rapidly.

Behind me, Brantley chuckled. "She likes you. I knew you two would get along."

Navar shifted and presented her broad back, twisting her neck to peer around at me.

"She's inviting you to ride. She doesn't do that for just anyone." Brantley's words breathed against my ear.

"I . . . I can't." Except Navar's playful joy coaxed me in ways none of Brantley's arguments could. The stiffness in my voice softened. "Can I?"

"She'll hold still for you. Sit astride her if that feels more secure. I'll be right behind you." Brantley shifted his hold on my waist before I could argue again. His grip was strong as he transferred me to Navar's smooth spine. "See? Like riding a pony."

"I've rarely done that either." I edged forward awkwardly, hoping to cling to Navar's neck. But she faced the sea, stretching her long neck along the surface. Muscles rippled beneath me. Was she preparing to move? "Wait!"

Brantley leapt to her back and knelt behind me. "I'll hold you. Stop squeezing her so hard with your legs."

I hadn't realized my heels were digging into the stenella's ribs. Did she have ribs? And why was I worrying about her anatomy?

She looked at us and gave a slow blink. Brantley raised one hand in the air and traced a slow circle with one finger.

Navar tilted her head, her back rolling in what felt like a sigh, but she seemed to concede that this was going to be a tedious swim. She glided so gently, it took a few minutes for me to realize we were traveling. I glanced around and saw the shore melting away.

My breath caught in my throat, lungs pumping unproductively. I was cut loose from our world! I squeezed my eyes closed, wanting the nightmare to end.

"Open your eyes." Brantley tightened one arm around my waist. "If you've never seen this before, it's as magical as star rain."

Leaning against the security of Brantley's chest, I persuaded my eyes to open. Navar turned, allowing me an easy view of land from a distance.

The island looked huge. Miles of shoreline stretching in both directions. I widened my gaze.

The island looked tiny. An insignificant world in a massive ocean.

Somewhere deep in the center, the Order was striving to turn and stabilize this mass of land, like ants trying to tame a gale or contain a rushing river. *Do they even realize how small we all are?*

A new fear rippled through me. If there was a Maker, how big must He be? No wonder a few words from His voice had overwhelmed me. Did He see us all as ridiculous insects, scurrying around His world like pests?

Farther from shore, the waves grew larger. Navar picked up speed, slicing through them easily. Spray wafted against my skin.

"Ready to herd some fish?"

"Do we have to be out this far?"

Brantley's laughter billowed over the sound of water swooshing past us. "This isn't far."

My fingers dug in to his arm, my legs still squeezing Navar's sides, but I managed a smile. "I suppose breakfast is a good plan."

"Atta girl."

Navar picked up speed, but with such graceful movements I forgot to be terrified. Every few minutes, she'd slow to look back at Brantley, who would signal with a wave of his hand. When a flock of gulls appeared on the horizon, he whistled and she changed direction. The wind caressed my face as we danced through the water, gliding and turning as if sharing a pattern with the ocean.

Brantley rested his chin on the top of my head. "We used to find schools of fish right off shore, but in recent years they've been harder to find. Another reason the rim villages can't afford the Order's taxes. In Windswell, people have been close to starving."

Navar began to zigzag, and my leg muscles cramped from their panicked grip. Even with Brantley's arm holding me in place, I could far too easily imagine being flung off to sink beneath the waves.

Brantley tightened his grip around my waist. "She's found them. Get ready."

"Ready?"

"Hold your breath."

"My breath? Why—?"

Seawater slammed into my face and choked me. The ocean had risen. No, we were diving. Frantic coughs expended the last of my air. I glimpsed a small school of copper fish before us. Navar darted left and right, chasing them toward land.

My lungs burned and I began to thrash against Brantley. *Air. I need air.*

Seconds later, Navar surfaced. I sputtered and spit out sweet water, gasping in each breath.

"I warned you to hold your breath." Brantley's casual amusement infuriated me. If I'd warmed to him during our days of traveling together, those feelings fled. Coughing and half-drowned, I hated him. Hated him for dragging me into the wild ocean and letting his creature pull us under to our deaths. Hated him for laughing at me.

I slammed my elbow back.

His air rushed out in a satisfying oomph. Let him feel starved for oxygen and see how he liked it.

Too late, I realized how vulnerable I was. To his credit, he didn't shove me off Navar or even release his secure hold on me. When he caught his breath, he leaned over my shoulder. "Did you think herders stayed on the surface? We go where the fish go."

I scooted forward, stiffening my spine. "Give me more warning next time."

He gave a wry chuckle. "Understood."

When we returned to the shore, Navar batted dozens of small fish up onto land. I'd never been so happy to touch the ground. I tugged on my shoes before stepping from the tangleroot to the dirt farther inland, but I was tempted to fall to my knees and kiss the bare ground. I picked up the cloak I'd left behind and threw it over my wet clothes.

"I'm still not sure of the closest village." Brantley gutted a fish and tossed it toward me. "Will you cook these while I go out and take another look?"

"Go." I shooed him off, glad to put distance between us. I didn't want him seeing how much my hands shook from the ride that had been all in a day's work for him.

He leapt onto Navar's back, and they raced out to sea. I paused from tending the fire to watch them. Each time Navar leaned into a turn, Brantley adjusted his stance. They moved like one.

When they turned to face the shore, Brantley shielded his eyes and scanned in all directions. Then he held up his fist and flung it open.

I squinted, not wanting to miss what they were doing.

Navar picked up speed, her body rising higher out of the water. Then with a splash, what I'd thought were fins along the sides of her body unfurled, opening out like wings. She rose into the air, gliding above the water. Brantley continued to search for bearings, then whistled something to Navar.

Fish charred over the flames, but I ignored our burning breakfast, awestruck. Navar and Brantley caught a gust of wind and gained elevation as they headed closer.

From the height of a cottage roof, Brantley whooped, sprang into the air, flipped and dove into the waiting waves. When he charged up out of the water, he shook his head, and droplets scattered like bits of glittering glass. His mount lowered to the surface and glided to where Brantley floated.

Navar's squeaks and gurgles rose over the lapping of the waves before she dove. Ripples marked her departure.

Brantley heaved himself onto land, as I gawked like an idiot. Was there nothing this man couldn't do? Diving underwater, flying over the waves?

He navigated the rolling ground and strode toward our fire, acknowledging my open mouth with a preening grin. Until acrid smoke made him wrinkle his nose. He grabbed a skewer of fish out of the flames. "I thought you were watching the breakfast."

"How high can she fly? Is she like a bird?"

He swung the skewer to extinguish flames that had charred the scales of one fish. "No, she can only glide a bit. Figured a higher view might help. And it did." He speared one of the cooked fish with his knife and offered it to me. "Hard to tell, because so much of the coastline looks the same, but I think we aren't far from Windswell. Now that you can ride, we should reach it in a few days."

I accepted the food from him, but not the plan. "You promised to take me to Undertow."

He settled to the ground and warmed his bare feet by the fire. "You're just full of demands, aren't you, dancer?" He blew on a fillet and then took a big bite. "I haven't forgotten. But we'll reach Windswell first. I need to find out if Bri got home safely."

Once he reunited with his family, he'd have no reason to help me look for mine. My fish stuck in my throat.

I pushed aside that worry and turned another skewer carefully along the edges of the flame. "Are there any villages along the way?" At his quizzical look, I shrugged. "It's just . . . I can't get Dancer Subsun out of my mind. She told me to search for a letter from the Maker. With all that's happened . . ." I blew out a breath. "As soon as we find a settlement, I want to ask if anyone knows of it."

He stabbed his knife into the ground, his expression suddenly closed. "Look, I'll get you to your village . . . against my better judgment. But I'm not getting involved in your silly quest for a Maker. Even if there were a Maker, He must be pretty ineffectual. He's let the Order take control of our entire world."

A fair argument. If Someone had formed our world, why did He leave it in the hands of the saltars? I massaged my forehead.

He rubbed his jaw and peered out through the drenched locks of his hair. "Stop worrying. You should be congratulating yourself. You rode a stenella for the first time. A noble effort." His lips twitched. "Even if you look like a drowned bog rat."

I looked down at myself. My braid had come undone, and wet hair fell across my face like tangleroot. At least my tunic and leggings were less grimy after their time underwater. I tried to frown, but started to giggle instead. "One day can I ride her while she flies?"

His brows lifted. The amusement in his eyes changed to something like admiration. "Sure. Once you're a more skilled rider. On our way to Windswell."

I managed a confident nod, although the fish I'd eaten seemed to be flopping in my belly. I would learn because I had no choice. That was a lesson won from my time in the Order. And if we spotted any settlements on our way, I would convince Brantley to let me ask questions about a Maker's letter.

WE RODE OVER THE WAVES FOR SEVERAL DAYS, CAMPING ON
land only at night. Sea spray splashed my bare feet as I drew honeyed air
deep into my lungs, letting it strengthen me. I had to admit that traveling
on Navar's back was more enjoyable than tromping through thick forests
and angry brambles. It helped that Brantley wanted to keep his pack
of supplies dry, so we didn't take any more frightening dives under the
surface. However, I continued to sit astride. I left the standing to Brantley.

On our third day, Brantley pointed out a small encampment set in
from the shore.

"Is it Windswell?" I asked, eager for a night with true shelter.

Brantley frowned. "It's Whitecap. We weren't as close as I thought. I
told you the shoreline is hard to read."

A new hope tickled the inside of my ribs. "Are we close to Undertow instead?"

"We'll still reach Windswell first."

I sighed. Would I never get closer to finding my home?

With a short whistle, Brantley directed Navar out to sea and scanned
the sky for gulls.

I twisted to see the village behind us. "Why aren't we landing? Isn't
Whitecap a safe place to stay?"

"Safe as anywhere. But we'll make more friends if we provide some
food first."

Of course. More fishing. Brantley located a small school and herded
them toward shore.

"We'd keep more of the school if we dove, but I don't want to take my supplies underwater."

"Or me."

He chuckled. "You survived last time."

Barely. But I kept my mouth shut, unwilling to provoke him.

We eased toward shore, and Navar swooped her head beneath the fish and tossed them into the air and onto land. A few landed on the band of tangleroot along the shore, the others on the stretch of beach farther in that was cluttered with tattered nets, slatted barrels, and a few children at play. A boy spotted us, waved, and ran inland toward the cottages nestled near sheltering willows and stunted pines. Beyond the tidy buildings, taller trees rose where the soil deepened. Yet even those stirred as the land undulated beneath. I heard their whispering boughs over the lapping of waves and squawk of seabirds. The buildings creaked and moaned with every roll beneath them. Like midrim villages, the cottages were formed of supple wood, but here, knots of rope held together the walls and roofs, so they had even more give.

Soon a crowd gathered on the shore and shouted greetings as they collected flopping fish into baskets. The children scurried about helping, their limbs too thin and fragile. Women hefted baskets against their hips, where their skirts held more patches than original fabric. A man no older than Brantley wound among the villagers with a stooped frame. Another man with a mottled rash across his face displayed missing teeth as he called an instruction. Hunger and disease had clearly been frequent companions of Whitecap.

When the entire catch had landed, Navar floated sideways against the tangleroot edge. Brantley leapt ashore and offered a helping hand to me. I balanced on the matted weeds and pulled on my slippers before following him up to more solid ground.

A wizened woman with a silver braid coiled around her head like a crown was the first to approach us. "Greetings, travelers, and thank you for the provision. After fishing dried up, our herder moved inland last year, so your gift is much needed."

Although no one looked hostile, the faces of the villagers were gaunt and lined with care and some leaned toward each other and shared suspicious whispers.

"I'm Brantley of Windswell, and this is . . ." He rubbed his jaw, where his whiskers had grown longer. "Um . . . Calara of Undertow."

The name sounded wrong. Calara Blue was my student name, and Dancer Calara had been my new designation, but I was no longer part of the Order. Yet what else could they call me? I'd once scrawled the word, "Carya," on the scrap of parchment, along with my village's name, but that could mean anything. My mother? Another village?

The woman didn't seem to notice Brantley's hesitation or my discomfort. She tipped her head slightly, then straightened with a regal posture any saltar would envy. "I'm Parisa of Whitecap, the matriarch here. Will you shelter with us tonight?"

Brantley offered a small bow with more respect than I'd ever seen him show. "Thank you. We've journeyed long."

We were swept into the busy preparations of a feast—probably the first they'd had in a long time. Men cleaned the fish, children skewered them, women stoked flames. Some of the villagers built a fire in the smokehouse to preserve the surplus catch, sending rich, meaty scents throughout the air. The busy community held dozens of homes and reminded me of the bustle of Middlemost.

Parisa invited me into the communal kitchen, where I marveled at the woven walls that rippled softly when waves rocked the ground. She set to work shaping batches of saltcakes, and I offered to help. Another of the few practical skills I'd learned in the Order. She asked about my journey, but when I remained vague, she didn't probe. Instead, she politely steered the conversation to the increasing number of storms each year and the welcome respite in weather of the past few days. "Perhaps the Order has found new patterns to calm the winds," she said.

Heat washed my face, and I turned away to arrange cakes in a baking dish. I'd given my life to serve villages like Whitecap by calming storms with my dance and then fled that responsibility. Was it any wonder that the High Saltar was desperate to find more dancers, in the face of the suffering villages were confronting?

I shook my head. The need was no excuse for Saltar Tiarel to steal children from their parents' arms, or to hobble novitiates she no longer found useful, or to drive dancers to madness. Did the Order care about the suffering of our people at all?

Carrying an armful of logs, Brantley marched into the kitchen, added fuel to the baking oven, then leaned on the table where I worked. "I've decided to stay a few days and do some serious fishing to build their stores."

More delays. But I couldn't argue. I wasn't in the center ground encouraging crops to grow or pushing violent weather out to sea, so at least I could support Brantley's efforts to help this village.

"That's a good idea," I said softly.

His eyes narrowed, as if he'd been expecting an argument. After sweeping me with his gaze, he nodded and left.

Parisa smiled. "Your young man is generous."

"Oh, he's not my—" How could I explain without revealing information that could endanger us? I handed a dish of saltcakes to the matriarch and nodded. "Yes, he is. He is the most honorable man I've known."

Footsteps sounded behind me, and I turned. Brantley had returned with an armload of kindling and stopped short, color painting his cheeks. Instead of offering his usual arrogant grin, he furrowed his brow. A stick clattered to the floor, and he tossed the rest of the wood into a bin beside the oven, then fled. One of the women nearby shot me a curious look.

Why did my praise send him running? Did he fear I relied on him too much? Did he think I mistook his kindness for more? My cheeks burned, and I hoped Parisa would assume it was simply from the heat of the kitchen fires.

Once I regained my composure, I settled into the kitchen work with Parisa and the other women. After so many days of travel with no companion but Brantley, I savored the sensation of swirling female conversation, laughter, and interaction. All the best memories of my time in the Order resurrected, which surprised me. I would never have expected this sense of community with women from a rim village. They weren't backward, contentious people as I'd been taught, in need of the harsh control of the Order to guide them. They were warm, funny, and generous.

When they offered me tsalla, a hot drink made of ocean water and local herbs, I put aside my fear of unfiltered water and found I loved the sweet citrusy comfort. Maybe I was a rimmer after all.

We stayed for three nights, and Parisa provided us with mats in her own home. Her brisk kindness filled me more than the meals she shared. She was in constant motion—washing and hanging laundry, stoking her fire, calling instructions to others. Yet she always had a tender pat for younglings, or a quiet encouragement to weary young mothers. More than once I wondered if my mother was like her. Perhaps even the matriarch of Undertow? I tucked those small hopes away.

I found small ways to contribute to the community, playing games with the toddlers and leading the older children in foraging expeditions. They taught me as much as I taught them, since many of the plants looked different growing in random clusters outside of the regimented containers of the Order. Still, I recognized a few useful herbs and harvested greens that added to each meal.

I also spent hours on a perpetual chore—binding the seams of buildings with new ropes. The constant motion frayed the ties so they needed to be frequently replaced. The task reminded me of patching the walls of the Order, only out here on the rim, the force of the sea was even more persistent.

Not everything was idyllic. Arguments broke out about the division of the catches that Brantley provided. Jealousy, gossip, and struggles for control invaded even the communal kitchen. And although the village welcomed our help, many remained suspicious and aloof in spite of my efforts to fit in. Like the ropes holding the buildings together, the good natures of the people here were fraying under the pressures of scarcity and fear.

On our last day, I found a quiet moment to speak with Parisa privately. We walked down to the shore to watch for Brantley.

"Brantley said it's taking longer to find fish with each trip." I shielded my eyes, squinting into the low-angled subsun.

Parisa settled onto a tuft of moss and drew up her knees. "I worry when a herder goes out so far. I fear he'll not find his way back."

We both shivered at that dire possibility, and I chewed my lower lip.

She glanced at me. "I'm sorry. I shouldn't have said that. I'm sure he'll be fine. But it's strange that the fish keep so far from the island these days. When I was a girl our herder stayed so close, we could watch him work."

"Troubling changes," I said quietly. The Order cared for our world, so even acknowledging the problems Whitecap faced felt disloyal. Yet I couldn't deny that the village was hungry, weather had been harsh, and fish were scarce. What was going wrong with Meriel? I thought of Nolana's simple trust in the Maker, and Dancer Subsun's fevered mention of His letter.

"Parisa, have you heard legends of the Maker?"

Her breath hissed in, and she faced me. "The Order forbids discussing the old stories."

I met her gaze, searching for any reassurance that I dare trust her. A hint of a twinkle lit her amber eyes.

"Yet there are stories?" I asked. Dredging up a bit more courage, I added, "And perhaps even a letter or a book that holds them?"

She assessed me, lips pressed together. It was her turn to decide whether to trust. Then she looked out over the ocean, as if listening for an answer to her own silent question. Small waves sloshed against the shore, and the land beneath us rocked. I softened my knees to maintain my balance, finding the movement almost soothing now.

"I've heard tell a letter remains. Somewhere hidden. Few remember it exists and fewer remember what it contains." Heavy sadness coated her words. "Would the words offer answers?" She shrugged.

I understood her resignation. What could a collection of old stories do to help our world, especially when the Order declared such works did not exist? What good would it do to learn more about a Maker when He was not welcome on our island?

A speck appeared on the horizon. Slowly it formed into the shape of a man. Navar rode so low in the water that Brantley seemed to glide on the surface. I smiled at the image.

Parisa stood. "Come, let's call the others to be ready to gather." As we walked toward the village center, she nudged me. "A strong and comely man you've found. No wonder you look at him so." When her teasing made me blush, she laughed.

I was thankful he was nowhere in earshot. If he ever knew how much fondness was forming in my heart toward him, he'd drop me at the nearest village and ride into the waves without me.

AFTER LEAVING WHITECAP, BRANTLEY AND I SETTLED INTO a pattern. We rode until we found an encampment. Brantley took me ashore and left his pack with me. Then he headed out to dive as deep as needed to herd fish to the shore.

Each place we stopped, I asked if anyone knew of the Maker's letter. In spite of the good will we garnered with Brantley's fishing efforts, I received only blank stares or suspicious frowns. If I tried to pursue my questions further, Brantley interrupted or pulled me away from the conversation, warning me not to cause trouble.

As we traveled, I learned more about the people of the rim. They struggled to survive and shared stories of cruel oppression; yet they held warm and loving families. Their homes, the forest, the plains, and the nearby waves were full of haphazard chaos that kept me uneasy. Yet many of the people who inhabited these wild places showed us kindness.

I also discovered that many people sang as they went about their daily tasks. In one village, the families gathered to watch the subsun set and to sing together. No wonder music was banned in the Order. It stirred and frightened me, and made me want to cry, and laugh, and hope. I longed to dance with it—far beyond the strict dictates of the patterns. I squelched that dangerous longing. I'd used a few simple movements to gentle the forest hound and get acquainted with Navar. But for all the smaller rules I'd broken, I was sure I'd perish if I ever fully danced outside the Order, especially to music.

DAYS STACKED INTO A FEW WEEKS AS WE TRAVELED THE rim. A few more villages dotted the shore, and we found shelter in most, bringing an offering of fish each time. Except the last; we left that village early in the morning before anyone was stirring. Since Brantley hadn't been able to herd any fish, we'd found little welcome when we arrived empty handed. Though we sheltered in a vacant hut, only thin reed mats separated us from the dirt floor, and Brantley had barely slept, guarding our paltry possessions all night. Still, even with a few unpleasant experiences with some of the less inviting villagers, I had a growing fondness for the rim. Anything was better than the harsh climate of the Order.

We sailed the waves all day, and I began to wonder if Windswell actually existed. Our endless days of riding the shoreline had given me a sense of the huge size of our world. Would we ever reach Windswell or find Undertow?

Today, barefoot and clad only in his trousers, pack slung over one shoulder, Brantley swayed as he stood on Navar's wide back. Rain sheeted down on us, but he seemed to revel in the downpour.

I huddled under my cloak, trying to keep the hem out of the sea. With the spray of waves and warm water lapping my legs—not to mention the rain—staying dry was a futile effort. My slippers, their laces tied together, rested around my neck where I could protect them and keep them handy to pull on as soon as we touched land.

Late in the day, the clouds broke enough for us to see the subsun lower toward the horizon. Brantley stood behind me and scanned the shore, then whistled a signal to Navar.

A cottage hugged the tree line not far from the water's edge, where a stooped, wiry man busied himself breaking kindling. When he saw us sailing in, he answered Brantley's wave by scurrying into his house.

"Not very friendly," I said. "Maybe we should keep going."

Brantley rocked as his balance adjusted. "Don't turn shy now, dancer. Varney is an old friend. He likely didn't see who I was."

Before I could offer more suggestions, Navar raced toward the shore, rearing back as she stopped short. I reeled backward, but Brantley caught me before I tumbled off.

"You really have to learn to swim." Shaking his head, Brantley held my elbow until I reached the shore. "You can't always rely on me to catch you if your mount takes an unexpected turn."

I shuddered. He was right, of course. The sweetness of the water and its thick, milky texture no longer terrified me, but being swept away into nothingness was a frequent nightmare.

"Fine. Soon."

"I'll hold you to that," he said.

I thrust my chin up. A ripple underfoot made me stumble, ruining my attempt at a determined stance. Hoping he hadn't noticed, I changed the subject. "Right now we have other things to think about. Go let your friend know who you are. And ask if he'll let me hang my cloak by the fire." I shook the garment, splattering Brantley.

He grinned, then strode to the hovel.

Thunder rumbled overhead, and a darker cloud rolled over us. Another burst of rain soaked through my hood.

"Ho, Varney! It's Brantley." He knocked on the door with casual confidence that expected to be welcomed anywhere.

My spirits lifted. Food and a chance to dry my things rested only inches away.

"Go away!" Varney yelled from within.

Brantley pounded once more. "No games, my friend, we've traveled far today."

"Not a game. Leave now."

All humor bled away as Brantley's brow pinched. "This can't be good," he said darkly.

Even though I longed for shelter and a hot meal, a shiver of foreboding made me tug Brantley's arm. "Let's move on. We can find a place to camp farther along the shore."

The rain plastered his wavy hair against his face, weighing it down so water dripped in his eyes. Those eyes held the same dark clouds as the sky. "I need to know what's happened. Wait here."

He reached for the door with an effort at his usual swagger, but his other hand clasped the hilt of the knife in his belt.

15

BRANTLEY PRESSED HIS SHOULDER AGAINST THE DOOR
and shoved. The small latch splintered and gave way. Even though
he'd told me to wait, I couldn't resist the allure of protection from the
relentless rain, so I slipped inside right behind him.

Varney was jabbing bits of kindling into his fire, the damp wood
stirring more smoke than warmth. My eyes watered and I blinked.

The old man straightened and attempted an angry glare in Brantley's
direction. "If you broke my lock, you're fixin' it." Then his rabbit gaze
darted toward me and away, and he gnawed one of his broken nails.

Brantley made a cautious scan of the tiny hut. A tattered fishing net
hung from one wall. On another, pegs held kettles and tools. A splintery
table and stool were the only furniture, and the sleeping mat held a
rumpled assortment of threadbare blankets that looked like they hadn't
been washed since I'd been born.

Not that I was in a position to judge. We'd had plenty of nights in the open
traveling from Middlemost, which made this shelter feel like pure luxury.

"Varney, what's wrong?" Brantley's fingers unclenched from his knife
hilt, but he kept his hand over it.

"We're only looking for protection from the rain." I stepped from
behind Brantley and spoke in my most soothing tone. "We'll leave first
thing in the morning."

My words did anything but soothe.

Varney squeaked, and he waved a stick of firewood, as if brushing
away a fly. "No, sorry. Can't help. Get her out of here."

Brantley tried a new tack. "Come on, friend, it's wet as the underside of our island out there." He chuckled and sank onto the lone stool. "You aren't going to make us set up camp in your yard, are you?"

Varney blanched. "Yes. No. I mean, you can't stay out there. You can't stay here at all. Move on before it's too late."

I felt sorry for the nervous man. He'd evidently lived alone too long.

Brantley's eyes narrowed. "Too late?"

Varney poked his last branch into the weak fire, hand trembling. "Soldiers been lookin' for dancers."

I gasped, but Brantley covered it with a bark of laughter. "So what does that have you all wound up about? No one would mistake you for a dancer."

His efforts to coax a bit of humor from his friend fell short. When Varney turned back to us, his sunken collarbone slumped further in resignation. He shook his head heavily. "You don't understand."

Brantley stretched out his legs, leaning back with his elbows on the table behind him. "Explain it to me."

"I grant you've helped me over the years. Supplies and such. Wish I could help. But you have no idea how close danger is. Why don't you just move along?"

"We're cold and tired. Besides, I'm worried about you. I don't know what has you spooked, but maybe you could use a friend."

Varney sighed and seemed to surrender to the inevitable. "Was about to fix some soup. Dry yourselves off by the fire. Only be a minute."

He scurried out the door, and I took advantage of his invitation before he could change his mind. After hanging my cloak on a peg, I crouched near the fire. "Your friend is sure jumpy. Is he always like this?"

"He's never been a very bold sort. But he always had a good heart. He moved away from Windswell years ago. Never told me why. I try to check in on him from time to time."

"So we're truly close to Windswell?" Plaintive hope and longing colored my voice.

My companion crouched beside me, warming his hands. "This has been hard on you, hasn't it?"

The unexpected compassion made my eyes sting. Or it could have been the smoke.

"Yes, we're close now," he said. "We should reach it tomorrow. Truly. Unless the soldiers Varney mentioned are nearby."

"And then you'll take me to Undertow?"

He frowned, his eyes searching mine. "Still don't trust me?"

Of course I trusted him. Riding Navar with him, watching his interactions with villagers, and learning about the world I'd never known, I'd discovered I had far more reason to trust him than the Order to which I'd pledged my life. But when we reached his home, why would he bother with helping me any longer? I opened my mouth to ask, but the door swung open and slammed against the wall.

A soggy gust of windblown rain invaded, followed by Varney, his arms full of flat potatoes and green tubers. As we'd moved from the center of the island toward the rim, all the root vegetables grew in flatter shapes, since the layer of soil was so much thinner.

He dumped the potatoes on the table and grabbed a kettle and knife from the wall. Chopping rapidly, he avoided looking at us. I edged beside him and pitched in, tearing herbs into small pieces to add to the pot.

He sniffed but otherwise didn't acknowledge me. After he set the kettle on the hearth to warm, he examined me with a merciless glower, taking in my mud-stained dancer garb and soft slippers. "Brantley, make your own self useful and fetch firewood," Varney said.

Brantley rubbed the small divot under his lips and hesitated. "You all right?" he asked me.

"I'm fine." I waved him off. If this nervous man had information for us, perhaps I could coax him to share in a private conversation.

As soon as Brantley left, Varney tugged at a strand of his greasy, brown-and-gray hair. "What are you doing so far from the Order, dancer?"

My stomach clenched. Weeks had passed since I'd heard that title spoken with so much contempt. Clearly my efforts to pose as a simple traveler weren't working. He knew what I was—or had been. Did Varney have a way to contact passing soldiers? Had he done so already? The people of the rim weren't exactly allies with the Order's soldiers, but a beleaguered soul might benefit from turning in an enemy. On our travels, I'd seen that the loyalty of some villagers could be purchased with a handful of food. We'd used that to our advantage, but so could the Order. I chose to answer his question as simply as possible to avoid giving him any reason to betray us. But I also wanted him to know I considered myself a rimmer.

"I'm seeking."

His staccato laugh was as nervous as pony hooves on cobblestone. "Seeking what?" He pushed scraps from the table onto a tin plate.

"My past, my home . . . and the Maker's letter."

His nervous twitching increased tenfold. He fumbled the plate, and it clattered onto the wood floor, scattering bits of stems and vegetable skins.

I knelt to help him pick up the mess, then rested a hand on his trembling arm. "Have you heard of it?"

Still crouching, he hunched forward. "'Tweren't my fault."

This wasn't the suspicion I'd seen in others when I asked about the letter. This was distress. He knew something.

"Please, tell me." I gently squeezed his arm, stilling the shaking.

He stopped gathering the fallen scraps and sank to the floor. I sat across from him, watching the play of emotions across his face.

When he finally met my gaze, deep regret pooled in his eyes. "I couldn't do it, you see. How could I, when the Order grew so awful powerful? So I hid away here."

My pulse quickened. "Couldn't do what?" My quest had faced nothing but stone walls since I'd spoken with Dancer Subsun. Varney's response was so different, I was certain I would finally learn something new.

The door blew open, and Brantley stumbled inside, arms loaded with firewood. He kicked the door shut and shot a curious glance at the two of us on the floor.

"Varney was telling me something about the Maker's letter."

Brantley rolled his eyes and busied himself stacking logs neatly near the fireplace.

Varney's spine curled forward. "It was my grandfather, you see. Right before he died." He bobbed his head toward Brantley, then hunched into his bony shoulders. "Remember him?"

"Sure. Good man. I used to watch him herd when I was a youngling." Brantley finished his woodpile and settled onto the stool near us. "You left Windswell right after he died."

Varney nodded, a quiver unsettling his jaw. "When he knew the illness would take him, he called me to his bedside." A small moan sounded in his chest. "'Twould have gone to my father. Why didn't my father live? He'd a done the job."

I shifted. "What job?"

"The letter," Varney choked out.

My breath quickened to keep up with my racing heart. "You know it?"

"I have it." He announced the remarkable news with cheeks colored by shame.

Hair lifted on the back of my neck. "Where is it?"

He grabbed my arm with sudden intensity. "Please. Will you take it? Take the calling with it?"

Brantley growled. "What calling?"

Varney impossibly sagged even lower, as if spineless. "Me old grandfather told me 'twould be my job. He woulda passed it to my father, but after me pa was lost at sea, he decided to wait and give the task to me. Visit the villages, he told me, and make everyone remember the stories."

Brantley brushed wet hair off his face. "I don't remember hearing tales of a letter growing up."

"Long before we was born, Grandfather had roamed the rim with the letter. But when he fell ill, there was no one to continue his work. The stories were forgotten."

A tiny puff of air escaped my throat. "And you were supposed to remind them."

Varney bounced his gaze between Brantley and me. "You understand, don't you? I couldn't. I thought maybe when the Order stopped sending soldiers to the villages . . . but time went by . . ."

Varney's justifications didn't interest me. The letter was real! That was all that mattered. Even Brantley looked a bit stunned.

"Where is it?" I asked again.

A shrewd squint squeezed Varney's eyes. "Oh, no. You can't just look at it and leave. If you want it so much, then you have to take the callin' too."

Brantley rocked forward. "Don't be ridiculous. If you were too afraid back then, what makes you think the task will be safe for this slip of a girl?"

I rose, body centered strongly over my feet. A wave rolled beneath us and the shack creaked, but I stood firm, now used to the motion. "Show me."

"You'll take it? You'll take it and fulfill the callin'?"

Brantley rubbed his forehead. "I'm telling you, she can't."

I rounded on him. "Whatever I do will be no worse than hiding the letter away so no one even believes it exists anymore. What if the pages truly tell about the Maker?"

Varney scrambled to his feet. "Oh, that it does. Powerful words. I stopped reading because . . . well, my failure accused me each time I looked at the words."

Pity swelled in my chest for the miserable, fear-ridden man. "You kept it safe. That's something. Maybe it was your destiny to wait until the right time."

Varney shook his head. "I failed."

"Where is the letter?" I asked for the third time, hands itching to shake the information out of him if he kept delaying.

"I'll get it." He darted out of the cottage like a copper fish.

"Should we follow him?" I asked. "Maybe he's running away."

"He seems genuinely eager to be rid of it. He'll be back." Brantley shook his head. "Who'd have thought? Varney of all people . . ." His gaze sharpened and turned on me. "And what now? Do you realize how much trouble this will cause? You don't even know what this calling will entail."

How could I explain my burning need to Brantley? My life had been built on lies. Perhaps the letter was merely another lie. But what if the pages held answers? Answers to what had gone wrong with the Order, the purpose of dance, the mystery of the Maker that Ginerva insisted was behind the voice I'd heard. "I have to read it. Then we can decide what to do."

"We?"

The simple question pulled me up short. After all our traveling together, my quest had become ours, at least in my mind. But in one more day we'd reach Windswell, and Brantley's journey would be complete.

I walked to the fire and stirred the bubbling stew, trying to form an answer.

Brantley pressed the heels of his hands over his eyes as if his head ached. "I don't like where this is heading."

Varney blew back in, clutching a leather-wrapped bundle against his chest. He held it out to me.

As I reached for it, he snatched it back. "Wait. You promise. You'll take this for good? You'll take on the responsibility?"

"Yes, yes," I said, over Brantley's low growl of objection.

Varney set the small bundle reverently on the table, then backed away. "It's all yours."

The relief in his voice stirred my apprehension, but I unfolded the leather with eager fingers.

My first glimpse was a disappointment. It looked like a thinner and smaller version of the history book I'd used when teaching in the Order: rough parchments bound together with a dull cover. I'd expected gems and precious metals, ornate art, instead of the simple words, "The Maker's Letter."

But I opened it and began to read.

16

THE PALE LETTERS OF THE FIRST PAGE WERE DIFFICULT TO make out in the dark cottage, especially with Brantley leaning over me.

"Do you have a torch or some candles?" I asked Varney. I didn't dare sit near the fireplace with this rare parchment.

Varney scurried to a rough-hewn box in the corner and returned with an uneven stub. After lighting the candle and dripping wax onto the table, he secured it in place and stepped back. "'Tis yours now. All yours. Understand?"

He didn't wait for a response. Instead, he reached for his tattered net and removed it from the wall.

"Where do you think you're going?" Brantley asked. "Night's fallen."

Varney gathered the tangle of fiber into an awkward bundle. "Gonna do some fishin'." A new lightness colored his voice.

"Now? It's dark."

"Rain's passed, and I have better luck at night, seein' as how I work from the shore, unlike some lazy people who let stenella do their work." His banter was a stark contrast to the weight of anxiety and guilt he'd worn earlier.

He hurried outside and slammed the door behind him. I turned again to the first page, wondering: what heavy burden could these pages impart that their mere transfer to another's hands could bring such a change? Perhaps I should close the cover now and turn away.

"What's it say?" Brantley's muscled arms surrounded me as he leaned in to look more closely. His breath warmed my ear. "I can read some, but that's hard to make out."

I wasn't surprised he struggled with the text. The villages along the rim had little need for reading. The skill was useful for the occasional deed or title, but parchment was precious, so books were rare, and few people wrote letters. The Order required everyone on Meriel to achieve a basic comprehension, in order to read the frequent proclamations sent from Middlemost. However, few advanced to the level of skill we novitiates achieved.

Finally, something I could do better than Brantley.

I pushed aside any hint of smugness and concentrated on the page. The script was ornate, with added curlicues, making it even more challenging to decipher. I had only read a few sentences when I gasped and straightened, my head almost hitting Brantley's chin.

"This was written by a dancer."

Brantley stepped away and grimaced. "Lies from the Order?"

"No. Not a dancer from the Order. It says, 'One day as I danced to the music of the waves, the voice of the Maker spoke. He called me to record His words so that future generations would remember His great love.'" I scooted the stool closer and turned the page. "If she danced near waves, she wasn't in the Order. Besides, no novitiate would be allowed to speak of a Maker."

Brantley gave a noncommittal grunt, but didn't come back to the table. He settled on a log near the fireplace, poking at potatoes in the stew. "I'll let you read in peace. You can tell me about it later."

I read slowly, soaking in each sentence. One by one, each paragraph tore down everything I'd been taught in the history books of the saltars. For years I'd dutifully recited, "The power of the Order is sufficient to shape the world." Yet this letter revealed a Maker who had formed our land with His own hands, and fashioned each plant and animal with intent and design.

The Order taught, "Only the worthy may direct our course." But who determined the worthy? Tiarel? The other saltars? The letter described the Maker as the only worthy One. One who gave each person worth because He cared for us. Warmth stirred in my chest. The saltars' sparing approval had been a cold pursuit, and never kindled the glow of loving arms wrapped around me as the words of this letter did.

My hand shook as I turned the page, my fingers speeding to trace the next line of revelation. My mind reeled, yet even though the words opposed everything I'd been taught, there was a deep drumbeat of truth to them, and I breathed them in.

If this letter was to be believed, the Maker had designed our world to ride the currents of a mighty ocean. He gifted the people He made with an echo of His creative power.

"Listen to this!" I couldn't resist sharing with Brantley. "'I gave some among you the gift of dance—a way to join with me in the caring for creation, and also a means to know me.' That's what the Maker told her. Imagine!"

Brantley blew on a spoonful of hot broth, then sipped it. "So this is just some long-lost manual for dancers?"

Already, I knew it was far more, but I didn't spare an answer. I kept reading.

Brantley offered a bowl of stew, but I waved it away, too enthralled. Time vanished and the cottage disappeared as the story unfolded . . . of a Maker whose one command to His people was that they remember Him. The love and longing, joy and promise, sorrow and hope poured from the pages with the same heart I had sensed in the center ground. His existence now stirred less fear in me. His letter made it clear that although He was far beyond my understanding, He invited His little creatures to know Him. I longed to rush straight to the center ground and meet Him there . . . to tell Him I was sorry I hadn't realized who He was . . . to thank Him for the dance, for the star rain, for flowers and bresh and breezes and all the things that had flooded me with a desire to thank Someone.

I carefully turned another page and read the next section twice. I glanced toward the fireplace. Brantley sprawled near the hearth, long lashes resting against his cheeks, and deep steady sighs rumbling from his chest. I hated to wake him, but I couldn't wait until morning to share this.

"Brantley?"

He opened bleary eyes, then shot upright, fumbling for his longknife. "What happened?"

"Nothing. You have to hear this."

He sank back against the wall, drew up one knee, and folded his arms over it. With a groan, he rested his head on his arms.

His lack of enthusiasm didn't trouble me. My knees bounced, and I drummed my fingers on the table's edge. "According to the letter, the Maker created the island to float in set currents. As it traveled over various areas, the roots of plants that reached to the sweet water drank from nutrients in each place to keep them healthy. And the world avoided major storms that stirred the ocean, because of the path it followed. And fish were bountiful as the island passed through their breeding grounds."

He rubbed his eyes. "That's nice."

I rested one hand on the page and turned to him. "It makes sense. You've said that fishing has gotten harder every year. The storms have only grown worse since we were children. This could explain why everything has changed. The Order keeps the world turning in one place."

He stifled a yawn and worked his jaw side to side. "You mean the Order is the cause of all our problems? Now that I can believe."

I bit my lip and returned to the letter. "I don't know. There are more pages . . ." Soon I was immersed again.

Truth, truth, and more truth. The words crackled like star rain, flaring with brilliance and color and beauty. Varney hadn't needed to warn me that I must keep the letter. Nothing would make me relinquish it now. There was much I didn't understand, and I had enough questions to fill as many pages as the letter. Yet what I could comprehend brought new light to my understanding of my world, and my life, and the dance. The candle shrank, and I read as fast as I could.

When I finished the last page, I closed the covers over the parchment, but my yearning continued to build. I longed to speak to the Maker who had poured out His heart in these long-forgotten pages. Brantley was asleep again, face boyish and peaceful at rest. I smiled, and drew his cloak over him. Then I tucked the letter beside him, where I knew it would be protected.

Kicking off my shoes, I ran outside onto the bare earth. Varney was nowhere in sight. He must have traveled to a favorite fishing spot. In the dark of middle night, only the stars guided my steps toward the shore. Damp earth squished between my toes, as if embracing me. Now that I had read the letter and heeded His call, shyness paralyzed me. I glanced back at the faint light in the hut's window, but then took a few more timid steps toward the shore. A fragile breeze swirled past, cooling my cheeks. How could I approach Him? Would His beauty and power destroy me?

As I thought of the words of deep love that I'd read, I struggled for words. "To hear Your voice may undo me. But I will die loving You."

Should I dance? I shook my head. I'd learned to use dance to assert my control over the world. He had intended dance to be very different. To be a joyful response to knowing Him. I couldn't use patterns to conjure His presence as if He were as malleable as a cloud or wave that could be steered.

So I waited. The last of the clouds had passed, and no hint of wind stirred the sea. I'd never seen the water so still. The mirrored surface reflected millions of stars, tiny pinpoints glimmering like gems above and below. Star rain would be a fitting celebration of all I'd discovered, but the stars weren't swelling and changing color.

Except for one.

From amid the stars, a glow of light lengthened out on the horizon—a human shape clothed in the glow of a million stars. Like a herder riding his mount, the brilliant column approached, but no stenella supported this figure. His feet traveled over the water.

My breath sped to rapid gasps. Collapse to my knees? Bury my face? Run? But I didn't want to look away.

"Come," He said in a voice like wind stirring in the pines.

Knees buckling, I stumbled toward the edge, balancing on the tangleroot underfoot. Every fiber of my being longed to hide, yet also craved His closeness.

"Draw near."

Quaking, my arms reached forward. Another inch and I'd tumble into the dark water.

"Who are You?" I asked, my voice trembling.

"You've heard my voice before."

This couldn't be the same voice I'd heard in the center ground, so large and fierce and terrifying. His words now were gentle as a lullaby.

His eyes sparkled from the midst of the light, and He smiled. "I am the Thunder and the Whisper. I am your Warrior and your Tender. I am your Maker, your Keeper, your Dancer. And you are Carya of Undertow."

"Carya?" I gasped. The stray word I had scratched onto a corner of parchment, not knowing what it meant. The long-forgotten name exploded into my heart.

"Your true name, given in love by your mother."

How could the Maker of our entire world care about one small dancer? My voice fractured. "You know my name?"

"I know *you*." The figure of light glowed even brighter, warm hues wavering outward. "You are mine. Draw near."

There was no stenella to ride out to where He waited. I couldn't swim. I had nothing to help me float. Surely He didn't expect me to plunge into the sea?

Bathed in the warmth that came from His light, those arguments fled.

I pressed through my foot, stepping forward onto the water that shimmered like polished marble. As my weight came down, the surface softened slightly, and rebounded, supporting me step after step, like the buoyant daygrass on the edges of the center ground. I ran forward the last few paces, throwing myself into His arms.

His arms caught me and lifted me, lifted us both. We soared upward. Deep, joyous laughter surrounded me. Beneath us, Varney's shack became a tiny smudge among the night-coated trees, and still we rose. The coastline spread out below us, and villages we had visited in past days. It should have been impossible to see much with only the stars for illumination, but the Maker's glow helped me see clearly. The island grew smaller beneath us. Paths that had taken us weeks to travel wound inland. Then the Order came into view, a dark stain in the center of the lush world. Even from this distance, even safe in the arms of the Maker, a shiver rippled through me, along with relief that I'd left that tortuous place far behind.

As if I were riding the primary sun, I saw the entire island, our world turning stagnantly in a vast ocean. Far out to sea, stenella glided, unfurling their fins before disappearing into the depths. Other strange and larger creatures swam languidly. Swirls of clouds gathered and parted, revealing what might have been another island thousands of miles from our world. The Maker's heart beat with love so powerful, I felt it throb through my veins. Now I loved the world too. Each plant, each creature, and each amazing and difficult and suffering person.

In a blink, we stood on the shore again.

"I showed you the vastness of the world; now I give you a new name. You are Carya of Meriel. No longer of one village or form or designation. You will share Me with all."

The outline of the figure beside me wavered. I could see Him, but even with trying, couldn't take Him all in. *I must be dreaming.* Perhaps I was sleeping at Varney's scuffed table, head in my arms, exhausted from reading deep into the night.

The Maker reached out, and I placed my hand in His. His grip was tangible and ethereal at the same time, in a way I couldn't comprehend. "My little dancer, will you carry my love to all the people of Meriel?"

I beamed. How could I do anything else? The joy flooding me would make me burst if I didn't share the news. All those years of thinking we were alone . . . struggling to control the world through our perfection. The truth was glorious. I would tell everyone I knew.

"Of course! Parisa of Whitecap will be so thrilled. And I can find Nolana when we reach Windswell tomorrow. And I must wake Brantley. He needs to see You for himself. And then when we reach Undertow—"

"Child, you will indeed travel the rim to remind people of what they've forgotten." The voice that pulsed like dance drums but also seemed to well up from inside me now held a tinge of sorrow. "Then you must take the truth to the center of Meriel. To the Order."

All my warmth and joy rushed away, and like a landed fish, I struggled to breathe. I sank to my knees, cold with dread. "Not there. Please. I can't go back there." Didn't He understand? The Order commanded obedience and fear throughout the world. They gloried in holding our island in place. If I questioned them, Tiarel would have me tossed into one of her wells to perish in the dark sea beneath the Order.

"In time long past, the dancers who formed the Order sought to be a blessing, to unite and equip those with the gift," He said.

I shivered. "But they are causing harm. Breaking the world."

"Because they are broken. They need the truth to make them whole."

My heart trembled. "I can't. Not me."

The world around me blurred into the background and the figure of light pervaded my vision. His words saturated my hearing like the swish of my own pulse in my ears as He spoke. "Don't be afraid."

That was the hardest command to embrace. I tried to tighten my back muscles, to stand strong, but still I shook my head. "They won't listen. Besides, I couldn't even find my way back to Middlemost alone."

"You won't travel alone."

"You mean Brantley? He won't have any interest in helping with this."

I could barely make out a patient smile on the face that glowed so brightly. "*I* will be with you."

A little of my faith and joy returned. Hand in hand with this glorious and powerful Maker, everyone would be quick to hear. One glimpse of Him, and they would believe. "Will You carry me as You just did, or will we walk? Or run along the sea?"

His hand touched my face, soothing as Ginerva's balm. "I will guide you. What was hidden will be revealed."

Even as the words floated in the air and repeated in my mind, the figure of the Maker glided away, across the water and toward the horizon. An early arc of the primary sun sent glowing hues skyward, and then dimmed as His brightness slipped past it.

"Don't go!" I scrambled to the edge, ready to run across the water after Him. The toes of one foot pierced the surface of the sea and sank beneath. The water no longer offered support.

I staggered back, barely preventing myself from tumbling into the depths.

I CROUCHED AND SCOOPED UP WATER, LETTING IT RUN through my fingers. It was mere liquid now. How had it supported my weight moments ago? A fish splashed, catching the spark of the rising sun. A few seabirds cawed and swooped out over the waves. The brilliant human figure disappeared past the horizon. Had it all been a dream?

Hinges creaked behind me. Brantley emerged from the cottage, holding the Maker's letter in one hand and rubbing sleep from his eyes with the other. "You're up early. What did you find out last night? And why'd you leave this with me?"

He looked grumpy and disheveled, and my heart sank. Here was my first challenge, my first opportunity to tell someone the message with which the Maker had charged me, and I didn't know where to begin. He would laugh in my face.

The lingering glow of the wondrous encounter coaxed me to set aside my fear, and I stepped forward. "It's all true." My words bubbled out. "I met the Maker. And He knew my name. I know it now. I'm Carya."

In the rising sunlight, Brantley's frown drew lines of shadow across his forehead. "Were you awake all night?"

"I . . . I think so. I finished the letter, then came out here to think. And He rode across the sea like the sun, and carried me to the sky above Meriel, and told me—"

"A dream?" Brantley pressed the back of his hand against my cheek. "Or a fever? You don't feel warm."

I placed my hand over his and met his gaze, willing him to believe me. "I don't fully understand. But He spoke to me. He asked me to do exactly what Varney said: to remind the villages of the Maker."

Brantley's worried eyes studied mine, and he blew out a frustrated huff. "You're a distraction. And you're naive as a newborn. But the truth is, I've gotten used to you. I don't want to see you harmed. If soldiers hear that you're reviving these old myths . . ." A thread of desperation wove through his familiar tone of irritation. "Don't do this. Please."

The way his voice roughened almost made me believe he cared for me, even though he'd made it repeatedly clear he viewed me as a nuisance whom he'd only promised to help.

"You don't need to worry." I pressed my hand to his chest, trying to offer reassurance. His strong and steady heartbeat rose like distant drumbeats, inviting me to the steps of a new pattern.

"Well, I do worry." A tendon flexed along his neck. "This course you're on . . . you don't understand the danger."

How easy it would be to leave the letter with Varney, find my family in Undertow, and live a quiet life.

How impossible it would be to turn back, now that I'd touched the hand of the Maker, heard His voice of love, and ached with Him for the brokenness of our world.

"I have to try," I said, stepping back from Brantley.

He thrust the bound parchment at me, as if it were a poisonous lanthrus plant. "I'm telling you, don't take this on."

A part of me wanted to beg his help. Yet the road before me would be full of danger, and I didn't want him to bear the cost of this calling along with me.

And I hadn't even told him the rest of my mission. If he knew that I would ultimately return to confront the Order, he'd probably send me to live with mad Dancer Subsun.

"Brantley, if you had seen Him you'd understand. I could read the letter to you—"

"I've got herding to do." He stalked away.

I understood his anger and frustration, but it still hurt. We'd built trust between us in our flight from Middlemost, yet now he wouldn't even listen.

While he and Navar were fishing, I used my old dancer hood scarf to bind the Maker's letter to my chest beneath my tunic. The leather covers, my tunic, and my cloak would hopefully protect the pages from any weather.

After breakfast, Brantley banked the fire and left a pot of fish soup warming beside it. "Doesn't look like Varney will come back until we've cleared out. Ready?"

Although exhaustion weighted my limbs and my eyes felt heavy and gritty, I nodded and walked outside.

Brantley bounded to the shore and stepped onto Navar's waiting back. "We should make it to Windswell by nightfall."

I managed a weary grin. "I've heard you say that before. You keep telling me we're almost there, but then we aren't."

He laughed, some of his dull anger toward me washing away. "Ready to try standing today while we ride?"

"I'd better not. If I fell, the letter would get wet."

A cloud blew across his features. "Right." He didn't even offer his hand as I stepped onto Navar and settled into my place near her neck.

We rode in strained silence for the first hour. The warm sun lulled me, and the repetitive swoosh of water brushing past soon had my eyelids drooping.

Hands grabbed my shoulders and tugged me upright, and I startled awake. "Wha-a . . . ?"

Brantley did nothing to hide his exasperation. "You were about to fall off."

The cloudy depths of the ocean stared up at me, and I shuddered. If I'd sunk below the surface, I would have died, but even more terrifying, the Maker's letter would have been lost.

Brantley lowered himself behind me. "Lean back. I'll hold you."

With his arms around me, I surrendered to my exhaustion. In spite of his frustration with me, Brantley was a good man. A very good man, I thought muzzily as I drifted off.

Sometime later, I was tempted to change my assessment. I opened my eyes and thought I was having another vision of flying over the world with the Maker. Then I woke fully and gasped. The ocean was a terrifying distance beneath us. I swiveled my head side to side, panicked.

Brantley's chuckle rumbled against my back. "Figured you wouldn't mind letting Navar glide if you weren't awake to see it." He leaned forward and peered around to check my expression. "We'll get there faster if we let her glide."

I swallowed, squeezing my legs against Navar's back in a death grip, about to protest. Then I thought better of it. What good were my bold intentions of confronting the Order's lies if I couldn't show courage about smaller things? "Good plan," I said, with only a small quaver.

He patted my shoulder. "Atta girl."

Even terrifying challenges can become routine in time. Navar lowered to the surface, folded in her fins, gathered strength from the current, then soared again, expanding smooth wings and catching an invisible draft of air. The first few times, I fought back a scream. But soon I grew accustomed to her flights, and used the opportunity to scan the shoreline with a bird's-eye view.

A day on the ocean had mellowed Brantley's mood. "We'll get there while the subsun is still high. A fine way to catch your first glimpse of Windswell."

"You love your village." I wondered if I'd feel the same when I was reunited with my family in Undertow. What would it feel like to have a place to belong that wasn't the Order?

"A fine place. Until the day soldiers came for our girls." His voice darkened.

My spirit tensed, wishing to hold back this story. Yet I had to know. "What happened?"

"He wouldn't let them take his daughter. I don't blame my brother for fighting. I would have done the same if I hadn't been out to sea that day. Still it was foolish. They ran him through and tossed him in the sea." Pain rasped in his throat. "Going up against a stronger force only ends in tragedy for everyone."

No wonder he held disdain for my plans. He had wisdom born

of experience. I squared my shoulders. I had truth born of the Maker. "Nolana said that . . . wait, what is her true name? Brianna never told me."

"Orianna. A tiny bundle of mischief, much like her mother. An amazing woman." His voice warmed with affection when he spoke of Bri, and an odd pang jabbed my heart.

"Cole loved her from the time we were all younglings. Everyone does." Navar dipped sharply, and Brantley threw an arm around my waist to secure me. "They'll love you, too. Windswell will be grateful you helped Bri and Orianna escape."

"Or they'll hate me for being a dancer from the Order." We'd hidden my background in our stops at other villages. Although a few people had guessed, no one had confronted me. We wouldn't have that luxury in Windswell. Not if Bri and Orianna had reached the village safely and told their tale. They knew me for who I'd been.

"I'll set them straight." Brantley kicked a splash of water skyward, and the droplets seemed to laugh as they scattered.

His good mood was infectious and helped me put my worries aside.

"See that crooked pine?" he asked a few minutes later.

I shielded my eyes and turned to see where he was pointing. "That one?"

"Marks the edge of the bay. Windswell will be coming into view right around that bend."

Navar glided down to the surface and sliced through the water, swimming rapidly. Brantley sprang to his feet. His eager posture made me wonder if he'd dive in and try to race Navar.

Windswell nestled beside a gentle cove that curved inland and protected the area from the larger waves that rolled in from the outer sea. Children frolicked along the shore, in and out of the water like playful frogs. Set back from the rim, neat cottages clustered under the shade of persea and citrus trees, and flowers dotted footpaths and yards. There were no constrained rows of containers like the gardens of the Order, but I'd started to appreciate the asymmetry of plants growing where they wished.

A late-day breeze tickled strands loose from my braid, and I struggled to tuck them back into place, eager to make a good first impression.

A small boy prepared to dive from the tangleroot, but spotted us. He whooped, and soon all the children stopped their play to watch us approach. A few swam out to meet us, while others ran toward the homes.

Navar held her long neck high and proud at the admiring oohs and ahhs of the children.

"We're home," Brantley said with a depth of warmth and satisfaction I'd never heard from him before.

I adjusted my cloak. Would he drop me on land and go off to fish? How would I explain my presence? Part of me smiled and greeted the children splashing near us, while the other part of me battled the riotous currents in my stomach.

A small girl jumped up and down. "Uncle Brant!" With her hair wet and darker from playing in the water, it took me a moment to recognize Nolana—no, Orianna.

We slid into shore, and Brantley sprang onto land. "There you are!" he called.

Bri's tousled blonde hair glinted as she ran from the gathering crowd and threw herself into Brantley's arms. She'd embraced him in Middlemost when he'd returned Orianna to her, but at the time I assumed she was his sister. Now I saw a different sort of love between them. Of course. After Cole was killed, she'd turned to Brantley for help. He was her hero, and clearly more. A strange regret pinched my heart.

Brantley greeted old friends from all directions, completely forgetting about me. I fumbled my way off Navar's back, landing on my hands and knees on the tangleroot. As I stood, my foot caught in my cloak and I stumbled, drawing giggles from the nearby children.

My travel companion glanced back, and his open, joyous expression dimmed. "Bri, you've already met—"

"Why'd you bring her here?" Brianna's sharp gaze cut me in two. Then she addressed the wider group. "She's a dancer." She spoke the title as if it tasted of poison.

My worst nightmare. The warm friendly faces around us closed up like the petals of a morning glory at nightfall. Murmurs spread, all in dark tones.

I pressed my hands over my chest and felt the reassuring bundle of the Maker's letter. I wasn't here to seek their love. I was here to offer them the Maker's love.

"Hello. My name is Carya of Undertow," I said.

"Teacher!" Orianna tore herself away from Brantley and ran to me. I scooped her up into a hug. When she raised her head, she grinned at the gathered villagers. "She looked out for me."

Brantley walked back and stood beside me, facing his friends and family. "She helped them escape. She's no longer with the Order."

"Well, where will we put her?" Bri's eyebrows pulled together. "She can't stay with you."

I wanted to roll my eyes. Brantley and I had traveled alone together for weeks. Fear for my life had overcome any squeamishness about propriety. Besides, as a dancer, I had long ago renounced the possibility of romance.

"Grandmother will keep her." Orianna pointed to a cottage set deeper into the woods. "That way."

The girl took my hand and drew me forward, but I paused in front of Bri to offer reassurance. "I won't stay long. I have a message to bring, but then I'll be on my way."

Her glare didn't soften.

Brantley frowned and spoke in a low voice. "I told you not to cause more danger for this village. Just keep quiet. Once I find out the situation here, I'll take you on to Undertow. Then you can do what you want."

I understood his concerns, but I could never ignore the task the Maker had given me. Especially here in Windswell where the letter had been protected for generations. They deserved to be the first to celebrate its rediscovery.

Before I could argue, Brantley turned away and asked one of the men how often soldiers had come through town, and how they'd hidden Orianna. As the child tugged me out of earshot, he was getting an update on the fish herds. Now that he was home, it looked like nothing would pry him away again. And after I defied him and told the village about the letter, he'd be even less likely to help me find Undertow.

"Teacher, look." Orianna released my hand and performed a beautiful fern pattern turn, humming a melody while she moved.

Instinct made me stiffen, ready to object. Music, carefree movements outside the Order, bare feet padding along uncovered earth—all were taboos that I'd been indoctrinated against for years. Then I remembered how much of my training had been shown to be false. I smiled and joined her in the final turn. "You remember."

"Ah, this one can't stop dancing." An older woman leaned against her doorframe, bent with age, but with crinkles fanning from her eyes. "Come away in. One of the younglings said Brantley brought a guest. My name is Fiola."

"I'm Carya of Undertow. Orianna thought you might have room for me for a few nights."

Orianna grinned, and tried a high-spirited kick. "Grandma, she was my teacher once. The only nice one."

"Of course. My granddaughter told me all about you." Fiola took my arm and led me into her neat cottage. Wooden plank walls stretched toward the thatched roof as if they were living trees supporting their branches. Dried herbs hung in tidy bundles high in the rafters. The arms of the chairs were worn smooth from years of use, and woven cushions invited guests to sink down for a rest. Shelves held pottery dishes and mugs, and colorful jars of elixirs or preserved food. The room exuded the same generous welcome as the grandmother's face.

She guided me to a rocking chair near the hearth. "I'll roll out an extra ticking, and you stay as long as you like. I'm ever so grateful you looked after Orianna."

"The Order should never have taken her."

Fiola presented me with a mug of tsalla, then settled into a chair beside me. Her pale eyes turned to me, tears welling. "I clung to Cole's body until the soldiers carried him away and tossed him in the sea like garbage.

I thought my heart couldn't possibly beat any longer. Losing him and my sweet granddaughter was too much to bear. But then this little one returned to us."

Orianna scrambled onto her lap, and Fiola pinched her cheek. "Off with you now, and let me get to know Carya."

The girl skipped to the door, then turned back. "See you later." Freckles lifted with her grin, and she ran outside.

"Are you hungry? I haven't made supper yet, but I could stir up a batch of something for you."

Her ready welcome reminded me of Ginerva, but Brantley's mother was older, with bird-thin bones. Instead of a fluff of white hair, her head was crowned with a thin gray braid. Her smile was lively, but she looked too frail to lift a spoon. The suffering of Windswell had clearly taken a toll on her health.

"No, please. Don't go to any trouble. It's just lovely to be on land again."

"I'm sure it hasn't been easy for you. What does a dancer do, who leaves the Order?"

"Mostly runs and hides." My cloak suddenly felt as if it were weighted with the water of a dozen rainfalls. I shrugged it off, but that didn't help. My shoulders still felt heavy. Her question reminded me of the mission given to me, and that I didn't know how to begin.

Her chair creaked as she leaned back. "Well, thank the Maker, He got you out of that place."

My head snapped toward her. Her mention of the Maker reminded me how Orianna had spoken of a grandmother who taught her about the Maker. Gratitude expanded inside my ribs like a deep breath. Somehow, the Maker had prepared a way and guided me to a person who still remembered Him.

I reached inside my tunic, unbound the letter, and pulled it out. "You know the Maker?"

Her eyes drooped. "Most are too afraid to speak of Him. They dismiss me as a foolish old woman, so I'm not a threat." She tapped bent fingers to her heart. "But it hurts me here. Hurts me to see what our world is becoming, how we've forgotten Him."

"This will help." I handed her the bound parchments.

She opened to the first page, rubbed her eyes, then held the letter out at arm's length, squinting. "Can't make it out."

I scooted to the edge of the chair. "It's the Maker's letter. Passed down from Varney's grandfather."

She straightened with a happy gasp. "I thought it had been lost. Varney, that scamp. I remember when he was a boy—such a nervous sort. Should never have gone to him. What's he been doing with it?"

"He hid the letter away. Never showed it to a soul."

She shook her head, then stroked the page, tears welling in her eyes. "What was hidden will be revealed. What was lost will be returned."

"After I read it, I . . . this sounds impossible to believe, but I . . . I saw Him. The Maker. He asked me to bring these words to the villages."

She clutched the pages to her chest. "But you can't take this with you. If anything happens to you, to this letter . . . we can't let it be lost again."

After nearly falling into the ocean earlier in the day, I'd had the same fear. "Could we make a copy for you to keep, before I travel onward?"

Fiola gripped the arms of her chair and pushed to her feet, scurrying to a cupboard on the wall. She pulled out two small pieces of parchment and a willow pen. "We'll need more." She pressed one finger against her pursed lips, then brightened. "There is one in our village who was always the best with reading and writing. You'll need to win her over first. She'll have more parchment tucked away and could even help with the work."

"Wonderful! Who is it?"

"My daughter-in-law. Brianna."

My throat constricted. The woman who loved Brantley and despised me.

DURING THE NEXT TWO DAYS, BRI REBUFFED EACH OF MY attempts to speak with her. With no source for parchment, the hours I could have spent copying the letter were wasted in fretting. Brantley, worried by the low stores of provisions at Windswell, busied himself with fishing and training Teague, a young lad who wanted to become a herder. He also took time to catch up with friends, and, I noticed, spent long hours with Brianna. He repaired thatch on her roof, stacked firewood, and loaded her smoker with fish. The villagers welcomed him at every threshold, sought his company all day and invited him to sit by the fire at night. I was happy for him, but part of me held a dull ache. While I caught glimpses of him enjoying time with everyone else, he avoided me.

One morning, I slipped outside moments before the primary sunrise, leaving Fiola snoring in her bed, and walked to the water's edge, barefoot. I'd taken to touching the earth freely, no longer afraid of the voice and eager for any words from the Maker.

True to habit, Brantley stood on the shore patting Navar, studying the horizon, and preparing to head out for fish.

Navar noticed me first and tossed her head with a wide grin, shaking droplets onto Brantley.

Brantley spun, and when he saw me, his eyes narrowed. "You're up early, dancer."

I offered a tentative smile. "I hoped to catch you before you left for the day."

"I'm busy. The sooner I restock supplies for the town, the sooner I can see you on your way."

I blanched. He truly couldn't wait to be rid of me.

He must have seen the hurt in my eyes, because his strong posture sagged and he softened the harsh edge to his voice. "Every day you're here puts Windswell in danger. You do understand that, don't you?"

"It's you who doesn't understand." Frustration tightened my muscles. "The Maker's letter is important. It—"

"Fine. Leave the letter here and one day when there's less risk, folks who are interested can pass it around."

"But that's not what—"

"Rumors have reached the village of soldiers approaching from the midrim. I promised the patriarch I'd bring in one more herd of fish, since food has been so scarce, but time is fleeting. Now, if you'll let me get to my fishing, we can leave tomorrow."

"Not until I—"

He bounded onto Navar's back and with a terse signal of his hand, she raced away, although she twisted her long neck to send me an apologetic glance.

I sank to the spongy tangleroot, dangling my feet in the milky water, water that stretched into infinity. I'd accomplished nothing here, and I'd run out of time. Brantley would drag me from the village by force tomorrow morning. Somehow I needed to share the letter. The people of Windswell had the right to know its contents.

I hurried back to the cottage, where Fiola was rising. My words tumbled out, full of confusion and frustration as I told her Brantley's plans. "And Brianna won't help me find parchment. She won't even talk with me. And even if I found a handful of people to listen, there's so little time. And . . ."

Fiola smoothed my hair back from my face. "Take a breath, little one. I have an idea. Why don't you start the morning fire? I'll be back soon."

She hobbled out slowly, wrapped in a cloak against the morning chill.

I appreciated her kindness, but there seemed little she could do. I tended the hearth and pulled herbs from a clay pot and set them to steep in a kettle near the flames.

By the time I prepared a few lopsided saltcakes, she bustled in the door, sniffed the aroma rising from the kettle, and gave me an approving smile.

"I've asked the patriarch to give you an audience with the village assembly. We usually meet once a week, but I explained you may not be here that long. He will send out word for everyone to gather just before the primary sunset."

A thrill of hope shot up my spine. "I can read the message and let the Maker speak for Himself."

She nodded and poured a mug of tsalla, then sank into her chair. Her rapid errand had left her breathing heavily. "And Brantley usually doesn't return from fishing until the subsunset, so he won't be here to interfere." Regret clouded her eyes. "That boy has been the joy of my life, but when he thinks he's right, arguing with him is like holding back a tidal wave."

I hid my disappointment. I had hoped after all our adventures together, Brantley would support me in this vital moment. But Fiola was right. Perhaps he'd only try to stop me. I summoned the last of my confidence. "Maybe if the assembly hears the letter, they'll let me stay and make a copy." And maybe when others accepted the truth, Brantley would finally listen, as well.

OUTSIDE THE LONGHOUSE IN THE SOFT GLOW OF THE subsun, I held the Maker's letter in one arm, and smoothed the fabric of the new tunic Fiola had made for me. No more clumsy peasant dress to tangle my ankles, or stained and torn dancer garb to remind others of my past. The caramel-colored fabric over new clean leggings gave the freedom of movement I preferred, yet helped me fit in with rim villagers. I hoped my appearance would disarm the folk when I spoke, at least enough so that they would let me share what the Maker had told me.

As I approached the steps leading to the entrance, Brantley emerged from the nearby woods. He was back early! His sudden appearance kindled a tiny hope in my heart. With him standing beside me, I'd have a chance to gain an open-minded hearing.

Brantley gripped my arm and yanked me away from the longhouse. "Fair warning. I'll do whatever I must to stop you. Stirring up our village will only lead to harm." The words gritted out, harsh as the rough stone that formed this building on the inland border of Windswell. They scraped over my heart, leaving a raw wound and brutally extinguishing my flicker of optimism.

I pried his bruising fingers from my arm. "I don't wish harm on anyone here. Forgetting the Maker caused the harm. Maybe after you hear—"

"There's nothing in there I want to hear." He flung a wild gesture toward the bound parchments and growled like an angry predator. Too bad I couldn't tame him as I had the forest hound.

I leveled my chin. "Your people can make their own decisions. But I can't leave until I've told them about the letter."

His jaw flexed. "You're still planning to throw yourself into the path of soldiers while you wander the island, endangering everyone you meet?"

Precious Maker, can't You make him see? My pulse throbbed in my temples, swelling into a dull ache.

"Carya, they're ready." Fiola peered out the doorway, stooped and fragile, especially compared to Brantley, yet strong in her own way. "Brantley, oh good!" she said, as if unaware of the tension in the air. "I'm glad you're here. Will you help me? My legs aren't holding up so well these days."

After shooting me one more warning glare, he went to help his mother find a seat.

I trailed behind, and my fingers spasmed in their fierce grip on the letter.

The long meeting hall seemed larger than it had appeared from outside, with rows of benches encircling the center. The sun had baked the pine walls all day, filling the air with forest scent and hints of smoke. The stern faces around the room reminded me of my testing day at the Order, and I wished my task were as simple as remembering and performing a pattern.

The patriarch introduced me and informed the gathered people that I'd requested an opportunity to speak. I searched his careworn features for a hint of either support or opposition, but as he took a seat, his expression was neutral and unreadable.

All eyes focused on me, some open and curious, others narrowed with speculation. Brantley leaned on the wall near the doorway and glowered. I looked away from him, hoping he wouldn't interrupt. The benches creaked as the earth shifted in response to an ocean roll beneath us.

I cleared my throat. "Many of you may remember Varney's grandfather. He had a very special charge, which he meant to pass along to his son."

A few heads nodded, one or two older men murmured agreement. They remembered the tragedy when Varney's father was lost.

I held up the letter, turning slowly. "This was the charge, and a few days ago, Varney gave it to me. But before I read it to you, I want to be honest." I risked another glance in Brantley's direction. "The Order disapproves of its contents."

A few dark chuckles sounded from the benches.

"Then we're sure to like it," a burly man muttered, eliciting more laughs.

My smile flickered, then faded. "I want to be clear. Even hearing these contents could be dangerous. If you'd rather not be part of this, please leave now."

I counted my breaths in the same way I had when holding a long pose in a difficult pattern.

In the potent silence, a foot scuffed. A young woman stood, pulling her husband up as well. Without a word, they left. A few older landkeepers shook their heads and walked out also.

One more breath. Another. Would they all dart away like copper fish? Too bad Navar wasn't here to herd them back together.

Brianna stood and lifted Orianna to her hip. She walked to the door and stopped, watching me. Orianna murmured something, and her mother nodded and leaned against the wall. If Bri walked out, I was sure many other village leaders would leave as well. Her stance near the door made it clear she would listen only until she chose to leave.

Fair enough.

A mother with several children ducked and scurried to the door, as if her crouched posture made her invisible. Instead the whole assembly saw her worried urging of her children as she hurried away.

I waited two slow breaths more. No one else moved. Brantley crossed his arms, but stayed.

Maker, please make Yourself known. We forgot You, but we need You.

I opened the first page and began to read.

When they heard the introduction about the dancer who penned these pages, grumbles rose from the benches. I'd considered skipping that part, since I knew it would only raise antagonism, but it seemed wrong to exclude a single page.

I read faster, passion fueling my voice. After I shared the story of how our world of Meriel was formed and set to travel on the wide oceans, I swallowed to ease my dry throat.

A few of the older villagers nodded approvingly, and I grasped that encouragement, turned a page, and read on.

Soon I was lost in the narrative of a loving Maker who warned His people not to forget Him, His plans for our world, and His longing to be known. The silence grew so thick that at one point I glanced up, wondering if the room had emptied. Instead, everyone listened so intently no other sounds dared interrupt.

I continued reading about the gifts bestowed on each person, some to dance and encourage the ongoing creation, others to keep the land, others to herd, others to cook, and teach, and build. My heart constricted when I thought of the way the Order had corrupted a gift and sought to place itself above all other callings, sought to control the way the gift of dance was used.

A droplet fell onto the last page. I touched my face, surprised to realize tears were pouring down my cheeks. I pressed my lips together and closed the letter. I didn't know what to do next. *Beloved Maker, this would be a good time for You to show Yourself to everyone gathered.*

No vivid light approached from the doorway, but Brianna's mouth hung open, the lines of resentment in her face melting away. I scanned the benches, where many faces mirrored my own tears.

I finally dared look at Brantley. His scowl pierced me like a soldier's sword. He lurched to his feet and left, the scrape of his bench echoing through the longhouse.

More tears slid down my cheeks, and I stifled a sob.

Fiola, undeterred by her son's abrupt departure, hobbled to the center. Enfolding me in her arms, she tilted her face upward. "What was lost is found. Oh, Maker, we are sorry our neglect and fear pushed You from our village. Forgive us. Grant us courage to live in truth. Truly, indeed."

"And truly, indeed," several people echoed in a hushed tone.

"Truly, indeed!" Fiola repeated with all the volume her frail body could muster.

"And truly, indeed!" The group spoke with more conviction.

A young woman with a babe in arms rose, lifting her gaze past the ceiling of the longhouse. "Precious Maker, we sent our girls away when the Order asked, forgetting that You alone are our Protector. Forgive us."

Murmured agreements floated up from the benches.

A gruff old man hefted himself to his feet, his voice breaking as he said, "We argued about which gifts are most worthy. I'm sorry."

As more people stood to speak, I helped Fiola back to her bench, and sat beside her. Although I didn't see Him in tangible form, the Maker was present, and I wanted to leave the center of the room to Him. Watching Him move throughout the villagers of Windswell was as awe-inspiring as seeing Him travel on light across the ocean or lift me above the world. This was a miracle hidden within the ordinary, but a miracle all the same.

Prayer after prayer rose from hearts broken in repentance and souls awakening.

A hand lightly rested on my back. I glanced up.

Brianna's eyes were reddened with tears. "Dearest Maker, I resented a dancer who only sought to share truth. Show me how to help her."

Gratitude filled me like a deep breath, and I stood to hug her.

"I'm sorry," she whispered.

"And I'm sorry for all the harm the dancers caused you."

The patriarch stood and cleared his throat. "This is an astounding discovery. Our village will make changes." He sounded congested, his nose clogged and an emotional hitch in his throat. "Let's celebrate that what was lost is now found."

Those in the longhouse poured out into the clearing. A man lit a bonfire and drew in some of the villagers who had left the meeting. Murmurs and quiet interactions built to laughter, hugs, and excited chatter. Mothers bounced children at their hips, and teens jostled each other for a place close to the fire.

I sat on the longhouse steps, soaking in the scene, and whispering my gratitude to the Maker for the way the village had embraced His letter.

In the shadows under a pine at the edge of the clearing, Brantley leaned against the trunk, also watching.

A woman brought out a stringed instrument and plucked a few notes. A cheer rose and she began to strum a folk song that made my toes tap. All those years music had been forbidden to me. Perhaps that had been one of the cruelest losses. I'd never known how powerful music could be.

A boy ran to Brantley and tugged his arm. I couldn't hear over the singing, but watched as Brantley shook his head, then after more urging, he finally shrugged and drew his whistle from a tunic pocket. Was he going to call Navar inland?

Still remaining in the shadows, Brantley added the high, clear notes of his whistle to the song. In a rhythm similar to a rain pattern, his melody skipped and jumped. A man grabbed his wife and swung her into the clearing. A group of boys joined hands and snaked around the bonfire, galloping and tugging at each other. More people moved and spun in any open space and the music urged them forward.

I pressed a fist to my mouth. What were they thinking? It was taboo for anyone to dance unless they trained for years in the Order. These were no formal patterns, but exuberant expressions. The Maker's letter had said that some had the gift of dance . . . the special sort of dance that the Maker infused with creative power. However, it hadn't actually said it was wrong for others to dance just for the joy of it. Yet a lifetime in the Order made me uneasy at the sight.

Uncovering the truth when I'd lived in lies for so long would be an ongoing process for me. I gnawed on my lip, but stayed to watch, wishing I dared join in.

As the rhythm built, everyone began to jump together, bouncing higher each time. How did untrained dancers get such elevation in their jumps? The longhouse steps swayed, and I realized the coordinated jumps were moving the earth like a sheet stretched and billowed between two washer girls.

A surprised laugh broke from my throat. Here was dancing that cast away loss and sorrow and left room for only rejoicing. My sort of dancing was clearly not the only way the Maker blessed His people.

19

THE SUBSUN SET AS NIGHT COVERED WINDSWELL MORE
deeply. The bonfire died out, musicians put away their instruments, and
tired villagers retreated to their homes. Brianna and I helped Fiola to
her cottage and poured her a mug of tsalla. Now that Brianna had heard
the contents of the letter, she agreed to help us create a copy.

"Will you speak again at the gathering tomorrow?" she asked me.

I shook my head. "It's not my place to steer any decisions. The Maker
simply asked me to share the letter. Windswell will figure things out, now
that they remember Him."

"Wise words from one so young." Fiola took a sip of her drink and
leaned back with a contented sigh. "Perhaps you'll be the one to help my
son hear the truth. Loss and anger have clogged his ears for too long, but
I've seen how you care for him."

Heat bloomed on my cheeks, and my gaze shot to Bri, hoping our
tentative truce wouldn't be broken by Fiola's assumptions. "I'm sure he'll
listen to Brianna. I'll be traveling on as soon as we can get a copy made."

Bri tucked a blonde braid behind her ear and smiled, seeming
unconcerned. "I have a few ideas for finding parchments so you can begin
work on a copy."

Over the next several days, I grew to appreciate the fiery woman
who'd dared travel to Middlemost to rescue her daughter. It was she
who informed Brantley that I couldn't leave yet. I was grateful I hadn't
witnessed that particular argument, but she earned even more of my
respect going toe-to-toe with him.

When we discovered there wasn't enough parchment in the village to complete all the pages of the letter, Brianna sent a team to harvest cattails, blending and pressing them into a different sort of paper. At her urging, her friends produced enough to create an extra copy after we finished the first.

I wrote as fast as I could without making mistakes, going through willow pen after willow pen. Brianna took turns as well, but insisted her writing skill was inferior and urged me to copy as many pages as I could until my hand curled in helpless exhaustion.

Brianna also kept me informed about Brantley's activities. While I worked on leaving behind the message of the letter, he worked on leaving Windswell a defensive strategy. If the village stood up to the Order and its rejection of the Maker, armed conflict could result—the same sort of clash that had taken the life of his brother. The thought made me uneasy, so I narrowed my focus to the page before me.

One morning Orianna scampered into the cottage, where I sat hunched over the table across from Fiola. She set an empty basket on the table. "Grandma, I went to dig up some of the root crop for you, but they haven't grown. Nothing but tiny nubs."

Her distress pulled me from my work. Fiola tapped the table and held me with her gaze. "What was it the letter said about the dance, about creating?"

I leafed back a few pages and read the section about the Maker's invitation to be part of His creative work, to respond in joy to His gifts. I was still uncertain about exactly what that meant. The Order had been formed to implement that call, but I no longer believed their work served the Maker. Perhaps dance held no more place in our world, now that it had been corrupted.

"Teacher, let's dance for the garden." Orianna rubbed one of her eyes with a dirt-streaked fist. The smudge left behind made her look like she had survived a fistfight.

I pushed my chair back a few inches from the table, then hesitated. "We could . . . maybe." I would be breaking the rules of the Order, but hopefully not the rules of the Maker. "Fiola," I asked, "can we ask the

Maker if I should dance a pattern for growing?"

She closed her eyes and leaned back with a smile. "Of course."

"It's just that I'm not used to speaking to Him. In the Order we were taught to speak to ourselves, to declare what we wished for and summon power through our perfection and our will."

Fiola snorted like an irritated pony. "A feeble patch of tangleroot to stand on. You've seen the Maker. Where would you rather put your trust?"

Put that way, it wasn't even a question. How had I ever believed that my will alone could shape reality? How had the Order come to believe they could control our world apart from the Maker?

I rested my head in my hands while Fiola prayed. "Guide this little dancer to use all she's learned in Your service. You know the needs of our table and of our village. We trust You to provide us food. Truly, indeed."

"And truly, indeed," I whispered.

Orianna led me to the garden patch Fiola shared with Brianna and another family. The vegetables were stubby and uneven. Many of the leaves carried blight, or had been gnawed by forest pests. Too bad Brantley wasn't the landkeeper he'd once claimed to be. Perhaps he would have known how to bring health to the plants.

Would my efforts make a difference? Even though I'd used tiny bits of movement to coax a forest hound or connect with Dancer Subsun or play with Orianna, I was daunted by the idea of dancing a full pattern out here away from the Order. I'd been taught that only a full group of dancers could perform the creating patterns, and only in the center ground. Another thought frightened me even more. I had always believed only the most worthy and perfect dared dance. The Order would judge me the most unworthy and imperfect.

Would the earth split and tumble me into the ocean beneath?

Thankfully, no other villagers were nearby to watch. Orianna settled under a tree, soles of her feet together and knees stretching open as if she were back in class.

I slanted my face to the warm touch of sunlight. "Stop me if this angers

You," I breathed.

I stepped between the rows, beginning harvest pattern. If I had a dozen dancers, our movements could have quickly covered the garden, but there was only me. I wondered what it might have been like in the time before the Maker's letter was forgotten. Had groups of dancers once used patterns in a humble way? Had they worked in a sort of unity like the Order, but in love instead of fear?

After so many hours of sitting at Fiola's table, my arms exalted in opening wide. Each kick of my legs was like a shout of celebration. The steps I'd learned seemed too small and contained, and when I began the second variation, I did something no dancer I knew had ever dared to do. My body absorbed inspiration from the garden, from the breeze, from the suns, and I added leaps and twirls and rapid prancing footfalls.

Like a stenella gliding over the surface of the waves, or a harrier bird banking into the wind, I experienced a new freedom. The steps I'd learned helped to launch me, but now I danced beyond the pattern.

As I finished my improvised variation, sweat dripped down my back, and my legs buckled from exhaustion. Orianna drummed her fingers lightly on the ground, and then for good measure raised her feet and fluttered them to the front, stirring puffs of dust. "You did it! Will you teach me how?"

Catching my breath, I blinked a few times. Broad leaves now stretched thickly amid the rows, and tubers grew so large they broke the surface of the ground. Orianna ran into the garden and pulled up one of the pebbly green rutish plants, shaking the dirt free. "Grandma will make a feast with these."

Laughter bubbled from my chest. In all the years of precision, perfection, and indoctrination, I'd never before grasped the joy of creating in this way, never saw such tangible effect from using my gift. I could only imagine what it would be like to unite with other dancers . . . not in an effort to empower the Order, but to celebrate the Maker. The villages wouldn't go hungry. The island could drift to new fishing grounds. Fierce storms could be averted. The possibilities left me giddy.

I helped Orianna harvest another row of rutish. "Go ahead and bring the bulbs to your grandmother. I want to rest a moment."

Orianna scooped the bounty into her basket and skipped away. I knelt among the plants as fatigue rolled through me. As glorious as the dance had been, it seemed to draw life from my breath and strength from my beating heart. I needed time to recover before rejoining the busy activity of the village.

I pressed a hand against my chest, coaxing the racing flutter to slow. Perhaps at least one of the proverbs I'd learned at the Order was true: Each gift required sacrifice. Sharing my gift had definitely taken a toll.

"There you are." Brantley stormed into the clearing. "You shouldn't be out here by your—"

"Look." I beamed and gestured to the flourishing garden. "I danced and it worked! The crops grew."

He scratched his head and shrugged. Obviously, he hadn't seen the dismal state of the vegetable patch moments ago. "I've been looking everywhere for you."

I rose and dusted off my knees. "Fiola could have told you where I was."

"Or you could have let me know you'd changed your plans." He glanced back, measuring the distance to the cottages.

I faced him and laughed. "Don't be such an old lady—"

Brantley froze, squinting past me into the undergrowth. Every muscle in his face tensed. A harsh whisper ground through his clenched jaw. "Run. Run now!"

I snapped my gaze over my shoulder to whatever had drawn his attention. Two armored soldiers broke from the cover of trees and sprinted toward us, swords drawn. Instead of fleeing, Brantley ran toward the first one, pulling his knife from his belt in a smooth movement. A shout tore from his chest. "Run!"

I stumbled a few steps toward the village path, but couldn't leave him to face this attack alone. These men weren't here to demand taxes or even steal girls. Murder burned in their eyes.

The first soldier swung his sword, but Brantley dodged, ducked under the blade, and grabbed the man's arm. The soldier stiffened and emitted a sharp gasp. Brantley pulled his knife back, blood dripping from the blade. He released his grip on his opponent, and the lifeless man crumbled to the ground.

The other soldier barely spared a glance at his comrade but ran toward me.

Brantley picked up the fallen sword, spun, and saw me, still wavering on the edge of the clearing. I whirled and ran for the closest tree. Perhaps I could climb out of reach.

Too late.

Cruel hands grabbed me. A beefy arm encircled my neck. The soldier jerked me back against him so hard, the studs of his breastplate cut into my back. He turned us both to face Brantley, who stalked toward us, muscles clenched with suppressed fire.

I tried to scream, but only a whimper escaped the choking arm at my throat. Then the soldier's grip shifted as he angled his sword so that the edge pressed against my belly. I couldn't move. Couldn't breathe.

"Drop the sword, rebel. I'll take her to the Order or run her through. Your choice." Fetid breath carried his growled threat.

Brantley advanced a few more steps, leading with the borrowed sword.

The soldier slid his blade and heat sliced across my stomach. I winced and bit back a shriek of pain.

He would kill me and then Brantley. I couldn't let it happen. "Leave!" I rasped out to Brantley. "I'll go with him."

Please, Holy Maker, let Brantley see sense. Don't let him throw his life away.

Brantley froze. Helpless rage contorted his face into the mask of a stranger. Splattered blood freckled his face, his clothes, his arms. Slowly he gave one tight nod, and made a great show of crouching and lowering his sword to the ground.

I tried to swallow but couldn't move even that much. Without his partner, the soldier couldn't control us both. "I'll come with you," I promised, forcing the whisper from my constricted throat. "If you don't hurt him." My fate was sealed, but at least I could save Brantley.

Brantley slowly straightened from laying down the sword and met my gaze. Midnight-blue storms clouded his eyes—and lightning flickered in their depths.

DESPERATION PROVIDED ONE MORE DROP OF STRENGTH. I twisted against the bruising arm at my throat, no longer afraid of the sword that had already seared my skin. I fought to grate out a few more words, as if I could reason with the brute. "I said I'd come with—"

In the space between two heartbeats, Brantley straightened. His other hand appeared from behind his back, raised as if to signal Navar. Air whooshed past my ear. The soldier's grip weakened.

I used the moment to wriggle away. What had happened?

A loud thud moved the earth as the man fell onto his back, thrashing, skin as white as a fish's belly.

Brantley's knife protruded from the soldier's throat.

I coughed and doubled over as I struggled to take in what had just happened. Brantley had thrown his knife, spearing the man as efficiently as he'd once dispatched a bog rat. He could have killed me!

"You all right?" Brantley threw the words my direction while kneeling beside the soldier, whose eyes and mouth were wide in shock.

He had asked me something, but I was too stunned for the question to make sense. "What?"

He motioned to my stomach. "Your wound."

I pulled my arm away from my tunic. Blood seeped, and I pressed my hand against my belly again. "Only a scratch."

Doubt registered on Brantley's face, but he turned his full attention on the soldier. Pressing his hand to the man's throat, he slowly pulled his knife free. Blood bubbled past his fingers, but he kept his grip, one knee digging into the man's chest. "What is the Order planning?"

The man stared past Brantley toward the sky. Did he feel death's fingers gripping his soul? He choked, and his lips shaped a weak sneer. "Know about . . . rebels . . . don't need rimmers no more . . ."

"What will they do?"

He sucked a pained fraction of air into his lungs. "Destroy . . . you . . . all."

"Nothing new there." He lifted his head in my direction. "And why do they want her?"

A rasping gurgle was the only answer. All life fled the soldier's eyes.

Brantley bit out a curse and stood, brushing his blood-soaked hands against his pants. He frowned down at the man, then turned to me. "At least we've gained a few weapons."

Who was this man who had just killed two soldiers? The deceitful landkeeper, the confident and joyous herder, or a ruthless warrior? I looked down. I didn't want to see him with hard lines shaping his face into callous fierceness and the blood of his foes painting his knife.

He stepped closer. At his touch, I cringed away. He muttered another curse, swept an arm around my shoulders, and hurried me to Fiola's cottage. He left me there to go retrieve the soldiers' weapons, bringing a few other men to help him hide their bodies in the sea.

Listening in silence to my broken account of the attack, Fiola bandaged my cut, which really wasn't much more than a scrape. The bleeding stopped once she cleaned and wrapped it. Then she gently washed the soldier's blood from the side of my face as short, tight sobs wracked me. Not from the sting of the wound, but from the shock of seeing men die. After I calmed, she handed me a mug of hot seawater, and I welcomed the rich, sweet tang. We'd survived. Everything would be all right now, I told myself over and over, yet couldn't stop the tremors in my hands.

As the fear and horror bled away, I welcomed a fog of numbness. Fiola had already started a stew with the tubers Orianna brought from the garden, and earthy scents wafted from the fireplace. A warm blanket woven from the fluffy fibers of a midrim plant wrapped my body. For the moment, I settled into a ragged sort of peace, clinging to the comfort of normality.

When Brantley returned, I was glad to see he had taken time to wash off the evidence of the battle. His clothes still bore stains, but at least his knife no longer dripped with blood. However, he now wore one of the soldier's swords, and the reminder of the brief battle made me shiver.

He paced, his large presence making the cottage seem small. "We've run out of time. We can't stay here. Our presence will only draw more trouble to the village."

I cleared my throat. "Maybe we could hide nearby—"

"They won't stop looking for you." He jabbed an accusing finger my direction—the same hand that had flung his knife in one lethal movement. "Besides, the inland watchman said the tax patrol is near."

My tenuous relief scattered like a cloud broken to pieces by a fierce gust. Would I always have to run one step ahead of fear? I cast off the blanket and stood. "I can hide here until I finish the second copy."

Brantley plowed a hand through his fair curls. "You don't understand. The whole village knows you're here."

"Well of course, I had to share the letter." Was he still angry about that?

"If even one person decides to tell the next passing soldier about the letter, or about you—out of fear or to bargain away their tax or whatever reason—you'll be dragged back to the Order."

The uneven stack of papers on the table called to me. Bri and I had finished the first copy for Windswell but had only begun the second. I grasped for a way to stay a little longer to complete my mission. Besides, now that I'd discovered a way my dancing could help, I wanted to encourage each garden plot in the village.

"Maybe I could—"

Brantley drew close, his voice low. "If you are betrayed, my mother and Bri will suffer too."

Further arguments caught in my throat. It was one thing to gamble with my own safety for a few more days in Windswell, but I couldn't risk harm to the family I'd grown to love. I reached for the letter. I'd sewn a simple pouch so I could carry the pages more easily, and I tucked the precious document inside and drew the long strap over my neck, letting it settle over my chest in the way new mothers carried their babes. After grabbing my cloak and slipping on my light shoes, I said, "I'm ready."

He frowned, as if not trusting my cooperation. Then he nodded, quick to take advantage of my agreement. "Hide those pages well," he told his mother. "And tell Bri to keep Orianna out of sight until the patrol leaves. I'll get word to you when I can."

Fiola pushed herself upright and hobbled to me. She pressed the heel of her hand against my forehead. "Go and move our world."

Goosebumps rose on my arms. The command I'd once heard from the High Saltar, a command that stirred fear and dread, was now a blessing that stirred hope and confidence. I gave her a gentle hug. "May the Maker watch over you."

Brantley brushed a light kiss on his mother's forehead. "Please be safe."

She touched his cheek. "And you."

He eased from her gentle touch, his face tightening as he turned to me. "Let's go."

After one more longing glance at the pages strewn across Fiola's table, I followed Brantley outside. Until this moment I hadn't been sure he would accompany me on my way to Undertow. Even now he might simply point me in the right direction and then return to his village.

To my surprise, he jogged to the path that led inland.

"Wait!" I called to his back, then followed when he wouldn't stop. "Wouldn't we get out of sight faster if we rode Navar?"

"Yes." He spoke over his shoulder and continued his track. "But my apprentice is out on a solo fishing trip. I'll whistle for Navar tonight when we're safely away from Windswell."

Catching his sense of urgency, I scrambled to keep up, the wound on my stomach throbbing as my pulse increased. "How close are the other soldiers?"

Shouts rose from the village behind us. A pony whinnied.

"Closer than we thought." Brantley grabbed my hand and ran faster. "They have mounts. Run!"

He came close to yanking my arm from its socket. Being dragged while dodging trees made the run more difficult than it needed to be, but now wasn't the time to explain rules of movement to him.

My feet flew as fast as possible. My muscles hadn't fully recovered from the garden dance, and my nerves still trembled from the shock of the soldiers' attack.

Brantley led us deeper into the woods. Underbrush slapped his face, then ricocheted to scrape across my cheek. Salty blood trickled over my lips. I tucked in my chin and kept going. Pain throbbed across my midsection and my throat burned from the bruises the soldier had left.

Galloping hooves advanced.

"Someone told them which way we went," Brantley said, his breathless gasp propelled by anger and betrayal.

We panted for air, ducking and weaving. This was hopeless. We couldn't outrun ponies. I risked a glance behind us. Armor glinted through the leaves. They'd see us in seconds.

I tugged my hand free. A wide willow drooped over a creek, and I slipped into its sheltering branches.

Brantley stumbled to a stop beside me, chest heaving. "Are you hurt? We have to keep moving."

I kicked off my shoes and put a finger over my lips.

Tack jangled nearby, and the dangerous scrape of a sword leaving its sheath chilled my blood. But I took a calming breath, hoping the wide tree would hide us a little longer.

I could think of only one way to evade the soldiers. We needed the cloak of fog. The Order didn't teach a pattern for that, so I wasn't sure where to begin, and any movement was difficult in this constrained space.

Maker, help me!

My legs drew wide semicircles, first to one side, then the other, inventing as I went along, trying to capture the rhythm of clouds mingling with night-cooled earth. Mist rose from the riverbed and encompassed us. With the air dense as soup, I grew bolder. Spinning with swooping dips, my arms welcomed the fog and urged it to thicken.

Sound muffled. The whole world seemed to dissolve.

I grabbed my shoes, took Brantley's hand, and led him across the creek before our way was completely covered by the mist underfoot.

Clear of the fog bank, I looked back. An impenetrable wall blocked the patrol from our view. More importantly, it blocked us from theirs. A smile spread across my face. "I thought that might help."

Bent forward with hands braced against his thighs, Brantley struggled to catch his breath. When he straightened, the pallor of his skin matched the fog. He stared at me as if he'd found a bizarre insect inside his porridge bowl.

"How did you . . . ?" He shook his head. "Never mind. Let's get out of here while we can."

Not a word of thanks for my quick thinking. I dropped my gaze. "Lead the way." He had every reason to be irritated. Once again I'd put people he loved in danger.

Lost in my thoughts, I walked after him for quite a way before realizing we'd left the sweet scent of the ocean far behind. Performing another dance—without the community of fellow dancers in the center ground—had taken a further toll on me, and weariness settled like a stifling blanket. "I thought we were going to the next rim village."

Brantley paused, pulling a twig off his trouser leg. "That's what they'll expect. If someone in Windswell betrayed us, they'll have revealed our plans. So we'll head to a midrim village instead."

I couldn't fault his logic, but my feet grew heavier as we trudged inland. Traveling by sea was so much easier. Would I ever reach Undertow and find my family? We passed a tall pine and a grove of shorter maples, then left the cover of forest to run across an exposed field.

After we pushed through brambles to enter another copse, Brantley shimmied up a smooth birch and checked the path behind us. He slid down and grinned. "Yep. We lost them. At least for now."

I brushed blood off my arm where thorns had broken the skin. "I didn't think I'd ever say this, but I miss Navar."

Brantley chuckled. "I knew you'd become a fan of the ocean. Soon as we have a chance, you have to learn to swim."

"One thing at a time."

He sank down, resting his back against the tree's trunk, then patted the earth. "Let's rest a bit."

I held my ground. "Are you still mad at me?"

Draping an arm over one knee, he lifted his chin. Clear blue eyes with swirls of cloudy ocean depths met my gaze. "I wasn't angry. Not at you."

"You could have fooled me."

"Not you. It's that letter." A hint of storm darkened his features.

I settled beside him and felt the warmth of him through my wrap. "But it's such good news. We can free the world from the abuses of the Order."

He hissed in a sharp breath. "So if there's a Maker, and this letter is so important, why did He let it go lost for so many years? Why didn't He stop the Order before they'd kidnapped children and hobbled women and bound the world to their rules?"

With a hand pressed against the pouch, my inadequacies rose up to taunt me because I had no explanation. "I don't know."

"And that's the problem, isn't it?" He rolled his shoulders, shrugging away the topic. A sly smile quirked his lips. "You've been holding out on me."

I leaned away. "What do you mean?"

"That fog thing you did. We could have used that a long time ago."

I smiled at the memory of dancing a garden into health and forming a cloudbank of protection. "I wish I'd known sooner."

"Didn't the Order teach you that stuff?"

A sigh softened my spine along the birch trunk. "They taught us patterns and formations. But until the Maker spoke to me, I didn't really understand how the dance works."

At the mention of the Maker, tendons flexed in his neck. "Now you do?"

"A little better," I said quietly. "It will take me time to discover all the truths I've missed. I grew up with so many lies."

When he turned to face me, compassion warmed away some of his icy stiffness. For a second, his features held the yearning vulnerability of a lost child. "I guess we all did."

There was so much more I could say. I wanted to plead with him to understand my call, to realize why I'd had to share the letter with his village, and why I insisted on a path that he viewed as reckless. But instinct warned me not to press. I held my peace.

A wind gust stirred the branches overhead, and leaves gave a warning rustle. A second later, clouds scudded together, blocking out the light of both suns.

"Let's keep moving." Brantley sprang to his feet.

We headed inland all day, our journey punctuated by short bursts of rain. We were both weary and bedraggled before Brantley decided we could safely set up camp.

Was this to be my new destiny? Fleeing one village after another, never knowing whom I could trust, staying one step ahead of Tiarel's soldiers? No wonder Brantley had tried to dissuade me.

"You were right." I pushed aside soggy underbrush, searching for dry sticks for our fire.

"About?" Brantley struck his firestone with the back of a knife and blew on the timid spark.

"This mission. I didn't fully realize what obeying the Maker would mean."

He reached for the bits of kindling I was gathering. "So you've changed your mind?" No hint of expression colored his tone. I couldn't tell if he was hopeful I'd give up my plans, or irritated at the trouble I'd caused so far.

After a slow breath, I drew back my shoulder blades. "I can't turn back. I won't. But now I understand why you fought me."

Crouching by the feeble blaze, his mouth quirked in a crooked grin. "It's a start."

Heat flushed my skin. Our tiny fire must be sending out more warmth than I'd realized.

21

I ONCE BELIEVED MY DESTINY WAS MEASURED IN INCHES. Each tiny movement scrutinized and judged. Each step imbued with the potential of success or failure as I strove to be accepted into the Order.

My new destiny was measured in miles. Long days of travel, weaving among midrim villages, cautiously skirting rim towns. Following a haphazard path. Now my goal was to read the Maker's letter to as many people as I could and to leave copies behind in any village where we lingered a few days. I discovered my heart savored this new calling even more than I'd once dreamed of dancing in the center ground; this new passion was broader, taller, deeper.

I was surprised that Brantley went along with this plan. I'd expected him to hurry us to Undertow so he could be free of me. Instead, he insisted we stay clear of the rim until he was sure there were no more soldiers on our trail, and then he intended to check on his family in Windswell.

While we traveled, I'd also expected him to protest any contact with villages along our route. But he, too, seemed to have a new agenda, one that he didn't discuss with me. Since I couldn't find my way to Undertow without him, I had to trust him. Whatever he was up to, our goals for the moment ran a parallel course.

We often slipped into a village and found someone who remembered the Maker and had prayed for help. Eager welcomes, grateful meals, and rapt attention seemed to await us in each new place. I took that as a sign I was squarely in the center of the Maker's plan. Everything was going better than I could have dreamed.

There were always some who scoffed, who argued, who turned away, but overall I marveled at the way the Maker had prepared a way for me.

Brantley embraced my cause . . . to a point. But while I focused on unveiling truth that had been lost, he held whispered conversations with clusters of village leaders. Whenever I saw him in the distance, my unease grew.

One morning, after we left a town that had provided refuge, I stopped on the trail and confronted him. "What are all these meetings you're having while I'm reading the letter to gatherings?"

"Finding out what they know. How many bands of soldiers Tiarel has patrolling, and where they were last seen." He fidgeted with a tie on his pack and turned away.

He was hiding something. "And?"

He eased his heavy pack from his shoulders and sighed. "Look. We agree the Order must be stopped, right?"

"Or reformed. Returned to what the Maker intended." I waved an arm back the way we'd come. "As more people of Meriel hear the truth, eventually the Order will have to change."

One of his eyebrows lifted. "Eventually? And in the meantime how many children will be stolen? How many fathers murdered? How many villages will starve? There's no time for 'eventually.'"

"We have to trust the Maker's plan—"

"No, that's your path. I won't interfere. But in the meantime, the village leaders have their own plans."

My stomach churned as if copper fish writhed inside. "What . . . what have you been doing?"

He faced me squarely, resolutely. "Raising an army. If all the villages unite and send men to confront the Order, they'll have to stop."

"But—"

"Look at it this way. If your Maker's plan succeeds, a rebellion will never be needed. The herders have a saying: 'Ride the current, but watch the winds.' I'll help you with your reforms, but if it doesn't work, we'll have a backup plan." He hitched up his pack and set out again.

I stared after him for a long moment. If I could have stopped his conspiring, I would have. But I knew better. Even the determination of a dancer couldn't match this man's resolve. The best way for me to prevent violence was to keep following the path the Maker had set for me. His truth would change everything. I jogged ahead to catch up. Brantley cast me a sideways glance. When I didn't argue with him, he offered me a grateful nod.

Day after day, we maintained our uneasy alliance. When he warned me to be more covert in my reading of the letter to villages, I listened to his advice and met with smaller gatherings hidden by the walls of longhouses. In turn, he stayed nearby while I read and waited until I finished before having discussions with the men about weapons and defense strategies and whatever battle plans he was stirring.

Between villages, Brantley and I shared quiet conversations on the trail by day and beside the campfire in the evenings. Despite my misgivings about his militant approach to stopping the Order, our talks forged a stronger bond and a growing trust.

One night, we sat near each other for warmth as stars emerged from the darkness, dotting the sky with light. "There!" I pointed upward over the center of the island, tracing an outline of stars. "See the shape of petals in bloom?"

"Nah. That's the ripple after a fish leaps and lands back in the water."

"No, it's definitely a flower. I always used to look for that pattern of stars when I'd sneak outside at night." Because of the turning of our world, the pictures were often in different quadrants, making it a challenge to identify my favorite constellations.

"Sneaking out? So you weren't the perfect rule follower after all?"

I smiled. "I tried. But there were nights I needed to hear myself think. And you? Did you *ever* follow any rules?"

He chuckled. "Oh, I tried for a while when I was young." He trailed off and tossed a twig into the flames. We watched sparks float in the silence before he continued. "Where did all the rule following get you, anyway?"

"It wasn't all bad. I loved learning patterns. They made sense. And I thought I could serve my people."

"You don't need the Order to do that."

I stared into the flames. He was right. I no longer needed the Order, but I did need the Maker. Now that I'd met Him, I felt more free to experiment with dance, using movements to help a berry bush to fruit when our supplies were low, or to bring rain on a bit of parched farmland in a village that needed our help. However, even those ways of helping didn't alleviate my impatience.

At last Brantley believed the soldiers had lost our trail completely, and he set our course for the coast near Windswell where he could signal for Navar. One morning he tossed me a saltcake covered with lint from his pack. "We'll be back at the ocean before you know it. Maybe even today."

I brushed off the hard biscuit and nibbled a bite. Grit scraped my teeth. I frowned. He'd been promising our imminent return to Windswell for days. "Stop doing that."

"Now what?"

"Being overly optimistic. Promising things you have no right to promise."

He squeezed the bridge of his nose. "I thought you wanted an estimate of when we'd reach Windswell."

"But you told me we were a day away before. And that was over a week ago."

"Life doesn't always run according to the Order bells. You can't schedule everything."

Was he right? Had my years of training made my temperament inflexible even while it taught my body to stretch and bend?

"Relax. We'll get there eventually." He hefted his pack and strode away from our campsite.

I glared at his back but grabbed my cloak and followed.

This time, his estimates were accurate. That same afternoon the breeze kicked up the sweet scent of the ocean, and my pulse quickened. As we broke through the trees, the view of the vast horizon stretched before us and I threw my arms wide in welcome.

Brantley laughed at my childlike glee, then flopped onto his stomach near the edge and blew a unique call on his whistle. He even dipped the end into the water and played more notes.

"Is Navar close enough to hear?" I settled cross-legged beside him, scanning the waves.

He sat up and put away his whistle. "Stenella can hear from vast distances, and even better underwater. Now we wait. She may be out with my apprentice and need to bring him home before she can answer the call. Or she may be a half-day's journey away from the island, visiting her pack."

A wistful longing brushed across my heart. "Do you think she misses her family when she's away?"

Brantley's eyes deepened to a darker blue as they reflected the sifting waves. "You'll find family soon. We'll reach Undertow any day now."

I threw him a teasing grin. "I've heard that before."

"I keep my promises." Light played against the surface and sparkled in his gaze.

We sat in companionable silence as the primary sun set behind us. During our journeys, the island had rotated so this coastline now faced the sunrise instead of the sunset.

"Do you ever wonder what's out beyond the horizon?" I asked softly.

Brantley chuckled. "I once determined to find out. I loaded a pack with food and took Navar out for much more than a day of fishing."

A cool breeze touched my neck, and I shivered. "How far did you go?"

"So far that the emptiness made me fear for my sanity. Days and days. I'd always wondered if there were other worlds adrift on the sea, but all I found was the vast sky and lonely waves."

What courage it must have taken to venture so far from the entire known world! "And then?"

"I ran out of food and turned back. Navar got me safely home. A little thinner, and no wiser about what lies beyond." He stood, frowning out to sea, the fading glow of the subsun lighting his curls and casting his face in shadow. "It's not like her to leave my call unanswered. Looks like one more night of camping."

Draping our cloaks over low pine boughs, we created a small shelter where we huddled. I'd grown used to makeshift beds and slept soundly. A feeling of absence woke me, along with the cool air of a vacant space. The glow of primary sunrise barely lit the sky as I crawled out of our tent.

Brantley stood a few yards away, one hand propped against a willow sapling, the other resting on the knife hilt tucked in his belt. Tight cords stood out on his neck, and his fingers flexed.

"Is something wrong?"

He spun on his heels and forced a smile. "No. Just watching for Navar." He turned back to scan the ocean again.

Combing my fingers through my tangled hair, I walked up to stand beside him. "I'm sure she'll be here soon."

"Of course." He rubbed the juncture where his neck met his collarbone.

"But you're worried." I touched his arm, willing him to be honest with me, to share whatever weight he was carrying.

He frowned at the horizon. "Even if she was working with a herder, they wouldn't stay out overnight. She's had time to answer my call five times over. Unless something happened to her."

Now that he'd revealed a glimpse of his raw fear, I almost wished he'd kept it hidden. Was Navar injured? Lost?

"I'm sure she's fine." But my words sounded vacuous, even to me.

Throughout the morning, Brantley lowered his whistle more times and put out the call only his stenella responded to. When Navar didn't appear after several hours, he strode away with a sudden sense of purpose. "Wait here," he called over his shoulder.

I scanned the ocean for Navar until my eyes burned. Every slight ripple on the surface quickened my heartbeat with hope, which sank when no stenella appeared.

Rustling noise pulled my gaze inland. Brantley dragged several long saplings into the clearing, where he whacked branches away with his knife. The vigorous work gave him an outlet for his worry, but why was he constructing a permanent shelter? We'd detoured long enough. We had to set our course toward a quick check on Windswell, and then finally on to Undertow.

I kept watch, saving my questions.

At last, Brantley paused in his work. Sweat glistened on his forehead, and he knelt at the water's edge and drank deeply of the sweet seawater. After splashing handfuls over his hair, he shook his head. His wet curls splattered water on me.

"Hey!" I laughed and backed away.

"Sorry."

It was a relief to see his grin again after all the hours of tension.

"Brantley, I think we should keep moving."

"I agree."

"Really?" I'd braced for an argument. "Then what are you building?"

He took my hand and settled on the edge, tugging me down beside him. I knew the signal. He was about to tell me something I didn't want to hear.

"We can't walk the rim from here to reach Windswell. The underbrush is too thick, and the tangleroot too narrow in most places."

Discouragement pressed me, even as light waves rolled me up and back. The conflicting sensations made me queasy. "You mean we'll head inland again?" I fought to keep my tone level, but couldn't hide my dismay.

"No. There's another way. We'll follow the coastline in the water."

"But Navar hasn't answered."

"So we'll swim."

I pulled away, panic squeezing my chest. "The Order was right. Drinking sweet water makes you touched in the head." My voice rose, tight and shrill. "You know I can't swim."

"You'll learn." His expression held calm resolve, and his tone brooked no arguments.

"But the Maker's letter . . . we can't leave it here. Besides I—"

He tipped his head toward the building project. "That's what the raft is for. It will hold our gear, and you can grab the edge for support."

A raft? I stared at the flimsy saplings, and slid my gaze to the limitless ocean and its cloudy depths. "No."

He stood and resumed his work. "Gather some reeds and braid them. We'll need to lash everything securely."

I gathered materials and began creating a rope, but all the while I kept up a stream of arguments and alternative ideas.

His only response was silence as he continued lining up slender branches. Eventually I ran out of words.

Far too quickly, the tiny raft took shape, uneven branches lashed together with clumsy knots.

"Could I ride on it?"

He shook his head. "It's too unstable. You'll be safer in the water."

The words *safe* and *water* did not belong together.

A hint of compassion warmed his eyes. "There's more chance of the raft capsizing if you're on it. Then what would happen to the letter?"

He was playing dirty. He knew I'd do anything to protect the letter.

"Why can't we go back inland?" I tried one last time.

He sent a worried gaze toward the horizon. "We need to get to Windswell fast. I have to find out what's happened to Navar."

My opposition softened. I didn't fully understand the implications of Navar's absence, but I understood how much Brantley cared about her. My affection for her had grown every day I'd ridden. I wanted to find her too.

I pulled off the pouch with the letter, then shed my cloak, shoes, and outer tunic. In my leggings and small undertunic, I could almost pass as a herder. "All right. Teach me."

His approving smile coaxed me to the edge.

When water lapped over my toes, I backed away a few steps. Was there a dance to turn the water solid? *Maker, couldn't you guide me on the surface, as You did the night I met You?*

"Slide into the water and hold this strand of tangleroot." He demonstrated, easing into the water without a splash. "I'll be right here."

I floundered into the water, scraping my chest in my desperate efforts to keep my upper body on land. I grappled for images of my early childhood when I'd perhaps enjoyed swimming, but the memories were deeply buried. My knuckles whitened as my fingers locked around a sturdy root. "Now what?" I squeaked.

To his credit, he didn't laugh.

"Kick your legs. That should be easy for you, dancer."

I convinced my legs to stop their frantic thrashing, and began to copy Brantley's actions. Slow, strong kicks supported me with surprising effectiveness. Once he was sure I could keep my head above water at the edge, he pulled the empty raft in beside me.

"Now try holding this."

I couldn't convince my hands to release the relative security of tangleroot to hold the fragile, untethered island Brantley had created. It bobbed and dipped with each ripple of the waves.

Brantley's patience shone as he helped me transfer my grip. "I'm right here. I'll hold you."

He treaded water behind me, not needing tangleroot or raft to stay afloat. His arms found my waist and the comfort of his reliable presence eased my hiccupping gasps. As my muscles softened, the water—and Brantley's arms—supported me. If I leaned too heavily on the edge of the raft, it tipped alarmingly. But as I learned to stretch out and allow the ocean to hold me, it steadied.

"Good. Keep doing exactly what you're doing."

Brantley nudged the raft against the shoreline, lifted himself onto land, and loaded our supplies.

"Wait. I don't . . . I can't . . . too soon . . ." My lungs didn't have enough breath to get out my protests.

After slipping into the water beside me, Brantley propelled the raft along the shoreline with powerful kicks. "Let me know when you get tired."

What if my grip weakened?

I should have let him teach me to swim weeks ago.

I should have learned to float without a raft before setting out.

I should never have left the Order.

That fickle thought pulled me up short. When challenges loomed, I couldn't second-guess the path that led me to this point, especially when my Maker had guided the journey.

I rested my cheek against the edge of the raft and embraced the sensation of milky liquid carrying me. My legs found a rhythm, not unlike performing a pattern. Repetitive movements quieted my worries, and I lost myself in the pure focus of swimming and pushing the raft.

Much later, a touch on my back startled me. I pulled my head up, which made my legs sink beneath me. I panicked and tugged too hard on the raft.

"Easy there." Brantley pointed to a large, tilted tree. "See that tree? We're almost there. The cove is around this outcropping."

I filled my lungs, which helped me float in place. "Let's keep going."

He grinned. "You continue to surprise me."

His respect fueled my determination, and I stretched out and resumed kicking.

As we entered the bay, no children frolicked in the water. Smoke wisps drifted from a few chimneys, but otherwise the village appeared deserted. We propelled the raft closer. One slight figure sat on the tangleroot with his back angled toward us, so intent on something in the water he didn't notice our approach.

We aimed his direction.

"No!" Brantley suddenly released his grip and dove under the water, swimming like an arrow.

I clung to the raft, nudging it forward in uneven jolts, while trying to see what had upset Brantley.

As I drew near, a dark stain coated the surface. Brantley swam through the discolored water and threw his arms around the listless shape floating near shore.

Navar!

I fluttered my legs, rushing to reach them.

"I tried to send her out." Brantley's apprentice, Teague, replaced a soggy bunch of moss, briefly revealing an ugly gash in Navar's side. "A few days ago a new band of soldiers arrived. They were rounding people up. I thought to ride her out until they left. But they saw me. I meant to signal her to flee, but got confused." Misery ran rivulets down the boy's face. "They threw a spear."

I stroked Navar's supple hide. Was she gone?

Her lids lifted halfway, but her violet eyes clouded like heavy fog, and then sank closed as she shuddered. A deep moan reverberated through the water.

Anguish carved dark shadows under Brantley's eyes as he stroked Navar and crooned to her.

Teague covered his face. "This is my fault."

Without turning from Navar, Brantley took time to comfort the lad. "It's not your fault."

I pressed my lips together, fighting back tears. Of course it wasn't Teague's fault. He was not the person who had drawn the soldiers' ire to this village. The fault was mine.

22

NAVAR SANK LOWER IN THE WATER, ONLY A SMALL HUMP OF her back breaking the surface. Winged fins extended from her sides, not for glorious flight but as a last effort to stay afloat. Without their support, it appeared she would sink into the depths. Her long neck held none of her usual energy, but stretched out along the water. Her eyes flickered a few times, glassy with pain.

I fluttered my legs, easing the raft closer.

Navar's agony reflected in Brantley's eyes, dark blue storms brewing in their depths. "Does Fiola know?" he asked Teague. "She might have a cure."

The apprentice reached for another handful of moss and passed it to Brantley. "She fled with the others. Most of the families scattered until the soldiers left, and some are staying away until they're sure it's safe again." Teague's neck corded, tension traveling down his arm to his clenched fist. "They were demanding more girls."

"And the village leaders refused?"

Teague's chest expanded and he nodded. "To a man. They took arms and stood together. Since the patrol was small, the soldiers backed down and left. But families with girls hid them, fearing the men would return with reinforcements. Otherwise Fiola would be here to use her herbs on Navar."

I inched closer. "Alcea leaves speed healing, at least for humans. They might help."

Brantley waved a hand at Teague. "Run to Fiola's cottage and see what you can find." He barely spared me a glance, obviously blaming me. He had every reason to hate me. If he'd never met me, soldiers wouldn't have targeted

Windswell. Villagers wouldn't have resisted. Navar wouldn't be dying.

Eager to be helpful, and perhaps also to escape Navar's suffering, Teague raced away, his lanky legs eating up the ground.

Alone with Brantley, I wanted to apologize for the Order, for the soldiers, for Navar's horrible wound. Nothing I could say would make a difference.

Instead I released the raft and wrapped my arms around Navar's neck, cooing into her floppy ears. "I'm sorry. Keep breathing. You'll be all right. We'll take care of you."

By some instinct, my legs bent together, rolling through a motion in the way Navar used her body to propel through the waves.

Maker of Meriel, teach me a new pattern. Teach me a dance of healing.

I forgot my fear of the water and turned in place, copying the movements I'd seen Navar perform. Releasing her, my arms unfurled like her side fins. I stretched my neck and reached toward the sky, then dove under her languid head and emerged on the other side. My movements echoed all the strong and graceful ways Navar had always danced through the water.

Brantley held compresses against his stenella's wound and paid no attention to me.

If nothing else, perhaps my swimming could distract her from the pain.

Navar lifted her chin, her luminous gaze following my movements. After finishing the stenella pattern I'd created, I stroked her soft withers and side. She inhaled deeply, lifting higher in the water.

I crawled onto my accustomed spot near her neck. "Yes, sweet Navar. Be whole."

Brantley pulled away a fistful of moss and gasped. Craning my neck, I looked back at the gash in her side.

The edges had drawn almost together. Fresh hide grew across the wound. Navar swiveled her neck and twisted to look. She nuzzled Brantley's chest and shoved him aside. A bewildered whistle rose from her throat, and then a joyous gurgle.

Brantley paddled back a few feet. He shook his head, then brushed his fingers across Navar's side. His expression swung from utter joy to a frown that could only mean disbelief. Lifting his head, he met my gaze. "I keep seeing things I can't accept."

I hugged Navar, then crossed the small span of water to clamber onto shore. "Sometimes the hardest things to believe are the ones most important to accept."

He circled Navar, checking for any other injuries, then pulled himself up to sit beside me. "Thank you. Will you watch her? I need to find out if anyone knows where my mother and Bri are hiding. I'll speak with any leaders still in the village."

"I won't leave her side."

He stood and dusted moss from his hands. "Looks like the time to oppose the Order is now, doesn't it?"

He strode away before I could answer. Another wriggle of unease twisted through my chest. The Maker had asked me to bring truth. I longed to undo the damage the Order's lies had brought our world and hoped the Maker would reform their methods. Brantley was trusting in a military opposition. The thought of war horrified me. Would it come to that?

Navar bleated and rested her chin on the edge of tangleroot where I sat.

I stroked her long ears. "I'm worried about him too."

BRANTLEY RECEIVED REASSURANCES ABOUT HIS FAMILY from the village leaders, and left messages for them. After restocking supplies and assuring that Navar was fit, Brantley and I abandoned our flimsy raft and resumed our accustomed places on the stenella's back to ride onward along the rim. I sat astride, whispering endearments to our mount, while Brantley stood behind me, scanning the shoreline.

"Next stop Undertow at last." Brantley shifted his balance and signaled Navar to glide. "Sorry it's taken so long to keep my promise."

"No one could have predicted all that's happened. I wonder what we'll find."

"Hopefully more strong arms to march against the Order."

My legs clenched against Navar's side as she glided above the waves. "That's not what the Maker—"

"Enough." Brantley threw his voice against the wind. "If the Maker had cared enough to stop the Order, I'd consider following Him. We agree that the Order must be stopped. You do it your way—"

"The Maker's way."

He broadened his stance as Navar caught a gust and swayed. "And I'll do it my way."

I gnawed on my lower lip. *Maker, could You meet with Brantley as You did with me? If he could see You, I know his heart would heal and he would trust You again.*

The ache in my chest came from more than fear about my mission. I also felt a deep concern for Brantley's pain and anger, a level of care that I didn't want to analyze. Yet no matter how much I cared, I could no more change his heart than I could make the suns move backward in the sky. Once again, I needed to practice trusting the Maker.

IN SPITE OF MY EAGERNESS TO REACH UNDERTOW, I WISHED Brantley would keep Navar on the surface. Each time she caught an updraft and rose toward the sky, my legs trembled from the effort of gripping her sides. Vertigo made the ocean spin beneath me, and I took to closing my eyes each time she left the water. Even with Navar's speed, we had to make camp on the shore two more nights before drawing close to Undertow.

The last afternoon, as we rode a strong updraft and soared above the sea, Brantley pointed out landmarks that told him we were near what I hoped was my home village. Tension built in my muscles, and my eyes strained for my first glimpse. Would I recognize any landmarks? Would there be people who remembered me? Perhaps the father whose shoulders I'd remembered riding?

"You keep edging forward like that, you'll fall right over Navar's head." Standing behind me, Brantley chuckled, but the warmth in his tone revealed sympathy for my eagerness.

What had once been a tiny clue, a word on a scrap of parchment, had grown to be a vivid hope. After being deferred by so many interruptions, my hope had only expanded. Would the village look like Windswell with neat cottages and flower-bordered paths? Soon I'd meet the family from which I'd been ripped away. What unique skills did they have? Were they landkeepers or herders or healers?

Happy fantasies played across my imagination in glorious color.

"Oh, no." Brantley's gasp pulled me back to reality. He sank to his knees behind me. "It can't be."

I followed his gaze toward the shore as Navar coasted down and sliced a landing on the water, carrying us within sight of a devastated village.

Burnt tree trunks rose like vicious pickets guarding an ash-strewn clearing. Only skeletons of homes remained, all gray and mottled and deserted. Carrion birds gathered in a tight row on the ridgeline of one cottage, cawing at our arrival. No hint of human life remained in what had once been a large village.

My hand found my throat. "This must be the wrong place."

His grip tightened on my shoulder, trying in his own way to offer comfort. "Wait here."

As soon as Navar reached the shoreline, Brantley leapt onto the rim and strode through the ruins.

I ignored his command and followed, my bare feet soon coated with cold ash. Deeper inland, we came to a large structure that still had partial walls. Brantley stepped inside the longhouse, then quickly returned, shaking his head.

"I told you"—he coughed—"to wait with Navar."

The odor of burnt and rain-soaked wood carried from the building and stopped my progress even before Brantley blocked my way. A scarred sign dangled from what had once been a doorway. I could make out the carved name, *Undertow*.

"What's inside?" I advanced one more step.

He drew me back toward the waterside clearing. "Nothing but ruin."

Pain lanced through me, and I fell to my knees. Charcoal dust stirred around me, dead and dismal as my ruined hope. "My people . . ." I gasped and covered my face, tears already splashing onto the earth.

"This was the work of the Order." Brantley stood stiff, his back turned to the ruins. "We have no choice. We have to rally the villages to fight. You see that, don't you?"

I hurt too much to see anything. Maybe he was right. Maybe there were no more options. Maybe in time anger would burn in me like it did in Brantley, and that would give me power to fight. But right now I felt only lost and as empty as the charred buildings. The Order had been my life. When I'd given that up, I'd clung to the fragile anticipation of finding a new place to belong, of reuniting with my village and family. To come this far . . .

I looked at my empty palms. What could I cling to now?

Brantley shifted his weight, backing away and then returning. I wanted him to leave so he wouldn't see my despair. But I also wanted him to stay and tether me to life. I hunched forward as silent sobs wracked my body.

After a few minutes, Brantley knelt beside me and rested his hand on my back. The warm touch in the midst of the cold desolation slowed my gasps of pain.

When only a few forlorn sniffles remained and my tears ceased, Brantley helped me to my feet. "If anyone escaped, they may have traveled inland. We'll look for a trail. At any rate, we'll need a place to camp tonight."

I nodded and shuffled behind him, my head drooping. When we passed the longhouse, I averted my gaze from the symbol of an entire village being completely destroyed. Fighting down nausea, I quickened my steps.

We crossed a field and entered a thicket of inland woods. "There." Brantley pointed at signs only he could decipher. "I'm sure some of the villagers escaped. We may still find them."

False hope was more painful than no hope. I closed my ears and my heart.

Maker, did You do this?

My fist pressed against the pouch at my chest.

Did You need to purge every good thing, every possibility from my life so that all I have left is this letter? Is that who You are? Crueler than the harshest saltar? Then why am I serving You?

23

AS WE TRUDGED INLAND IN THE DEEPENING TWILIGHT, I was grateful for Brantley's silence. Absorbed in my doubt and pain, I bumped against him when he stopped.

"Listen," he hissed.

Irregular murmurs floated on the air ahead. Not the steady mumble of water dodging around rocks in a stream or the chatter of a flock of starlings.

Human voices.

We crept forward, ducking from cover to cover, attempting to find the source without being seen. A thin voice rose, then broke off. A child. An infant cried, then quieted amid nervous shushing.

The sounds came from within a deep circle of pines. Thick branches draped from tight-spaced trunks, and propped-up limbs covered the gaps. A crude but effective shelter. We circled the trees and caught a flicker of light through a seam. A hint of smoke wafted toward us.

"They should be more careful. If we found them this easily, the soldiers—"

"Hold!" A lad near as young as Orianna sprang from a tree, landing in front of us and brandishing a tarnished sword he could barely lift. Rigid silence ended the murmurs from within the circle of trees.

Brantley raised his hands. "We're friends. We seek the villagers of Undertow."

The boy swiped a hand under his runny nose and let his sword droop. "No villagers left."

A cough and rustle from within belied his words.

Brantley pulled me forward. "This woman is from Undertow. Wrested from her parents as a child."

The boy chewed his lower lip and squinted at me. "Don't know her."

"I was taken before you were born. Held by the Order. I'm hoping to find my family." My throat thickened, and I had to blink several times to remind my tears I'd given them too much freedom already today.

A wizened hand pushed aside the concealing branches, and an old woman emerged. Gray hair coiled above her neck, and she stood tall as the pines. "Pert," she said sharply, "resume your watch."

The boy clambered through the branches and out of sight.

"Your name?" The matriarch studied me.

I stared back. Could she be my mother? Her face triggered no memory. "I'm Carya of Undertow. Stolen from the village some fifteen years ago. At least I think this was my village."

Even under the deepening shadows, the woman's face paled. "You're a dancer?" I should have been used to the suspicion and disdain—I'd heard it often enough over the weeks since leaving the Order. But coming from the matriarch of my home village, it crushed me.

I shook my head. "Not anymore. I've escaped the Order."

She stared at me hard, skepticism darkening her gaze. "So perhaps it was you they were looking for?"

Horror contracted my ribs. Could all this be my fault?

Brantley put an arm around my shoulder. "We've witnessed other damage the Order's soldiers have done, but they've never razed an entire village to the ground like this."

"Not true." She gazed toward the island's center. "We had word that Foleshill was also burned." Turning to Brantley, she asked, "And you? Who are you and what do you seek?"

"Brantley of Windswell." His hand rested on his knife hilt. "I seek to destroy the Order and return our world to the villages."

Her eyes widened. "An ambitious goal." Then she sighed and her proud posture slumped. When she spoke again, her voice was edged with bleakness. "I am Reena, the current matriarch. You're welcome to enter and see the remnant of Undertow."

This wasn't the warm acceptance I'd hoped for. More a resignation from a woman past the point of caring about danger.

Brantley strode past her, ducking beneath a low branch. I followed, but then stopped and touched her arm. "Do you know my father or mother? Is there anyone here who remembers me?"

She studied me again, and her expression softened. She placed her hand over mine. "Yes, little one. You were not forgotten."

"My family, are they . . . ?"

"Come." She patted my hand and led me into the clearing.

Families clustered around tiny fires that raised only a cautious glow. Brantley crouched by a circle of young men and was quickly deep in hushed discussion. A baby whimpered, and his mother bounced him, her arms as thin as willow branches and her cheeks sunken. Starvation and exhaustion proclaimed their presence every direction I turned. And the horrible lethargy of grief. No doubt each person here mourned for family members who had died in the attack on the village.

Resolve kindled in my chest. Now that we'd found my people, Brantley could herd fish for them. I could dance and stir the local berries and fruits to replenish what had been destroyed. We would help them rebuild the village and fortify it against the Order.

Reena guided me past the other small groups. Most of the people were too weighted by grief to show much interest in our arrival.

She stopped near the edge of the enclave. "Your only remaining family is your mother. Each year she spoke in the longhouse to the elders, asking them to stand up to the Order. She had no recourse, but she spoke your name. She continued to speak it. Even when your father traveled inland to learn of your fate and didn't return. She bore all loss, all struggle, holding on to the hope you would return."

My pulse quickened as I struggled to comprehend. My father had been lost? I'd feel that wound later. Right now, excitement crowded out all else. "My mother is here?"

Reena's arms surrounded me in a gentle hug. "I'm sorry." She stepped aside and indicated a figure on the ground, hidden by shadow under the shelter of pine boughs. A makeshift bed had been created with tattered blankets. The woman tossed and moaned.

I fell to my knees, searching the haggard face. "Mother?"

Her eyes didn't open, but she stilled. Sweat glistened on her forehead, and I pressed my hand to her skin. The fury of two suns burned within her body. "What's wrong?"

"The fever took many who survived the attack. Most perished quickly." Reena handed me a cloth soaked with sweet water.

I stroked my mother's face, squeezed droplets from the cloth on her dry lips. "But some recovered?"

Reena's hand touched my back. "No. She has lasted longer than the others, but there is no hope for her."

I would not accept that. Could not. I soaked in every inch of her, longing for the connection that had been severed so long ago. Even haggard from disease, her face held precious reflections of my own: strong jawline, high cheeks, fine hair. Her locks were tangled and drenched in sweat. Gently, I smoothed them back from her face.

"Mother. It's me. Carya. I've escaped from the Order. Please wake up."

Her eyes opened briefly, glazed with fever. Another moan vibrated in her chest, and she moved again, thrashing as if the very air tormented her. Finally she drew a deep rattling gasp and went limp.

Was she gone? I rubbed her arm, caressed her face. "Mother?" A hint of breath still warmed her lips.

Reena brought a fresh bowl of water and another cloth. "She may wake again. They do. Especially near the end."

The end? No.

I'd discovered a healing dance for Navar, surely I could do something for my mother.

Maker, restore her. Grant her life. This was surely why You spared her. So I could find her.

A flicker of conscience reminded me how angry I was at the Maker after witnessing the devastation of Undertow, and the questions my heart had flung at Him. Would He even want to help me now?

Never mind. The Order taught that when we focused our full will on an outcome, we had all the power needed within ourselves.

I stood and lifted my arms in and out like strong lungs. Small light steps brought to mind the beating of a young heart, so I pummeled the earth with my feet. I built to large movements, springing into explosive leaps, then rolling onto the ground, feeling damp leaves beneath my back. I sprang upward again and repeated the pattern. Villagers turned from their fires, doubtless believing a mad woman was in their midst. I ignored them and danced until my muscles screamed. Still I danced, desperately willing with every bit of my human strength. Live! Live!

When I'd depleted every bit of strength, I collapsed to my knees beside her again, lungs heaving for air. Her eyes would open now. They would. I knew it. Here was my destiny at work. Saving my own mother.

Her body lay still as death. A flicker of doubt licked my soul, but I stamped it out. I gathered her into my arms as she lay across my lap. "Mother?"

Her lids quivered.

Yes! She wasn't gone!

Then her eyes opened. Glorious, beautiful eyes. Clear as my memory fragments had shown me.

"Carya?" Her hoarse voice swelled with wonder. One weak hand reached up to touch my cheek.

"Yes, I'm home. Thank you for never forgetting me. I'll take care of you now. We'll get you well. And then we'll make sure the Order never steals another child." Still breathing hard, I pulled her closer, infusing years of love and longing into my embrace.

"Carya."

I pulled back so I could stare at her beautiful face again.

"Yes, yes it's me."

Her hand trailed down my face and rested on the pouch that hung from my neck. She smiled. "My daughter."

I would never need another gift in the world. Her love, her words, were everything. Joy pulsed through me.

Then she closed her eyes, sighed, and relaxed in my arms.

I hugged her again, thinking she was settling into restoring slumber.

After I lowered her to the blanket, I wrung out the cloth and dabbed her forehead again. Under my fingers, her skin felt cooler. Good. The fever had broken.

But there was a strange gray cast to her skin.

"Mother?" I placed my ear near her mouth, searching for a hint of exhalation.

"Little one, she's gone." Reena spoke from behind me in a voice coated with regret and tenderness. "But you gave her joy for her last moment."

Gone? That didn't make sense. Hadn't I been drawn here to save her? Hadn't I danced with all my will and skill? Dazed, numb, I continued to stare at her, waiting for a change. Waiting for hope.

Strong hands tried to coax me away, but I shrugged him off and kept my vigil. Perhaps if I didn't move, this wouldn't have happened. Perhaps if I waited long enough ...

Oh, Maker! I need You. I can't bear this!

My fist clenched over the Maker's letter, where my mother's hand had last touched me. Minute by minute, hour by hour, the dark night consumed me, broke me, tore me open. All was lost. I couldn't move for the pain, couldn't cry.

Finally, as soft waves of light rolled into the dawn, I learned that I did indeed have tears left. Silent, soft, salty, they rolled down my face. In the morning light, the truth could no longer be denied.

My mother was dead.

To the villagers, her loss was one more tragedy among the many. To me, watching her leave me was the end of every hope.

A warm presence settled beside me. A familiar arm encircled my shoulders and pulled me into his side. "I'm sorry," Brantley said quietly.

I was so shattered and weary, I let my head droop against his shoulder. I couldn't refuse a small comfort. He shared my pain, held me, waited.

Waited for what? I couldn't bring myself to make a plan or a decision. I knew the villagers needed help, but my brain seemed frozen, incapable of knowing what to do.

As the camp came to life behind us, Brantley ran his thumb over my face, wiping away the last tears. "You have another reason for being here."

I lifted a bewildered gaze to him.

Tranquil ocean depths swam in his eyes. "Read them the letter."

24

HOW DARE BRANTLEY REMIND ME OF MY CALLING TO SHARE the letter, when he had never believed in the Maker's words?

My grief coalesced into an urgency to flee. I needed to turn from my failure, my loss. I needed to get away from Brantley's scrutiny and Reena's sympathy. I needed to see the vast ocean.

I sprang up, but my knee buckled. Something had twisted in my wild and desperate dance and now sent a sharp warning through the joint. All my muscles had stiffened in my nightlong vigil, too.

"Whoa, there." Brantley's arm steadied me by grabbing my elbow.

I wrenched away from him.

Limping out of the sheltering pines, I stumbled each time the earth rolled underfoot. I dragged myself along the near-invisible footpath, past the burnt-out longhouse, and across the ashen earth of the former village.

I sat on the edge of matted tangleroot, dangling my feet into the water. Beneath the rippling surface, the stain of soot still coated my feet and legs. I pulled my gaze away from the sad reminder of destruction.

The primary sun painted sharp amber and coral streaks across the rich blue of the morning waves. The sunrise reminded me of the glowing pillar of light that had ridden across the deep and revealed the Maker to me. If only He would show Himself like that again.

I looked around. Brantley hadn't followed me. No one else had ventured through the ruins of the village, so I dared give vent to my pain, glaring out over the sea. "You left me! Where were You last night? I begged You. I danced to give my mother life."

I squinted toward the horizon, hoping He would become tangible again. When He'd met me with a physical presence, it had been so much easier to trust Him. Instead, the water stirred, rushing a current over my feet strong enough to wash away the dark ashes. The bruises from the frantic dance on uneven ground faded and disappeared.

"No." I pulled my legs from the water. "Don't heal me. Go heal my mother."

She is restored. The words were soft as a breath brushing across my cheek, and I wasn't sure if it was the Maker's voice or my own fragile hope. I decided to cling to the thought. My mother was indeed restored. I longed for encounters with the Maker, and she now had the blessing of being constantly in His presence.

My hand pressed against my heart. "I believe You. But it's so hard to see You here, where there is so much loss and hurt." I gestured to the broken village behind me, and the whole island beyond. "What do I do next?"

Why ask when you already know?

Did I know? I eased my weary feet back into the water and let His touch continue to heal. The water buffed my feet, as cleaning and comforting as when Ginerva had massaged my wounded ankle. My whole body felt new strength.

He had asked me to bring His letter to the villages, and my own people still hadn't heard the precious words. Grief had stolen my senses for a time, but my calling hadn't changed. Even Brantley knew that.

The crunch of footsteps sounded behind me, and I turned. Brantley stopped several yards away, looking at me through his lashes, scuffing the ground uncertainly.

I smiled in welcome and patted the island's edge at my side.

He let out a relieved breath and sat. "I'm sorry you had such a brief time with your mother. Do you . . . do you feel the Maker failed you?"

The water had stopped stirring, no visions unfurled across the sky, no more quiet words spoke into my heart. Yet I knew the Maker was present.

"I did," I admitted, turning my gaze out to sea again, "for a while. But it was the Order who failed me. They taught me that the greatest power comes from my strength of will."

He leaned forward and scrubbed his hands in the water. "I hold no trust for the Order, but relying on strength of will sounds like truth to me."

"No, it's the core of their lie. Our strength is not in the dance or our perfection or our focused will. The Maker is the power."

He met my gaze, small furrows between his eyes. But he didn't scoff. "Will you be all right if I summon Navar and do some fishing?"

"Of course. The people are starving."

He stood, wiped his damp hands on his tunic, and offered a hand to me.

I let him help me up. An unexpected wave rocked the ground and I fell toward him. His arms caught me easily. Instead of setting me back on my feet, he held me for a long, quiet moment. His chin rested on the top of my head.

The comfort of the Maker had been wonderful, but His comfort given through human arms was especially precious.

"Thank you," I whispered to them both.

HOURS LATER, I SAT ON A FALLEN LOG SURROUNDED BY THE miserable remnants of Undertow. Brantley had refused to go fishing until I promised to rest. By the time I woke from a few hours of sleep, he had returned with baskets of fish, and roasted fillets now sated empty bellies. However, the food did little to satisfy the empty and aching hearts. Everyone in the clearing had lost loved ones in the soldiers' attack or the disease that ravaged them afterwards. Looking around at the tattered remnants of her village, Reena agreed to my offer to share the Maker's words with what was left of Undertow.

Reena moved around the clearing, murmuring and gesturing toward me as she spoke with each cluster of people. Quietly, the villagers banked their fires and came to sit near me, spreading their cloaks on the damp ground.

My gaze shifted toward the bedding where my mother had died. How could I offer any comfort when my own grief was so raw? *Help me, Maker.*

"Some weeks ago, we"—I nodded toward Brantley, who sat on the ground near me—"found a man from Windswell who had preserved the Maker's letter, carefully passed down through the generations."

A man coughed, then scoffed. "How do we know the man didn't write it himself?"

Brantley stifled a smile at the suggestion of Varney composing the letter. "I can attest that he didn't create it. Beyond that . . ." he shrugged.

I took the pouch from around my neck and pulled out the bound parchment. "You can judge for yourself. I didn't know what to think when I first read the letter. But then the Maker met with me."

Children's eyes widened. Some people leaned forward. Others studied the ground. Except for the deeper pain of grief that curved my shoulders, this conversation was like so many others I'd had with the rim and midrange villages.

"We forgot Him." I held up a scorched bowl I had unearthed in the ruins near the sea and brought back to the clearing. "And we crowded our hearts with other things." I poured out filthy water, green algae, and bits of charcoal. "Most of my life, I believed my purpose was to serve the Order."

Dark murmurs rose from the villagers.

I lifted a hand. "And I finally learned that was wrong. But leaving them behind left me so empty I thought I couldn't go on. The Maker is teaching me that an empty vessel can be filled with Him."

I smiled at Pert, who crouched nearby, and gave him our prearranged signal. He jumped up with a pitcher of sweet seawater and sloshed it into the bowl. He scratched his ribs, then bowed to the gathered audience with a flourish.

Chuckles rose from the crowd. I handed the bowl to Brantley who took a sip and passed it on. As the water circulated throughout the group, I unfolded the letter.

"All I ask is that you allow me to read the Maker's letter."

Once again, the words of love and longing captured me as I read. My worries about Undertow's response faded into the background. My grief hadn't left, but it became a gentle dance of evening shadow blended into a pattern of sunrise, that only enhanced the sense of blessings to come. My fear also shrank. The tasks ahead that had seemed so frightening lost some of their power. The Maker loved me. He would never leave me.

DURING THE NEXT SEVERAL DAYS, BRANTLEY ASSISTED IN the work of clearing the old site of the town and tearing down charred ruins. Part of the longhouse still stood, so as people overcame their fear of further attacks, they moved into it for shelter. I danced over the charred stalks of grain and trampled beds of tubers and rejoiced as they returned to life. Those who remained skeptical about the Maker's existence still appreciated the return of food.

Renewed with hope, the villagers began to rebuild. Soon the song of saws and hammers rose and fell through the day.

Although the work was hard, the daily routine was comforting. I built friendships, learned more about my family-that-had-been, and could have happily settled in Undertow for the rest of my life.

Brantley also seemed to thrive. Each morning he rose early to ride out on Navar and was able to find at least a few schools of fish before digging in to the restoration of the town, pitching in wherever he was needed.

One afternoon, I brought a load of blankets and supplies from the inland campsite to the village. Brantley worked on the roof of the longhouse, pounding new beams into place. Hair tousled and too shaggy, muscles strong and tireless, he walked across the ridgepole with the balance of an experienced herder. My breath caught as I watched him. Probably just worried about his safety up there.

Reena came and stood beside me, collecting the armload of blankets. "You and your man have given our village—*your* village—new life."

"Oh, he's not my . . ."

Brantley spotted me and gave a jaunty wave.

"Mm-hmm," Reena murmured before walking away.

THAT EVENING THE SUBSUN FINISHED ITS JOURNEY OFF TO
the left side of the horizon, reminding me of the ever-changing angle
caused by our world's rotation. I sat on the lip of land, dangling my legs
and letting the cool water refresh my feet.

Far from me, in the very center of the island, the Order continued to
turn us all. They held our land fast, unable to ride the currents as the
Maker intended.

"Please free Meriel." I whispered the prayer. "You can do that. I know
it's Your will. And You are stronger than the Order."

*It is My will, and I am able. But I have invited you to be part of the
unfolding. Are you willing?*

I looked behind me at the blossoming village and the people who
had become dear to me already. Part of me had hoped the Maker had
forgotten that He'd told me to confront the Order. Regret drew a sigh
from my chest. "Must I leave already?"

He waited. Every sound muffled, as if the world stilled in holy silence.

I gathered my feeble faith and looked back out to the vast unknown. "I
am Your empty bowl. Fill me with Your task."

I will fill you with Myself.

Stars twinkled by the time Brantley found me where I was still
resting in the presence of the One who would never leave me. This quiet
communion built strength in me for the painful choices ahead.

"I asked again," he said, dropping down beside me, "but no parchment
survived the attack and the fires."

I was touched that he understood my desire to write out copies of the letter for each village we visited. This village needed His words more than most.

"I could travel back to Windswell and get supplies," he said.

The eagerness in his tone made my stomach tighten. "Is that what you want to do?"

"We've made good progress on rebuilding Undertow's supplies here. And I promised Reena that when Navar next births, we'll bring the calf to them so they can train up a herder. I've done all I can here for now."

He shifted his position, then drummed his fingers on his leg. He was restless. Ready to return to his life. I'd commandeered him for far too long.

Another wrench of loss twisted under my heart. I fought to sound cheerful and accommodating. "Well then, I think you should return to Windswell. Although you don't need to send parchment back. I won't be staying here long enough."

I rose and dusted my hands against my leggings.

"What do you mean?" he asked.

"It's time for me to head inland. The Maker made clear that it's time for me to bring His truth to the Order."

He stood and blocked my path. "Just like that?"

Even in the darkness I could see the lines of his brow, the clench of his jaw. What was he upset about now? I had done all I could to make things easier for him, yet he was still irritated.

"You only offered to help me reach my village, and you've done that and more. It's time for you to return to your life. Isn't that what you want?"

"What do *you* want?"

I wanted him to stay with me, to help me with this last most frightening task, but that wasn't fair to him. He would only resent all the sacrifices he'd made to help me.

Trying to be brave, I raised my chin. "It's time for me to continue this quest alone."

He took a step back. "So now that you've gotten what you want, I'm dismissed?"

"Brantley, I appreciate all you've—"

"You appreciate me?" His voice had turned flat and cold.

I reached out to touch his arm. "I only mean that—"

"You've made yourself clear." He pulled away. "I'll leave in the morning."

And he walked away.

25

THE NEXT MORNING, I STOOD NEAR THE NOW-EMPTY clearing where the village had camped after their attack. Enough structures had been rebuilt for the people of Undertow to reclaim their location near the sea. Inland, shadows of deep forest murmured of danger. I stared into their depths, into the uncertainties of my next journey. In the past weeks I'd visited many midrange and rim villages, shared the Maker's letter with hundreds of people. I would have been content to continue that pilgrimage for the rest of my days. But no matter how many times I suggested that to Him, the Maker's answer was resolute. It was time to complete my mission. Time to confront the Order.

Footsteps crunched behind me. Reena approached and crossed her arms. Her long tunic was tattered, and dark crescents rimmed her eyes from days of relentless work. Yet she carried herself with the regal bearing of a saltar. "Why is Brantley packing all his gear?"

I pressed my lips together, then managed a neutral tone. "He's needed back home. He believes your village is well on the way to sustaining itself again."

She frowned. "It's not our village I'm worried about. Are you leaving too? I thought you were staying for another few days."

"Oh, I am. I still want to try our plan." Reena and I had discussed a way to allow Undertow to keep the Maker's letter alive. We would assign various villagers one paragraph each of the letter to memorize, so their people could keep the words with them even without parchment. Two days should be sufficient, and then I'd head to Middlemost.

She ran a hand over her forehead. "I don't understand. Is Brantley coming back for you?"

Why did she have to probe this vulnerable wound? A bee circled overhead, then aimed for a wildflower peeking from the composting leaves at the edge of the clearing. I watched it to avoid meeting Reena's gaze. "No, he has his own life to lead."

"He won't protect you as you travel inland? What happened?"

"Nothing." I tucked a strand of hair behind my ear. "Perhaps continuing alone will help me trust the Maker more deeply."

She snorted. "Maybe you think suffering alone is noble. But making sacrifices the Maker hasn't asked you to make isn't noble. It's playing the martyr."

Her words stung, and my vision swam as I stubbornly focused on the bee and its lonely quest to draw a bit of sweetness from the dank forest. "I'm not trying to be noble. I'm terrified of what lies ahead. But he . . . but I . . ."

She stepped closer and I braced myself against her tender concern. Instead, she grasped my upper arms. "I thought you had a splash of sense, even for one so young."

My mouth gaped.

She gave me a sharp shake. "Go talk to him. Now."

I shook my head. "I've kept him from his people too long. I can't ask him to follow where I'm going next."

"Then don't ask. But don't push him away, either. Do you reject the light of the suns or the nourishment of the rains when the Maker grants them?"

"But I only—"

"Brantley doesn't want to leave any more than you want him to go."

Could she be right? Brantley had been a gift from the Maker ever since I'd left the Order. But did Brantley want to be included in the next step of my calling? A plan he didn't even believe in?

Reena turned me toward the village by my shoulders and gave a small shove. "Go. Now. Before you are left standing alone with regret as your only companion."

Her words propelled me to walk with hesitant steps down the path and past the longhouse. The odor of smoke still lingered from the ash-strewn ground and burnt timbers of destroyed cottages. But the breeze carried honeyed sweetness from the sea. Had I been wrong? Had I pushed away a friend, a dear ally? I couldn't be sure. But I hated to have him leave when we were on bad terms. At least we could part as friends. My steps hastened, until I was running past the newly repaired seaward cottages.

Too late. Far out in the ocean, Navar's long neck stretched upward, a figure silhouetted on her back.

I whistled and waved, but the stenella continued on her way. The enormity of my loss choked me. A small whimper of dismay escaped my throat, and I curled forward, hugging my stomach.

"What's wrong? Are you ill?" Brantley's deep voice sounded behind me.

I swung around and rubbed my eyes, but I wasn't hallucinating. He stood two paces from me, frowning with equal parts concern and irritation. A smudge of dirt lined his unshaved jawline, and his fair hair was wet and tangled.

I pointed out to the waves. "Who's riding Navar?"

"The lad I've been training. Their future herder. Why? Did you need me?"

Did I need him? If he only knew. "I . . . I . . ." How many times had I stood so near him during our travels, his hair tousled from a morning swim, soft bristles dusting his face, eyes alight with colors of sky and sea? He had become a comfortable friend, yet now a new awareness had grown in me, leaving me awkward and unable to find simple words.

He sighed. "Have you changed your mind about the parchment? Do you need me to return to Windswell?"

I shook my head.

"So this is a guessing game?" His annoyed growl finally returned my ability to speak.

"Why are you mad at me?" I said.

His head pulled back. "I'm not."

"Yes, you are. Last night when I told you to go back to your life, I only—"

"Oh, please." He stiffened. "Let's not go over that again."

And then I saw it. His irritation hid a flicker of hurt. I'd used his help and then dismissed him like a High Saltar waving away an attendant. He deserved so much more from me. He deserved truth.

"It's time for me to go to the Order." I didn't hide the quaver in my voice. "And I'm terrified. And I don't want to go alone. I don't even know how to find my way back." I tried to laugh, but it came out as a tiny sob.

The tight cast of his frame softened, but he still looked wary. "Then why are you sending me away?"

I dug my toes into the thin layer of dirt, misery sweeping over me. "You sounded so eager to go home, and you've done so much already." Now that I'd begun, I couldn't stem the flow of words. "And I can't ask you to take these risks, and I thought I was relying on you too much, and I know you don't believe in this cause . . ."

His bark of laughter drowned me out. "I suggested returning to Windswell to get some parchments for you, remember? You're the one who grabbed at the chance to be rid of me for good."

I dared to meet his gaze. "I can't ask you to do more."

He rolled his eyes. "Dancer, don't you know by now that I can make my own choices?" He lightly tapped my nose.

I was relieved to see his playful good humor return; however, I was still reluctant to draw him into my dangers. I stepped toward the rim, where the dirt gave way to a mat of tangleroot. Small waves played with the woven vines. I stared out toward the horizon and the dance of seabirds over the frothy waves. "You aren't even sure there is a Maker."

"I'm not sure there isn't. Can't that be enough for now?"

"I don't know."

He shrugged, as if his shoulders could throw off any fear or risk. "We share the desire to end the Order's power over our world. I've asked those with weapons to meet me inland in three weeks' time. You and I both plan to confront the Order. We may as well do it together."

The Maker hadn't told me to raise an army against the Order. True,

I'd watched as Brantley had followed his own agenda when we'd visited villages, but I hadn't known he'd made such concrete plans already. The man was a rogue.

My brow puckered. "I don't think—"

Water splashed us both, drenching our clothes. Navar gurgled at the shoreline as if pleased, then dipped her head and tossed fat fish with glimmering scales onto the land.

Brantley laughed and bounded toward the closest. He gave a whistle, and a handful of children raced from the cottages to help gather the catch. After the bounty was collected, Navar stretched her neck over the lip of land where we stood. Brantley fed her one of the choicest fish heads and stroked her neck. "Guess we won't be traveling back to Windswell after all, my girl." Then he turned to me. "When will you be ready to head inland?"

"Two days," I said hesitantly, still worried that we were at cross-purposes. His efforts to raise an army would only interfere with my task to speak to the saltars and show them the Maker's letter. "How long will it take to reach Middlemost?"

He gave Navar a last pat before she swam off, her tail fin showering us with one more splash for good measure. "Depends. If we have to avoid patrols or deal with other hazards, it could take longer, but if we take a direct route, I'd guess about two weeks."

I nodded. That would give me time to approach the Order and carry out the Maker's wishes before the rimmers mounted a civil war.

"AT LEAST LEARN TO USE A KNIFE." BRANTLEY STRODE ALONG beside me on the tamped earth forming a path toward the next village. We'd been on the road for several days, and his irritation was as well-worn and comfortable to me as soft-soled shoes.

I smiled at him. "That's not the sort of battle the Maker has asked of me."

He adjusted his wide leather belt that held a sword. He no longer looked the part of a carefree herder. His purposeful strides and alert demeanor seemed more like that of a soldier or protector.

"We'll likely encounter soldiers before we reach the Order. What if you're attacked? Besides, there are other dangers in the wilds. Forest hounds and . . ."

I raised a brow.

He rolled his eyes. "Never mind. But using a knife is still a basic skill every rimmer learns." He stopped by a fallen tree coated with moss. "Let's rest a few minutes."

Grateful, I sank onto the soft surface, hugging one knee to my chest. I stretched my foot up to the sky, lowered it, and hugged my other knee.

Brantley kept running a finger around the collar of his tunic and checking the knots on his knife hilt.

"What's wrong?" I asked.

He shifted his weight, but still couldn't seem to settle. "I hate going inland."

I drew a deep breath. The air was heavy with vegetation instead of the citrusy sweetness of ocean. We were already too far from the shore.

"I miss it too." I leaned forward and ran my palm against the earth. "It feels too solid underfoot. Less alive."

He offered an appreciative grin. "You've found your rim roots, have you?"

"I've found a lot of things. My name. My family." I sobered. "Although none are left."

He shifted again, this time facing me. "Carya, all of Undertow is your family now. Reena wanted to send their strongest men to accompany us."

I shook my head. "She needs every able-bodied person to rebuild Undertow and defend it."

"Leaving no one to defend you."

I tilted my head. "I have you. You've kept me safe this far."

Furrows drew brief shadows on Brantley's forehead. He reached behind his back and drew his knife. "Here. Throw at that stump." He slapped the hilt into my hand.

I balanced the unfamiliar weight and imagined I could still see a soldier's blood staining the blade. Cold tendrils wove up my back. I didn't want to learn to use a weapon. I didn't even want to touch it.

I flung the knife toward the stump just to be rid of it.

After a blurred spin, it sank precisely into the upper edge of the stump.

Brantley pulled back from me. "How did you . . . ? Well, you are full of surprises, aren't you?" He retrieved his knife. "Let me see that again."

I stood and crossed my arms. "No. Let's keep moving. We have a long way to go."

He stared me down, but I met his gaze with equal determination. At last he put away the knife and gave a broad gesture with his arm. "Lead on, dancer."

As our feet ate up the rolling ground, I probed his plans. "Are you worried that the Order might know how you are inciting the villages? That someone will recognize you when we reach Middlemost?"

He grinned. "Now you're thinking like a strategist. Yes, the closer we get to the Order, the more power they control. But I made a lot of allies in Middlemost. Few are loyal to the Order. At least at heart. Some pay lip service because the High Saltar is a good customer. But they well know that the coin she spends comes from their own taxes. Their girls have also been coerced away or stolen."

"You think they'll stand with you? If it comes to that?" I still held hope that the Maker's plan would unfold long before Brantley's rebellion.

He squinted at me. "Some will hide in their homes at any signs of trouble. A few might try to betray us. But don't worry. We have enough allies to make our point."

I could have told him that it would take more than a coalition of villagers to convince the High Saltar of anything.

As we continued to walk inland, I was always alert to approaching danger, always aware that an impossible task lay ahead of me, always wrestling tormenting questions.

Days and nights passed, too slowly and too rapidly. Each morning I'd slip away from our camp at first light and pray. I poured out my questions and doubts to the Maker. I begged for reassurance that I was on the correct path. Yet now I heard only silence. Did the Maker only speak to me on the rim? I'd heard His powerful voice in the center ground, though I hadn't known Him then. So, no, He spoke when and where He willed.

Why was He silent and invisible now?

As we neared Middlemost, I took an early watch while Brantley slept. Coaxing a tiny bit of warmth from our campfire, I once again prayed.

Holy Maker of all, I'm setting out on the task to which You've called me. But I'm small and afraid. I need to hear Your voice again. I want to be sure of my next step.

I opened the letter and turned through the pages, tracing my fingers over the precious words. Like the dawning sunrise, I realized He *was* still speaking to me. His words were alive and met me with encouragement and truth. I still longed for an audible voice and a tangible touch, but if this was how He chose to speak to me, I would strive to be content.

"Thank You for creating our world," I whispered. "Thank You for loving Your children. Help me trust You even when I can't see You."

"So He's left you?" Brantley's sleepy voice growled from his place beside the fire.

"Never," I said. Faith swelled a bit more in my heart as I gave my firm answer.

Brantley stirred and sat, brushing his disheveled hair back from his face. "How can you be sure that what you experienced before wasn't a fevered dream? If you can't see Him, how do you know He's even listening to you?"

Brantley's questions were always sharp and pointed and threw my thoughts into a tangle. Yet I knew I'd face much more difficult questions from High Saltar Tiarel. *Dear Tender of my soul, please give me the right words.*

"The Order claims our world just happened into being. Don't tell me you agree with them? When you ride Navar, don't you sense that there must be a Maker behind the immense ocean and the glorious sky?"

He lurched to his feet and shook out his cloak. "I almost want to trust your Maker's letter, if only to spite the Order." He chuckled. "I guess time will tell who's right."

He strode to the nearby creek for his morning ablutions.

I folded his cloak and stuffed it in the pack. For now, I'd need to be content with his uncertainties. *But please make Yourself real to Brantley. Somehow. In some way. And to all the people of Meriel.*

Silence hung heavy over the campsite, and the weight of the task ahead rounded my back. The Maker was reaching out to His people, but what would be the cost? And would I have the courage to bear it?

26

MIDDLEMOST WAS SMALLER THAN I REMEMBERED. AND LARGER.
Although I had spent little time there during my years in the Order, I
knew the town enough to expect a sense of familiarity, of coming home.
Instead every building looked out of balance, like a dancer with an
injured limb.

As we entered the town early in the morning, the wide ring of buildings
bustled with frantic activity, harsh voices, and the sharp crack of a whip
against a pony's flank. A tantalizing aroma of bresh and salt cakes floated
from the chimneys of a bakery but was soon smothered by the scent of hot
metal from the smithy and the hay and dung from one of the local stables
as I followed Brantley through the narrow streets. Each time we turned a
corner, the tower of the Order loomed from its central place, observing
all, controlling all.

We'd traded berries at a midrange village, so I now owned a cloak with
a deep hood. Few would identify me as a dancer. My skin was no longer
the pale hue of a novitiate, my braids were unkempt, and although I was
still slender, some of my muscles had filled out. More importantly, I no
longer moved with the delicate precision of a dancer. I didn't stride as
carelessly as Brantley, but my gait had definitely been reshaped by all the
miles of walking over varied terrain.

"A colleague is meeting me at the Fernshadow Inn," Brantley said in a
low voice. "Might already be here." By colleague he undoubtedly meant
a co-conspirator, another village leader bent on revolution and violence.

I pressed my lips together and stopped. "I want to talk to Starfire. Go
on ahead."

He frowned and rubbed the several days' growth of beard that made him look even rougher than usual. Even his fair hair was darkened with dirt and had lost its carefree waves. Every part of him wore the weight of his plans and the uncertain future of our world.

A knot in my gut twisted more tightly, but I forced a smile. "I can meet you at the inn later." I darted away before he could argue. Clinging to shadows, I scurried around a corner. When I glanced up, the Order glared down again, the only building of such height in our world, more imposing than I'd remembered. I dipped my chin and tugged my hood forward, determined to ignore its menacing glower of superiority.

Reaching the stable where Starfire worked, I waited across the street, lowered a pack from my shoulder, and pretended to rummage in it while I eyed the entrance. Several ponies rested in the fenced paddock, some saddled and some without gear—although they all looked equally despondent.

The oafish tender appeared in the corral, arguing with a merchant before they settled on a price and the merchant rode off on a mangy pony. The owner took no notice of me, but counted his coins with a greedy smile. He shouted something into the stable and sauntered away toward the nearest tavern.

I crossed the street and cautiously approached the door. One of the ponies snorted, and I paused to stroke his muzzle. He bumped his nose against my chest, and his limpid eyes reminded me of Navar. How I missed the stenella. I even missed the sweet, tangy spray of the sea against my skin as we cut through the waves and the exhilarating swoop in my stomach as she glided up and down. Would I ever see her again?

I gave the pony one more absent pat and stepped into the fog of stable smells and dimness. Odors of manure, wet straw, and horse sweat hung in the air. A slim figure at the far end was mucking out a stall with energetic pulls of a rake. I tiptoed closer. "Starfire?"

The person startled and turned. A gangly lad, smudged with dirt and suspicions, thrust his chin out. "Whaddya want? The tender ain't here."

"I-I'm sorry to disturb you. I was looking for Starfire."

His face pinched with the effort of thought, then cleared. "Oh, she be the one a few times ago. Heard tell they took her back to dance. They sure use up a lot of dancers." He scratched his rib cage and shuffled forward, peering at my face. "Hey, are you one of them? What are you doing down here?"

My stomach contracted, making me catch in a sudden breath. "No, no. Just looking for a friend. Sorry for bothering you."

I fled to the comfort of the ponies in the yard, hoping the stable boy would lose interest and forget he'd seen me. Starfire was a dancer now? Months ago, the news would have delighted me. Now only dread swam through my veins, spreading a frigid tremor. Tiarel was destroying women, sending them to wrestle Meriel's course from the hands of the Maker, a task as foolish as a toddler trying to wrench away his father's knife. If Ginerva had been right, when they failed and their minds broke, they were banished like Dancer Subsun . . . or worse.

The rumors of a pit in Tiarel's inner office—cut directly into the sea below—conjured horrible images. Even the friendly ponies offered no more comfort. I scurried away, head down. Closer to the inn, crowds jostled me. Middlemost had always been a full and busy place, but there seemed to be more people about than I remembered.

A man elbowed past. He looked familiar. A father from Undertow? A landkeeper from Windswell? I pulled against the nearest wall, one hand pressed over my heart that pounded wildly against the pouch I carried. Brantley's rebellion was already gathering. Did the Order suspect? Were the conspirators able to stay hidden among the bustle of the town? More importantly, were they keeping their intentions hidden?

I tried to breathe, but the threat of blood and destruction tainted the air.

No quiet glen invited me to seek the Maker and rest in His presence. Instead, I raised a nervous prayer in the midst of the chaos. "What do I do now?"

Only silence answered me. A silence so heavy it blunted the din of the streets. A silence that squeezed my heart in a tight fist, wringing out the last drops of faith.

I'd never felt so lost and bewildered. "I've come here. I've done what You asked of me. Tell me what to do now. Please."

Unbidden, my gaze traveled upward to the windows of the tower. I wasn't being fully honest with my Maker. I'd come *close* to the halls of the Order where He'd called me. But how could I take any more steps if He didn't make His presence clear to me? Did I have the strength to cross the open space from Middlemost to the grounds?

If I headed to the inn, Brantley could make the choices. Where I was bereft of plans, he had a bounty of them.

A young face appeared at one of the tower windows, then disappeared. The Order housed so many children torn from their homes, indoctrinated. This very hour novitiates were being convinced that they were gods, that their will was supreme, that if they achieved perfection, they would control the world. Those children needed to hear the truth about the Maker.

A woman carrying a heavy basket bumped me and pressed past without apology. I realized I'd moved away from the wall and into the street. I changed my course away from the inn and kept walking, closing the distance to the edge of town until nothing but bare earth and daygrass stretched up the slope to the Order.

I aspired to march forward with great courage and resolve. When the Maker had carried me above our world, guided me onto the water, spoke words rich in love and strength, I imagined striding toward the Order to tell them about the Maker's letter.

But it had been many days since He had met with me. My steps were timid as I walked up the slope, my gaze down and my body weighted with fear and doubt. Perhaps the Maker had been nothing but fevered dreams. And how could mere words change the course of the mighty Order? Perhaps Brantley had the best strategy: an all-out war against those in power.

As I trudged closer, the faint pulse of the Order's drums rode the wind. I paused and tilted my head. The pattern was leeward storm. I pulled my cloak around me. That pattern was rarely used . . . only if our world was suffering drought. With all the rain in recent weeks, that was not the case. Why would the High Saltar inflict this dangerous weather on Meriel?

Dark clouds already gathered over the tower. A harsh gust tore my hood from my head. The approaching storm helped me to hurry as I battled the buffeting wind. Perhaps this opposition was a gift from the Maker. It certainly motivated me to move and gave me no time to entertain my fears.

By the time I reached the outer garden walls, rain sheeted down, angling outward. I ran, half swimming through the deluge, through an arched entry, and past the school's cultivated beds where I used to linger as a student.

Alcea flowers and calara reeds alike bent and broke in the downpour. Gasping for breath, I no longer debated an approach. I pushed open the nearest door and stepped into the place that had been my cherished world for most of my life.

The angry drum pattern pulsed through the whole building, while sticks clattered a different rhythm in one of the school's rehearsal halls. In the midst of the storm, classes continued as always. A saltar shouted something to her students, a young voice asked a question, an attendant crossed the far end of the hall and turned toward the saltars' office without seeing me. Before me, the stone stairway led upward to the sleeping quarters and classrooms.

I shook droplets from my cloak and brushed back my wet hair. Indecision cut through me like a broken rhythm. What next? *Maker, You promised to never leave me, but I'm not seeing You or hearing You. How do I know where to go?*

I had two choices: I could storm down the curved hall and into the High Saltar's office to confront her. Or I could look for Starfire. Maybe she could help me decide my next steps.

I tiptoed up the stairs and found one of the balconies overlooking the center ground. The faithful dancers below formed precise patterns and moved with strength. Since the storm blew outward, there was only a thin layer of mud to impede their steps. While hiding in the shadows, I watched each face in the cloud-darkened light but didn't spot Starfire.

Good. Perhaps she was resting in her room. She was the one face I looked forward to seeing in this place. I slipped through the dining hall and to the door that led to the dancers' wing. At the threshold, all the old taboos pounded with my pulse and the relentless drums. I was no longer a dancer of the Order. I wasn't worthy to enter.

From the kitchen, a cook called to an attendant. They'd be bringing out lunch soon. If I lingered here in the dining hall, I'd be discovered. No more time to hesitate. I pushed open the door and shut it quietly behind me. Familiar halls greeted me, along with the banners of each form's color.

Since Starfire wasn't out in the center ground, she was either resting in her room or rehearsing with her group. I stopped at the main rehearsal hall and peeked in. Saltar River's back was to the door as she harangued the dancers. All the women were concentrating on holding an extension facing the left wall, so no one spotted me.

Iris was there, and other familiar dancers, but no sign of Starfire. If she had been brought in to replace me, would they have given her my old room? Footsteps approached, and I ducked into a laundry alcove, hiding behind a large basket. The steps continued on toward the dancers' dining hall.

After leaning out to look both directions, I took a deep breath and ran to my old room. I found the reed pattern carved on the door and pushed it open an inch. Then another. A slight figure slept under a blanket. Auburn hair spread across the pillow.

I'd found her! I breathed a prayer of thanks to the Maker, entered the room, and quietly closed the door behind me. Touching her shoulder, I whispered, "Starfire?"

She bolted up in one sudden movement, panic turning her freckles dark against her pale skin. I remembered the stress of living here. The constant fear of making a mistake.

"Shhh. Starfire, it's all right. It's me . . ." I was about to use my true name, but realized it would mean nothing to her. "You knew me as Calara."

A spontaneous flare of welcome brought a smile to her face, but then she covered her mouth. "How? How can you be here? I thought . . ." Her voice quavered.

"I've found something wonderful. The Maker's letter. I'm here to tell the saltars about it."

She shoved aside her bedding and stood, her movements stiff and abrupt. "You shouldn't be here." Her muscles were so rigid she seemed to push me away without even touching me. She looked past me.

"What's wrong?"

She turned away. The hem of her long sleep tunic shifted, revealing scars on her ankles.

"Please go. I've broken a million rules even speaking to you."

"What have they done to you? Starfire, please look at me."

She sniffed in a tight breath through her nose. "I am not Starfire. I am Dancer Calara."

Of course. She had taken my place, my room, my name. "I remember when we both longed for this," I said softly.

Did her shoulders soften? Her troubled gaze met mine, then darted away.

I dared a small step toward her. "I found them. My village, my family. I was stolen from them when I was tiny. Maybe you were too. Maybe you have a family somewhere outside the Order."

Her jaw clenched and she stared at the door.

I edged sideways into her line of sight. If she would only look at me, if one ounce of our friendship and laughter remained, if . . .

She looked straight through me. "Only the worthy may serve the Order." Her singsong voice drew chills across my flesh.

"Starfire, don't be that way. I understand you face danger by talking to me. But I had to let you know—"

She thrust one palm toward me. "Leave. Now."

"I will, but first let me tell you. Remember how we—"

"I mean it." Her voice hissed low through her teeth. "I'll fetch an attendant."

The blow of betrayal and loss hit like the hilt of a knife driving into my chest. I stepped back, sagging around the pain. "All right. I'm leaving. Maybe you could meet me later in the . . ."

She covered her ears, visage fierce, eyes unseeing.

I searched for any flicker, any hint, that my dear friend was still inside the resolute body of this dancer.

One tear poised in the corner of her eye, the only glimpse of Starfire that remained.

27

TEARS BLURRED MY VISION AS I STUMBLED AWAY FROM Starfire's room. Outside the wind howled as the leeward storm unleashed its anger, and a shutter cracked against stone.

I'd rather be outside in the tempest than trapped in this miserable tower that had stolen everything—even my best friend. Would Starfire report my presence? Even now she could shout for prefects to drag me before Tiarel. And the High Saltar could make me disappear before I'd ever have a chance to speak to the Order. I should have joined Brantley at the inn. When I'd stood in Middlemost and looked at the tower, I'd believed that I had to approach before I lost all courage. Perhaps my impulsive choice had been foolish.

I retraced my steps, rounding a curve near the laundry alcove. A chubby figure backed out, her arms full of neatly folded tunics. I sidled away, but not rapidly enough.

She bumped into me and whirled with a fierce frown. "Here, now! You aren't allowed in the dancers' quarters. Deliveries use the kitchen." The fluff of white hair and the soft lines of her face belied her harsh words.

My panic gave way to recognition. "Ginerva!"

She squinted at me, then dropped her stack of laundry. "Can it be?"

By law she should refuse to acknowledge me. Instead she enfolded me in plump arms. Her welcome brought all my loneliness and fear to the surface, and I sniffed back my tears, allowing myself this one blissful moment of comfort.

She pulled back, head swiveling like a nervous harrier bird. "In here." She tugged me into the alcove. After retrieving the clothes, she pulled a curtain over the alcove before cradling my face in her hands. "How?"

"You were right. About so much. The Maker led me to His letter, and He . . ." The enormity of that encounter washed over me again. I coaxed a deep breath from my tense lungs. "I've read His words."

My shoulders drew back. I pulled the pouch from beneath my cloak and removed the letter. Here at last was an ally. Someone who could advise me and help me. I held out the precious pages.

She threw up her arms. "Put that away!"

"Don't you want to—?"

"Fool girl. Why would you bring that here? Tiarel would delight in destroying it."

My fingers fumbled as I tucked the letter back into the pouch. I'd feared for my life coming back to the Order. I'd feared the danger of being drawn back in to the pride, the control, the lies. But I hadn't thought of this letter being destroyed. Doubts rose again. Had I misremembered what the Maker had asked me to do? The last time He'd spoken to me, I'd been grief-stricken over my mother's death. Exhausted. Confused. No one had believed this was a wise course. Now even this dear attendant thought I had made a huge mistake by coming here.

I sagged against the alcove wall, leaning on one of the laundry baskets. "He told me to read the letter to the villages. To help them remember what has been lost."

Ginerva squeezed the bridge of her nose. "Then why are you here?"

"Because then He told me it was time to bring the truth to the Order."

Her mouth opened, then she pressed her lips into as firm a line as her rounded face could create. Her eyes closed and she dropped her head forward as if deep in thought. When she raised her chin, she reached out. "May I see it? Long have I waited for this day."

I handed the pouch to her.

She removed the letter and turned the pages, touching the words reverently. "But why would He let you bring it here? It was forgotten for a generation, but now it could be destroyed forever."

I shook my head. "It won't be destroyed. We've made copies at most of the villages where I stayed. People all over Meriel have heard the truth. They remember the Maker now. Even if she burns these pages, she can't thwart His purposes."

Ginerva tilted her head and offered a soft smile. "You speak like one who has walked in His steps, little one." Then sadness puddled in her eyes. "But even if Tiarel can't erase His words, she will certainly seek to erase you."

I gave a tight nod. "I know. What should I do?"

Her eyes widened. "Why are you asking me? Ask the Maker. What has He told you?"

"Nothing more." I brushed my hands over my throbbing temples, dislodging the cloak's hood. Admitting His silence to Ginerva stirred all my fear and doubt again. "You've known Him longer. Why would He set me on a course, and then give me no details of how to proceed?"

Ginerva touched a finger lightly to my forehead. "Use the brain He gave you, and be willing to listen when He does speak. And take comfort in knowing He will not abandon you. Now, to gain an audience with the saltars, you'll need to approach Tiarel . . . but not when she's alone."

"I know. That's my fear. She could have me killed and never let anyone in the Order hear the message I'm bringing."

I shifted my weight from heel to toe and back again. No closer to a plan, every second I lingered here endangered Ginerva. "I could go back to Middlemost and wait. But there's not much time. Rimmers are gathering in town. Their solution is to destroy the Order. If I don't share the letter soon, there may be no one left to hear it."

Ginerva sniffed. "As if ridding Meriel of dancers will benefit anyone. We need truth, not destruction."

"Where will Tiarel have lunch today?"

"She's scheduled to oversee the school's lunch."

I pursed my lips. "And when she's at the head table, most of the saltars are with her."

"But you won't find many allies among the students. They are the most desperate to please the Order."

"I know. Yet I may have more of a chance to address the saltars there. They won't want to expose their cruelty in front of all the forms. That may give me a small window to speak."

Ginerva's face puckered with worry lines. "I suppose I could get you into the kitchen. If you stay hidden until the meal is served . . ."

Could I do it? Should I? *Holy Maker, guide me, please.*

Ginerva tugged my hood up and forward, shielding my face as much as possible. "Well, we can't stay here."

"You don't need to come with me. I know the way to the school's kitchen."

She crossed her pudgy arms. "You'll fit in better if I'm with you."

"Perhaps, but . . ." I didn't want to draw her into this dangerous task.

"Let's go." She picked up an empty basket and took my arm, hustling me from the alcove and down the hall toward the school.

Two attendants strode past, but I kept my head down, and they didn't stop us. The dining hall was still empty, although the bell for lunch gave its first chime as we scurried past tables to the kitchen.

Several serving girls brushed past us, their baskets wafting the aroma of bresh for the head table and saltcakes for everyone else. I took refuge in the kitchen, Ginvera using her bulk to block me from any curious glances. She chatted amiably with one of the cooks, offering sympathy for the bad weather. Stray rain found its way down the chimney to harass the cooking flames and spit a protest to the heat.

In the dining hall, the voices of students built, benches scraped, tables filled. I waited until everyone fell quiet, indicating the saltars had entered.

I touched Ginerva's arm.

She stepped aside and faced me. "Are you sure?"

Truthfully, I wasn't sure of anything. But I nodded and left the kitchen.

As expected, the head table was now full of saltars, women I had respected and learned from all my life. The attendants had served the food and were returning to the kitchen.

I walked against the current of their passing, drawing the attention of Saltar Kemp. She nudged Saltar River and pointed at me—a hooded figure daring to interrupt the flow of lunch routines.

High Saltar Tiarel had still not taken notice of me, and rose to address the room. Her mouth opened, then snapped shut as she saw me where I stopped, resolute, before the high table.

In spite of my quavering knees, I tossed back my hood and drew forth the Maker's letter. "Greetings, saltars of the Order. I've been asked to bring you this letter."

Deep within the tower, drums throbbed from the center ground. From without, rain bounced loudly against eaves and cobblestones. I was grateful for the sounds that covered the horrible silence that gripped the dining hall.

Tiarel planted her fists on the table, and she leaned forward. Her eyebrows tented in recognition. She hadn't forgotten the fledgling dancer who had fled the Order after one shift. Schemes and counter-schemes played out behind her eyes.

"You may deliver your letter to my office after lunch." Her voice was flat, without inflection, giving away nothing.

Going alone to her office was exactly what I needed to avoid. Desperation gave me courage to act. I turned my back on her and addressed the students' tables. "The letter is for everyone." I raised the pages above my head. "The Maker of Meriel—the Maker of each one of us—wrote this. It was forgotten, but it's time to remember."

Familiar faces stared at me. The youngest forms with their scarlet hood scarves clustered at tables farthest from the head table. They peered around each other, squirmed in their seats, unrestrained in their curiosity. Other tables reflected varied responses: uneasiness at a disruption in routine, confusion, worried whispers. Nearby, the older students in the blue form showed greater discipline. Straight, unmoving, staring ahead. I recognized Furrow Blue and a few others from my class. The bravest woman cut a quick glance toward me, then resumed her blank forward stare.

Murmurs rose behind me. Two prefects moved my direction from the side of the room. My opportunity was slipping away. I faced the head table again, trying to summon boldness from my constricted throat. "He has asked me to share His words with all of you." The prefects drew near, and one grabbed my arm.

My stomach lurched, panic coiling upward to strangle my best intentions. *Holy Maker, help me. Don't let this opportunity be lost.*

Tiarel held up her hand and the man released me. I pulled myself tall, ready to meet her tirade, her threats. Instead, she feigned a motherly smile. "Students, don't be afraid to look on this outcast. She deserves our pity. Learn well. This is the sort of raving that is manifested by those who fail as dancers."

Raving? No, I brought only the fact of the Maker's love. Strength flowed through my limbs and I found the tiny kernel of courage I thought I'd lost. I ignored Tiarel and appealed to the other saltars at the table. "If the Order is founded on truth, surely you aren't afraid to listen. *Are* you afraid? I request a hearing with the saltars."

A new inhale of silence held the room in thrall. A hearing of the saltars was a rare and powerful event. Tiarel would never allow it.

A light laugh bubbled from Tiarel's throat. "Granted."

She'd surprised me again. The sensation was like pushing hard against a door that suddenly gave way too easily. I nearly stumbled. "Thank you."

"The prefects will escort you to my office to wait."

I stiffened. "How do I know you won't just . . . chase me away?"

Gasps rose from the young dancers at the tables. Questioning the integrity of the High Saltar was treasonous. But then, so was fleeing the Order or speaking of the Maker.

Tiarel's smile tightened a fraction, but she calmly took her seat. "You have my word among all these witnesses. You will have a hearing before the saltars today when afternoon classes are finished."

What was Tiarel planning? She must be incredibly confident in her control over the Order to permit a hearing. I allowed myself a whisper of hope. I'd be able to share the letter with the saltars and they'd discover the true purpose of the dance. Together we'd free our world and bring peace between the Order and the villages. With the island traveling the currents again, we'd find ample fishing and weather to support our farms. This was going more smoothly than I'd ever dared dream.

Perhaps too smoothly.

Trust me.

The Maker's whisper explained nothing, but helped my tight limbs unlock enough to walk. I followed the prefects down the aisle, pausing to dip my head at the youngest form and the girls I had briefly taught. Some gave timid waves, but then glanced nervously at the head table.

"Students." Saltar River stood. "I realize this interruption is confusing, since you know we must not acknowledge an outcast. However, the High Saltar in her wisdom is able to make exceptions. We will leave it to her to resolve this. You must not lose focus. Eat, return to class, and dedicate yourself to perfection."

Spoons scraped against wooden bowls and the relief in the room was palpable. The students were grateful to be told what to do, to return to the norm, to understand their place.

Part of me missed that reliable security.

I shook my head and followed the prefects from the hall. Security that eliminated all freedom was an imposter. Could I be brave enough to inspire the Order to a new way? Would the letter turn the tide?

UNDER THE PIERCING GLARE OF TWO PREFECTS, I SCARCELY
dared move as I waited in a straight-backed chair in Tiarel's office. A
closed door marked the far corner of the room, and ceremonial robes
hung from pegs on the wall behind a large table. Through the open
door to my right, I could see the outer area where the desks of the other
saltars lined up in familiar order. As a young novitiate I'd stood before
Saltar Kemp, overwhelmed at the honor of being invited to teach. How
much my life had changed in the months since then!

Yet the Order remained the same. Before me, the High Saltar's table
held the same instruments I'd once glimpsed from afar: brass measures
to mark the position of the stars, wind gauges, a large box of willow pens.
Parchment maps splayed across the surface. From where I sat, a few
village names were legible. I wanted to edge closer to decipher what the
circles and marks indicated. A cold knot formed in my throat. The notes
didn't look like records of crops or taxes. They looked like battle plans.

I massaged my neck. There was still time to prevent all-out war. Tiarel
had promised, and all the saltars had heard her. I had no faith in Tiarel's
word, but given in front of the entire Order, even she couldn't revoke
the promised hearing. They would let me read the letter, and that would
forestall the danger scrawled across the maps.

Moving slowly so as not to aggravate my guards, I angled the chair
toward the full-length window facing the center ground. While I was a
novitiate, I'd envied the clear view the High Saltar had of the dancers
at ground level. As a dancer, I'd feared this window where she watched,
eager to spot the smallest error.

Right now, the women in the grounds were splattered with mud. Their faces were drawn and exhausted as they continued the difficult leeward storm pattern. The drums had repeated the long rhythm three full times already. Even one cycle of leeward storm could leave a dancer gasping for breath, but three times? The effort it took to coax this violent storm and then maintain its force showed in the dancers' limbs as they grew heavy with exhaustion. My own muscles ached in sympathy.

Yet despite pelting rain and harsh movements, I still found breathtaking beauty in the sight of the women moving together, creating intricate patterns, connecting with the world—the world the Maker had designed.

I rubbed my forehead. All that misplaced effort. They were working so hard and missing the whole point. The dancers commanded the world and thought no force was higher. And although their work was rich with duty and perfection and striving, it was poor in love.

They didn't even realize why Tiarel had chosen this pattern. Her motive wasn't to nourish plants suffering from drought, but to repel her enemies. The dancers were suffering, the villages outside were suffering, the whole of Meriel was suffering—and it didn't need to be this way.

I touched the pouch with the Maker's letter. I had hours to wait before the end of the day's classes and my hearing with the saltars. If I read the history again, perhaps the truth would give me the courage I needed. But before I drew out the pages, Tiarel entered with her precise, silent tread. I stood and tipped my head respectfully.

"Ah, I see you've been watching the vital work of the Order. The calling you pledged to serve." Tiarel's seawater-sweet voice now carried a bitter bite.

I swallowed. "I've found a higher calling."

She strode to her desk. "There is no higher calling. You rejected us and all the years we invested in you." She pulled a gleaming silver dagger from a drawer and came to stand before me. Her gaze shifted to each of the prefects, and with that subtle movement they closed in and grabbed me.

I strained against them, my eyes widening and fixing on Tiarel's face.

"You promised me a hearing."

Her lips curled. "Of course. You'll have your hearing. But first I have an important issue to deal with. You betrayed your vows. Outcasts aren't allowed to leave the Order to endanger the world with their abilities intact."

Horror bloomed across my chest as I guessed her intent. I struggled, almost wrenching one arm free. One of the men threw a beefy arm around my neck and pinned both arms painfully behind me. The other gripped my legs like manacles. Tiarel crouched.

I fought for breath. "Wait! You don't need to—"

A searing line cut across the back of my ankle. A strangled scream rose from my throat. Pain, sharp and hot, unlike any I'd ever felt, severed me from sanity. Shock stopped my efforts to breathe and black mist clouded my vision.

The prefects released me, and my wounded leg collapsed, unable to bear my weight. I crumbled to the ground, grabbing the wound as if my hands could reknit skin and muscle and stem the blood. Jagged sobs wracked me.

Inches from my face, Tiarel still crouched. She held up her knife, wet with my blood. "I look forward to the hearing you requested."

And she smiled.

A sharp jerk of her chin directed the prefects. "Take her within and clean up this mess."

The men jerked me upright, each movement sending fresh torture through my tendon. They dragged me through the door. Through the haze of pain, I remembered the rumors that the inner room contained a well into the ocean. Perhaps my death awaited. The suffering was so intense I would welcome that escape.

MINUTES OR HOURS LATER, A SOFT VOICE BROKE THROUGH

the roaring pain.

"Oh, little one. Would that I could have stopped this," Ginerva said.

I turned my head slowly. I'd learned the smallest action could drive the flame in my leg to an inferno. Every beat of my heart traced lines of fire up my leg. Blood seeped through my fingers as they held the wound, as if somehow I could also hold myself together after being torn apart.

Ginerva knelt beside me, a basket over her arm. Compassion flooded her eyes and almost undid me again. I squeezed my lips together, determined to stop the groans that escaped with each breath. She pried my hands away from my ankle. The touch of air across the deep cut triggered another gasp. I buried my head in my arms to fight back a scream.

"This will help," she soothed.

I didn't respond, too busy surviving each beat of my pulse, each tight breath, each second of agony. How could a cut, even one so deep and damaging, create this fire that crept through my whole being? Did Tiarel's blade carry poison?

From my distant place of shock, I felt Ginerva blot away blood, dab on one of her potions, and firmly wrap the wound.

"It doesn't help," I moaned. But the fact that I could speak proved her salve was helping, at least a small amount. I opened my eyes. "Did they summon you so I wouldn't get more blood on Tiarel's floor?"

Her soft arms supported my upper back and helped me sit. "No. When the High Saltar had you taken to her office, I feared the worst. I told the prefects out there that Tiarel had sent me."

"You lied?" No, no, no! I couldn't face having more people suffer because of me.

She shrugged. "I'm a simple-headed old woman. Easily muddled. Perhaps I misunderstood."

Her feigned confusion almost coaxed a smile to my lips. Then my gaze dropped toward the bandage. Hobbled. Worse than my physical suffering, a deeper pain grabbed my soul. "I'll never be able to dance again. I won't be able to hear the Maker."

Her arms squeezed me, rocking me gently. "Hush. Where there is life, there is hope."

The low voices of guards mumbled from Tiarel's office. I squeezed her arm. "She mustn't find you here."

Ginerva gathered her poultices and bandages and covered the basket. "Tiarel assumes you won't have the nerve or strength for a hearing with the saltars tonight. She's wrong. I brought you this." My old attendant reached for a twisted staff resting against the wall and placed it in my hand. Before I could thank her, she toddled from the room.

Bracing myself with the staff, I got my good foot under me. In class we'd often practiced rising on one leg to build strength. Still, the action of standing, even without taking weight on my wounded ankle, sent new waves of flame up my leg. Nausea roiled through me, and my throat tightened.

How would I ever speak to the saltars like this? Deformed, defective, shamed and broken. Why would they listen to anything I had to say about a Maker who loved us?

Where had His love been for me?

I drew the pouch from around my neck and dropped it to the floor. The stone walls of the small room seemed to close in. One tiny window allowed a feeble hint of cloud-shrouded light. No furnishings interrupted the stark gray surroundings of this inner room, but a trapdoor set in the floor hinted that the rumors of a well might be true. How many had disappeared from this room over the years?

Pulling my gaze upward, I leaned more weight onto the staff.

"You promised to be with me," I whispered to the Maker, throat burning from holding back screams. "Look at me now."

A low rumble from the dying storm echoed.

"Please speak to me again. Show me how to go on." My voice broke, my heart raw and exposed. The colors of anger faded into an aching plea. I hopped one painful stride so I could lean a hand against the wall near the window. "You told me to bring Your letter to the Order, but I can't."

Memories glided across my vision like the rain drawing patterns on the window. The Maker calling me to come to Him across the water. Ridiculous. Yet He made it possible. The Maker asking me to read the letter to the villages. Implausible. Yet He gave me Brantley as a guide, and allies and eager ears in each town.

But presenting to the saltars was even more impossible. The letter was beautiful and truthful, but with a representative as scorned and pathetic as me, no one in the Order would have reason to listen. I eased to the floor and pulled out the bound parchment. The words swam as I tried to read. The pain was too insistent. I couldn't focus, couldn't concentrate. Each sharp pang through my leg made me groan, "No!" Each time I glanced at the bandage with blood already seeping through, I gasped, "No!" As the drums pulsed through my stolen hopes of dancing again, I whispered, "No!"

Accepting His purpose was impossible. Yet wrestling against Him was torment. "Help me. Make me willing." In my heart, I called out to the Maker until I had no words left.

Slowly, my soul stopped thrashing and allowed warm arms of love to hold me, although He remained silent. I rested my head on my arms, sprawled on the floor, empty of my confusion, my doubt, my resistance. "Yes," I said quietly, even though I wasn't sure He was listening. "If this is what it will take to free our world, I'm Yours."

SHADOWS STRETCHED ACROSS THE SMALL COLD CELL AS
the primary sun set. The insistent drums had slowed, and the wind and
pouring rain dwindled. Dancers couldn't maintain the violent storm
patterns forever. The rhythm that pulsed through the building now was
a slow, circular pattern, simply holding the world in place.

I touched the bandage around my ankle. Our poor island was as
hobbled as me.

I propped against a wall, rubbed away my tears, and tried to plan a
compelling speech to make before the saltars of the Order. I'd lost my
home, my friends, my purpose, and now my ability to dance. If my effort
to share the Maker's words failed, all that sacrifice would be for nothing.

When even the subsun sank low, I wondered if Tiarel had gone back
on her word. Classes were over for the day. She should have summoned
me to the hearing before now. Using the staff, I hoisted to my feet and
stretched up on my good leg to peer out the window. Fires and smoke
flickered down in Middlemost. More than I ever remembered seeing at
dusk. And nearer than they should appear.

I squeezed my gritty eyes and looked out again. The flames were close.
Those weren't campfires of travelers in the town square or puffs of smoke
from hearths. In the deepening gloom, I made out the figures of men and
women, many holding torches. They advanced from the ring of the town.

Brantley's rebellion?

Remembering him brought a stab as sharp as my wounded tendon.
What had he thought when I hadn't joined him at the inn? The last he
knew, I was planning to find Star at the tender's. Had he worried when I

never returned? Perhaps he'd guessed that I'd made my way to the Order. Maybe he even believed I'd returned to them freely, still bound by loyalty and a lifetime of service. If I disappeared, he'd never know the truth. And he'd never know how much he meant to me.

Sounds rang from the outer saltars' office and approached. Scuffling and raised voices lifted from the High Saltar's inner room. I limped from the window and pressed my ear against the door, trying to make out what was happening. Through the thick wood, Tiarel's voice carried, ordering prefects to defensive positions. Saltar Kemp spoke with a querulous high tone. I couldn't make out the words, but recognized Saltar River's shrill voice interrupting her.

The door flew open, and I hopped back an awkward step.

Two prefects grabbed my arms and yanked me into Tiarel's office. I kept a grip on my staff and struggled to keep my good foot under me. The jarring movement caused new fire to shoot through my wound, and I bit my lip to hold back a gasp.

Tiarel was waving away several saltars. "Of course I prepared for this. I've had soldiers gathering knowledge in every village. Do you think the Order hasn't faced opposition before? But we control the dancers, so we control our world. Disgruntled peasants can't change that."

Saltar Kemp shot a glance my way, then pressed her lips together, the warmth of regret flaring in her eyes. Saltar River's eyes cut to the bloodstained bandage on my ankle before she sniffed and turned away.

Tiarel drew herself up to her full, imposing height and pointed at me. "For those who doubt the wisdom of your High Saltar, look upon this answer."

I wouldn't let Tiarel use me as a prop in her schemes. "I was promised a hearing. It's not too late. I have important—"

"Bring her." Tiarel flicked her hand as if brushing aside an insect, and strode toward the hall.

The soldiers dragged me along.

I gasped in a breath, struggling to hop without sending jarring shards through my severed tendon. A flurry of saltars surrounded us as Tiarel led the strange procession out the tower doors, through the garden, and to the primary archway. Beyond the courtyard, soldiers and prefects took up positions to stem the approaching tide.

Poised, regal, displaying no hint of fear, Tiarel confronted the threatening horde. Prefects with torches formed a semicircle around her, creating a pool of light, her white robe stark against the backdrop of armored men. "Send forward Brantley of Windswell."

Silence descended over the crowd like flowing water extinguishing a flame.

Her chest rose. "Oh, yes. We know who has stirred up this harmful opposition. Step forward if you dare."

The advance halted, leaving the distance of a dining hall's length separating us from the villagers. Although the High Saltar's words had commanded attention, they didn't seem to intimidate any of the rimmers. Muscular herders and farmers held torches high. Long knives gleamed from the belts of some. Others brandished scythes or hoes. They waited in stillness like an adamant wall. If the wrong word were spoken now, that wall of brave men would close in and crush everyone in the Order. Or Tiarel's soldiers would tear into that bastion and destroy it person by person.

Over the persistent and distant pulse of the drums inside, a rustle announced a man's approach. The villagers stepped aside and Brantley emerged. He'd taken time to clean up from our weeks in the wild. Shaven, in a clean tunic, his sword catching reflections of flame, he was no humble herder, but a leader of men.

He didn't let Tiarel continue to direct the conversation. "We demand the release of our villages' daughters. The Order no longer serves our world." Confidence and a current of anger rang through his voice, in spite of facing armed soldiers with only a ragtag group of villagers.

"The Order alone has saved the world." The High Saltar's high pitch would have seemed a feeble response if not for the army behind her.

Brantley firmed his stance and set his jaw. "By demanding that everyone in this world serve the Order? You've bled our lands dry and broken our families. You've chosen our world's path without any consent of her people.

That ends tonight."

"Your ill-advised rebellion is the only thing that will end tonight." Tiarel sneered and turned her gaze to the villagers before her. "Are you rash enough to think you've surprised us? Those loyal to the Order have kept us informed of this rimmer's attempt to stir up trouble. We know all about Brantley of Windswell. This man you follow is a coward and a fool. He cares nothing for your villages or the damage he is causing. His mind has been clouded by a desire for revenge, ever since his unhinged brother threw himself in front of a soldier's spear. He wants us to return the novitiates to their villages, but they don't want to go. They embrace the high honor of protecting Meriel, of learning to serve her."

Brantley's bearing held strong, but some of the men shifted. Uneasy murmurs welled and spread. I could guess their thoughts. Was it true that Brantley's motives had nothing to do with protecting the villages? Would the girls they had come to free refuse to leave? And if Tiarel knew about the opposition leaders, what retribution had she sent to their villages already? How would their families suffer? Could they still retreat? Sideways glances reflected the paranoia that the High Saltar had planted. The armed villagers measured each other, wondering who among them had given reports to Tiarel's soldiers.

The High Saltar took advantage of the brewing uncertainty. She flicked a finger, and the soldiers pulled me forward. Ignoring the crowd, she focused on Brantley. "Withdraw now, or she dies."

His gaze met mine for a precious eternity. Desperation and frustration swam in his eyes. I was ruining his plans and giving Tiarel leverage against him. But beneath the surface, I read something deeper in his face: a yearning, a promise, a silent "trust me."

I tugged against the guards, but couldn't break their grip.

Brantley's focus widened. He took in my crooked stance and the bandaged leg. He turned toward Tiarel, rage flickering across his face with the torchlight. If he hadn't been tethered by her threat to kill me, Brantley would have run her through.

Even worse, when he turned back to me, pity shaded his eyes. I'd become an object of wretchedness to him. I twisted away, unable to see him look at me that way. Straining against my captors, I focused on the other saltars. "You are all witnesses. She promised me a hearing." A powerful reminder. A High Saltar's promise had to be trustworthy or her entire leadership was thrown into question.

A few of the saltars drew back from Tiarel. Furrowed brows and wringing hands proclaimed their confusion. Uncertainty hovered in the air over both groups now, a better flavor than relentless division. There was still time to sway the others of the Order, as well as the rebels.

A man beside Brantley stepped forward. "The only thing they'll listen to is the sound of our weapons tearing this place down stone by stone."

Brantley clamped a hand on the man's shoulder. "Peace. Let the dancer speak."

The weight of dozens of pairs of eyes—furious, skeptical, hopeful, impatient—all rested on me. I couldn't bear the heaviness.

Maker, help me!

Brantley's eyes narrowed. His terse nod prompted me to speak before the moment was lost. I cleared my throat. "The Maker's letter has been found. Some of you have heard its truth. Before you destroy each other, let me read it."

The tenuous mood of the crowds softened, like a wave pulling back from the shoreline. Could it be this easy? Could this be the moment for which the Maker had called me to speak truth?

"Impossible." Tiarel's shrill word wiped away any conciliation. "We will never allow her to deceive more people with these myths."

"If they are myths, why are you so afraid of them?" Brantley asked calmly.

Tiarel's chin lifted and she smiled like a mother correcting a disappointing child. "Despite the suffering it costs us, the Order will ever protect Meriel from lies. Yet this is how you reward us."

Among the rebels, several heads dipped. By sheer reflex, the power of her role and what I'd been taught all my life sent shame coursing through me. How dared I oppose her? But oppose her, I must.

I pulled myself to my full height. "You are the one speaking lies! The dance was never meant to be contained in the center ground. It was never meant for only a select few. And it wasn't meant to hold our world in bondage."

Tiarel drew her dagger and handed it to one of the soldiers. "Kill her."

Brantley drew his sword, but he'd never reach me in time. The crowd held its breath while the gleaming blade hovered in the soldier's hand.

You are a dancer. The quiet and beloved voice whispered to my heart.

"Wait! I can prove it." I gasped the words out, but they carried with surprising volume.

The soldier paused. Brantley stood down, watched and waited.

I drew myself as tall on my good leg as I could, gripping the staff and confronting Tiarel. "Look at me. Cripple, outcast. Yet I will dance and invite the Maker's gifts on the land. You'll see Him work. If He does not, the rebels will return to their villages, and you may take my life."

Several saltars gasped, and Tiarel laughed.

"No." Brantley ground out his words. "Don't do this."

Threads entangled and tightened around my heart, but I squared my shoulders. "Surely that's a fair challenge. If I'm proven right, you'll grant me the hearing to read the Maker's letter to everyone in the Order."

The High Saltar stepped toward me and removed her dagger from the soldier's grip. The constricting cords in my chest loosened and I drew a deep breath. Until I saw Tiarel's expression.

A predatory smirk bloomed across her face. "You're right. A challenge will put your heresy to rest once and for all." She raised her voice. "You've all witnessed her terms."

"Indeed, High Saltar," the saltars and prefects recited in unison.

Grumbles of assent returned from the villagers close enough to hear our discussion.

"Agreed." Tiarel flicked her hands in a graceful dismissal. "We must wait for the light of our suns so that all can bear witness. You are invited to gather in the Order's outer courtyard tomorrow as the subsun rises."

Serene in her control of every situation, she whirled and walked away, and even though no wind blew across the field, her robes billowed and rippled, as if she strode in a perpetual breeze, conjured at her whim.

I leaned toward Brantley, wishing I could touch him across the void between us. "Trust me. I—"

Soldiers dragged me back toward the Order before I could say more. As the villagers withdrew, the torchlight left heavy darkness behind, revealing only the rough image of Brantley's form as he stood alone, shaking his head.

Once inside the Order again, Tiarel's benevolent-mother façade dropped away. "Get her out of my sight." Her demand was punctuated by a crisp flick of her hand and a sneer.

The other saltars huddled together and followed Tiarel toward the offices. Prefects hurried to their assigned posts. No novitiates dared peek down from the stairway in spite of the uproar and strange events that had occurred outside. In moments, I was alone in the entry hall with two soldiers. One of them scratched his beard, and the other shrugged. They were clearly at a loss about what to do with me.

Ginerva emerged from the shadows. "May I be of help? I have a room prepared for her."

I longed to run into her arms, but instead took a small step forward, looking to the soldiers for permission.

One of the men puffed out his chest. "We'll have to stand guard. The High Saltar would disappear us if she escaped."

"Of course. This way." Ginerva's nonthreatening demeanor convinced them, and my guards and I followed her into the dancers' wing. The guards should have known that an outcast would never be allowed within, but in a day of so many strange events, they seemed eager to tuck me out of the way.

Ginerva followed me into the small room. The guards stomped around the space, even pulling up the ticking to be sure no weapons lurked beneath. Then they withdrew.

As soon as the door closed, I sank to the mattress and allowed a tremor to roll through my weary frame.

"Do you plan to flee?" Ginerva whispered, even as she pulled items from her pockets.

"No. I made a challenge and I will honor it." I forced false confidence into my tone.

Ginerva's soft hands were already unwrapping the bandage. I leaned back on my elbows and hissed in a tight breath, but then surrendered to her ministrations. She applied fresh ointment and bandages, gently rotating my ankle. "Do this each day. Don't let the joint stiffen as you heal."

"Will that really make a difference?"

She lifted her troubled eyes to mine. "I watched from an alcove. The High Saltar is much too pleased with herself."

"But everyone witnessed the bargain. She can't back out."

Her white hair bobbed as she nodded. "Perhaps she assumes you are too crippled to stand, much less dance. But . . ."

"You think she has something else planned?" I would drive myself mad trying to unravel Tiarel's intentions.

"And that's not your only problem." Ginerva tucked her bandages and poultices into a basket. "How long can you hold back the tide of anger against the Order?"

"Especially when I want to swim in that current myself." I flexed my foot a few times. Even without bearing weight, it shrieked at the small movements. "The anger the villagers feel is well-earned. Yet the Maker hasn't called for the Order to be destroyed but to fulfill its proper purpose."

Ginerva sniffed. "Leaving neither side happy."

I shrugged wearily. "One step at a time. First I earn the right to read the letter to all the saltars. I'll leave it to the Maker to change hearts."

Her hand rested softly on my arm. "That would be wonderful." But resignation and doubt shaded her voice. Years of waiting for change and watching the abuses of the Order made hope a fragile thread for her.

I hugged her. "Take heart. The story isn't finished yet."

AFTER GINERVA LEFT, I CLOSED MY EYES AND EXHALED, exhausted from holding myself together. Subtle tremors rolled up and down my spine, reminding me of the way the waves teased the ground when I had traveled at the rim. My time of riding across the wide and unpredictable ocean felt lifetimes away. A newly emerging part of my soul missed those open currents.

But another part of me longed for the time when life was simple, when I had a place to belong and everything made sense. I opened my eyes and sought comfort in the stark orderliness of my room. In this large edifice, the floor subdued the movements of the ground. The drums beat consistent patterns. Novitiates followed schedules. Everyone knew her role. Despite Tiarel's cruelty, the tug of the familiar tempted me.

I gingerly wrapped another layer of bandage over my throbbing wound. What was I thinking? I could never belong here again. All I'd ever had to offer was my dancing, and I was no longer a dancer.

"One last time," I whispered. "Dear Maker, please show up tomorrow."

If He didn't make Himself known, I'd never have a chance to share His letter. The rimmers would attack the Order. People would die. Whatever the outcome of that battle, our world would continue to be bound—either by faulty laws or by chaos.

I curled up on the mattress and pulled a coarse blanket over my shoulders. In spite of my throbbing leg and the looming test ahead, a strange peace surrounded me, much softer and more comforting than the bedding. Live or die, the Maker loved me. Whatever happened tomorrow, He could still bring about His purposes.

I was almost asleep when I heard a thud against the wall outside. Had Ginerva returned? Or did Tiarel regret her promise? Had she sent soldiers to kill me?

Scrabbling sounded at the lock, and I grabbed my staff and pressed to my feet. The door flew open and a cloaked figure rushed inside and scooped me up. Muscled arms held me tight against a broad chest that smelled of leather and seawater.

"Stop!" I pounded his head with my stick, connecting sharply with his skull.

He fumbled me, holding me with one arm while fending off my cane with the other. Still, he eased me down carefully and pushed back his hood. "Ow! Cut it out, dancer. I'm here to rescue you." Brantley rubbed the crown of his head, further tangling his mop of curls. "But we have to move fast."

Typical. I had a plan to forestall a war, and he felt he had to rescue me. I glared at him. "I'm not going anywhere."

He grabbed my arms and gave me a rough shake. "Wake up. It's too late for that. I know you've done remarkable things with your dancing before, but now . . ." He swallowed and fixed his focus on my bandaged leg. Pity and resignation flickered across his face.

His compassion nearly broke me, and the heat of shame crept up my neck. "But now . . . ?" I demanded he finish his sentence.

He squared his jaw and met my gaze. "You can barely stand. Admit it. Your deal with Tiarel is an exercise in futility." His tone softened. "Let me get you to safety before our alliance invades tomorrow."

I couldn't stay angry with him. His path wasn't mine, but he'd risked everything to come for me. I placed a hand over his heart. Even through his tunic, I felt the warmth of his body, the strength of his muscles, the passion in his blood. "No," I said simply.

He seized my arm again, but I jerked away, almost toppling over. "Don't make this harder, Brantley. I'm where I need to be."

He narrowed his eyes. "Back in the Order? Is this what it was all for?

You think they'll welcome you back? I should have known this is what you wanted."

I gasped. I thought I'd felt every kind of pain imaginable this past day, but I was wrong. A thorn pierced and tore at my soul. "Is that what you think of me?"

"Why not?" He scowled. "You're back where you belong. You used me to guide you back here so you can be one of them again."

"How can you say that? You know it's not true." I searched his face for any sign he didn't believe his own accusations. "I'm only here to serve the Maker."

A hint of color rose on his cheeks, giving lie to his words. He rubbed the back of his neck as if to keep his hands busy so he wouldn't grab me again. "So prove it." He glanced toward the hallway. "Come with me. Now."

I drew a slow breath. "You shouldn't have come."

"I had to." He reached out and cupped my face in his hands. Powerful currents played in the depths of his ocean-colored eyes. "I can't watch you die tomorrow." His voice broke.

With our faces only inches apart, I sought a way to comfort and reassure him. Gently, my lips touched his, then I burrowed into his chest and savored the strength and protection of his embrace.

"Nothing I say will convince you, will it?" he murmured.

I shook my head, not trusting myself to speak.

"How do you expect me to trust the Maker when He asks such things of you?"

I leaned into his chest. "I don't know."

A moan rose from the guard collapsed in the hallway. Brantley released me. "The soldier is coming to. Last chance. You can still escape."

I shook my head, letting all my affection shine from my eyes. "I can't. Please go. Stay safe. And ask the Maker to help me be brave."

He looked like he wanted to say more, but then clamped his jaw and nodded. In the space of a breath he slipped away. I sank down to the bed, wrapping my arms around myself to hold in the last traces of his warmth.

THE PRIMARY SUN WOKE THE WORLD, BRIGHTLY UNAWARE
of the angry rimmers encircling the Order, or Tiarel's plans to keep
control, or my quailing fears. Ginerva brought bresh loaves and fruit to
strengthen me, but my throat was too constricted to get any food down.
My bold proposal to dance for the Maker seemed ridiculous in the light
of day.

As the subsun began to chase the first sun across the sky, two prefects
arrived to escort me to the center ground. I tightened the scarf over my
hair, and brushed off my mottled tunic and leggings. I looked nothing
like the pristine dancer I'd once aspired to become. Even with my staff, I
could barely support my own weight.

The men led me to the entrance from the dancers' wing and stopped
there. Only dancers or drummers could step past the threshold. I was
neither. I braced myself for the ground to split and swallow me at my
presumption as I hobbled into the grounds—imperfect, outcast, unnamed.
But under my bare feet, the earth and daygrass welcomed me.

Tiarel and all the saltars formed an impressive border around the edge
of the clearing. White-garbed dancers continued their work, ignoring this
unheard-of intrusion into the sacred space. The morning turning pattern
kept them tightly in the center. They danced the very steps that fought
the Maker's purpose, chaining our world into place. As they pivoted, I
recognized friends I'd trained with my whole life. Under one white scarf,
Starfire held her expression, cold and impassive. Her presence was
another thorn piercing my heart, and as it bled, I felt even weaker.

Tiarel took control, easily raising her voice over the drums. "Village
leaders will observe from my office to bear witness to the truth. Your
rebellion must end. The Order must be supported."

Rimmers were here? I glanced up, but saw only novitiates in tunics
of every hue peering down from balconies. Finally, I spotted the

representatives, watching from the large window in Tiarel's office. They each wore a green scarf of truce knotted around their necks. I doubted that ancient tradition would protect them if I failed. Tiarel's soldiers would never let them leave. A Windswell elder edged aside, allowing Brantley to step forward near the glass. Seeing him here was both comfort and agony. I wanted to talk to him once more, to seek his understanding or approval for my course. But I didn't dare allow myself that distraction. I hobbled a few steps further into the grounds. One lone cripple against the might of the Order.

Saltar River raised her arm, pointing her finger at me as if it were a sword. "I protest this desecration of our consecrated place."

Tiarel frowned. "Your opinions have been noted. The decision is made. The rimmers have pledged that when this outcast's delusion is proven, they will return home and continue to send girls as candidates for our vital Order."

I gasped. That would be worse than civil war. If I failed today, there would be no one to stand against the Order. Our world would continue to be bound and would eventually die. The Maker would be forgotten again. My heart pounded; my legs shook.

A light breeze found its way to me and brushed my face. *"This is not your battle, dear child."* The Maker's voice whispered to my heart, so gentle I wondered if I was imagining it. *"The truth does not rely on the strength of your legs, the wisdom of your mind, or the skill of your tongue."*

"What are you waiting for?" Tiarel asked. "Show us your mythical Maker."

I shut out the crowds, friend or foe. I turned my gaze skyward. Only one arm was free, since I needed the other to hold my staff. But I danced with that free arm, swaying in a gentle approximation of the opening movements of the calara pattern.

Tiarel's laughter rang out, harsh and loud as a dinner bell.

I fought to ignore her derision. Centered over my good foot, I swiveled my body to one side and then the other, opening my arms in an expansive gesture that would have been beautiful if I hadn't needed to hop awkwardly to keep my balance.

The drums fought me, pounding their fixed pattern. Then another sound rose from all around me. The saltars had drawn out the rhythm sticks they used in class, and added more power to the driving beat.

I pushed against the noise, trying bits of one pattern and then another.

Tiarel raised her hand, and the drums stopped mid-beat. The dancers in the center froze. Would she finally allow this to be a fair test? Would she let me invite the Maker's presence without her interference?

She chopped her arm downward. Instantly the drums and dancers began a new pattern. Leeward storm again.

The wind picked up and clouds scudded overhead, blocking both suns. I resumed my feeble motions, but rain sheeted down. The tempo grew faster, and the center ground became slick with mud. I limped to the left and stretched my arms, lifting my damaged leg behind me, fire pulsing through the wound. I pushed weakly against the storm with patterns of sun and warmth, but when I raised my face to the sky, the rain threatened to drown me. Soon the mud sucked at my feet, making each movement even more impossible. I returned to the edge where the daygrass gave some purchase. Palms up, I again offered the simplest of movement.

The storm continued to beat me down, my wet headscarf plastering my head.

I sank to my knees. *I'm so sorry. I've failed You. I don't know what to do.*

Beneath me, the earth shuddered. *"Let me teach you a new dance."* The deep voice of the Maker rumbled from the core of our world. *"My dance."*

The wind tugged at my tunic, but the gale no longer attacked me. Instead, courage breathed over me, through me, into me. Then even the awareness of courage gave way to the simple joy of being with Him.

The pulsating drums faded into an unimportant background. Music like distant birdsong guided me. From my knees, I stroked the beloved earth of Meriel, lowered myself even further, prostrate on the ground. Yes! This was His dance. The Maker who formed a world from the clay of

His love. The Maker who offered Himself to His people. The Maker who reached out again and again to rescue His children.

I rolled to my back and my arms reached skyward. Tucking my good foot under me, I arched and let my heart reach up in response. I curled, contracted, then released with a spring that brought me to my feet. He gave, I responded, He called, I answered. My movements echoed the story of His letter.

The saltars continued to tap their sticks, their faces expressionless under the downpour. They weren't hearing the powerful music.

But I heard every note. I smiled.

Too full of love to contain myself to any pattern now, I spun a series of turns around the dancers who continued their work in the middle. Each time I pushed off my bad leg, the sharp reminder of Tiarel's knife tried to distract me. The pain called out, but it was muted under the exquisite delight of moving with Him.

The ground that was usually so stable here in the middle of our world began to ripple. A few dancers stumbled, missed a motion or two. I leapt, and the earth propelled me upward, then cushioned me as I landed.

This wasn't any pattern the Order had ever taught. Yet the storm scattered and the suns burst into the space again. As my leaps carried me around, I glimpsed Tiarel's face. She waved her hands frantically, insisting on an even faster tempo. Her arrogant confidence gave way to panic. The other saltars' faces reflected even more alarm. Over the pounding drums and the rumbles of the earth, Tiarel shouted, "Resume the turning!" The rhythm shifted again, faster and faster. Even the saltars turned in place, adding their efforts to those of the others. Prefects in balconies banged staffs against the floors as novitiates on each level joined, spinning in place. Their frenzied acts were an obscene parody of the gift of dance the Maker had bestowed when He made our world.

Should I dance faster? Leap higher?

"*Stand and watch.*" The Maker's words breathed into my heart. I finished the circle of leaps, and held my ground.

As if His hand rested on my shoulder, He gently turned me in one slow rotation. I saw everyone with vivid clarity. The smallest girls, barely able to see over the balcony on the top floors. Burly prefects and exhausted attendants. Saltars with their angry sticks. Dancers drenched from sweat and rain, faces drawn with desperation. Ragtag rimmers watching in confusion. Brantley, dear precious Brantley, worry and doubt painted across his face.

Compassion welled up in me, as if the Maker poured one tiny drop of His ocean into my heart. He loved His children. Even these angry, prideful ones who resisted Him at every turn. Even me.

Please let them see You.

"Unbound!" His deep voice resonated through the earth. The dancers in the center tried to obey Tiarel's command to perform the turning pattern, but a few stumbled. Some covered their ears. Others fell to their knees. The drums ceased, and one of the drummers fled the center ground.

"Fight it!" Tiarel stomped her feet, as if her will could hold the world in place. New cracks splintered along the stone walls. Her voice no longer carried over the groans and shudders of the earth, but she kept flailing.

The very world seemed about to rend apart.

Then He whispered, *"Now."*

CASTING ASIDE MY STAFF, I FLUNG MY WHOLE BEING INTO
the love of my Maker.

He swirled me around, breathed through me. His presence blazed
brighter than both our suns. His voice consumed me with sounds sweeter
than morning birdsong. His love drew me forward with the strength of a
hundred dancers, so compelling that even my crippled leg obeyed.

Forsaking the edges of the space, I danced right through the center.

The last remnants of the Order's symmetry fractured. Many dancers
backed away. Others reached to grab me but caught only air. Their pattern
broke completely, and before they could resume, the earth groaned and
shifted. This time everyone heard.

Tiarel's face whitened, her tight eyebrows and pursed mouth standing
out like the tiny embroidery stitches on her gown. A couple saltars
grabbed the tower wall, and the ground roiled again. A stone jarred loose
from an upper balcony and tumbled down. A dancer screamed and ran
to the door.

Heedless of the chaos, I spun toward the center again and stopped. I
felt our world break free with a last quiver as it sailed forward on a new
current. My feet touched the earth's joy, and I skipped lightly in place,
savoring the exhilaration, the rightness of the moment.

Shifting my gaze down, I saw one dancer sitting and hugging her
knees. A strand of auburn hair had escaped from her sodden headscarf. I
reached for her hand. Starfire lifted her chin.

I smiled at her, and the panic left her eyes. Mischief scampered over
her face, and she took my hand. Perhaps she thought that if our world

was crumbling away underfoot, she may as well perish while dancing. Or maybe she welcomed the voice of the Maker reminding us of who we were meant to be. Whatever the reason, she joined my steps as we lightly sprang forward in a long-forgotten pattern of trust. We invited other dancers and many joined in. A low thrumming of the ocean below provided the only rhythm we needed.

We moved with shapes and designs that were new and free of any desire to control. We weren't ruling the world; we were celebrating the Maker's creation. Harrier birds and forest hounds, soft clouds and prickly lanthrus, fountain fish and stenella, wind and waves. Our island world sailed forward again.

My lifetime of longing to be a dancer could never have been fulfilled by the rigid rules of the Order or by movements separated from the Maker of the dance. Somehow all along, my spirit had longed for this true movement and connection. I savored the freedom of my limbs, but also of our island, no longer intimidated by the saltars or worried for the rimmers. The Maker was here and all would be well.

Out of the corner of my eye, I saw Saltar Kemp take a few unsteady steps away from the wall. A smile of wonder tugged at her wrinkled cheeks, and she lifted one arthritic hand toward the sky. But other saltars cringed or tossed their heads, as if driven to madness by hearing and resisting the Maker's call. Tiarel crouched tight against the wall, hands over her ears, and mouth open in a silent scream. Saltar River helped her up and guided her to the door into the dancers' wing.

As the world shook free of its shackles, a new deeper rumble sounded. A child screamed from an upper floor. Those who had been looking down from balconies ran back into the tower, and shouts rose from the windows that faced outward.

Had the rimmer army decided not to wait for the report of the delegation? Or was some other disaster approaching? I ran inside, out of the dancers' wing, and to the old familiar stairway to see what was causing the distress. Several saltars and a few dancers came with me.

Taking the steps two at a time, I paused each time the tower shook. I raced past children, some crying, some clutching each other, past the horrible storage closet where I'd once been punished, and to the ladder that led to the roof. Once I reached the highest point of the ringed building, I scanned the horizon in all directions. The rending sound became a crackling, crumbling, tearing roar. Was our island no longer capable of sailing the waves? Were we about to rip apart?

There! I spotted the source of the sound. Approaching from the rim, a finger of water rent the land. Awestruck, I gripped the parapet. The newly formed river chose a careful course, winding between trees. As it neared Middlemost, I held my breath.

Guided by the Maker's hand, the tear eased between a stable and a smithy, separating them with a creek that soon became a river flowing in a deep crevice.

The channel moved closer. The tear cut all the way down to expose the ocean.

Would it split the Order tower in two?

The saltars who had followed me up to the roof huddled behind me. "Do something!" one of them cried.

I closed my eyes and listened for the Maker's guidance.

"Join me," I told them, holding hands with the two closest saltars. Soon a row of us stood together. We raised our arms, in a wide stance, then leaned first to one side and then the other. We weren't touching the earth; we weren't opposing the water. We were simply inviting the Maker to protect Meriel, and all the people in Middlemost and this tower.

As land opened below us, we could see down into the dark water. The last finger of the crevice moved to the archway of the garden, then stopped. Buildings groaned in protest, a wall creaked, but then everything fell silent. A relieved sigh poured through the saltars, and we let our arms go limp. Our world was forever changed, perhaps scarred as I was. But we were not destroyed. Perhaps later the Maker would explain this strange occurrence. I had no doubt there was a purpose to anything He allowed.

I climbed back down the ladder and peered into the center ground from one of the balconies. Now that the rumbling and shaking had ceased, one drummer who had remained thrummed a playful rhythm, eyes closed to listen to the tempo of the new current our world was riding. The dozen or so dancers who hadn't fled in fear picked up the beat and flitted like carefree birds, seeming to fly as they darted around each other.

Laughter bubbled in my throat and I tore down the stairs to get back to that beautiful and changed place. The center ground no longer frightened me. The daygrass tickled my feet, and I found Starfire, took her hand, and joined her skipping steps.

Then Starfire gasped, and we all stopped. Overhead, another impossible event exploded in the sky. Star rain fell, even though it was midmorning. The sparkles were brilliant enough to see even in sunlight. We laughed, caught handfuls of light, tossed the glittering sand back into the air, and watched as the essence of stars coated our tunics. The white uniforms of the official dancers became iridescent. Even their mud-spattered leggings were beautiful in the shifting colors.

The door from the dancer wing opened and Ginerva took a few timid steps onto the center ground. She met my eyes. "If the Order had everything else wrong, were they wrong to only allow the perfect ones out here?"

I didn't know how to answer. So many things were changing so swiftly. Instinct—or the Maker's spirit in my heart—caused me to beckon her forward. "The Maker's letter says He welcomes everyone to share His dance."

Her eyes brightened like the star rain, and she tapped the earth softly with one foot. Saltar Kemp saw her and gasped, then looked to me. A mere attendant setting foot on the sacred ground? I shrugged. The implications would take time to sort out. For now, I beckoned everyone in sight to the grounds.

My work wasn't finished. I reluctantly pulled myself away from the celebration in the center ground and hurried inside, through the hall, and to Tiarel's office where the rimmers had been watching. Brianna stood with hands pressed against the glass, and turned when I entered. "I believed something would happen—but this?" Some of the village elders sat on the floor, gripping the doorframes or furniture as if unsure of what would happen next.

Brantley strode toward me, gathering me into a hug that squeezed the breath from my lungs. "What's happening? What does it all mean?"

"Meriel is free. And we've won the right to read the Maker's letter to the Order—to everyone."

He shook his head. "I saw everything, and I still can't believe my eyes." He held me at arms' length and looked down. "And your leg? You leapt and ran. Impossible."

I shook my head, bemused. I'd forgotten all about my hobbled leg. Was I permanently healed, or had it been a temporary gift in a time of need? The question didn't seem important. I could live the rest of my life fueled by the memory of today's one dance and be content.

I laughed and stepped to the window. Dancers still improvised in delightful new steps. Some who had fled ventured back in to the center ground. I spotted Iris, the dancer who had endured shackles. She sprang with the lightest steps of all, seeming to hover at the height of each leap. Ginerva held hands with Saltar Kemp and they tiptoed in childlike circles.

"Where did Tiarel go?" I asked.

Brantley draped an arm across my shoulders. "She came through and into an inner office."

"Will she honor the test? Will she let me read the Maker's letter to everyone in the Order?"

He frowned. "I don't think she's in a state to decide anything. From the wildness in her eyes, she didn't seem in her right mind."

Outside, more attendants and even a prefect or two joined the frolicking in the star rain. I turned from the window with a sigh. I would have loved to dance out there all day, but I needed to complete the task the Maker had asked of me. "The whole school gathers for the noon meal. I'll ring the bell and also call in the dancers and attendants from their wing. But first I'll make sure Tiarel won't prevent it."

"Not by yourself." Brantley's grip on my shoulder tightened.

I smiled up at him, then sobered. I was enjoying his protectiveness far too much. Even though many things were changing, the Order's original purpose had been valuable, and I'd pledged to serve the world as a dancer. That required forsaking all human attachments.

I slipped from his grasp and marched to the inner office, leaving behind his help and the sigh he gave. Saltar River crouched by the open trapdoor, her hooked nose and posture giving her the appearance of a carrion bird. Other than her, the room was empty. A chill raised gooseflesh on my arms. "Where is the High Saltar?"

Saltar River cut her burning gaze at me. "This is your fault. You invited the madness."

Her anger was as potent as a leeward wind and blew me a tiny step back. I felt Brantley's reassuring hand on my back to steady me. He'd followed me, and I couldn't find it in myself to reject his support.

"Where is she?" I asked again.

River straightened to her full lanky height and jabbed a long finger toward me. "She fought the voice, but couldn't overcome it. I tried to stop her, but wasn't quick enough. She threw herself into the sea."

I crouched by the trapdoor, peering into the depths. The well was cut through the tallest layer of our island clear through to the ocean. Deep in the darkness below, water rushed by faster than the liveliest stream. Anyone entering the sea would have been swept far under our island.

"Why?" My voice broke. She chose death over truth and freedom. Even though she'd tried to destroy me, I couldn't shake my years of reverence for her. She'd guided the Order because she believed in it. If only she'd left one sliver of her heart open to consider the truth of the Maker who set our world into motion, who had a different purpose for the dance, and who had loved her. It wasn't His voice that drove her mad, it was her adamant opposition to Him. She set her will against Him with such fury, His very presence made her destroy herself rather than accept what she'd experienced.

Inexplicable tears stung my eyes. I reached down as if I could touch the water, sweet and cool so far below. But only empty air trickled past my fingers.

Brantley pulled me back. "Save your compassion for others. Rumor was that she sent many through that trapdoor."

I managed a stiff nod. He was right. After all the pain she'd caused, there was a justice in her end. Yet I still grieved for her. And I sensed the Maker did, as well.

Brantley stepped around me and closed the trapdoor. The loud clank as it slammed down made me shiver. How many deaths had this door witnessed?

Saltar River brushed her hands on her tunic. The grief that had rimmed her eyes seemed sincere but faded quickly, and she jutted her chest forward. "I'm the High Saltar now. Leave the Order. You've done enough damage."

I planted my feet and faced her. "Not until I've read the Maker's letter to everyone."

Her fists clenched, flexing arm muscles strong enough to shove Tiarel to her death. I would never know what had really happened between the two of them in this inner room. Whether Saltar River was grieving her mentor or gloating over her quick action to take power, I'd do all I could to prevent her from controlling the Order. I spun on my heel and left the room where the blood from my injury had once seeped through my fingers and stained the floor. A pang from my ankle pierced upward, and I clenched my teeth, willing it away. Moments earlier, I'd danced with freedom and strength. Surely the damaged tendon was healed.

Saltar River followed and shrieked when she saw the center ground through the office window. Even more dancers were improvising new patterns, and a handful of bold rimmers had found their way to the door and stood, swaying, arms reaching upward in the space that had always been forbidden. "This desecration is your fault." Her fist clenched and rested against the glass. "Every evil that befalls our world will be on your head."

She couldn't intimidate me, not when the Maker's presence was still so tangible. A laugh bubbled free, and I didn't bother responding. Instead,

I headed to the dining hall, Brantley staying close beside me. I rang the bell for lunch. A worried attendant poked his head from the kitchen. "The meal isn't ready yet."

I smiled. "Don't worry. We're gathering early for a special event. You can serve the meal after that. And whoever can be spared can sit in the dining hall and listen too."

The lad's eyebrows disappeared under his bangs, but he gave a quick nod and ducked back into the kitchen.

I stood near the head table and stared out at the many empty chairs.

Brantley braced one foot on a bench. "Will they come?"

Allowing myself a quaver of doubt, I met his level gaze. "I don't know."

32

I'D FACED VILLAGES WHERE PEOPLE HAD BEEN BATTERED BY weather, crippled by scarcity, and brutalized by the Order. Yet their faces had lit with hope and joy as they heard the Maker's letter. Reading the letter inside the Order was different. Very different.

The firm, uncompromising walls of stone rose around me. A line of older students filed in, maintaining their precise walk as they took their table. The younger forms soon followed. Inexperienced, they hid their confusion with less skill. I saw the fear in their eyes. Every day of the Order followed the same pattern, but today everything had changed. The very ground had broken open.

Saltar Kemp strode in with a light step and found her chair at the front of the room. Several other saltars followed her from the dancers' wing. Some timidly, some with determination. Most of them offered me tentative nods. Then Saltar River stormed in. She paused near me, spearing me with her glare. After she glanced around at the other saltars smiling in support of me, she backed away and pulled out the High Saltar's chair. The legs screeched along the platform as she slid into place. She held her spine as rigid as the many rules that had shaped my life here. A bit of my confidence faltered.

Oh, my Keeper, let Your words form a new pattern in our hearts today. We thought we could thwart Your plan, but we are as feeble as flower petals. We need You to direct our world—and our lives.

I continued to pray silently as more rows of novitiates filed in. The traditions of structure had their uses. Everyone assembled efficiently and without speaking. Only the scrape or creak of a bench broke the stillness.

I pulled the letter from the pouch around my neck and unrolled the parchment, but my hands trembled.

"Hard to believe this will make a difference," Brantley whispered, tugging the collar of his formal tunic. "But then I'd never have thought a scrawny dancer could square off against the whole Order and free our world."

I shook my head. I hadn't freed our world. Brantley's misstatement steered my thoughts to the One who had led me to this moment. My chest lifted. "It was the Maker who freed our world, and the Maker who will speak today. Not me."

He gave me a crooked smile and small bow before moving to the side of the room and leaning against the wall. I narrowed my eyes. The man knew me too well. He'd flattered me on purpose, knowing that I'd remind him about the Maker, and therefore remind myself. He was too clever by far.

I shook my head and took a breath, absorbing a strange sound. Silence. No regular shift of drummers and dancers worked in the center ground, so the pulsating rhythm that had always undergirded my life here was strangely absent. Behind me at the head table, saltars waited, pretending a composure they had lost, but still fighting to hold on to their control, hands tucked into wide, white sleeves. If they couldn't control our world, at least they would keep their expressions calm and confident.

Rows of novitiates stared at me, shaken by the strange events they'd witnessed. Their eyes cried out questions. Why was an outcast allowed to touch the center ground? Why were dancers creating new patterns? Why had the whole world shaken? Would the rift in the earth move forward and tear our island in two? Did the interruption to the patterns mean destruction, as they'd always been taught?

Compassion welled in my heart, as I remembered sitting on those hard benches, the weight of the world on my shoulders, believing I could make myself worthy if I tried harder. I hoped for a better future for these novitiates.

"I've come to bring good news." Fingers trembling, I opened the pages. The parchment crackled, soft and familiar. Then, as I'd done in village after village, I began reading the letter.

The youngest children absorbed the words the most easily, expressions wide and eager, as if a beautiful bedtime story had been proclaimed as truth. Perhaps like Orianna, some of them had grandparents who had whispered stories of the Maker to them, and they still remembered. The older children kept shooting gazes to the head table, looking for a reaction from the saltars. They wouldn't nod or smile or ask questions without the guidance of their instructors. The blue novitiates, including Furrow, sat the most stiffly. I knew what was churning through their minds, like the waves deep under our world. *Not now. Why must everything change? I've worked too hard to reach this point.*

When I glanced behind me to the head table, Saltar River's lips pressed into a hard line, and a vein at her temple pulsed in its own furious rhythm. I paused, swallowed, and remembered the beautiful way the Maker had made His presence known. Our world was free. The dancers, the rimmers, were all free. They just didn't know it yet.

I continued to read. Even the usual clatter of pots and spoons from the kitchen fell quiet.

My leg gave a twinge, then throbbed. I hadn't had time to peer beneath the bandage. My ankle had supported me when I needed to dance. That should be enough blessing for me. Yet I pressed back a whimper as the pain returned. My palms began to sweat, moistening the leaves of the letter.

Page by page, sentence by sentence, I focused my determination on letting the Maker's letter speak. I'd think about my own fears and needs later.

When I finished the last word, I wanted to close my eyes. Instead I dared to look at all the faces around me. Tears ran down many cheeks, the glistening drops speaking of wonder and new possibilities. Bodies relaxed forward as if remembering how to breathe. Dismay shadowed the eyes at the saltar's table as many of them realized the tragic direction the Order had taken. Few showed outright doubt, because everyone had witnessed the breaking of the pattern, the great rending moment when our world surged forward in freedom. They had seen the strange star rain that fell in a clear morning sky.

And they saw a wounded dancer leap for joy in My presence, the Maker whispered to my heart.

My own eyes flooded at His words. The injury that had shaken my trust in His love had been worth the pain. My weakness helped show His mercy and power to everyone in the Order. But now that the purpose was fulfilled, why was blood oozing through the bandage once again? Why not leave me perfectly restored?

A breeze tugged at the windows with a soft rattle. New cracks traced veins across the masonry of the walls. Scents of stew and burning saltcakes wafted from the kitchen. I waited, allowing each person to absorb what had been heard.

Saltar River stood, her outstretched arm quivering, fingers pulled into claws by taut muscles. "Prefects, take this outcast to my office."

Brantley straightened, reminding everyone of his presence in the room. No one else moved.

"Call the soldiers!" Spittle flew from the new High Saltar's lips. "I said get rid of her!" Her voice reached an irritating shriek, and those who glanced at her wore expressions of pity instead of reverence.

Saltar Kemp stood, the lines of age in her face framing a gentle smile toward me. "We thank you for sharing this important message with us. The saltars will meet to discuss our response. Obviously the Order needs to change."

Red blotches rose on River's cheeks. "There is nothing to discuss! We will resume the patterns and stop the dangerous course of our world. We'll hold it in place again." She clapped her hands. "Everyone, return to your classes. Prefects, clear out the intruders who don't belong in the center ground. Call the soldiers to halt the invasion if necessary. Dancers, perform the turning pattern."

Over her shouting and gesturing, the other saltars rose and gathered in a huddle, ignoring her. Saltar Tangleroot slipped away and approached me. "We need your input. Will you advise us as we meet?"

Me? Advise the saltars of the Order? My soul warmed that they were taking the Maker's letter to heart, but as I took a limping step forward, unworthiness drowned me like a stenella's underwater dive. A hand touched my arm. "Only if I accompany her," Brantley said protectively. "I still represent the interests of the rim villages."

I didn't fear for my safety. Not anymore. But he jerked his chin toward Saltar River, who was storming back and forth, tugging arms of other saltars and continuing to hiss commands. She would push me through the trapdoor with no compunction, given half a chance.

I nodded. "Where shall we meet?"

Saltar Kemp joined us. "We still have guests in the offices. Let's use the large rehearsal hall in the school."

Tangleroot nodded and scurried over to tell the other saltars. One of them was trying to calm River, so in the relative quiet while River stopped shrieking, Saltar Kemp addressed the novitiates. "Form Blue, please pair up and take a younger form into your care. There will be no classes today. You are free to enjoy the gardens or gather in classrooms or your rooms. Keep the children away from the edge of the new canyon." The many-colored tunics quickly dispersed, and the white-clad dancers returned to their wing.

I walked into the room that had once produced so much hope and terror—for me and all the students who had trained here. The vast rehearsal hall held echoes of leaps I'd performed, and meticulous steps I'd perfected, but always with fear and pride driving me. Never the love and joy I'd experienced in the center ground.

My bare feet again pressed along the cold marble surface, but now my bad leg couldn't articulate the movement as it once had. The saltars ignored the bench where they sat for judging novitiates. Instead they clustered in a circle in the center of the room like first-form children. The incongruous sight made me shake my head.

Even though the Maker had confirmed His presence, even though He'd enabled me to dance with Him, even though everyone in the Order had listened to His letter, a strange melancholy descended over me. The lower half of my leggings were damp and spattered with mud. I was exhausted, my leg ached, and I wanted to find a quiet room where I could sleep.

Instead, questions flew at me.

"Should the Order be closed?"

"What does it mean?"

"Who will guide the world now?"

"Where will we be swept to?"

I felt like I'd been tasked with teaching the youngest novitiates again. My temples throbbed. Brantley dragged a low stool forward and I sank down gratefully, even more aware of the stabbing in my tendon.

"I think . . ." I let my gaze travel over the drums and rhythm sticks in the corner, the courtyard gardens beyond high arched windows, and the worried faces of the saltars. "Much will change. The best thing to do is to seek the Maker's guidance."

Saltar Kemp entered, out of breath. "Thank you for waiting. I had to stop in the office. I remembered something." She held an old book in her arms, and when she brushed off the embossed leather cover, she sneezed. Sunlight suspended dust motes in the air like the sparkle of star rain.

Inwardly, I groaned. No one needed reminding of the Order's dictates. Hadn't we moved beyond that?

Instead of opening the book and reiterating dictates, she gave me a reassuring nod. "Please read the part of the letter again about the dance."

I fumbled for the page and read. "'The dance is a gift. A blessing. An invitation to enter the creating and nurturing of this world.'"

Color dotted Saltar Kemp's wrinkled cheeks. "Sometimes it is the holiest blessings that we're tempted to turn into idols. We've utterly forgotten our past." She found a faded page in her book and showed a sketch to the group as if we were first forms in a history lesson. "Our Order was first formed to worship the Maker and use patterns to steer the island to various oceans where nutrients and fish were plentiful.

Instead we locked it in place, determined to wrest control. Even worse, we corrupted His gift of dance with layers of rules and requirements. We need to make copies of this letter." Saltar Kemp gestured to the parchment I still clutched.

Even behind the solid doors of the rehearsal hall, shrill threads of River's voice carried from the offices as she ranted to everyone and was obeyed by no one.

"And we need a new High Saltar," Tangleroot said in an undertone.

Another of the saltars knelt by my feet. "This dancer brought us forgotten truth. Let her lead us."

Murmurs of agreement rose around me like a rising wave, and horrified me.

"No!" I stiffened my spine. "The Maker asked me to bring you what was lost, not to lead. If He allows, I'll gladly dance for Him—with other dancers from the Order here, or wherever He leads me. But I'm not called to this." I waved my hand, encompassing the whole tower, the student rooms, the prefects and attendants.

Protests splashed against me. "But everything has changed."

"We need someone new to guide us."

"You know the most about the letter."

With my good foot, I edged my stool back a few inches. "No."

"Are you sure?" Brantley asked, as if he could see me ruling the Order, and by extension, our whole world.

I faced him in disbelief. Did he really know me so little?

He shrugged one shoulder. "I had to ask. After all that's happened, I wasn't sure what you planned next."

I pulled off my headscarf and raked a hand through my hair. "That's just it. It's not about my plans. I want to serve the Maker, but . . ." I paused to listen for His nudging in my heart. "This isn't where I belong anymore."

Brantley pressed his lips in a firm line as if holding back a smile. A spark that I couldn't interpret lit his eyes, but he only gave me a tight nod.

I turned back to the saltars. "Select a new High Saltar who can deal fairly with the villages, who will restore the Order to its true purpose, who can guide the novitiates in learning about the Maker. Someone who understands the work of teaching and organizing."

Tangleroot looked at Saltar Kemp. Soon other faces turned her way as well. Color rose in her cheeks, and she shook her head.

I reached for her hand. "Please. Consider it. I can't think of a better person to reform the Order."

Worry knit her brows together. "With Tiarel gone, we'll need a leader with strength." She lifted her gnarled hands as if to give proof of her frailty.

I smiled. "The Order needs a leader who longs to serve. You can't tell me that isn't you."

She glanced around at the other saltars.

"Please, Saltar Kemp. You've always held the respect of all of the Order," said one.

"You can't let Saltar River seize control. You know she'd rule with more cruelty than even Tiarel," said Tangleroot.

An older saltar gasped at this stark criticism of the former High Saltar, but then she nodded. "We need a new leader for this new direction."

Saltar Kemp squeezed my hand and searched my eyes. "Are you sure you won't lead us? You have had more time to study the Maker's letter. You can dance with more power than the entire Order combined."

I shook my head, weariness making even that movement difficult. "It wasn't *my* power. The Maker invited me to be part of His work, and He accomplished His purpose. But now He invites you."

Beside me, Brantley yawned. He probably found all this discussion about the Maker's plans tedious.

"I accept," Saltar Kemp said quietly. "And before we continue our discussion, my first recommendation is that we offer a room to this remarkable dancer, where she can rest and have her wound tended."

Brantley surged to his feet. "Most sensible idea I've heard for a while."

I stood, grateful for his support as I wobbled. Kemp signaled for an attendant, Brantley wrapped an arm around my waist, and they guided me back toward the dancers' wing.

My gait grew heavier with each step. When we reached the hall to the dancers' quarters I stopped. "Brantley, you aren't allowed in here."

He barked a laugh. "They'll survive."

The hall was deserted anyway as he helped me to the room. Ginerva hurried toward us, having torn herself away from the center ground at last. Her face glistened from the exertion of dancing, and perhaps from some holy tears. The glowing expression fell as she saw me. "Oh, poor lamb." She elbowed Brantley out of the way. "I'll care for her."

He raised his hands in surrender. "Good. But"—he lifted my chin and stared deep into my eyes—"don't go anywhere after you've rested. We have things to say."

Ginerva gave me little time to stare at his back as he strode away, but his words lingered. He'd more than honored his promise to guide me. All that remained to say was our goodbyes.

Somehow that thought was one too many to bear.

33

"WHY DO I FEEL SO EMPTY? EVERYTHING HAS BEEN MADE right." I squirmed as Ginerva applied another poultice to my ankle the next afternoon. I'd lain down for a nap and slept through the night. Rest had restored some of my strength, but my melancholy hadn't eased. I felt guilty for my heavy gloom. The whole Order seemed to ring with new hope, but I hid inside the walls of the borrowed dancer cell. I had every reason for joy, but the sharp ache of my leg permeated my whole being. I wrinkled my nose against the overly sweet scent of the poultice. "I know I should feel grateful."

She wiped her hands on a linen towel and gave me a nurturing squeeze. "You're exhausted, is all. And yes, much has been made right, but it hasn't been without cost. Feel what you need to feel. The Maker understands."

I managed a half-hearted nod.

She pressed a mug into my hand. "Have some soup. Saltar Kemp would like to meet with you, but I told her you needed some hot food first. Oh, and that young man of yours has been hovering around. He met with the rimmers, and they've returned to their camps and inns in Middlemost, but he refuses to leave."

A heavier wave of sorrow rolled through my chest. "He wants to say goodbye."

Ginerva snorted. "He doesn't have the look of a man waiting to fare thee well."

A flicker of curiosity cut through my lassitude. "What *does* he look like?"

"Eat." She guided the mug of soup to my lips.

I submitted, rolling bits of cooked tubers around my tongue. Not as refreshing as rimmer soups made with fresh seawater, but the meal did strengthen me, at least enough to unravel the reasons I felt deflated. I'd focused so long on reaching the Order, on fulfilling the impossible task of freeing our world, on sharing the letter, but I'd never thought beyond. Now that the confrontation was over, I had no idea what to do next. Would the Maker ever meet with me again? Was my usefulness at an end? I was certain that refusing to become High Saltar was the right decision. My old mentor would fill the role far better than I ever could. But what would become of me now?

I lowered my foot to the floor and tried putting weight on it, then winced.

"Stop that," Ginerva said. "Give it time to rest."

I managed a wan smile. "I'll have nothing but time now. But you know rest won't repair a hobbled tendon, not enough for me to dance again."

Her mouth pursed, opened, then she thought better of what she had planned to say and sighed instead. With a last pat on my shoulder, she bustled to the door. "Remember. Saltar Kemp is waiting at the office when you're ready."

I lingered over the soup and brought my questions to the Maker. I told Him how difficult it was for me to recover from the marvels He'd performed, the depths of fear and heights of ecstasy I'd experienced, and my confusion about where I fit now. I didn't hear the mighty Voice but did sense gentle arms wrap me in love. With that light touch, I was finally ready to take my staff and limp to the office.

In the doorway, I couldn't help but remember being called here as a novitiate, when a busy Saltar Kemp had assigned me a teaching task. I'd been consumed with reverence for the High Saltar, full of eagerness to prove my worth, and horrified I might make a misstep. I shook my head. I'd been so young, so indoctrinated. *Maker, if the current novitiates stay, let them serve in truth and joy and humility instead of the fear and competition that dogged my every step.*

In the outer office, a handful of attendants were cleaning and reorganizing desks, and several saltars interrupted their animated discussion to smile and nod at me. I hobbled through to the High Saltar's office. Saltar Kemp stood by the full-length window facing the center ground, watching with the soft smile of a grandmother observing children at play. Instead of the formal embroidered robes of the High Saltar, she wore a simple white tunic and leggings. The drummers were back at work with a vigorous harvest pattern. Dancers performed the steps but added occasional spontaneous improvisations. An attendant and even a young novitiate also gamboled along the daygrass near the edges.

Saltar Kemp turned her sparkling eyes toward me. "What do you think? Can we still value training and work together as a community, while also allowing a place for freedom and welcome for anyone to dance?"

My heart swelled. "It seems like a beautiful combination."

She beckoned me toward a chair, and we settled in for a long and fruitful conversation. She had uncovered lost patterns that had been designed as thanks and worship to the Maker, and wanted to teach these to the novitiates from their earliest age. Her ambitious plans included a larger garden to provide more food for the Order, so they would rely less on gifts and taxes from the villages. She had already abolished the policy of stealing children for the Order. We discussed allowing families to move inland to be near their children who wished to train in the Order.

I shared everything I'd learned on my travels: the attacks on Foleshill and Undertow, the suffering even the midrange villages faced because of heavy taxes, the distrust of the rimmers. Most of the saltars had never known the extent of Tiarel's abuses.

I learned that after frantic efforts to regain control, Saltar River had stormed from the Order, along with four prefects who were loyal to her, and a handful of the saltars. My brow furrowed. "Was it wise to let her leave? Seems she'll cause trouble in the future."

Saltar Kemp's face fell, but she hastened to reassure me. "If we forced her to stay, we'd be no better than the former Order. I doubt she'll find much support wherever she goes."

Maybe she was right. How could Saltar River interfere anymore? Too much had altered along with the massive shift of our world.

Saltar Kemp was eager to tell me that the negotiations with the representatives from the rim villages had been fruitful. "One of the rimmers has offered to help us create parchments, so we can produce many copies of the Maker's letter. Did you meet Brianna of Windswell on your travels?"

I beamed. "Yes, I did." I marveled that Bri could extend forgiveness after the Order had wounded her family. Enough forgiveness even to offer her help.

Maker, you free our hearts as well as our world.

"If we focus on teaching writing skills in the younger forms, by the time they are in the tenth form they could spend some time each day working on that project." As we talked, it was clear the Maker had restored a vision to her of what the Order could truly be—worshiping Him, serving the people of Meriel, and helping share His letter. Some dancers had chosen to leave the Order and find their home villages, but enough were staying to continue to aid our world from the central ground. A sense of peace began to brush away the remnants of wistful sadness I'd been feeling. Until her next question.

"And what are your plans, Carya of Undertow?"

My ribs contracted, and I fingered the hem of the white tunic Ginerva had provided. "I don't know."

"I would love your help teaching the new patterns to the children who stay with us."

Her offer was sincere and touching, but as I weighed that option, I finally sensed a hint of direction—a different direction.

My shoulders eased back. "Thank you. Perhaps one day. Right now I think my place is with my birth village. Once my leg is strong enough to travel, I'd like to return there and help where I can."

Sympathy swam in her eyes. "All the better," she said. "We need representatives from the Order to help the rim villages. They have years of struggle to overcome. Let me know how I can help you and your village."

We talked for hours more, and my spirits continued to lift as I saw the ripples of goodness that the Maker's intervention had brought. When I took my leave, she was dusting off more old books of forsaken patterns. Her eagerness made me smile.

I wandered out to the gardens, dreaming about the expansion she had planned. She'd need new landkeepers. Too bad Brantley didn't actually have those skills.

Uneven fences had been hastily constructed along the edge of the new canyon. Dislodged cobblestones littered the area where the earth had split. I limped as close as I dared. I could only wonder why the Maker had carved this mark across half our island.

A scrabbling sound drew me forward, and I peered down to the water below. Someone had ignored the fences and found uneven footholds to climb down. Fair, tousled hair glinted in the late-afternoon subsun. "Brantley!"

He looked up and flashed a grin. "Wait there. I'll help you down."

Again, I found myself wanting to skitter away from a challenge that he coaxed me to face. I couldn't resist him. With his steady arm supporting me, I picked my way down to the river. A splash erupted and a familiar long neck and floppy ears rose from the water.

"Navar!" I reached forward and hugged her. "How did you get here?"

Brantley all but swaggered as he stepped onto her back. "She's the fastest stenella I've seen. I whistled for her after the big confrontation yesterday morning, and she followed the new river up in mere hours. Do you realize what this means? Herders from the rim can travel back and forth in a day instead of weeks using this river."

More incredible changes. The Order would no longer be an isolated tower but connected to the shore and the ocean that cradled our world.

I settled on the ground and traced my fingers through the water. Muffled by the canyon walls, the drums finished one pattern and began another. For most of my memory, those drums had provided the heartbeat of my life. Always present in the background. Strong and reliable.

I glanced up. Brantley pressed his face against Navar's neck and crooned praises. His formal tunic had already rumpled and gathered smudges from his climbing. Water splattered his trousers. Affection swelled under my ribs, followed by a sharp pang. In these past months, he'd become like the drums. Steady, trusted, and so constant that I hadn't realized how much I relied on him until I pictured his absence. Yet now our traveling together was over.

As if feeling my perusal, Brantley turned his gaze toward me. With a last pat for Navar, he stepped back onto land and settled beside me. "So did Saltar Kemp convince you to stay?"

I shook my head. "I'll help her for a few weeks while my ankle heals, but then I plan to go home and serve my village."

He drew a deep, satisfied breath. "A fine plan. Then again, and I hate to admit it, this"—his gesture took in my neat head scarf, clean tunic and leggings—"suits you. When I saw you in the center ground . . ." He cleared his throat. "You're meant to dance like a bird is meant to fly."

I pulled my knees closer and touched the bandage around my ankle. "Not anymore."

Shadows danced in the depths of his eyes, and he rested a hand on my shoulder. I couldn't stomach the compassion, so I pulled away.

"What's wrong?" he asked.

"I don't want your pity." The words sounded harsh as they came through the tangle in my throat.

He laughed. "Pity? I've never met a woman less in need of pity."

I searched his face, looking for the lie, but could find none.

Instead, a warm smile met me openly. "You still don't realize what you've done, do you? You don't realize who you are. You've more courage than the wildest herder. Yet you also have a heart as big as the ocean."

His words unraveled the knot in my chest, and a flood of warmth swept me. His respect and approval meant more to me than the praise of a High Saltar.

My skin flushed, and I adjusted a fold on my bandage. "I'm glad I found you before you left. I wanted to tell you that I'm grateful for all your help."

"Grateful?" He leaned back on his elbows, and as lines bunched at his brow, I feared I'd made him angry. But then he laughed hard enough that his blond waves of hair bounced. "All right. Grateful. I'll take that for now."

"For now?" Confusion throbbed behind my forehead. He'd once been insulted by my expression of gratitude, but today he seemed only amused.

He chuckled again. "I guess it's how the Order trained you. When you're focused on one thing, you don't notice anything else around you, do you?"

"I . . . I suppose." What on Meriel was he talking about?

He shifted, kneeling in front of me. One hand smoothed a wrinkle in my scarf and lingered against my face. "Carya of Undertow, we both have our villages to serve. I understand that. But we're going to find a way to serve them together."

A honeybird fluttered beneath my breastbone. "Together?" My whisper floated on the breeze and hung between us.

He shrugged and offered a crooked grin. "I've gotten used to having you around." Then the mask of humor fell away, and his ocean-blue gaze grabbed mine, all the depths of his soul exposed for a fleeting moment. "I don't want another day to go by without you in my life."

Heat rushed to my skin, my eyes widened.

He brushed a soft kiss on my forehead. "I'm sorry. You've been through a lot and need some time. I shouldn't have spoken so soon," he added with a wry grin.

Together, he'd said. The picture flooded my imagination in vibrant color. The wings in my chest beat even more frantically, as if begging to be set free.

He was waiting for my response.

"I don't know what to say. Of course I care for you . . ." And so much more. I admired him, trusted him, savored my memories of even the most brutal days on the trail because I'd been with him. I loved him. But even as I admitted the truth to myself, objections pinned my wings and placed my dreams firmly back in a nest. I had pledged to forsake all attachments. I no longer felt bound to serve the Order, but I wanted to—needed to—serve the Maker the rest of my life. Was this a horrible temptation I must fight, or was this a gift the Maker was offering me? What did Brantley and I have in common? And why would he saddle himself with a crippled wife who had no practical skills?

His gaze never left me, and I was certain that even my years of dancer training were failing to keep my emotions from flitting across my face. Love, longing, doubt, uncertainty.

His smile was tender and understanding. One callused finger rubbed away the worry lines from my forehead. "It's a start," he said. "I can wait." He launched to his feet and helped me up. His eyes sparkled and his posture declared his confidence.

I wanted to explain why his dream would never work, prevent him from false hope, but I didn't have the heart.

When we reached the lip of the canyon, we walked to the trellised archway and watched the last rays of subsun paint the buildings of Middlemost. Far beyond in the woods, a forest hound lifted a mournful howl.

Brantley shook his head. "That day in the clearing when you tamed the hound, I thought my heart would never beat normally again."

I sighed at the happy memory of discovering I was still a dancer, even apart from the Order. Perhaps I was still a dancer even apart from healthy limbs. "He was sweet."

"Maker, help me," Brantley said under his breath. "What have I gotten myself into?"

The bell rang from within the Order, a frantic stream of sound, far too early for dinner. "Something's wrong." I planted my walking stick and hurried as best I could into the Order. Brantley edged along my other side and offered his arm. The support helped me limp quickly over the cobblestones.

Saltar Kemp met us in the entry hall. "The attendant on watch saw something strange. I'm heading up to the telescope now."

"We'll come with you," Brantley said, not waiting for my response. I stiffened. If we planned to work together, I'd have to talk to him about his bossiness. At the thought of the clashes ahead between us, a secret joy bubbled in my chest.

My progress on the stairs was slow and painful, so Brantley swept me into his arms and carried me up the final flights to the roof. A young attendant squinted into the large brass instrument. When we approached, he backed away. "Look!"

Saltar Kemp peered through. "Did you check the lens? It looks like a smudge."

The youth frowned. "The glass is clean. There's something there."

"But that's impossible," she said.

Brantley took a turn staring into the telescope and gave a low whistle. "Look at that." His arm around my waist supported me as I positioned myself to take my turn.

Through the curved lenses, the whole world seemed to expand and move toward us. Disoriented by this glimpse, it took me a minute to see what had caused all the excitement.

Out to sea, some distance beyond the rim of our world, the outline of a large shape came into focus: shoreline, trees, a slope leading inland. My breath caught. "Another world."

"But there is no other world," Saltar Kemp said quietly. She shook her head. "How much more do we have to learn?"

Ignoring our consternation, Brantley leaned on the parapet and stared out to the horizon, as if he could see the new land with his naked eyes. "Meriel is free now. We must have drifted on the current near another world." He turned and took my hand. "I'm going to explore it. Will you come with me?"

Who could guess what this new discovery meant? What adventures or dangers waited on that new island? Could this be part of the Maker's plan?

I'm with you wherever you go.

The gentle reassurance quickened my pulse. I peeked again into the telescope. A new world. A new love. A new direction. My future sailed before me and I was ready to dive into the current. I stepped away and took a deep breath. With my weight on my good leg, I twirled once, lifting my hands to the smiling sky. Then I faced Brantley and took a deep breath. "Let's go."

GLOSSARY

ALCEA FLOWER — Delicate, sweet-scented blossoms.

ATTENDANTS — Servants who work in the Order.

BRESH — A flaky, buttery roll. Luxurious treat eaten by dancers.

CALARA REED — Well rooted, supple reeds growing near water. (Calara pattern is one of the most complicated.)

CENTER GROUND — The huge open field in the very center of the island, where the dancers of the Order perform the patterns that keep the island turning around its core.

COPPER FISH — Small, glittery fish that swim in large schools and provide food for rim villages.

DAYGRASS — a soft, mossy grass that springs up overnight.

FOLESHILL — A midrange village that refused to pay their Order taxes and incited a brief rebellion, which interrupted testing day.

FORMS — Various levels within the Order's school. First-form children are generally around seven years old and work up through the ranks to the fifteenth form (twenty-one years of age) and if successful can join the Order as dancers. Some dancers later become saltars.

FOUNTAIN FISH — Pink-and-green-striped bronze fish, kept as pets or in fountains.

HERDER — One who herds fish from the ocean waters so they can be gathered by rim villagers.

LANDKEEPER — A person who gardens, farms, cares for plants.

LANTHRUS — A plant with prickly leaves that cause blisters and fever, but when dried is useful for pain.

MAKER, THE — The forgotten one who created the oceans, the island world, and everything in them.

MERIEL — The name of Carya's world (the island floating in a vast, featureless ocean universe).

MIDDLEMOST — The largest city, in the center of Meriel, surrounding the Order.

NOVITIATES — Girls training to become dancers of the Order.

ORDER, THE — The organization of novitiates, dancers, saltars, prefects, and attendants that directs the course of the world through the dance. Located in the very center of Meriel, in a large edifice that encircles the center ground. They pass down the patterns through the generations.

PATTERNS — Precise dances and formations named for various natural elements or plants. To be accepted into the Order, each dancer must prove she can perform any pattern flawlessly.

PERSEA FRUIT — Knobby-skinned, meaty fruit with a pit.

PREFECT — Support staff for the Order school, they enforce rules, help saltars, etc.

RIM — The undulating outer edges of the island world.

RIMMERS — Sometimes derogatory term for those who live in rim villages.

RUTISH PLANT — A tuber that has a pebbly green skin and is good in stews.

SALIS — A midrange village where castoffs from the Order sometimes found refuge.

SALTARS — The leaders and top teachers of the Order.

SALTCAKES — Dry, crumbly biscuits.

STAR RAIN — A magical occurrence on rare evenings when stars burst in the air and glittering light rains down.

STENELLA — Sea creatures with long necks and wide spreading side fins that can glide over the water as well as dive under.

SWEET WATER — Ocean water that tastes sweet and citrusy. Loved by the rim villages, but feared and filtered by those in the inland towns.

TANGLEROOT — The matted, intertwined vines that form the outer edge of the island.

TENDER — Someone who cares for domesticated animals, especially ponies.

TSALLA — Sweet ocean water brewed with herbs.

ACKNOWLEDGMENTS

MY THANKS TO C.S. LEWIS, WHOSE NOVEL *PERELANDRA* captured my imagination so many years ago. I adapted his imaginative concept of floating islands. Eternal gratitude to my agent, Steve Laube, who suggested I write a fantasy series drawing from my background in dance. Fun ensued immediately. Deepest appreciation to my editor, Reagen Reed, who brings so much care, respect, and wisdom to making my stories stronger, and to copy editor Lindsay Franklin whose attention to detail polished each page.

Immense thanks go to the friends who offered prayer support. You carried me through the years of work on this new series. Special thanks to writing buddies Chawna, Patti, and Michelle for in-depth edits, and to Amy, Angela, Beth, Jenni, Ted, and Joyce for reading the full manuscript and offering such helpful critique. I'm also grateful to writing buddies who shared insights on specific chapters or scenes. Thanks to Stacy, Brenda, Carol, Haleigh, Brennan, and John.

As always, Ted, you continue to be the model for all my heroes. Thank you for your strength, compassion, and integrity. My love to Joel, Jennelle, Kaeti, Raphael, Joshua, and Jenni. You fill my heart. I couldn't do this without your support and encouragement. And to Mom and Carl, the Hinck clan, and all extended family: I appreciate you so much. Huge thanks to friends who put up with me and my yammering about imaginary worlds and the struggles of writing.

Above all else, thank you to my Maker, from whom all blessings flow. May the truth of His grace free souls as we discover or rediscover His letter.

AUTHOR BIOGRAPHY

SHARON HINCK WRITES "STORIES FOR THE HERO IN ALL OF US," novels praised for their strong spiritual themes, emotional resonance, and imaginative blend of genres.

She earned an M.A. in Communication (with a major in theatre and thesis in dance) from Regent University and spent ten years as the artistic director of a Christian dance company. That ministry included three short-term mission trips to Hong Kong to teach and choreograph for a Y.W.A.M. dance/evangelism team. She taught classical ballet and liturgical dance for twenty years, and led workshops on dance in worship.

She's been a church youth worker, a dancer/choreographer, a church organist, a speaker, a crafting workshop teacher, and a homeschool mom. One day she'll figure out what to be when she grows up.

When she's not wrestling with words, she enjoys serving as an adjunct professor for M.F.A. writing students, speaking at churches and conferences, and has taught at Minnesota Christian Writer's Guild and the national conference of the American Christian Fiction Writers and Realm Makers.

A wife, mom of four, and delighted new grandmother of three, she lives in Minnesota and is a member at St. Michael's Lutheran Church.

Feel free to visit her at sharonhinck.com.